In the Stars Rewritten

KIM SWIZZ

In the Stars Rewritten is a work of fiction. Unless otherwise indicated, all the names, characters, businesses, places, events, and incidents in this book are either the product of the author's imagination or used in a fictitious manner. Any resemblance to actual persons, living or dead, or actual events is purely coincidental.

Copyright 2025 by Kimberly Swiszcz

ISBN (trade paperback) 979-8-9910534-2-6

ISBN (ebook) 979-8-9910534-3-3

This book or parts thereof may not be reproduced in any form, stored in any retrieval system, used by any artificial intelligence ("AI") program or AI learning program, or transmitted in any form by any means – electronic, mechanical, photocopy, recording, or otherwise – without prior written permission of the author, except as provided by United States of America copyright law.

Cover Art by Ink and Laurel

Interior book formatting by Grace Elena

Developmental editing by Annie Meagle at Spare Words Novel Editing

Copy editing and proofreading by Hannah at April Editorial

Books by Kim Swizz

<u>Wilcox Grove Stories</u>:

Barefoot Lake

In the Stars Rewritten

For anyone who has been told you're too much.
Keep on shining.

Playlist

Nice to Meet You – Myles Smith
Messy – Lola Young
Ordinary – Alex Warren
Close to You – Gracie Abrams
Beautiful Things – Benson Boone
Little Things – One Direction
Everything Has Changed – Taylor Swift (feat. Ed Sheeran)
Wherever You Go – GAITS
Home – Edward Sharpe & The Magnetic Zeros
champagne problems – Taylor Swift
The scientist – Bea and her Business
I'm Yours – Jason Mraz
Stargazing – Myles Smith
Home (soft version) – Good Neighbours
Stars Will Align – Kygo, Imagine Dragons
Beloved – Ben Barnes

Author's Note

In the Stars Rewritten is intended for adult readers aged eighteen or older and contains explicit language and intimate scenes.

Some readers prefer to dive into a story without any hints about where it may go, while others prefer a heads-up regarding certain topics. There is no right or wrong way to read a book, so readers can find full content warnings and a spice guide at the back of the book after Acknowledgements.

Prologue

PIPER

LAST OCTOBER

I lean forward, so I can look down the dark wood bar and check on Alice. My heart leaps when I see her animated expression, hands waving around while she tells some story to one of the women I met earlier. I think her name is Hannah?

Alice fought me when I suggested coming out tonight, but she needed this.

When I surprised Alice with my arrival this morning, I expected to find her sad—her mom, Rain, just died at the end of summer. The day after her mom's funeral, Alice left her shit fiancé and temporarily moved into the lake house Rain left behind here in Wilcox Grove.

Like I said, sad is something I expected, but Alice has always been a friendly person, so I didn't bank on finding her so very *alone*. It scared me. Seeing Alice happy here tonight is good, very good.

"Hey," a smooth voice says on my other side, pulling me out of my thoughts.

I turn and find myself almost nose-to-nose with my new

friend, Scott. I met him on my bus ride up to Wilcox Grove this morning, and I must say I am pleased Alice's fears of him being a serial killer are seemingly unwarranted. His piercing blue eyes hold my gaze, and a smirk slowly tips up his lips when I don't move away. *Really* pleased.

"What can I do for you, Scotty?" I ask. Flirting with him all night has been thoroughly enjoyable. I'm only visiting, but it still feels nice to be wanted.

"No, Piper. The question is what can *I* do for *you*?" This man has the balls to lick his lips.

I bet he would be a damn fun ride. Fun guys from bars, or busses I suppose, are usually just my type.

Never one to back down in these kinds of situations, especially when fueled by shots, I slide off my stool, bumping against him when he doesn't step back. I internally wince when I realize how much taller than Scott my heels make me. I'd be taller than him even without them, and most guys lose interest when they realize I'm a tree. Maybe I should have stayed seated.

But when Scott's eyes trail down my body and back up without shame, his pupils are so wide the sparkling blue is barely a rim around them. Maybe the game isn't over yet.

I reach my hand between us and take hold of the open front of his flannel shirt, the backs of my fingers rubbing against the t-shirt stretched over his chest as I move down the material. I can feel his heart hammering.

I'm about to tell Scott exactly what he can do for me when Penny, the bartender, loudly announces that karaoke sign-ups are available for the last hour the bar is open.

"Sorry, Scotty. Next time," I say with a wink before I pivot away from him and yell for Alice's attention.

I grab Alice's arm when I trip over my own feet scrambling toward her and almost take her down with me.

"Alice," I gasp, elated. "You *have* to sing Spice Girls with me!"

My best friend's eyes go wide.

"No. I actually do not," she says with a smile.

"But you do! You're my best friend. You can't make me do this alone. It's against the rules."

Alice's smile falls, and I can see her trying to find a way out of my guilt trip. She does look terrified, and I kind of feel bad for making her think she has to sing with me if she really doesn't want to. I'm about to take it back when I feel a warm hand on my hip.

"I'll go with you." Scott's voice is once again at my ear, and I like it just as much as before. Maybe even more once I see the relief on Alice's face from his offer.

I turn and throw my arms around his neck, squealing my thanks. As I'm falling against him, I worry once again about having overdone it. Alice survived my attack moments ago, but Scott... Well, Scott is actually incredibly solid. He doesn't falter an inch, catching my full weight with ease.

Once I release him—he surely wasn't going to be the first one to let go—I drag him to the karaoke machine set up in a corner.

"Do you know any Spice Girls songs?" I ask as I scroll through the options.

"I might? But just pick whatever you want. I'll figure it out," he assures me.

This guy just might be too sweet for my messiness. I push the thought out of my mind as I select our song and hold the microphone between us. Scott's hand wraps around mine. Sure, I'm taller, but my hand feels dainty under his.

Scott does not, in fact, know the words to "Wannabe," but that doesn't lessen his enthusiasm one bit. The man commits. We're terrible, but I have the best time. We're both clinging to each other as we walk back in stitches, laughing at ourselves.

Of course, my too-long limbs betray me again, and I stumble. Scott keeps me up, but not before I bump into the back of a blonde girl's chair, jostling her and causing her to spill the beer in her hand.

"Oh shit. I'm so sorry," I say immediately, but the damage seems to be done. Next thing I know, some oaf is on his feet, and Scott's pushing me behind him.

This asshole is itching to start something with Scott, and I can tell from his tone there's history here. He says something about Scott's dead parents, and I feel a rush of protectiveness. I didn't know Scott lost his parents, but it's obvious that's a low blow. Next thing I know, the guy hits Scott, knocking him to the ground, and the chick calls me a slut.

I stand, coming face to face with the woman, a crowd clustering around us.

"What did you just call me?" I question, shocked by how high school this whole thing feels. The girl doesn't back down. Instead, she raises both of her hands and shoves me, hard, into the bar stool behind me.

The group presses in, and I'm not the only one of Scott's friends around him now. I push back, trying to get this woman off me, and we both fall to the ground.

Next thing I know, I've got blondie pinned under me with her hair gripped tight in one fist. I'm pretty sure my other fist just hit her. Alice is trying to pull me up, but I really want to hit the girl again. I reel back and...

Are those police sirens?

CHAPTER 1

Piper

"Pea-brained, small-dicked, egotistical…" I grumble.

I notice a woman on the other side of the bus aisle scooch closer to her window and further away from me. Maybe my grumbling isn't as quiet as I think it is. I've been on this bus for over three hours, and I'm still as livid as I was when I stormed out of work this afternoon.

Everybody has their limit, and Bernard, the library's under-qualified, self-important director, found mine today. I've been dreaming of rage-quitting for months, and it feels damn good to finally have done it. Flipping him off on my way out might not have been the most professional move, but I still don't regret it. It's far less than he deserved.

"What he deserved was a swift kick to his—" I see the woman's eyes widen and cut myself off.

I cross my arms and huff as I flop against the side of the bus. I put my earbuds in and turn the volume all the way up, determined to put Bernard out of my mind.

I try to keep my grumbling to a minimum once I crawl into a taxi outside the train station in northern New Hampshire. The privacy of the vehicle also means a lack of anonymity for the curses I am putting upon Bernard's house. Instead, I look out the window for the forty-minute drive to Alice's house in Wilcox Grove, telling myself to find serenity in the golden hour glow.

The last time I took this ride, it was peak leaf peeping season, and the trees were all vibrant shades of red, yellow, and orange. Now, with summer just around the corner, the road is lined with bushy branches of rich greens and everything has that fresh, damp scent.

Alice has told me multiple times over the last several months that this place has healing properties, but this is the first moment I might believe her. As I watch signs of mass development slip away, it feels like I can breathe easier. Bernard is still a dipshit, but that doesn't weigh on me as heavily. By the time the asphalt beneath the tires turns to gravel, I feel good.

I'm free from a job that felt like it was killing me, I'm about to see my best friend, and I have a world of opportunities in front of me. That last one is a little intimidating, but I'm choosing to focus on the positive aspects it offers.

It's dark when I finally climb out of my cab, but I feel fantastic. Alice lives off a gravel road in the middle of the woods, so I keep my eyes peeled for critters, but everything is tranquil and quiet. Well, except for the cab driver. He looks like he thought I might have been leading him to his death at a cabin in the woods. He certainly speeds off like he's relieved to be getting out of here alive.

I take a deep breath and look around. For being in the middle of nowhere, the space is surprisingly well-lit by the full moon climbing into the sky.

I look up at the two-story, dark brown home and sigh with relief when I see an upstairs light on. After my unexpected voluntary unemployment, I packed up my things and took off to see the one person I need right now. I texted Alice a couple of times since storming out of the and tried calling her from the bus and then the station, but I haven't been able to get a hold of her. Thankfully, it looks like she's home. Chances are her phone is just wedged between the couch cushions, forgotten.

Alice's house is the twin to its neighbor, her boyfriend Jake's house. Both rustic homes have small grass lawns before their front doors, but the rear of the houses is where the beauty lies. Out back, both homes have narrow wooden porches and large, stone patios before a slope of grass that leads down to the breathtaking Barefoot Lake. The glittering expanse is actually just one part of an enormous collection of interconnected sections of water that make up the lake, and its beauty blows the mind of this city-living girl.

Alice inherited this home last year after Rain passed away from a long battle with cancer. Rain had purchased the property shortly after getting her diagnosis five years prior, searching for peace in her remaining years. I think she found that and more in Wilcox Grove. Then Alice did. And now I hope it's my turn.

Something rustles out of sight in the leaves, and I decide that's plenty of nature for me. After walking across the grass, I heave my duffel bag further up on my shoulder and drag my suitcase up the few steps to the front door. I knock and wait, but there's no answer. When a second attempt still doesn't yield an answer, I hop back down the steps and find the tiny fake rock against the house. I lift it to pull the small pill bottle from the ground and remove the spare key.

"Alice, it's Piper!" I holler once I'm inside. I dump my bags and backpack in a pile beside the door and slip off my shoes. The front entrance leads into the living room, but I can see through to the kitchen at the back of the house. The door to the library beside the kitchen is ajar, and I can see the light is off.

The only other room down here is a bathroom, and that's also empty.

Alice and I met eleven years ago, when I was an eager little eighteen-year-old freshman in college and she was the coolest sophomore resident assistant in my dorm building. We've been sisters ever since, so I have no qualms about letting myself further into her house.

As I approach the base of the stairs, I can hear the shower running upstairs. At least that explains why there was no answer to my knocking. The old plumbing in the house results in rumbling pipes making it nearly impossible to hear anything from inside the shower.

I head up to announce my presence more effectively and pray her boyfriend Jake isn't in there with her. I didn't notice whether there were signs of life next door before coming in here. As I reach the top of the stairs, I hear the water shut off.

"Ali—" I start to call Alice's name again when the bathroom door slams against the wall, and a projectile flies at my head while a loud, indecipherable shout fills the space.

"OW!" I yelp, rubbing the spot on my forehead where a large shampoo bottle just smacked into me. "What the hell?"

I slowly look up from the bottle on the floor and find surprisingly hairy legs, a towel, and then a very naked, very male chest. Once I reach the definitely-not-Alice-shaped-person's face, realization dawns on me. Alice must have already fully moved in with Jake. He just asked her to move in last week. I didn't realize she'd be able to complete the move so quickly. The plan was for Scott to stay in this house when he came back to Wilcox Grove from New York City. After nearly getting arrested last year, Alice and I learned that my bus friend, Scott, is Jake's younger brother.

"Piper, I'm so sorry!" Scott rushes over to me, guilt painted all over his face. "Are you ok?"

He reaches out for my hair and gently touches his fingers to the tender spot on my head. I won't pretend I'm not immediately hyper-aware of the contact.

"Hi Scott. Yeah, I'm fine. Thankfully, your choice of weapon isn't too dangerous, but what's the big idea with assaulting me?"

"I *obviously* didn't know it was you. You can't blame me. I was here alone, I didn't expect anybody, Alice and Jake are out of town, and I used to listen to true crime podcasts. I think I acted rationally, all things considered." Scott must realize he's still touching my head because he drops his arm. One of his hands goes to the towel around his waist, making sure the end is securely tucked in.

I follow the movement and wish I hadn't. When Scott and I met last year, I could obviously see he's an attractive man, but this nearly naked, wet version of him is doing things to my brain. I watch a drop of water slice down his abs to get absorbed in the low-slung towel and swallow hard.

Then my brain picks up what he just said.

"Did you say Alice and Jake are *out of town*?"

"Yeah, they wanted to celebrate moving in together, so they left earlier today and won't be back until the day after tomorrow. They took the puppy camping, I think."

Alice had fulfilled Jake's lifelong dream of having a golden retriever by gifting him one for his birthday a week ago.

"They wanted to celebrate moving in together by leaving the house that they now live in together? That makes no sense. *And* she didn't tell me?" I struggle to picture Alice camping. Neither of us has ever really been a nature girl, but she did say it's grown on her since she moved here. Not really my thing. Nature is pretty and needs to be protected, but I think it should also remain outside while we remain inside.

Scott shrugs, and I notice the definition of his shoulders. I blink and look away.

Sure, I was ready to jump his bones last October, but that was before I learned he's Jake's only living family. With how things are going between Jake and Alice, it's likely Scott will at least tangentially be in my life forever. As a love 'em and leave 'em kind of girl, having lingering dudes isn't a good idea, especially sweet dudes like Scott.

"Well, shit. I was hoping to crash with Alice. I kind of rage-quit my job today and moved out of my apartment."

"I mean, you're welcome to stay here until she gets back and you can figure things out," Scott quickly offers. "It sounds like there's a story here, and I want to hear it."

"Is the house still a vengeful demon?" I ask, remembering how the thing seemed to have it out for Alice when she first moved in last year. I swear *everything* in this house was broken.

Scott chuckles, seemingly having heard the stories. "Jake did a lot of repairs, and it is much more docile now."

I don't know why I even pretend to think about it. I already know the house has two bedrooms.

"Then, yes. You're a lifesaver. Thank you."

Scott's face splits into a grin, and he seems truly happy to have me staying. I'm overcome with a rush of immediate comfort.

"Let me get some pants first, but do you want some wine?"

I smile back at him.

"Do you have anything stronger?"

CHAPTER 2

Piper

"You *actually* flipped him off? Did he see?" A couple of hours later, Scott has an arm squeezing across his stomach, both of us sore from laughing so hard.

"It was right in his face before I walked out. Unless he's blind, he saw. I should have stayed longer and told him everything I thought about his sexist policies and his stupid ideas for the library." I tip my head back and slide down the couch until I'm sufficiently molded into the cushions.

"I'd say we should make a drinking game out of him and take a shot every time he did something illegal or unethical, but I think we'd both die." Scott's cheeks are flushed from the multiple margaritas he's had, and I expect mine look the same.

"Let's do one anyway," I suggest, heaving myself forward to grab the blue tequila bottle off the coffee table.

Are my words mushing together? They feel like they're mushing together. Before margaritas, we started with a shot each —mine to soothe my burning rage and Scott's in solidarity.

Scott leans forward beside me and holds out his empty glass.

"What're we cheersing?" he asks. Scott's words are smushing, too.

Smushing.

I laugh at the word and dump some tequila into Scott's cup. That felt like a shot-ish amount.

"To Bernard's hopeful future herpes," I cry out before knocking the bottle against Scott's knuckles, completely missing the glass I was aiming for, and taking a swig. It doesn't really make sense, but I know Scott knows what I mean.

Words are hard.

"To Bernard's herpes," Scott echoes and takes his shot, lying back and throwing his arm out across the back of the couch.

I'm still laughing when I fall over and rest my head against the inside of Scott's elbow. I'm worried tequila is going to come out my nose, and I can only imagine how painful that would be.

"I'm gonna do it," I announce suddenly. I start wriggling around until I can extract my phone from my back pocket. I pull it up, but it refuses to read my face. Stupid phone.

"Do what?" Scott rolls his head toward me and furrows his brow.

"I'm going to call Bernard and tell him all those things I didn't say before." My password *won't... work*! Ah-HA! It finally lets me in.

"Ohhhhh no you're not."

From behind me, Scott's arm bends over my shoulder and snatches my phone right out of my hands. He tosses it to his other hand and holds it as far away from me as he can. I launch across his lap, reaching for it.

"He deserves to know!"

Scott stretches his arm high above his head, and I start clambering up his body. I realize where I am when I put all my weight on the hand pressing into Scott's stomach, and his breath puffs out against my ear. I freeze.

Oh.

This is a bad idea. A bad idea. A bad...

Scott's free hand slides up the outside of my thigh as I turn to face him, finding only the thinnest ring of blue around wide pupils. I remember him looking like this at the bar last year. I remember wanting to kiss him.

"Hi," I breathe.

"Piper…" It sounds like a warning.

This is a *bad idea.*

I let my knees, one on each side of his thighs, slowly slide apart until I'm seated in his lap. I see Scott's jaw clench as his eyes flutter closed, and I slide my hand from his stomach up his chest.

"Piper." Scott's voice is rough now, and his eyes find mine again. "Are you sober enough for—"

"Shut up."

The words rush out of me just before I tilt my head down and crash my lips against Scott's. His response is encouraging, eager. His fingers squeeze into my leg.

In a moment of clarity, I pull back, and Scott leans forward when I do, seemingly reluctant to let me go.

"Are you—" I pull air into my lungs. Consent is important. "I don't want to pressure y—"

"Shut up," he says my words back to me. I hear my phone thud to the floor behind the couch before both of Scott's hands slip into my back pockets, and he presses me against him.

The sound that escapes me is positively feral.

I curl over him again, rolling my hips while my teeth find his ear, his neck, his collarbone.

"Scott, I—" I don't know what I planned to say. I'm not sure I had a plan at all, just need.

"Hold on," he instructs and pulls his hands out of my pockets to wrap one arm around my waist and the other under my ass. He stands in one swift movement, and my ankles hook behind his back, my hands clamped on his shoulders.

"Oh fuck," he breathes, and I look down to see I'm sitting so high on his waist, he's basically eye level with my chest. He loosens his grip so I can slide down, and the friction sets me on fire.

"Upstairs, now," I demand, and thread my fingers into his hair. He hums in response and takes the stairs two at a time.

Once we're in Scott's room, I expect to be thrown on the bed, but he turns and sits at the edge, keeping me astride him.

"I want to watch you," he explains before reaching over his shoulder to yank off his shirt. I follow his lead and by the time he's taken his off, mine is gone too, and my hands are behind me, unhooking my bra.

"Good, because I like being on top," I answer.

"Fuuuuck," Scott drags out this time when I slide the straps off my arms and drop my bra behind him on the bed.

His head descends to one breast, while his hand grips the other, rolling my nipple under the pad of his thumb. I've never had a lot going on in that area, but Scott makes me feel like I'm perfect.

I gasp at a sharp sting and look down to see Scott smiling devilishly up at me, having just nipped at my skin.

"Too much, princess?" he asks. *Princess? Me?*

Scott drags the flat of his tongue across the faint mark he made, and every thought leaves my brain.

"Just enough," I groan, arching and pressing myself further into his mouth.

I shove my hand into the miniscule gap between us and pop open the button on my shorts. The zipper grinds open as I move my hand inside and down, chasing the pressure I need. Between us, the back of my hand rubs against Scott's hard length as I pinch my clit, and both of us moan at the same time, the vibration of Scott's spreading across my chest like a wave.

He shifts his lips to my other nipple and clamps over it,

sucking and licking with fervor. I immediately wonder what that would feel like between my legs, and my whole body shudders. I rock my hips against my hand, against him. Scott's free hand is back on my ass as he helps me chase my release, just on the edge of pain, while he worships my breasts.

"I need to get inside you, so you're going to have to come, Piper," he breathes out between teasing bites down my sternum. "Can you do that for me?"

"Uh huh," is all I can manage, but it's enough.

"That's my perfect girl," Scott mumbles against my skin before he draws my nipple back between his lips. The hand that isn't on my ass moves to my back, where he grips me like he's afraid I'll slip away. His fingertips draw lines of electricity across my shoulder blade, and I expect to find more marks on my skin when he grips under my arm to help me lift and fall against him.

It's all too much—his mouth, his hands, my fingers, the rough denim. I combust. I must have closed my eyes, because I find Scott looking reverently at me when I open them.

I'm still breathing hard, but I gasp out, "more."

I stand on shaky legs and kick my underwear and shorts off in one go while Scott strips just as quickly and pulls himself further up the bed. When he looks back at me, he freezes.

"I have died and gone to heaven," he mutters.

"Not yet," I say and crawl over him.

I straddle his thighs and take his length in my hand. His hips buck to meet my stroke, and I repeat the motion.

"Condom," I say.

Scott's arm flies out to the side, and his fingertips tap against the nightstand.

"Drawer," he says through clenched teeth.

I stretch across Scott's body to reach the drawer and return with a condom. I rip it open and roll it on him, not hesitating before I position myself over him and sink down in one smooth motion. I don't think it's the tequila making my head spin. I feel *so* unbelievably *full*.

I put my hands on Scott's chest so I can lift up, but he grips my wrists hard enough to draw my attention to his face.

"Need a minute."

He breathes very slowly and purposefully, and I've never felt more powerful. I can't help it, I shift my hips the tiniest amount, and his desperate gasp feels like a reward.

"Please, Scott?" I beg, digging my nails into his skin and tilting my head to the side.

"Ok." He nods before saying it again. "Ok. Lift up."

I tip forward and lift, prepared to sink back on to him, but Scott raises his hips and drives into me and—*Oh.*

He finds a rhythm that hits this spot inside me over and over again, and all I can do is hang on and say his name like a prayer. He releases a wrist and moves his hand between us, holding me at the crease of my thigh for stability and brushing against my abused clit. I am swollen and sensitive, and I will not last long.

"Scott, I—" Again, I don't know what I was going to say, but he slows.

He removes his hand from my leg and brings his thumb to my mouth. I wrap my lips around it, drawing it into my mouth and lapping at the pad of his finger with my tongue. He pulls the wet digit from my lips and replaces it against my clit, where he presses slow, delicious circles.

Scott begins moving again, keeping the rhythm with his thumb, and I am already tipping right on the edge. I think he can tell, because he drives into me brutally. I can take it. I *need* it. I crash, squeezing around him. I feel every inch of him when he explodes inside me. As I come down from my high, Scott releases me slowly, and I tip off him, gravity pulling me onto the mattress next to him face down, limp, and spent.

Scott turns his head and gently kisses my hair, rubbing a

soothing hand down my spine. I practically purr. I feel the bed dip as he gets up and hear rustling and running water a moment later. He returns, crouching beside the bed, and I crack open my eyes.

"Drink," he says, holding the cup of water before me. I prop myself up enough to follow his instructions before setting the empty cup on the nightstand and moving to pull his sheets over me.

"Nuh uh," Scott says, and I see that dangerous smirk again.

He slides a knuckle from my shoulder, down my side, over my bare ass, and to my leg. He walks down the bed as he goes, suddenly grasping my ankle at the bottom of the bed and flipping me over. He takes my other ankle and pulls me down the bed, until my ass is right at its edge. I watch as he sinks to his knees.

"I'm not finished with you yet."

CHAPTER 3

Piper

When I wake up the next morning, I'm possibly still a little drunk. I roll over, and the room keeps moving after I've stopped. At least, I think I've stopped.

Oh yeah, she's tipsy, world.

The headache hasn't hit yet, but I know I'm going to feel like crap pretty soon. My mouth is dry and tastes like something died in it.

I press the heels of my palms into my eyes in an attempt to stabilize my world. It doesn't work. Everything still feels like it's moving.

No, something is *actually* moving next to me.

I remember a flash of last night and groan quietly. Moving one hand away from my face, I crack an eye open. All the clutter is gone, but the furniture is unmistakable. I'm in Alice's old room… now Scott's room. And the warm, naked body next to my equally naked body is his.

Yep, we did that. And *damn* was it good.

I slowly turn my head toward Scott and see him sprawled on his stomach, face turned away from me. Having settled again, he's now motionless other than his rhythmic, soft breathing. He's mercifully still asleep.

I allow myself to admire the expanse of his lightly tanned back for just a moment before I shift into magician mode and try to levitate my way out of this bed without disturbing him. Last night was a blast, but it was also a huge mistake, and I need to get the hell out of here so I can begin pretending it never happened—immediately.

To call myself a "relationship person" would be a blatant lie. I've casually seen guys before, sure, but it never goes anywhere, and I've stopped trying to get anything long-term to work. They lose interest, I fly down a toxic spiral of meaningless hookups to remind myself I don't care, and I usually finish it all off with a haircut.

Something like that simply isn't an option with Scott. He's Jake's brother. Jake and Alice are probably going to get married. Alice is my sister for all intents and purposes. Everything is so… It just can't happen. I can't drag this man into my inevitable mess.

What happened, happened, and I can't undo it. The best thing to do now is just delete it from my memory forever.

I quickly find my underwear and shorts on the floor and snatch them up with lightning speed, purposefully avoiding looking in any mirror, not needing to see the marks I can feel all over myself. My shirt is flung in a corner, but my bra is trapped under Scott's leg, which is sticking out from his sheet. Scott shifts when I tiptoe back toward the bed, so… nope.

The bra is dead to me. RIP. I'm glad it wasn't one of my nice ones. Goodbye.

Fleeing down the stairs, I stop just long enough to grab clean clothes from my bags by the door, dress, spray on some deodorant, pop a mint in my mouth, and shove my feet into my shoes. Before leaving, I scan the room for my cell phone, remembering it ended up on the floor behind the couch. I snatch it up and roll my bags back out the front door, slipping down the porch steps as quietly as possible and realizing I have nowhere to go.

Scott said Alice and Jake won't be back until tomorrow, and I am in this tiny town by myself without a car. I consider trying to break into Jake and Alice's house next door before the answer slaps me in the face. Grateful Bob is just a few houses down.

Grateful Bob is objectively the coolest guy I've ever met. He's lived in this town for forever and literally just does and says whatever the fuck he wants. He could be anywhere between sixty and one hundred years old, but he's not at all frail looking. Instead, he's sturdy and not just physically. He has long, white hair that he keeps tied back in a low ponytail and is basically never without his patch-covered denim jacket—each patch giving a hint about a piece of his long life. The kind of man who seems like he'd have advice about anything. He also knows everything about everybody in this town. He's like a sage or blunt life guide.

Grateful Bob is also a bit odd. He's *never* just Bob, but as far as I'm aware, nobody knows the true story behind his nickname since he makes up a new tale every time somebody asks. And he has a massive collection of loon paraphernalia. Whatever makes you happy, bro.

Most importantly, I learned he was friends with Rain and basically made it his job to watch over Alice as soon as she arrived in Wilcox Grove, a kindness for which I will always be, well, grateful. I've learned through Alice he's one of those rare authentically good people. He is a good listener but will also offer a kick in the pants when one is warranted. I immediately got that vibe when we met last fall, and Alice has confirmed it repeatedly over the months that followed. I'm confident he'll know what I should do until Alice is home or at least give me a safe place to land.

There are openings in the trees around the lake with two houses in each of them and a single road that connects the offshoots around this part of the lake. It's this solitary dirt road I'll be trudging down with most of my worldly possessions. The walk isn't too long, but I'm dreading making it with all my bags and legs that are already sore because of… reasons. It takes a significant amount of effort to drag everything down the gravel road, but I'm determined.

The early morning sunlight is sneaking through the trees that seem to bend over the road, making a safe little cocoon over me. Dew clings to everything, sparkling when a determined ray finds its way through the branches overhead. Birds are singing and chattering all around, and I'm reminded once again how very far I am from the brownstone I rented back in Boston.

When I eventually make it to the opening in the trees leading to Grateful Bob's house, I find the man I'm looking for standing by the door to his truck, telltale denim jacket right where it should be. He must hear the ruckus I'm making (sorry everyone) because he starts and looks right at me.

I may not know why he is called Grateful Bob, but I sure as shit am grateful he's here right now.

"Hi, Grateful Bob," I say at a reasonable volume for the early hour and hurry—as much as I can in my pack mule state—over to him.

"Piper?" he questions, confusion painting his face.

I'm impressed he remembers my name. We only met one time early last October. On the other hand, I did get in a bar fight the night prior alongside Alice and Scott, and we nearly needed him to pick us up from the police station at two in the morning, so I guess that would be memorable.

"Good morning and sorry for intruding. I came up here a bit suddenly to crash with Alice, but Scott told me she's away with Jake until tomorrow, and I was kind of wondering if I could hang with you for a bit until I figure out a plan." Having just reminded myself I've only met Grateful Bob once, I realize barging in on his life is a bit brazen.

The old man smiles kindly, and my worry drips away. He has a special way of making people feel at ease.

"You're Alice's people. Of course you have a place with me."

Alice hasn't even been here a year yet, and it warms me to my toes to see her so quickly welcomed. She deserves a whole flock of people on her side. Still, I don't want to take advantage of that kindness.

"Are you sure? I don't want to impose, but a ride into town would be a huge help, so maybe I can find a place to stay until Alice is back."

"I'm sure. It's no trouble at all." He easily lifts my large rolling suitcase and sets it in the bed of the truck. Maybe he's not *that* old? I swear that bag weighs a ton. "I'm headed to Barefoot Bake for some breakfast. Why don't you come along with me?"

"Hannah and Leslie's place? After all I've heard Alice say about Hannah's baking, there's no way I'd turn that down." I hurry around the truck and hop in without hesitation, shoving my other bags on the passenger side floor. I smile when I see the loon print blanket tucked around the bench seat and the loon on the air freshener hanging from the rear-view mirror. I wonder if he got them specially made.

The man of the hour is chuckling as he climbs behind the wheel. I'm used to people finding me a little silly and enjoy that I can bring that amusement.

I fire off a quick text to Alice.

ME

I hope you're having the best time, but we need to talk as SOON as you're back! I'm hanging with Grateful Bob for now.

Then, I dig out some ibuprofen from my bag and swallow them dry.

We bump along the road in silence for a minute until we

pass the gap in the trees leading to Jake's and Alice's (now Scott's, I guess) houses. Grateful Bob jerks his head toward the opening.

"I'm surprised you got a hold of Scott already today. That boy isn't usually a morning person."

"Oh, no. I talked to him last night."

Grateful Bob turns his head just a bit to survey me with an all-knowing gaze, and I wonder how much mascara is smudged under my eyes. I really should have stopped in Scott's bathroom before bailing.

As I think about my early morning arrival, laden with bags, looking the way I do, I quickly realize what I just revealed with my overshare.

"Hm," is all he says, nodding his head as he focuses back on the road.

Somehow, I'm positive he knows. And now I want to die. But, after a few more minutes in silence, I think I just might have escaped any questioning.

No dice.

"Do you want to talk—"

"NOPE." I cut him off abruptly and feel the heat rising up my neck to my cheeks. He laughs again. I'm a freaking *riot* this morning, I guess.

"Alrighty then. How about you tell me what sent you up here in the first place?"

He really is a gem.

"Ugh, yes! Last year, the library director left and the powers that be decided to replace her with someone external, without even interviewing anybody from the library. He came in with guns blazing and without a single brain cell in his stupid tiny head. He's inexperienced, sexist, narcissistic, manipulative—basically think of every bad trait a person could have, and you've got this weasel snake's personality."

Grateful Bob makes a face like we're downwind of a cow farm. "And you couldn't get rid of him?"

"I don't know if he's got dirt on people in high places, or if they're just too stupid or lazy to address the problem, but no matter how many people left, nobody in a position of authority seemed to accept Bernard is the problem. I was trying to hold out as a point of pride and to protect the library, but it was just too much. I feel guilty about bailing, but staying wasn't an option."

"I'm guessing you feel guilty because you're a good person and not because you did anything wrong."

"I can see what was happening clearly enough to know it wasn't on me, but I think I'll mourn how it used to be before Bernard for a while. At least I know I won't regret telling him exactly where he could stick his attitude and terrible ideas as I left."

Now we're both laughing, and Grateful Bob is easily parallel parking his truck on the street outside a perfect-looking bakery with **Barefoot Bake** burned into the wooden sign across the building. Next door, a matching sign reading **Literary Lake** sits above a window display filled with books.

The two shops sit right in the middle of the main street that runs through town. It's got a quintessential small-town vibe, lined with family-owned shops, many of which were likely passed down for generations. There isn't a chain store in sight. But we did pass a drugstore, a flower shop, a pizzeria, and a small law office in a pretty, old Victorian house. Somebody is watering window boxes filled with daisies a few stores away, and a crossing guard is guiding kids a bit further down the road. It's so cute I could scream.

"I might have paid good money to be a fly on that wall," Grateful Bob says, pulling me back into our conversation as he puts the truck in park and turns off the engine.

"My lease with my roommate was ending soon anyway—

she's moving in with her boyfriend—so I just kind of left. And now here I am. If Alice will have me, I might stick around for a while and see if I can be as happy here as she is. I've missed her." I snap my mouth shut when I realize I'm tipping over into over-sharing again.

My gracious driver doesn't let on that he's annoyed by my yapping yet, though. I've hopefully cut myself off in time. Instead, he nods to the café.

"I think one of Hannah's muffins is a good start if you're looking to fall in love with Wilcox Grove."

We hop out of the truck when Barefoot Bake's front door flies open. Hannah, who I also met on bar fight night, is standing in the doorway looking panicked with her jacket hanging off one arm. She's about to take off, but she abruptly stops.

"Shit! The café," she says loud enough I can hear her even though she doesn't seem to be speaking to anybody in particular.

"Hannah?" Grateful Bob rushes up to her, using a calm voice one might use with a spooked animal. "What's wrong?"

"Oh my god—Grateful Bob! Leslie got hurt doing some downhill mountain biking thing with her friends, and she's at the hospital. I don't know what happened, but they said she had to be taken by helicopter. I need to go, but—" She looks back and forth between the café and some point down the road. Maybe her car? I can't imagine how she's feeling. Leslie is her wife

Thankfully, Grateful Bob seems to understand. "I'll take care of things here. Don't you worry. You need to go."

He looks over Hannah's shoulder and into the café. He quickly seems to spot what he's looking for.

"Marty!" he calls, and a young woman comes over to the door. I'm pretty sure I've heard Alice mention Marty. I think she works with Jake.

"I need you to drive Hannah to the hospital. Can you do that?"

The girl nods furiously. She takes Hannah's forearm gently

and guides her fully out of the café, prying Hannah's two sets of keys from her hand at the same time. Marty hands one bunch, likely the store keys, to Grateful Bob and keeps Hannah's car keys. Hannah still looks stunned. I'm not sure she's fully understanding until she looks back over her shoulder and whispers, "Thank you."

I've just been standing stupidly on the sidewalk by the truck, but I scurry to him when Grateful Bob waves me over.

"I know you were going to look for a place to stay tonight, so you're welcome to stay on my couch, but I'm going to need your help in there. You up for it?"

"Absolutely," I assure him. I tie up my hair, and the two of us jump into the fray.

CHAPTER 4

Scott

I feel like a doofus, but I actually wake up with a smile on my face. I didn't think that happened outside of cheesy movies, but here I am, grinning like an idiot. I stretch languidly as I roll onto my back and notice I'm alone in my bed. I can tell from the silence in the house that my bedmate isn't just lingering in another room.

Piper's absence is disappointing but not surprising. I doubt I was on her agenda when she came to Wilcox Grove last night. Our decision-making was impaired and impulsive, but I have no regrets. Piper is an incredible woman, and that was an incredible night.

It might sound unbelievable, but I've known there's something special about Piper since the moment I laid eyes on her last fall.

I shove a water bottle in my bag as I approach the bus station doors so I can head back to my hometown, already regretting my decision not to just drive from New York to New Hampshire. I thought it would be better to take the train and then a bus, where I could work for the long trip. Plus, I like people and weirdly like public transportation for the people watching it offers. But I'd *forgotten how annoying the transfer in Boston could be if my train had any delays and got in late. This train in particular had a massive delay and got in <u>very</u> late, leaving me to take the first bus in the wee hours of the next morning from Boston for the last leg of my trip.*

As soon as I get on the rumbling monstrosity, a muffled but cheerful laugh draws my attention. I find the source quickly—a stunning woman in a window seat about halfway down the aisle trying to stifle her laughter behind her hand. Cozy in leggings and a hoodie that's basically swallowing her, with a head of wild curls piled on top of her head in a bun, she's folded herself into the too-small bucket seat, her long legs tucked up in front of her and a paperback book propped on her knees.

It's way too early in the morning, still dark outside, and most people, myself included, are barely conscious or are chugging coffee to stay awake, but she's already alert and lively. Her eyes are glittering with wonder as they fly down each page, and I can see blush across her cheeks, likely from trying to stop herself from grinning so hard. That smile seems to light up this dim and dingy bus. Something about her just seems so alive. She's breathtaking.

I don't realize I've stopped moving until a man behind me not-so-subtly nudges me forward. I'm not a creep, so I don't try to sit next to her, but I do mentally claim the row across from her as my own. When I get close, I put my hand on the back of the seat beside hers.

"Anybody sitting here?" I ask when she looks up, gesturing to the empty two seats across the aisle from her.

Her brows pull together, and her smile falters as she sees the same two empty seats that I do.

"Um... no?" she says warily, probably because my question was both stupid and unnecessary, but I've committed now.

"Thanks," I say genuinely and smile even though it feels like

neither my expression nor any other will compare to her joy. Still, her lips quirk back up, and her eyes soften. I'm calling it a win.

She goes back to her book, and I take my seat, shoving my bag into the overhead space, but keeping my tablet with me. I had planned on sleeping for as much of the ride as I could, but now I'm unwilling to lose a minute with this woman. I'm completely captivated, and I have no clue why she's affected me so much, so fast.

I'm not here to be an asshole and disturb her peace, so as the bus jolts and starts our journey north, I mind my own business and continue working on a design that's been bugging me for a few days. It just doesn't feel "right" yet.

Even though I try to focus on my drawing, I'm still hyper aware of the woman just a few feet away from me. About an hour into our journey, she starts squirming and the heel of one of her legs suddenly slides off her seat, her socked foot hitting the bus floor with a loud thud.

Out of the corner of my eye, I see her head jerk up and look around to see who noticed her little disturbance. Answer? Nobody. It's a bus. Nobody cares.

She sets her book on the empty seat beside her and lowers her other foot to the floor so she can rifle through one of her bags. I swear her whole arm disappears into the tote while she struggles to pull something out. With a hearty yank, she wins the battle, but her phone goes flying out of the top of the bag and miraculously lands right by my feet.

I look at her fully now, and see the guiltiest expression looking back at me, a makeup bag clutched in her hand.

"I'm so sorry," she dramatically whispers at me. A lot of other passengers on the bus are trying to get some sleep in like I'd initially planned on doing.

I wave off her concern and retrieve her phone. I scoot into the aisle seat on my side of the bus and set my tablet on my vacated chair before reaching over to hand back the device.

"I'm sorry," she apologizes again, taking it from me. "I'm such a disaster literally all the time."

She seems to have forgotten she thought I was a weirdo before this ride started. I'm grateful.

"Nah." I try to portray the embodiment of nonchalance. "It's very normal in my culture to introduce yourself by throwing a personal belonging at somebody else."

I fling my stylus across the aisle, and it lands beside her discarded book.

"I'm Scott."

She smiles a soft smile, looking down at the pen. It's just as perfect as her big smile from earlier. She picks up my stylus and her book, sliding into the aisle seat on her side. She holds the pen out to me.

"I'm Piper."

I hope Piper left to avoid a potentially awkward morning after and not because she's upset or regretting last night. She doesn't seem like the kind of woman who does anything she doesn't want to, regardless of whether tequila is part of the equation. But I still want to make sure she's ok.

I pull up her contact, quickly updating the name before trying to call her. It rings out and goes to voicemail. At least she didn't see my call and decline it. I fire off a text in case she just hates answering the phone.

ME

> Hey. Where'd you take off to? Is everything ok?

I get out of bed, brush my teeth, go downstairs, make coffee, and come back up to get dressed before checking my phone again. There's no reply.

It's after nine in the morning, so I dial Jake's number without fear of waking him. After several rings, my brother picks up.

"Hey, what's wrong?"

He's such a worrywart.

"Good morning, Jake. I hope you're having a lovely morning, too," I tease. The line stays completely silent. I sigh. "Everything's fine. I was just wondering if Alice had a chance to check her phone. Piper came up here last night, not knowing you whisked Alice away, and I'm wondering if the two of them connected yet."

"Hold on."

My brother is a man of many words. If his business spending time almost exclusively with plants doesn't work out, he should consider public speaking.

The connection starts breaking up, but I hear most of his recounting my question to Alice followed by Alice's surprised "oh!" in the background.

"We *barely* have service out here." The audio cuts in and out like it's trying to prove his point. "She'll try calling her now. Thanks for the heads up."

"Does Alice know where she's at? I can check up on her."

After a pause he says, "She's with Grateful Bob."

"Thanks! Since I can barely hear you, I'll let you go. I'll see you tomorrow. Love you, bro."

"Love you, too, Scotty. See you."

I guess I'm off to find Grateful Bob.

CHAPTER 5

Piper

"Each book follows one of the brothers or somebody in their lives. You don't have to read them in order, but they all exist in the same world and are consecutive. If you like hot country men, you'll *love* these," I gush.

The young woman's eyes are wide with anticipation as she carries the entire series up to the register. I'm in my element, talking about books. Because Literary Lake is attached to Barefoot Bake (I adore the cheesy names and Hannah and Leslie's affinity for rhyming and alliteration), the bookstore is busy when the café is, which is basically all morning.

A rustic brick archway connects the two shops seamlessly, and the portion of the bookstore just on our side of the archway offers a seating area used by readers and diners alike. Literary Lake opens later than the café, but a lot of the patrons use the seating area on the bookstore side as they enjoy their caffeine and pastries, so there's been plenty to do since I arrived. The store, like the café, is peppered with plants in all different kinds of pottery that need watering and some TLC, too.

A couple of hours after she left, Hannah called to let us know

Leslie was going to be ok but had broken several bones in a fall. I don't know how news got around so quickly, but it's been unbelievable to see so much support from the people in their lives. Throughout the day, dozens of townspeople have wandered in with premade meals, cards, or just well-wishes for us to pass along. Most have also lent a hand when they stopped in—taking out the trash, cleaning tables, collecting books from tables to be re-shelved. There have been a lot of moving pieces, but it's been thrilling.

I'm so appreciative of Mads, one of Literary Lake's regular booksellers, giving me a rapid-fire rundown of the store after Hannah took off this morning. She's been manning the register because when I was at the till, I spent more time asking her questions than helping customers. Wilcox Grove doesn't have its own public library branch, so the store functions as an unofficial library with a section of used books upstairs available for borrowing. I have yet to master the check-in/check-out system used here.

I've been primarily on the floor, cleaning, shelving, and helping with recommendations. I even spent extra time with the middle school librarian, Molly, helping her put together a list for her summer reading program. Periodically, I've checked in with Grateful Bob on the café side, but his system of organized chaos seems to be working without my interference. He has support from two of Hannah's and Leslie's employees, and I haven't smelled anything burning, so I think it's been going well.

Today is the most fun I've had in a while.

I'm watching Wilcox Grove's newest romance reader carry her books out of the store, when I feel a prickle on the back of my neck. I turn around to figure out whose eyes are on me and spot Scott leaning against that brick archway, a paper coffee cup in his hand.

Damn, he looks good.

He's shorter than my six-foot height, but with his confidence, you'd never notice it. My eyes trail up his body, from his black boots to his dark wash jeans, to his white v-neck. Some might think the outfit is simple, but I guess I like simple. He's lean, and I know first-hand he's a lot stronger than he looks. When I first met him, his hair was buzzed, but he's let it grow out since then, and while the sides are still cut short, his dark locks are just long enough on top to show their curls. My gaze moves down to his eyes, and I can't hold his stare. Instead, my focus falls on his lips, quirked in a cocky smirk, and an image flashes in my mind of those lips on my skin last night, trailing up my sternum between my—

I immediately pivot and face the opposite direction to hide my reddening cheeks, happy to pretend I wasn't just openly ogling that man for a solid minute, just as happy as I am to pretend last night didn't happen. As I get to work straightening some perfectly straight books, I can still feel Scott's eyes on me. His chuckle at my refusal to acknowledge him carries easily between the stacks to me.

I'm not proud to say it, but I scamper away, deeper into the store and further from that damn archway. I'm desperately seeking somebody I can help when I hear footsteps coming in my direction. I will *not* turn around. I grab an armful of returns off one of our carts and stubbornly face a bookcase.

I'm looking at the cover of the first book so I can figure out where it goes, but I seem to have forgotten how to read.

"You're not running from me, are you?"

Suddenly, Scott is directly behind me, and I can feel his breath moving my hair.

"No." Thankfully, my voice sounds steadier than I feel.

"Piper, come on. Look at me." His voice has a pleading undertone, enough to make me turn and meet his gaze.

"Can I help you?" I'm aloof and a little cold. I feel badly about it, but I can't help it. I need to protect myself.

Scott's face falls. He reaches forward and takes the stack of books from me, easily holding them balanced on one large palm. My gaze slips from his and falls to the books. The cup he was holding is gone. He lifts his other hand and gently turns my face back to him with a single finger on my chin.

"Being serious, Piper. Are you ok?"

"Oh!" From his tone, I suddenly realize he's legitimately worried he did something wrong with me last night. "Scott, no—I mean, yes. I'm fine. Really. Are you ok?"

"Are you kidding? I'm fucking fantastic." Just like that, his megawatt smile is back.

"I really am ok, but that can't happen again." My wall pops right back up.

"Sure it can. It's simple. When you're done here, you just come with me back to—"

"Scott!" I hiss, looking around to make sure nobody's suddenly wandered into earshot. "That's not what I meant, and you know it. We shouldn't have, and we *cannot* again."

"You can't tell me you didn't have a good time. From the sounds you were making, I'm pretty sure you did."

My eyes must be as big as dinner plates, even though he's lowered his voice to barely above a whisper. "You cannot *say* shit like that! I—It was—You were… good. That is *not* the point."

Talking about it sends my mind right back into Scott's bed. I swear I can feel the pressure of his fingers gripping my—

No! Stop that!

Now I'm chastising my own brain.

Scott has a cool smirk on his lips, and I can't believe how unbothered he is about all of this. I feel like every one of my nerve endings is electrified.

"Look, I have a lot to do here. I don't think Hannah even realized she was leaving the store in my hands, and I will not let her down. You need to go. I'm not good for you."

The image of my first boyfriend on my porch forces its way into my mind. I'm standing there, fifteen years old, in the homecoming dress I spent hours searching for, trying to comprehend what he means when he says *You're exhausting, Piper. You can't expect anybody to want to put up with you.* Instead of picking me up for the dance, he breaks up with me. I stand frozen even after he drives away until my mother asks me to close the door before I let bugs in. I go up to my room and shred the dress with scissors.

Scott's brows draw together, like he's displeased, but he doesn't answer. Instead, he picks up the first book from the stack in his hand, flipping it over to check the section listed by the price sticker and then stepping around me to shelve it.

"What do you think you're doing?" I ask.

"I've clocked a decent number of hours in this bookstore, and I'm pretty proficient when it comes to the alphabet, so I'm helping."

He doesn't even look at me when he says it, continuing to completely ignore how frazzled I am. Maybe it's possible he's oblivious? He also doesn't comment on me saying I'm bad for him.

"Don't you have something else to do?"

"Nope," he says, popping the p. "I like being around you, even if you're having a bit of a freak-out. It's not entirely surprising, but it *is* fairly amusing."

My mouth drops open. I simply cannot have him here. I snatch the remaining books out of his hands.

"I'm glad I'm such great entertainment," I breathe, exasperated. "If you want to be helpful, go find Grateful Bob in the café. It's lunchtime, so I'm sure he'll find something for you to do. I'm officially banning you from the bookstore."

I snap my feet together and point back toward the café.

He holds up his hands in mock surrender. "I'll go, I'll go. But you're it for me, princess. You just need to let me show you."

His chuckle carries to my ears yet again as he smoothly walks away. The audacity of this man!

CHAPTER 6

Scott

I follow Piper's instructions and seek Grateful Bob out at Barefoot Bake. He immediately puts me to work cleaning tables, running trays of mugs through the dishwasher in the back, and circling with regular and decaf coffee refills. He's known me my whole life and has no qualms about telling me what to do. He helped me and Jake a lot after our parents died and is basically family.

Even though I can't see Piper while I'm working, just knowing she's in the same building has me excited. I haven't gone a day without thinking about her since we met seven months ago. From the second I laid eyes on her, I felt inexplicably drawn into her orbit.

Since parting after the whole bar-fight-slash-police-station incident, we texted a few times—she checked in on the status of my face after I used it to block Troy's fist and we exchanged major holiday well wishes—but I never dreamed I'd have the chance to be near her again for an extended period of time. I lived in New York, and she lived in Boston. I'd crowned her "the one that got away."

But she's not away. We're both here, and yesterday I got a taste of what it's like to have her.

She sat on my couch with her bare feet wedged under my thigh, and she'd become so animated when she ranted about her shit ex-boss that I was tempted to drive down to Boston in the middle of the night just to find the guy and hit him upside the head with a book.

Then, she told me other little bits of her life, about college with Alice, about going off to get her master's degree in a new state all by herself. I couldn't get enough. I wanted to know anything she was willing to share, but she seemed hesitant to do so.

We drank, we chatted, and we laughed.

Piper is unlike any woman I've ever met or am likely to meet in my lifetime. I'd be a damn fool to let her go again.

A small crash has me looking over toward the bookstore. Piper is crouched near one of the seats just through the archway, picking up a book from the floor and handing it back to the chair's occupant.

She's smiling at them, and I swear all the light in this place is coming from her. Her hair is pulled back in a low bun, but running around all morning has caused some of her dark curls to fall free.

She unfolds herself from the floor, and I admire the miles of her legs. She's wearing tan pants that hug her perfect ass and a coral tank top that makes her copper skin glow. She makes me think of summer, just around the corner.

I'm still staring when her warm brown eyes dart to me. I jump, having been caught. I step up to a nearby table to refill an empty coffee mug and end up pouring scalding coffee all over my hand and the table.

I see Piper move toward me out of the corner of my eye while

I'm shaking my hand off and hissing, pretending it doesn't feel like my flesh is peeling from my bones.

"I'm good," I say loud enough for her to hear me and give her a thumbs up. Piper only rolls her eyes in response.

I'm so not good. I'm in deep.

I'm impressed I don't cause myself further bodily injury during the day since I keep getting distracted by Piper. I'll catch the sound of her voice or her ethereal laugh, and my eyes will automatically seek her out. She fits in so easily here, kindly welcoming and helping even the most odious members of Wilcox Grove society.

She fits in here, like a missing puzzle piece, and others are just as hypnotized as I am. It seems like almost everybody finds a reason to speak with her, and the other booksellers defer to her, even though she's newest on the block. She seems to handle everything with ease.

Even with all my daydreaming and Piper-watching, Grateful Bob has kept me busy, so I'm tired to my bones when we're cleaning up the bakery just after six. He and Piper have been here all day, so I can't imagine how they feel.

Usually, Literary Lake stays open later than the bakery, which stops serving at five, but Grateful Bob made the executive decision to close both stores together after the manager on duty this evening called out. Piper insisted she could keep going until the bookstore's closing time at nine, but Grateful Bob won't allow it.

"I'm really happy to stay," she says again, following the older man from table to table. "I don't want to mess with Hannah's and Leslie's usual store hours."

"I'm no labor law expert, but it feels like it should be illegal to have you here any longer. Plus, I already sent your booksellers home. You did good today, kid. Real good. Now it's time to get out of here."

They've been arguing for several minutes, and Piper finally gives in.

"You're sure?"

"I'm positive," he says, looking through a set of keys. "Bring the cash to the back—I've got a safe key on here—and then we can get going."

Piper retrieves the cash drawer from the bookstore and walks it back over.

That's my cue.

"Piper," I say, sliding up next to her. "I'd be happy to drive you back."

She doesn't look at me.

"I'm all set. I'll go with Grateful Bob. Thanks."

I follow her through the kitchen and into the office at the back of the building where she hands off the cash drawer. Grateful Bob starts muttering to himself as he counts it.

I lean close to Piper, so I can whisper without being overheard.

"Why? You afraid of what will happen if we're alone together again?"

I think I see her shiver.

"No!" she exclaims, finally looking at me out of the corner of her eye. "Because nothing will happen."

It's not clear whether she's trying to convince me or herself.

"Then let me drive you back. Alice and Jake will be here tomorrow. You can stay in the guest room. No funny business. I promise."

Grateful Bob finishes tallying the cash and looks up at us.

"It'll be much more comfortable than at my house. All I have to offer is a couch, but it's yours if you'd like it," he says to Piper.

Damn. He's got good hearing for an old guy.

Piper opens her mouth, likely ready to object, but seems to struggle to find a reason to decline my offer. She sighs and snaps her jaw shut.

CHAPTER 7

Piper

S cott's eyes sparkle playfully, but his expression is authentic. I think he meant it when he said *no funny business*. Still, my pride wants me to dig my heels in.

"Come on, Piper," he teases. "If you're not afraid, what's the harm?"

Apparently my competitive side easily overrides my prideful one.

"Fine. I'm fine, and this is *fine*." I can hear myself getting riled up, and I take a breath to calm down. "Thank you for your offer, Scott. The spare room would be lovely."

My voice is girly and prim and entirely fake. I don't care. There is nothing between me and Scott, and there will be absolutely no issue with me staying at his house.

"Good!" Scott hides a laugh behind his fist, and we all begin moving toward the front door, Grateful Bob eyeing us both warily.

"You need a hand with your bags?" Scott asks.

"Nope!" I turn on my heel and stubbornly stomp to Grateful Bob's truck.

I pull the passenger door handle as I reach the truck, but

Grateful Bob has caught up and presses a hand against the door to stop me.

"You know," he starts softly. "I threatened Jake last year when he was being an idiot about his feelings for Alice. Don't make me have that talk with you about Scott. He's a good boy with a good heart. He doesn't deserve to be played around with."

The fight goes out of me, and I pivot to look into his eyes, hoping I can properly convey my intentions to steer clear of Scott. I know how painful shattering Scott's misguided perception of me would be.

"I know. I won't. You have my word," I promise.

He nods curtly before opening the door for me and then moving to pull my suitcase from the bed of the truck. I love that I'm now in a place where we don't even need to lock the car doors.

I swing my bags over my shoulders and follow Grateful Bob, who's already carrying the massive suitcase like it weighs five pounds. Scott comes over to relieve him of the burden and lifts the bag even easier into the back of his shiny black SUV.

Scott's shit-eating grin tells me he thinks he won this battle. He holds open the passenger door and dramatically bows when I get close. I remember him making the same move when we met up at the Corner Post bar last fall, and I fight back a smile. It's so *so* easy to like Scott.

He knows what's good for him because he keeps his mouth shut as I climb inside his car and shove my bags on the floor. Wordlessly, he slips the duffle off my feet and deposits it in the back seat, so I'm no longer squished.

After we wave goodbye to Grateful Bob, Scott gets into the driver's seat and pulls out of his parking spot, heading the opposite way of the house.

"I ordered takeout from Papa's," he explains before I can ask, referencing an Italian restaurant Alice is obsessed with. Jake took her there on their first official date.

"You had enough time to order it while I was grabbing my bags?" I ask, wondering if there will be enough for two but not wanting to ask it outright.

"No. I ordered it fifteen minutes ago. Don't worry. I got a lot of different things because I didn't know what you'd like. It's all delicious, so I guarantee something will be a winner."

My eyebrows pinch together.

"Fifteen minutes ago, I was still planning to stay with Grateful Bob. How'd you know I'd agree to stay with you?"

Scott smirks like he's keeping a secret. "I knew."

A few minutes later, Scott pulls up in front of the restaurant and hops out to grab our food. I immediately start fidgeting… well, snooping. I pop open the center console but find only some spare napkins and plasticware. Boring. I flip around to check the back seat, but the only thing back there is my bag. The glove box is similarly neat, containing car paperwork, a phone charger, a tire pressure gauge, and a roadside emergency flashlight tool thingy.

My eye catches on the driver's manual cover. Scott drives a Range Rover, and it's only a couple of years old. Everything still smells new and clean and *expensive*. Not at all like chemical-filled cheap leather. I'm pretty sure this is a *niiiiiice* car, and it certainly doesn't look second-hand.

I'm just starting to think this vehicle is an odd and very costly choice for somebody who, until recently, lived in New York City, when Scott returns with several paper bags in his hands. He slides the bags onto the floor behind the driver's seat, and all I can think about is the heavenly smell quickly filling the car.

My stomach embarrassingly sings the song of its people, grumbling and growling the entire, though mercifully short, drive back to Scott's house. I glance over at Jake and Alice's place, but the lights are still out. It was wishful thinking to hope they'd be back early.

Scott pulls toward the side of his house to park in front of the garage, sandwiched between the house and the woods. As soon as the headlights shine on the slightly warped garage door, a small, furry creature scurries along the building and disappears between the trees.

Even though I'm safely in an enclosed vehicle, I still squawk and pull my feet up onto my seat, like the raccoon is about to nibble on my toes. As he slams the brakes, Scott's attention flies to me.

"What's wrong?" he asks, and I feel incredibly silly.

"The raccoon startled me," I admit.

"The raccoon? Out there? You know we're inside an enclosed car, right?" His confusion isn't unreasonable.

"I *really* hate nature." I doubt I can keep the look of distaste off my face.

"You're joking." The outrage is clear in his voice as he eases the car forward again to finish parking.

"I most certainly am not. I like my life clean and bug and rodent free."

"There's so much more to nature than bugs and rodents, though." Scott cuts the engine and starts to get out of the car, so I follow suit after scrutinizing the tree line for any beady little eyes.

When I meet Scott at the house's side door, me carrying my two smaller bags, him carrying enough food to feed the Italian army, he continues his rebuttal.

"Hiking and camping are how I find peace. Nature is calm and beautiful in their simplicity."

"*Oh yeah*. I've always found the lack of indoor plumbing to be exceedingly peaceful," I tease sarcastically.

When the new door easily swings in, I can't help but smile. When Alice arrived up here, this door in particular sucked. It would only open when it felt like it, no matter how much jiggling and heaving were imposed on it. Eventually, it needed a full replacement when both Jake and Alice fell against it to get away from a charging moose that was interrupted in its inspection of the garage door.

"You know the only reason this house has a working side door is because a moose, *nature*, almost killed Alice last year, right?" I continue. That moose is also responsible for the multiple dents still in the garage door.

"But it didn't, and the way I understand it, that near-death experience helped Alice and Jake get closer." Scott is a hopeless, wild-critter-loving romantic.

We keep bantering as I follow him inside, while he retrieves my suitcase, as we unpack dinner, while we eat, and after, when we sit on the couch and ignore whatever we decided to put on the television. It's nice, lighthearted.

He meant it before. There's no funny business. It's just an enjoyable evening in each other's company. Eventually, Scott lugs my big bag upstairs for me, to the room I stayed in when I visited Alice. As I follow him, I refuse to look past his open bedroom door on the other side of the bathroom, afraid I'll see the sheets on his bed just as rumpled as I'd left them this morning.

Scott either doesn't notice my struggle, or he ignores it. He's the picture of professionalism.

"I'm still in the process of unpacking, but there are towels and washcloths in the linen closet and soap and hair stuff are still under the sink, so help yourself. I think some of them might even be yours that Alice had here." Scott steps into the bathroom to open the cabinet under the sink as he speaks, showing me where everything is. "I'll be downstairs if you need anything."

"Thanks for letting me stay here. It really is a big help," I admit before he leaves. It's annoying that he was right, but this is nice.

"Anytime," he replies and pads down the steps.

After showering, doing my nighttime skincare and haircare routine, and changing for bed, I swallow my instinct to hide away and slip downstairs to say goodnight like a polite roommate. He's in the room that Rain had set up as a library when she first moved up to Wilcox Grove. The windows facing the lake out back are open, and a warm, late spring wind gently sweeps inside.

As I approach, I spot Scott crouched on the floor, finishing putting together a desk. I quickly survey the room and see the many built-in bookcases are still mostly empty. It's a shame.

"What do you think?" he asks, as he seems to effortlessly flip the large piece of furniture upright.

I watch the way his tense muscles stretch the sleeves of his shirt and enjoy the way his sweat makes the material stick to his shoulders and back.

"I think it looks very nice," I say, my mouth suddenly quite dry.

CHAPTER 8

Piper

When I wake up, I can tell it's at least mid-morning. Yesterday was tiring. I was a good kind of tired, though. I stretch lazily in the bed, enjoying the extremely soft sheets. They're definitely not the same ones that were here when I visited Alice. Scott must have brought or purchased them.

Now that I think about it, the towel I used last night was similarly plush and luxurious, as were the sheets on *his* bed. Is he a secret fancy man? All things considered, I know very little about him and the life he had in New York.

The rest of the guest room largely looks the same as I remember, with a dark wooden dresser, a few shelves for knickknacks, and a gold framed, full-length mirror. Some boxes, which I assume must be Scott's, are neatly stacked against the wall.

Light streams in from the gap in the curtains. Since the main bedroom is at the back of the house and has the lake view, this window looks out front and over the garage toward the forest.

I'm about to get out of bed when I realize the shower is running. There's no way I'm risking bumping into Scott clad only in a towel again, so I stay put. I'm not being lazy. I simply cannot risk getting up yet. I don't make the rules.

Since I'm trapped in this cloud of a bed anyway, I flop over and snatch my phone from the nightstand. I'm surprised to see a flood of text messages from Alice. Some appear to be from yesterday. They must have come through all at once at some point in the middle of the night.

ALICE

> You're in Wilcox Grove? Why? What happened? Are you ok? Jake is on the phone with Scott now.

> Ugh. I don't think any of these are going to actually go through!

> Why are you staying with Grateful Bob? Did Scott not offer you the spare room at Mom's house? I'll throttle him!

The last few are time stamped from early this morning.

> I have reception!!! Are you up?

> I'm taking that as a no. I just talked to Hannah. Call her when you see this.

> Are you still not up? Piperrrrrrrrr.

> Oh! I guess you need Hannah's number. Here you go!

I chuckle as I type out a response. I love that girl. I tell her I can't wait to see her and assure her I'm calling Hannah ASAP. The bar loads most of the way across my screen, but the message stays in limbo. Alice must be back off the grid again.

After saving the number Alice sent over, I call Hannah.

"Hello?" She sounds absolutely exhausted.

"Hey, Hannah? It's Piper. How's Leslie?"

"Piper, hi! Leslie's ok." I hear shuffling footsteps and the snick of a door closing. When Hannah speaks again, her voice is a little louder. "She's resting now. They did surgery to set both of her legs. They had to put in all kinds of hardware, so that should be the worst of it. Once they're sure she's stable, we'll get to go home, but she'll have a lot of healing and then physical therapy. We're so lucky she didn't land on her head. If she had—" Hannah's voice cuts off, and she tries to cover her sob with a cough.

"But she didn't. She's going to be ok." My words feel insignificant in light of the scare Hannah had and the long recovery ahead of Leslie, but I don't know what else to say.

"Yeah. She's going to be ok," Hannah clings to that sentence like it's a lifeline. The line is quiet, just the sound of our breathing. I couldn't imagine loving somebody as much as Hannah clearly loves Leslie and seeing them hurt like this. I hope she knows I'm here for them both.

After a minute or two, Hannah clears her throat.

"Thank you," she says softly, like the company of being on the line with her helped. I hope it did. "And thank you for yesterday. I talked to Grateful Bob earlier, and he said you were a force to be reckoned with in the bookstore."

"I was more than happy to help. Literary Lake is a *dream*, and your employees are solid. He's exaggerating though. I just helped out."

"He's not the only one to say something. Mads and Molly and a bunch of other people raved about you and Grateful Bob stepping in, too."

"Well, thank you. It was kind of them to say something. But, I mean it. Being there was good for me, too. I had almost forgotten how much I love being around books. My old boss kind of sucked the joy out of everything."

"You're setting me up perfectly here," Hannah says, and I

hold my breath. Could she be…? "Grateful Bob said it sounded like you'd be in town at least for a while, and I was wondering if you had time to come back to the store today to discuss the possibility of you working there more permanently. If you're interested?"

I am so proud of myself for resisting the urge to scream into the phone. Hannah doesn't need that right now. I can't keep the excitement out of my voice, though.

"I'm extremely interested!"

Literary Lake is exactly the kind of environment I always pictured myself working in. Sure, it's a store and my degree is in *library* science, but it has the community-building feel of a library, and a really cool book lending program, too. It's peaceful without being boring and emanates safety.

Plus, as a practical matter, I need another job. I have student loan debt, and the freelance editing I do isn't going to cut it if I want to pay more than the constantly accruing interest and still be able to do silly things like eating.

Hannah's sigh of relief is audible.

"You are a godsend, Piper. Could you meet me at the store in like an hour, hour and a half? I need to grab some things for me and Leslie from the house anyway, and it's right by the store. We can talk through some details in person?"

"I'll see you there. Thank you so much for this opportunity. Please tell Leslie I'm thinking of her and hope she feels better as quickly as possible."

"I will. Thank you too, Piper. Really. I don't know what I would have done if you said no."

Once I hang up, I fall back on the bed and kick my feet. *Yes!!!*

The last thing I want to do is be late for my meeting with Hannah, so I need to get a move on. I stop my happy dance and listen. Silence. I creep over to the door and open it just a crack.

The bathroom door is ajar, and it seems like I'm the only one upstairs.

After getting dressed, I scurry into the bathroom to wash my face and brush my teeth. Sitting on the counter is my bra from yesterday morning beside a note in small, neat handwriting.

I believe this is yours, princess.

I snatch the bra and note up and fling them into my room before quietly closing the door. Back in the bathroom, I take off my bonnet and spray some water in my hair so I can gently roll the waves around my fingers to convince them to match the curls.

By the time I'm satisfied, something downstairs smells amazing. I look over at the stairs and hesitate. I've never lived with a man before or stayed with one other than for naked sleepovers. Scott won't be naked, right? I mean, why would he be? People don't just walk around naked when they have guests. That's ridiculous. I shake my head like the motion can clear the nonsense from my brain. I'm at least 87 percent nonsense, though, so it's hopeless.

I take a breath to steel myself and head downstairs, following my nose to the table situated between the kitchen and living room. It's covered in a full spread—pancakes, eggs, bacon, sausage, potatoes, and a jug of orange juice. Is that fresh-squeezed?

Scott turns from his spot at the sink and smiles when his eyes fall on me. When he chuckles, I realize I'm frozen beside the couch with my mouth open. I snap it shut. I also decide I will *not* be mentioning the bra situation.

"Breakfast is served," he says, pulling the dish towel from his shoulder with a flourish.

"This is…" I try to find the right word. "Incredible. You didn't do all this just for me, did you?"

Scott just shrugs. "I like to cook. Jake taught me after…" He trails off.

He means after Jake moved back home to be Scott's guardian. Their parents died when Jake was twenty and Scott was just twelve. Jake left college to return home for Scott and never looked back.

Scott clears his throat and continues. "Jake had learned some stuff from Mom when he was in high school, and kind of threw himself into cooking once he came back home. I liked to help him after school. I think it helped us connect. I dunno. I think it was easier to talk through things when our hands were busy."

My throat feels thick and the bridge of my nose stings. In the grand scheme of things, Scott and I basically just met, but this man is standing before me, laying himself bare. Vulnerable. Grateful Bob was right. He has a *very* good heart.

Not knowing what else to say to that, I look back to the food and offer a pathetic, "Thank you."

Scott overlooks the fact that I'm awkward and stiff next to his open soul. I don't know how to *do* this, and he should have somebody who does. I don't deserve his care and kindness when I offer so little, and I'm only about to ask for even more.

"Sit. Dig in," he insists, taking a seat himself.

"I feel like a schmuck, asking for a favor after you did all this, but would I be able to get a ride to the bookstore after we eat? Hannah asked to talk to me about a job." I slide onto a chair across from Scott and start building a small mountain of potatoes on my plate. "I could ask Grateful Bob or see if I can get a cab or something if you're busy."

"I'd be happy to take you. Congrats on the job!" I look up and see Scott looks genuinely pleased for me.

I suddenly realize it's a Monday morning, and I have no clue how Scott spends his time. "Are you sure? Do you have a job or something to do, somewhere to be?"

Shoving a piece of bacon in his mouth, Scott lazily waves his fork like he hasn't a care in the world. Once he swallows, he explains, "I'm a graphic designer and almost all of my work is remote."

I douse my potatoes in ketchup. I can't think of a more polite way to ask, so I get straight to the point. "What does a graphic designer do, exactly?"

Scott smiles like he finds my lack of tact to be charming. That won't last.

"I make logos, marketing materials, social media posts, and other illustrations or graphics for all kinds of clients."

"And the clients don't want to see that you're working? Who are they?"

"Some are individual people, some are massive corporations, and some are marketing companies that have their own clients. Sometimes, I go in to see the suits, but for the most part, so long as I meet my deadlines, I work on my own schedule." He shrugs like it's no big deal to be so independent at such a young age.

Alice had told me Scott drew Jake's tattoos, but I hadn't realized he was still so creative, professionally even.

"Damn," I said, not attempting to hide the awe in my voice. I'm impressed by him even if he isn't impressed by himself. "You must be good to have that level of freedom."

"The trust came with time, I think. I started small when I was still a student and grew mostly through word of mouth. My clients know they can rely on me, and I know they'll come to me with good projects. It's mutually beneficial."

I think he's blushing. It's sweet. I quickly look at my plate and pretend not to notice.

"I'm surprised you came back here, though. New York sounds like the kind of place you'd want to be for what you do. Wouldn't there be new opportunities on every corner?"

"There were." Scott nods thoughtfully. "I liked the city. I

moved there for college, and when I was a student, I even loved it. I graduated young, at twenty, and I hustled hard. But it felt like I aged ten years in the last two. Living there was like being in a constant state of 'on.' Every single thing was dialed all the way up. It's loud, busy, stressful, expensive."

He hesitates for just a moment before adding, "Lonely. It's wild how I could be surrounded by so many people, without a square foot of my own to stand in and still feel so completely alone."

"Then coming home was the perfect choice. What I understand from Alice's stories, it's impossible to feel alone here." I smile, thinking of yesterday at the bookstore. "From my one day here, I can see this town is a family."

Picking up another piece of bacon, Scott returns my smile. "Yeah, it's good here. Hopefully you don't think of *everybody* as family, though."

I roll my eyes at his raised eyebrows, but I can't stop the laugh from spilling past my lips.

CHAPTER 9

W hen I park in front of Barefoot Bake, Piper looks out the passenger window toward the building but doesn't move to get out of the car.

"Is everything ok?" I ask tentatively.

Piper looks back at me with her eyebrows furrowed.

"I think I'm nervous." She says it like nervousness is a highly contagious illness she's been avoiding her entire life. "I feel so stupid."

"No. You're not allowed to say things like that," I protest, refusing to hear her speak about herself that way. "Being nervous means you care. There's *nothing* stupid about that. But you have nothing to worry about. Hannah is very reasonable, and you did great yesterday. Everybody said so, and I saw it myself."

"Yeah?"

If she needs the reassurance, I'll always be happy to give it.

"Yeah. Go get 'em. Plus, I'll be at a table getting some work done, so I can be a getaway driver if things go sideways. Just shout 'pickles,' and I'll cause a diversion."

"Pickles?" She raises one eyebrow at me, sounding dubious.

"Pickles." It's the first word that came to mind.

Her lips tip up, and she nods. She shakes out her arms before rolling her shoulders back, psyching herself up. "Deal. Let's go."

The second we walk through the café door, Hannah throws her arms around Piper's neck, and I know Piper will be just fine. Hannah gives me a small smile over Piper's shoulder before the two of them head to Hannah's office to chat.

After I order a coffee in a mug the size of my head from Paul the barista, I take up residence in an armchair just past the archway into the bookstore. The space is cozy and welcoming. The tables and chairs have a hodgepodge vibe, but it works in the space, removing any clinical stiffness that a lot of the modern places in New York exude, with their shiny chrome and sharp corners.

I pull out my tablet to put the finishing touches on a poster about protecting your privacy on the internet for some college computer labs. It's not the most glamorous project, but it's important information for freshmen who think they're suddenly geniuses because they're of age to vote.

I'm sending out the poster design for approval when Hannah leads Piper into the bookstore. They meet up with Mads and move deeper between the shelves, chattering away at a mile a minute. It's almost physically painful to resist staring, but I'm doing my best to mind my own business.

I must get lost in my work because it's at least half an hour later when I look up again. Like I'm drawn to her, I find Piper quickly enough to see her gaze dart away. I pointedly look down at my screen and get back to drawing. Every few minutes, she looks back over—I can feel it—but I don't seek her out again. I don't want to make her self-conscious.

I finally allow myself the tiniest peek out of the corner of my eye and see Piper at the register with Mads. Piper's lip is caught between her teeth and a look of pure concentration is on her face. After a few seconds, her expression lights up, and Mads bumps her shoulder in camaraderie. I look away again, trying to play it cool. This is good. I want her to feel settled here, safe.

"Hey, lover boy," Hannah says quietly as she walks up to my workspace. Her eagle eyes don't miss a thing.

"Yes?" I'm not going to deny it.

"Do you know what you're doing with all that?" She jerks her head toward Piper.

"Probably not." I shrug. I'm not too proud to admit that. "But I've got to try."

With one hand, she refills my coffee from the pot. In the other, now extended toward me, she holds two plastic cups with iced drinks in them.

"Drop these off to the girls," Hannah instructs, a knowing look in her eyes. She's a romantic through-and-through, and the support is encouraging. Maybe that means I'm not completely out of my league. Just *mostly*. "Could you also ask Piper to come check in with me? I'm going to head back to Leslie in a few, and I want to make sure she's all set for now."

Hannah and I both know it would be easiest for her to deliver the coffee and check in, but I happily take the excuse to go talk to Piper. I leave my coffee on the table, snatch up the two plastic cups, and once I learn Piper's coffee preferences from Hannah, leap out of my seat, hurrying off to complete my task.

"Helloooo ladies," I say with dramatic swagger as I approach the registers. They look up together, eyes alight.

"I'm doing it!" Piper exclaims proudly, pointing at the computer screen. She's completely in her element and looks like she's floating on air.

"Alright!" I congratulate, setting one of the cups down and holding up my hand for a high five. The crack of our palms connecting is loud and satisfying in the quiet store. "I come bearing fuel," I say, picking the cup back up and holding one out to each woman.

"Bless you," Mads says, before taking a large gulp. Piper follows suit.

"It's perfection. Thank you," she practically purrs. I feel the hair on the back of my neck raise at the sound.

"You're both very welcome. Piper, Hannah is taking off and asked if you could check in with her before she goes."

Piper rounds the counter and starts walking back to the café with me. She bumps against my shoulder the same way Mads had nudged her earlier, happy and playful.

"Did you volunteer to come get me just so you could check up on me?" she questions teasingly.

"I didn't," I honestly say. "Hannah asked me to be her messenger, and I was happy to oblige. How are things going, though?"

"They couldn't be better," she says, casually placing her hand on my arm, and I'm thrilled for her… and for me. I swear I see stars in her eyes.

I slow as we approach my table. "This is my stop."

I'm trying to think of something clever to say when the café door bursts open, and Alice flies in like a hurricane, head turning this way and that, eyes round and manic. Piper springs away from me, the ghost of her touch leaving a burning print on my arm.

"Scott! Piper!" Alice exclaims, looking between us so quickly I almost miss it, before bounding over. She gives me a one-armed hug and a quick kiss on the cheek before leaping on Piper, who catches her rocket of a body easily. She doesn't even spill her coffee.

"I'm so sorry I wasn't here to meet you. Are you ok? Is Bernard dead? I'll bury the body with you. How was it helping at the store?—Oh my God, Hannah!" Alice disentangles herself from her best friend and flees into the back of the café without waiting for an answer to any of her questions. "Hannah, is Leslie ok?" Alice's voice carries to us from out of sight.

Piper and I are both looking at where Alice disappeared in stunned silence. Piper breaks first, folding and dropping her free hand to her knee as she cackles. "Damn, I really love that girl," she gets out between wheezes. She composes herself and straightens up. "I'm going to go give Hannah some backup."

"It seems like you're in good hands. Are you good here if I head home to unpack some more and get to work with the big monitor?" I ask.

"I'm great. Thank you for everything."

I wink in response. Her eye roll is expected, but no less enjoyable.

CHAPTER 10

Scott

Once I'm back home and working at my desk with my full, multi-monitor setup, I expect the productivity to flow through me. Instead, I find my mind drifting back to dark brown curls and full-body laughter.

I get up and make myself a sandwich, pacing the first floor while I eat it, trying to get the creative juices flowing or something like that. I turn on the television just to turn it back off. I open all the downstairs windows, including the one at the back of the library, to let in the warm breeze and the sounds of the lake, do twenty jumping jacks, and commit to focusing on my work before sitting back in my highly ergonomic chair. I buckle down and miraculously fall into a rhythm. I start working on a marketing campaign for a fantasy book launch, and I disappear into the drawings, completely losing track of myself.

I feel like I've been shaken awake when I hear tires crunching the gravel outside. Despite the blue light filter over my screens, my eyes burn, so I blink hard and drag my hands down my face.

When I hear a car door slam, I hurry to the front door and poke my head out to snoop. I'm surprised to see the sky is already a soft, muted blue and glance at my watch. It's almost seven. Damn.

I spot Jake's truck poking out from beside his house, and decide the brotherly thing to do is to go greet my dear old bro. I'm out of the work bubble, and I know there's no going back into it again right now.

Jake's unloading grocery bags, so I jog up to him and take the load from his hands when he turns to face me. He throws an arm around me and firmly thumps his hand against my back as his only greeting. Jake isn't a chatty man, but he's always been solid and dependable for me. His love doesn't need words.

He follows me into his house through the side door with the rest of the bags, and we deposit them on his large kitchen island. Waffles, the new puppy, starts making a ruckus in his crate, and Jake's whole face softens as he takes in that perfect little fur baby. He collects a couple of dog cookies and stands before the enormous crate.

Waffles is several months old, but still a puppy, so Alice and Jake are still working on his training. Jake holds up his fist with the cookies inside so Waffles can see, and the dog immediately settles, sitting primly and looking up adoringly at Jake.

"Good boy," Jake praises calmly before squatting to give Waffles his first little treat. "Stay," he says firmly before opening the crate door. He holds up his palm and takes two steps back from the open crate. Waffles taps his front paws, clearly eager to run to Jake. My brother spots the restraint and smiles, shoulders relaxing.

"Alright, you. Come here," he says, squatting back down so he can scoop up the fuzz ball that launches himself into Jake's arms. The dog's wet nose is going wild at Jake's fist, eager for his second reward. Jake relents and Waffles's tail furiously whips back and forth. My brother has *always* wanted a dog, and it warms every inch of my heart to see these two so happy.

"He seems to be doing well," I eventually say, after enjoying watching my responsible, serious brother get stomped on by giant puppy paws. "How was the trip?"

"It was good. Really good." I know Jake is thinking of Alice, because he's got this dreamy look on his face that only started appearing after he met her. He snaps out of his daydream. "It seems like there was more action here than with us, though. What's up with Piper? And Hannah and Leslie?"

Like they're on autopilot, my hands start unloading the bags as I update my brother on Leslie's status. Jake disentangles himself from Waffles, washes his hands, and comes to stand beside me. Old habits die hard, because we're moving around one another in the kitchen just as easily as we did when we still lived together. The familiarity is comforting.

I'm telling Jake about how Piper is thriving at Literary Lake when a chuckle escapes him. I cut off.

"What is it?"

He shakes his head as he stands from sliding a pan of chicken parm into the oven. "You're still completely gone for that woman," he says, sliding his eyes over to me.

"Sure am." I smile widely. Being gone for a woman like Piper is nothing to be ashamed of.

A deep furrow appears between Jake's eyebrows, and my smile falters. I know that look from when he was in charge and I was a kid. I've just been busted. For what? I have no clue, but I'm in trouble. Jake's eyes narrow as he scrutinizes me, and I feel the instinct to bolt.

His expression morphs into one of shock. "You *slept* with her!" he suddenly hisses.

"Uhhhhhh." I really don't know what to say here. I have no clue how he figured that out, but I feel pretty sure Piper doesn't want people to know. At the same time, I *don't* lie to Jake. Not telling him something is very different from outright lying. I cannot do the latter. My eyes dart around the room like Waffles will suddenly gain the ability to speak and come to my rescue.

No such luck. The space is filled with a very loud silence.

Leaning back against the counter, Jake sets down the pot he had chosen for linguine and crosses his arms. If it weren't for the topic we're about to discuss, I'd feel twelve again.

"There's no point in denying it," he says, calm again. "It wasn't a question."

I rub the back of my neck and shrug. "Would you believe me if I said it just kind of… happened?"

"Of course I would," Jake says flatly. "Why didn't you say something?"

Jake's confidence in me hits me like a freight train, and I feel how lucky I am to know without question he has my back.

"I don't think she wants it to get out. She said it was a one-time thing, and"—I cringe, already knowing Jake isn't going to like what I say next—"that it shouldn't have happened."

"You're *that* bad?" Jake smirks, teasing me.

I pick up the dish towel from the island behind me and chuck it at his face, disappointment flooding me when he catches it easily.

"There were no complaints about performance, thank you very much." I huff, exasperated. "I think she's scared of things going wrong since we're connected through you and Alice. I'm happy to give her time."

"Be careful, little brother. What if she really thinks it was a mistake?" There's the concern I expected.

"Then we'll just be friends, and I'll pine for her for the rest of my life," I answer, but I can see Jake doesn't find my sense of humor to be very funny. "I'd never pressure her."

"That's not what I'm worried about." His face does yet another transformation, and he looks like a concerned father. Jake's gonna be a great dad someday.

"You don't have to worry about me. I was just kidding about the pining."

"Were you, though? This wouldn't be the first time you jumped into water without checking for sharks first."

He's not wrong. It's possible I've told him I found "the one" more than once before but thinking of how I felt those other times just makes me even *more* sure Piper is different. This feeling is *different*.

"Of course. It's not like that this time," I say, making a noncommittal gesture.

"I don't want you getting in over your head if Piper's made her intentions clear. Because if she's serious, you're just going to get hurt. You know you're a romantic, Scott. You always have been, and sometimes that makes you see things through rose-colored glasses, maybe seeing what you want instead of what's really there. You shouldn't have anything with her unless you're sure she wants what you want."

"I'll be careful. I promise. But Piper is a once-in-a-lifetime kind of woman. I can't not even try."

"Just don't try so hard that you lose yourself or scare her off. You can be a little intense."

"I know. And I won't." I mean it. This isn't just about me or Piper. She's Alice's best friend and if Alice is going to be permanent in Jake's life like I think she is, our lives are all tangled together. I don't want to make stupid mistakes here.

I guess Jake is satisfied because he nods, conceding and picking the pot back up so he can fill it with water. With the matter settled, I get to work on a spinach, strawberry, and goat cheese salad. We work well together, like always.

Steam is billowing up from the sink as Jake strains the pasta when the distinct sound of a car parking outside has both me and Jake whipping our heads toward the side door. I wonder if he notices we have the same dopey grins on our faces at the sound of Alice and Piper's laughter coming from the other side of the door.

After they tumble inside, Alice offers a sweet, "Hello, boys."

"Ladies," Jake and I respond in unison.

The women giggle some more. Alice pats my shoulder as she slides around me before launching herself at Jake, flinging her arms around his neck. He easily catches her with one arm around her back, and she plants a kiss on his cheek.

"Welcome home, Ace," he murmurs.

I look away, feeling like I'm intruding, and find Piper. I catch her gazing at them, an expression that looks a lot like longing on her face. She notices me watching her and quickly looks down, busying herself with untying and taking off her shoes.

"Can we help with anything?" Alice asks before breathing in deeply. "Something smells amazing."

Jake sets Alice back on her feet. "Could you set up the table out back, please? I think it's warm enough to eat out there, if you want to."

"Yup! Come on, Pipe." Alice turns towards the back of the house. Jake swats her backside and she squeals, delighted, as she skips out the door, Waffles on her heels.

Piper and I lock eyes again, eyebrows raised high. Should we just, like, go?

Jake starts when he looks back at me, like he'd forgotten he and Alice weren't alone, and awkwardly clears his throat. Piper quickly snatches up a roll of paper towels and silverware, luckily finding the right drawer on the first try.

"You done with that salad, Scotty?" Jake asks, clearing his throat a second time and *still* completely failing at sounding normal.

I've been done with the salad for like ten minutes, and he knows that. What a dingbat.

"Yep. I'll take it out." I follow Piper out the back door while she tries to hide her stifled laugh. It comes out as a snort.

Alice finishes arranging and dusting off the chairs, and we all make a couple more trips inside for serving spoons, glasses, drinks, the chicken parm, and the pasta.

Jake and Alice sit beside one another, with Piper and me on the other side of the table. When we all dig in, it feels like we're a family.

"I have a bit of an announcement," Piper says once everybody has a full plate. "Hannah offered me a job running Literary Lake, and I accepted, so I'll be staying in Wilcox Grove for the foreseeable future."

Alice is basically vibrating in her seat with excitement, so it's clear Piper already told her all about this in the time since I left the bookstore. Alice still pushes back her chair and comes around the table to hug Piper from behind. Jake and I offer our more subdued, but no less authentic, congratulations too.

Alice and Jake lock eyes for a moment before Jake discretely nods his head.

"And you'll stay in our extra bedroom, of course," Alice says.

Piper's hands come up to squeeze Alice's forearms, banded across Piper's chest.

"Thank you! I was hoping you'd let me crash."

I try to school my expression, but disappointment floods me. I was hoping she'd stay where she is now, with me.

Be cool, Scott. Don't leap before you look.

It's going to be my mantra of the summer. I try to fix my face into a supportive smile.

"Before the semester starts, I'm just working on class prep and helping some high school kids with SAT prep, so I'm happy to come by whenever I can to help at the bookstore or the bakery, too. Just let me know what I can do," Alice says as she retakes her seat.

I'm tempted to volunteer my time too, but I reel it in. Cool as a cucumber.

"Best part of being an adult is never having to worry about the SATs again," I say. "What classes will you be teaching this fall?" I ask Alice. I can think about things other than Piper. Nothing to worry about.

As Alice answers, I find myself looking over to Piper more than I should and mentally scold myself each time. Jake is his usual quiet self, but Alice, Piper, and I talk through the rest of the meal, and I focus on keeping my eyes off Wilcox Grove's newest resident.

After we finish, Alice and Jake collect our plates and promise to return with coffee for everyone. Jake holds the door to the house open for Alice, who slips under his arm with a playful laugh. He bends to kiss the top of her head as she does.

Once the screen door closes behind the lovebirds, and it's just the two of us, I turn to Piper.

"Do you really want to live in a house with *that* all the time? These houses are old and the walls are *not* very thick. You're going to hear a lot more of Alice's life than even a best friend wants to hear. Trust me." I pause, and she doesn't immediately scream and flee. "You can keep staying with me. There's an extra bedroom, and it's not like I'm charging rent, so the price is perfect."

"I don't know if living with you is such a good idea," Piper says, her voice unusually small.

"What are you afraid of?" I hope it's not me. Have I *already* pushed too hard? Am I pushing too hard right now? Maybe Jake was right.

"That you'll stop liking me."

Wait, what?

CHAPTER 11

Piper

Scott's looking at me like I just asked him to do complicated calculus in his head. Maybe that's a bad example. I wouldn't be surprised if he was very good at math.

I feel exposed, laying my flaws out for Scott to see, but I *need* him to understand. I can't let him have hope this is going to work out someday if he just tries harder. It wouldn't be fair, and it wouldn't be kind.

It might be a cliché, but it's not him. It's me.

"I'm a lot, Scott. Like, a lot, a lot. When people first meet me, they think I'm fun, but then they get to know me, and they always want me to be less. I'm loud, and I'm messy, and I'm chaotic, and I rarely know where my brain is going. I am who I am, and I accept that. But I know I'm hard to be around and even harder to be *with*. I've been told it to my face more times than I can admit without completely humiliating myself. And I don't want to see the look in your eyes when *you* decide I'm too much."

I stare at the table, finding Scott's gaze too difficult to hold. He doesn't speak for a moment, and I wonder if he's going through all our interactions, seeing all the grating parts of me he previously overlooked.

"That has to be one of the most outrageous things I've ever heard," he finally says. His stern, nearly angry tone makes me look back up. His expression is almost… heartbroken.

"It sounds to me like you've been around a lot of assholes who didn't appreciate you for all that you are. You're not too much, Piper," he continues. "They're just not enough."

I blink at him, momentarily stunned into silence. Sadly, he's mistaken.

"Stay at the house with me. I promise it'll be better than hearing my brother all over Alice every night." He blanches but continues. "And I think it'll be fun. Let me show you what it's like to be treated the right way."

I press my lips together as I roll the idea around in my brain. He stays silent, letting me work through it myself. I'm about to double down and decline again when a shrill laugh breaks the silence.

"Jake! Stop it!" Alice's voice carries clearly from inside, playful and flirty. Scott gags a little bit more. But their PDA might be his saving grace. I make a face as my eyes slide to the screen door, more giggles drifting out to us. I don't want to know what those poor mugs of coffee are witnessing right now.

I love Alice, but she needs her own space with Jake right now. I would be a wet blanket on their new home together.

"Ok." I nod firmly. If I maintain boundaries and remain on my best behavior, I might be able to make this work. "I'll stay with you. But no wooing. We're just roommates."

I won't string him along.

"I think you're missing out, princess," Scott says.

"I mean it. I make bad decisions, and I won't have you caught up in those mistakes," I insist. I need him to hear me.

He holds up his hands in surrender.

"Ok, ok. I'll take it."

I'm still not convinced he believes me, but I do trust Scott not to overstep. With time, he'll understand.

Scott smiles even though I know I'm mean mugging him a little bit. Then he winks. I know he's only teasing, and I can't stop my smile. I still shake my head at his idiocy.

"Roommates," Scott says, holding out his hand.

I eye it warily, but after a pause, shake it.

In my sleepy daze, I briefly think the soft tapping that's waking me up is from a bird at my window, and I'm about to embrace my true calling as Snow White. Except—scratch that—I'd freak the fuck out if there was a whole crew of woodland creatures in my room.

I pry open my eyes and thank all that is holy that I'm helping with the bookstore and not Barefoot Bake because I could not imagine getting up before the sun every single day. There's early, and then there's bakery early. Also, I can't bake to save my life, so there's that.

I slowly claw far enough into consciousness to realize the tapping is coming from my door and groan out a mumble-growl that might vaguely resemble the words "come in" if you speak hibernating bear. Scott seems to be fluent in whatever sound I made, because the door slowly opens a second later, and his face appears.

"Hey, I'm so sorry to wake you, but I did bring coffee as a peace offering." He's speaking softly. Likely another skill learned from hibernating bear survival training. That sounds like something people who grew up here would have done.

I sit up at the promise of coffee and reach grabby hands out toward my roomie, I mean, toward the cup he's holding. "Gimme," I politely demand.

He shuffles into the room and places the mug in my hands before backing up to the half-opened door, careful not to invade my space. The mug is chilled. The cold is a welcome surprise since I expected him to have made hot coffee, like everybody does, but I prefer my coffee iced. I take a long drink.

"It's quite literally perfect." I hum. "How did you know how I take it?"

Scott lifts one shoulder in nonchalance. "I asked Hannah what you got yesterday."

It's the smallest gesture, but it hits me somewhere deep and frozen. I just might hear a crack in the ice, but before I can thank him, Scott continues.

"I also got an email from Bets at the post office early this morning. Your boxes arrived. Since you sent them to Alice at this address, she reached out to me."

After I stormed out of the library, I went back to my apartment, threw all my stuff into boxes, and dropped them at the post office. I knew even then wasn't just a visit to see Alice. I was coming to Wilcox Grove in hopes of staying.

"Oh, thank you. I'll go pick them up after I finish at the bookstore this afternoon." Mads is picking me up this morning, but I haven't figured out my way home yet. I'm trying to think of a plan—maybe renting a car I can't really afford—when Scott surprises me yet again.

"Don't worry about it. I went to pick them up already. That's why I woke you up early. I wanted you to have time to make sure everything is accounted for before you have to leave for work."

I don't think he even notices how kind that was of him to do. With the way he's talking, I think it's second nature for him to just... help.

"I—you didn't have to do that. And Grateful Bob told me

you're not a morning person, either, so especially because of that, thank you."

I didn't send much and the post office isn't far, but it's sweet, and I don't know what to say. I can't seem to even pick a place to look, and my eyes flit between my mug, the mirror where I can see creases from the sheets pressed into my face, and Scott's softly smiling face.

"I'm happy to help, no matter the time of day. And I know you don't have a car." He nudges the bedroom door all the way open. "Everything is stacked in the hallway, but let me know if you need help moving anything."

I only nod before pulling my bonnet off and gently finger-combing through my hair with the hand not holding my coffee, suddenly desperate for something to do with my hands.

"Well, I'll leave you to get ready," he says, turning to give me privacy.

Thankfully, my manners kick in enough to jump start my brain again, and I get some words out. "Thank you, again. For all of this." I lift my mug toward the stack of boxes just outside my door.

Scott awkwardly salutes me before heading down the stairs.

I toss back the covers and set my coffee on the nightstand before venturing into the hallway to examine my boxes. I use a key to cut through the tape and flip them open. Summer clothes. Winter clothes. A towel set. A couple pairs of shoes. My favorite mug. And my books—my few, precious books. I flip one open and breathe in as I fan through the pages.

I am simply just a girl.

My roommate in Boston had already lived in the apartment we shared before I moved in, so it came fully furnished, and she already had basically all the shared kitchen stuff, so I needed very little. Because of how small the space was and how tight I was on cash, I wasn't very incentivized to accumulate stuff. It all seems to have made it here without issue.

I drag the boxes into my room and shove them against the wall before getting ready for the day. I check my phone and ignore a text from my dad. He's *not* happy I left Boston to come up here and is making that displeasure well known. Super.

When I lumber down the steps, I find the table again set for breakfast, with an egg sandwich on a bagel next to a yogurt cup waiting in front of the chair I've come to know as mine.

"Ok, you've got to let me do something for you in exchange for all these favors. I don't know what, but the scales are imbalanced right now," I say as I take my seat. I don't like feeling indebted to anybody, even though Scott hasn't given me any indication that he'd hold his generosity over my head.

"This isn't a 'tit for tat' thing," he says between bites of his own sandwich. "I meant it when I said I like cooking. Knowing somebody is enjoying my food makes it even better."

He's so nonchalant as he says it, scrolling through something on his phone at the same time, that I want to believe him, but I struggle to accept he isn't secretly keeping score. Everybody always does. I rack my brain for something I can do to contribute here.

"Then I'm at least paying for groceries," I insist. Financially, it might not be my best choice, but I'm not *completely* broke, and I'm starting full time at Literary Lake today. "And I want to talk about rent. I know you said there isn't any, but that doesn't feel right. So, let's hash out the details of me staying here."

Scott glances up at me and must see the apprehension all over my face. He sets down his phone and gives me his undivided attention. "If you really want to pay for groceries the next time we go to the store because it'll make you more comfortable, ok, but it's not necessary, and it won't be a regular thing. We'll split them going forward. There's no rent, and I won't be changing my mind on that, but we can split utilities, cable, and internet."

"I have to pay rent. I'm taking up space in your house."

"Alice owns this house outright and isn't charging me rent, so it would feel like highway robbery if I charged you. I don't need the money, and she just asks that I take care of the place, so as long as you're ok with that stipulation, we're square. Don't make me feel like your landlord, please."

His eyes plead with me, and I find my resolve crumbling. His frankness *really* makes me want to believe him, even if part of me still worries it's a trap.

I can try.

"Ok. I buy next round of groceries, and we split utilities and other bills." I nod with finality before picking up my breakfast sandwich and diving in.

When I finish eating, I stand and take both of our plates over to the sink. I rinse them and load them into the dishwasher, catching Scott turned around in his seat to watch me.

"Thanks," he says quickly looking away, like he's pretending he wasn't just busted staring. "Do you need a ride to the bookstore this morning?"

I shake my head. "Mads is going to pick me up."

"Do you have a plan for getting home?"

I hesitate because I know Scott is going to offer to pick me up, and I feel like a complete mooch already.

"I'm finalizing a car rental today," I lie instead.

"A rental? Just indefinitely? That's going to cost a fortune." Scott stands now, aghast. He walks over to the line of hooks behind the door and retrieves his car keys. He tosses them to me, and I only catch them because it's a reflex. I do not want them. This is so much worse than offering to pick me up after my shift is done.

"You should use my car," Scott says.

I quickly launch the keys back at him. "No," I reply unwaveringly.

"Yes." The keys barely touch his skin before he's flung them back in my direction. This time, I duck to the side and let the keys crash to the kitchen floor, where they slide until they stop against a cabinet.

"No," I repeat firmly, losing my patience. I cover my face with my hands like I can escape if I don't look at Scott. This has been a very emotionally stressful morning for me. Scott's kindness is unnerving, and my trust issues are beaming like a superpowered neon sign.

I hear my roommate's sock-clad steps approach me and the gentle touch of his fingertips on my wrists as he coaxes my hands from my face.

"I really don't want to upset you," he murmurs. "But listen. I work from home. If I need a ride, the Trans Am is next door in the garage. The Range Rover is a good car. It's safe. It's not like ten-minute drives are going to put real wear and tear on it. Use it. Please."

I look into Scott's kind eyes. I think they're his secret weapon because they seem to display every feeling he has *and* steal my ability to say no. I cringe when I think of Scott's shiny, clean, beautiful, *expensive* car.

"I don't want to mess it up," I admit.

"It's just a car," he whispers, not needing to speak any louder with how closely we're standing. He releases me to retrieve the keys before returning to my side. We both turn to the door when we hear what must be Mads's car outside. "Since Mads is here this morning, I'll come pick you up after work today, and we can go grocery shopping."

I don't understand how he can be so casual about a car that costs as much as his does (I googled it), but I nod. This is an acceptable concession.

"And then for your next shift, you'll take the car." There's a subtle sternness to his tone. He's not asking. It's unexpected from sweet Scott, and I feel goosebumps erupt on my arms at the authority in his tone. It suits him. "Some days we can carpool if I know I'm going to be out. This doesn't need to be a big thing. We'll just share the car."

I find myself nodding again, just because I need to go. Mads gives her horn a quick honk out front.

"Ok," he says simply and steps aside so I can head to the front door. I check my jeans pockets for my phone, little wallet, and house key. Good to go.

I look back at Scott. "I thought I said no wooing."

He smirks.

"This isn't wooing, princess. You'd know if I was wooing you."

I don't have an answer for that, so I pull on my shoes by the door and start to head out. With my hand on the door, I suddenly remember a story Alice told me about that Trans Am, a sporty little thing that had belonged to Jake and Scott's father.

"Oh, by the way?" I throw over my shoulder. "You might want to get the Trans Am detailed after what Jake and Alice did in it."

I see a look of confusion transform Scott's face before the realization hits, and I flee out the door.

I can still hear Scott's "WHAT?!" echo from inside.

CHAPTER 12

Piper

Mads's eyes look slightly alarmed as I sprint to her car, cackling like a banshee. I fling open the passenger door and dive in, slamming it behind me. Mads immediately picks up what I'm putting down, throwing her car into drive and spinning out as she punches the gas. We both shriek like lunatics.

Once we hit the paved road a couple of minutes later, Mads lets off the accelerator, and we're both gasping for air, continuing to laugh together.

"Ok, I love the vibe, but care to tell me why I'm playing the part of getaway driver?" Mads finally asks.

Her willingness to go along with my nuttiness without a prior explanation is more touching than it should be, and suddenly I feel stupid for flying off the handle without reason. I sober quickly.

"I'm really sorry. I guess I just kind of did it for fun," I say, unable to meet her eyes. "It was dumb."

Mads glances over at me before punching me in the shoulder. "It *was* fun Piper."

This is the good part, when people think I'm *fun*. Fun isn't what people want long term, though.

I see my father standing in my bedroom doorway. He had missed another one of my volleyball games because he volunteered to cover a surgery for another anesthesiologist, and I'd been lying with my head in Mom's lap, crying about it. He just got home, and my mother had called him up to talk to me, knowing how upset I was. *You need to stop playing around, Piper Jane. You're not going to be a professional volleyball player, so it's time to grow up and get serious about your future. I love you, and I want more than this for you.* My mother squeezed my hand sympathetically. It didn't help.

Back in the car I smile tentatively, trying to ignore my father's voice in my ears. Mads rolls down the windows so we can ride the rest of the way to Literary Lake with the wind in our hair.

Once we're at the store, Mads gets to work opening the register while I park myself at one of the small tables with the store's laptop and begin going through inventory and sales records.

Yesterday, Hannah told me that Leslie has never been much of a "book person," so I was encouraged to provide feedback for filling any gaps I thought the store might have. As I work my way through recent receiving and sales reports, I worry there may be many.

Currently, the businesses heavily rely on Barefoot Bake's profitability to remain afloat, but I think there are a lot of opportunities for Literary Lake to carry more of the load.

I'm a little old fashioned, so I buy myself a new emotional support notebook from our shelves and begin brainstorming. If Hannah and Leslie agree with making some changes, I'll have my work cut out for me. I'd love to update our inventory system and publisher contacts, clean up the store's inventory, and start planning and hosting events in the café space after Barefoot Bake closes in the early evening.

I'm eager to prove my worth to Hannah and Leslie, so I get to work updating publisher accounts and setting up social media for the store on all the major platforms. I even make some dummy posts to give an idea of what we could do with an online presence. Then I start brainstorming event ideas—game nights, movie nights, book release parties, author signings, trivia nights.

It's only when Alice shows up at my table with a ham and cheese croissant and a glass of water for me that I realize it's well past lunchtime. I didn't even know she'd stopped by. I blink up at her and the store comes back into focus around me. I haven't been this excited about work in a long time, and it feels good.

"Ah, there she is," Alice teases. "I thought we lost you for a bit there."

"Honestly? You might have." I press the heels of my hands into my closed eyes until I see spots in the darkness. "How long have you been here? What did I miss?"

"Not very long, and you've missed absolutely nothing." Alice sighs, flopping into the chair across from me. She absentmindedly looks at my open notebook on the table, covered in half-formulated ideas and a mess of crisscrossed arrows and scribbles. "I think I've missed a lot, though. May I?" she asks, gesturing to the notebook.

I nod, even though the messy page is a little embarrassing. My system only makes sense to me, and I always make things much prettier before letting anybody else see. This is like seeing how sausage gets made. Alice has stuck by me and my mess for years, though, so it's a little easier to let her into my chaos.

While Alice flips through the many pages of notes I've made, I fire a text off to Hannah to see if she has time to talk about some of my ideas this afternoon, even if just over the phone. I stand and stretch, not realizing how immobile I must have been sitting until every one of my joints loudly cracks and pops. I shove half of the croissant in my mouth in one bite.

"Piper," Alice says, drawing my attention back to her. She's still looking at my scrawl. "You've got some *really* good ideas in here."

I fill all the way up with pride. I love working with books, and I don't think I'm bad at it, but it's nice to feel like my calling wasn't squashed by Bernard and his cockroach-like tendencies.

"I just hope Hannah and Leslie think so, too," I say wistfully and reclaim my seat.

"They will. I know it." It's impossible not to feel good in the face of Alice's never-ending positivity.

My phone begins dancing across the small table as it buzzes with an incoming call. I feel a rush of nerves as Hannah's name pops up on the illuminated screen. I guess she has time to talk now. Alice follows my gaze and stands, holding out my notebook to me.

"I'd wish you luck, but you don't need it. Wow her," she says softly, jerking her head toward the phone. "I'm going to head out."

Alice kisses me quickly on the cheek before leaving, and I snatch up the device before Hannah gets sent to voicemail.

"Hey, Hannah. How's Leslie?"

"She's the *worst* patient ever! We'd be able to get out of here if Leslie could quit ripping her stitches," Hannah replies over Leslie's protests and cries of boredom in the background. "What can I do for you? Is now a good time to chat?"

"It's perfect. Thanks for getting back to me so quickly. I was hoping to run some bookstore ideas by both of you before I over-stepped."

"We both already have a really good feeling about you, so I

doubt there will be an issue, but lay it on us. You're on speaker now."

I take a deep breath and dive in, rambling a little once I get going. Excitement quickly overpowers nerves, and I can feel myself get more animated as I talk through the potential I see for Literary Lake. The space and community Hannah and Leslie have created are already so special. I just want to take them to the next level.

The women let me work through my list without comment, and by the end of it, I'm out of breath, and my heart is thundering in my chest. The silence on the line continues for a beat after I stop speaking, and I worry I've either dropped the connection or irreparably insulted their prior management so badly that they're debating ways to dump my lifeless body without getting caught.

I finally hear muffled murmuring from the phone, telling me the call didn't drop. Does this mean it's option number two?

"Do it." Leslie's voice is clear now.

"Do it?" Did I hear correctly? "Which part?"

"All of it," Hannah chimes in. "I think you might be the answer to our prayers."

"Me?" This can't be right. The connection *must* be bad.

"We opened the café because Hannah is a genius in the kitchen. Then, we bought the bookstore because the old guy who owned it was selling, and we didn't want to risk having a crappy neighbor. Neither of us really knew what we were doing. We just did it. Like, books are great, and—um—yay books, but we've been winging it. Pretty poorly, from the sound of things." Leslie sounds a bit winded by the end of her explanation. She really does need her rest.

"You've been doing great here. You seem to have a loyal staff and a great community that is dedicated to you both. I'm just really excited about the prospect of being able to offer them more. I don't want to pressure you though. Are you sure?"

"Positive," Hannah takes back over. "I can give you access to our budget, and some financial projections Leslie's been maintaining. If you stay within that, you're welcome to try new things and see what sticks."

"Ok. Yes, I can do that. I won't let you down. Thank you." Their blanket permission and faith in me are both intimidating and flattering.

"Nah, thank *you* for caring." There's more rustling in the background, and I hear Leslie's complaint about Hannah fussing. "We're going to go so I can try to get my wife to *rest*."

"I'll keep you posted. Listen to Hannah, Leslie," I advise, and we end the call.

I stare at the dark phone for several minutes in complete awe of the golden ticket I've just been handed. A ping from the laptop pulls me out of my trance. It's an email with the financial details from Hannah and Leslie.

Pulling up the calendar app so I can try to plan things out, I dive right in.

The rest of the ham and cheese croissant is sadly forgotten.

In the middle of my day, I spent some time on the floor, learning the store, talking to customers, and supporting booksellers, but I did plop back down for more planning after a few hours. My eyes sting when I finally close the laptop. My eyebrows pinch together as I notice the golden hour sun streaming in through the windows. Damn, I lost time twice in one day. What the hell time is it?

A quick glance into the café tells me it's closed, so it must be after five. I look around the bookstore and find it's peacefully quiet. Mads is nowhere to be seen, but Scott is parked behind the register, elbows on the counter and an empty mug hanging lazily from one finger. He grins as my eyes rove over him.

I really need to talk to somebody about my apparent lack of awareness. It can't be good for running a business.

I push to a stand only to slap my hands back on the table when I realize the lower portion of one of my legs is completely asleep.

That lack of awareness also can't be good for my body. Yeesh.

Slowly and with much support from our bookshelves, I hobble toward Scott.

"Hey," I greet him. "What are you doing here?"

"I told you I'd come pick you up after you were done here today, remember?"

"It's already time to go?" I feel like I've just stumbled out of a car wreck, mildly confused and majorly suspicious.

"I think you were off duty over an hour ago. Emily is upstairs organizing something in lending with Jack and Amy," he explains, referencing the evening manager and two of our booksellers.

I check the time on my phone. He's right. I should have taken off almost two hours ago.

"How long have you been here?"

"I like it here," he avoids answering. I expect he was early for the end of my scheduled shift and has been around for a *while*.

I flush with embarrassment and guilt. This guy keeps showing up for me, and I keep abusing his kindness.

"Scott, I'm so sorry. You should have shaken me back into reality. I didn't mean to have you waiting around here for me."

"None of that, Piper. I'm a big boy, and if I wanted to take off, I could have used my words and let you know. It's not your job to take care of me or read my mind."

I blink at the simplicity of his statement. "I—uh—thank you?"

He laughs, finding my confusion amusing. "Did you want to finish anything else up?"

I shake my head, still feeling sheepish. "No. I think I'd like to go home."

He raises his eyebrows.

"To your house," I quickly amend, but I know I am anything but smooth.

It's just an expression. *Really!*

CHAPTER 13

Scott

Piper is quiet as we head to the car, like she's afraid of letting a dirty word like "home" slip again. Maybe it meant nothing, but maybe, just maybe, it meant she could like it here. I know *I* like her here.

I tentatively crack the windows once we're on the road and watch Piper's entire demeanor relax. When I roll them all the way down, she even closes her eyes. I don't think she realizes she's smiling. Maybe she doesn't hate *all* of nature as much as she thinks.

Moving slowly, like anything more could break the delicate peace, I click on the radio and gradually turn it up until we can hear the slow opening notes of "Beautiful Things." Piper begins mouthing the words, and I'm hit with a memory of our duet at karaoke last fall. The night might not have ended the best but seeing her open up like that will be burned in my brain forever. She's silent now, but I'm determined to get her to let go again this summer.

The drive to the grocery store is short, and the way Piper's eyes pop open in surprise when we park tells me she forgot we were stopping here.

"Is it still ok with you if we grab some things before heading back?"

"Of course." She recovers and hops out of the car like a springbok. It's a "me thing," but I dislike that I didn't have the chance to get her door for her. One of the most vivid memories I have of my parents is my dad always opening every door for my mom. When they were together, June Preston didn't touch a door handle. My dad, Danny, wouldn't hear of it.

I obviously know Piper isn't my wife. She's my roommate, reluctant friend at best. But the urge is there nonetheless. It's even stronger because Piper doesn't seem to expect anybody to take care of her. *Maybe* she'd let Alice fret over her, but I doubt anybody else would get to see even a hint of vulnerability.

I remind myself it's not my place. Piper can take care of herself.

Don't be so intense.

As we grab a cart outside the store, I ask whether Piper has any ideas for what we should get.

"Um… food?" she offers. "I'm sorry. I'm absolutely no help. I don't cook, and I've never planned out what I'm going to eat. I just grab random things and eat them at the same time, calling it a meal. I am the poster child for girl dinner."

I smile and lead the way inside, determined not to make her feel inadequate. "The world is our oyster, then. Though, I'll admit I don't like actual oysters. They're slimy, and I do not get the appeal at all."

"Agree we can skip the actual oysters," she says, and I hope I can pull more of her likes and dislikes out of her.

A few aisles in, I realize I'm out of luck. She's completely clammed up and has taken to blindly agreeing with whatever I suggest we get. Eventually, she even moves away from vocal responses, just humming and nodding. We finish as quickly as possible. She still wants to pay for our haul, and I don't argue. We agreed, and I respect that.

We load the car, and I immediately roll down the windows and put the radio back on. Piper closes her eyes and turns her face toward the wind rushing in. She looks peaceful, stunning really, and I tear my gaze away before I accidentally drive us off the road. However, I can't help but notice she stays that way the whole drive home.

Back at the house, Piper hops out of the car before I can even close my door, but when we end up at the side door at the same time, both laden with grocery bags, I at least get to hold *that* door open for her.

In a friendly roomie way. Nothing more.

I'm being so cool about all of this.

After I close the door, I see Piper standing uncomfortably near the table full of bags, holding the new pack of toilet paper. We make eye contact, and she looks like she's thinking a thousand things at once.

"I'mgonnagounpacksome." The words rush out of her as she sprints from the room and clambers up the stairs. She's like a skittish deer.

I'm unpacking our bags when there's a thundering boom from upstairs.

"I'm ok!" she calls out.

A *clumsy*, skittish deer.

With the groceries put away, I retreat into the library to get some more work done, quietly closing the door behind me. Piper will tell me if she needs something. I do not need to hover.

It's maybe an hour later when I hear the very familiar sound of fruitless rummaging through the fridge. In the early days when it was just me and Jake, I was a professional rummager. Until Jake and I learned our way around the kitchen together, I made more messes than meals.

Creeping over to the library door, I quietly crack it open and peek out. The angle isn't great to see the kitchen, but I can more clearly hear Piper's exasperated sigh as bowls, pots, and bottles clang together.

I meander my way out of my work cave until I see Piper bent over, most of her body hidden in the fridge. This woman and her ass have been sent to torment me. I'm sure of it.

I quickly look away and realize contents of the fridge are covering every flat surface in the kitchen.

"Piper? Whatcha doin'?" I cautiously ask.

She jumps, smacking her head on the freezer door, the rattling of the various bottles left in the fridge barely covering the sound of the swear she lets loose.

"Sorry, I didn't mean to startle you," I say, wincing because that sounded like it hurt.

"It's all good. Par for the course. I'm not a graceful person," she assures me as she tenderly prods at the top of her head, hissing when she finds the spot.

I crouch to catch her gaze. "Are you sure? Do you want ice?" Her eyes are beginning to water.

Waving me off, she stands. "I'm good, I'm good. Don't bother." She's blinking furiously and a flush is spreading across her cheeks.

"Well, at least take a seat." I jerk my head toward the table, but Piper just looks at me like I'm nuts. I move my hands to my hips giving her my best stern expression until I realize I'm mimicking "serious Jake" from his disciplining days. I drop my arms.

Piper huffs but flops into a chair. Once she's properly situated, I look around the kitchen.

"What was the plan here?" I ask.

"I didn't really have one," she admits, staring at the table like it's the most impressive piece of art she's ever seen. "I felt bad for abandoning you when we got back, and I was hoping if I could see everything we had, inspiration would hit, and I'd suddenly become a master chef so I could make *you* a meal for once."

The kindness of her mission isn't lost on me, even if execution didn't exactly pan out. And I can't deny her knit brow is endearing. I take in the ingredients we've got.

"Ok, let's do this. That is, if you'll have me," I offer.

"The whole point is that I wanted to do this *for* you," Piper says, peeking up at me.

"And I'll leave if you'd like me to, but I think it could be fun if we made something together."

"Yeah?" she asks, straightening up.

"Yeah."

She chuckles, and the sound is like music. "Alright. What do we make?"

"Would you like something hot or cold tonight?"

Piper thoughtfully looks out the kitchen window at the darkening sky. The air is thick and muggy. "Cold," she decides.

I dig through the pile of fruits and vegetables and keep nearly everything out, replacing only a few items into the fridge. Piper is warily eyeing the pile I left on the counter. When I pull the blender down from on top of the fridge, she looks like she might be regretting this whole cooking adventure with me.

"You remember the part where I said I don't know what I'm doing, right? That wasn't an exaggeration." She sounds genuinely worried. "Maybe I should just watch."

"You can do this. Trust me." She's still eyeing me like I'm playing a prank on her. "We're going to make a Thai beef and noodle salad and some gazpacho. I know they don't really 'go together,' but I won't tell if you don't."

"Those sound… complicated?" she says.

"They're not. I promise. And I'll walk you through everything. Can you wash those while I clean up some?" I ask, pointing to the produce I separated out.

Piper stands and scoops up the bags to take them to the sink. The unruly mass fights back, and one tumbles to the floor. Piper's face falls.

"Crap," she says as she places the rest of the load beside the sink. "I'm sorry."

"It's just an onion. No harm, no foul." I retrieve the runaway bag and bring it to her. This insecure side of Piper is a new one, like she's *terrified* of messing up.

Her ears are flushed, but she takes the onion without further protest. As she washes, I set up chopping stations for us both.

I dramatically extend my arm toward one seat. "After you, ma'am."

Piper lowers herself into the chair like it's sitting on a pressure trigger, and the wrong move will send her sky high.

"I'll work on the salad. For the gazpacho, everything is going in a blender, so we just need cucumber, tomatoes, and peppers cut into big chunks, if that works for you?"

"That's it?"

"We'll add a few more things to the blender, but yeah. That's basically it."

Piper nods and looks hopeful. She scoots her chair forward and bumps the table. The metal bowl I'd put out for Piper tips to the side and careens to the ground, making the world's loudest crash. Piper jumps at the sound, spinning toward it, sweeping her arm across the table, sending her knife and several tomatoes to the floor, too. Piper then jumps up, and her chair tips over backward.

The whole scene feels like something out of a cartoon, and I'm tempted to laugh at the unfortunate chain of events until I see Piper's face. She looks like somebody bracing for a punishment.

When she turns toward me, I see panic in her eyes, and I cannot understand where it came from.

"Fuck! I'm sorry. I told you I'm a walking disaster. You didn't listen." Her tone is angry, but I can tell it's masking embarrassment and shame.

"Piper, it's ok. It was an acci-"

"You know what? I quit," she cuts me off, sounding disgusted with herself. "I'm just going to do dishes after as my contribution to this. It'll be better for us both if I get out of your way."

Her intense reaction breaks my heart. It tells me something—or someone—tried to break *her* at some point.

"If you really don't want to, I won't force you, but I'd like you to stay," I say. I won't let her think I don't want her here.

"I'm not the right person to help. I'm making it worse," Piper counters, putting the tomatoes back on the table before picking up the bowl and knife and dropping them into the sink. She's stubborn and terribly unkind to herself. I'm not a fan of anybody being mean to Piper, even Piper.

I get a new bowl, walk over to Piper, and gently take her hand to guide her back to the table. Surprisingly, she lets me.

"You're not. I promise." Prickly Piper doesn't scare me.

She sits with a huff, and I stand behind her, gently sliding her chair in. I get a new knife and hand it to her. I nod encouragingly until she picks up the pepper and starts chopping, focusing on it like she's performing surgery. I can see her breathing slow as she works, her chest rhythmically rising and lowering.

"See? You can do this," I say after she's finished.

It isn't until she turns her head toward me that I realize how close we are and take a step back, reminding myself of boundaries, even as I smell my bodywash on her. A very male feeling hits me when I realize she stole my soap. I lock that feeling away tight. It has no place in this fragile friendship.

"You can do this. And if you change your mind, just say pickles, and I've got you," I say once I've returned my focus to our cooking mission.

That still feels a little too tense for cooking, so I reel in even further. I pat her stiffly on the head. "You're doing a good job."

She raises one eyebrow and looks at me like I'm insane.

Ok, cool. She noticed how weird the head pat was, too. Excellent.

"Yeah?" she asks anyway.

"Yeah," I answer. It seems to be becoming our thing.

And I *really* like that we have something that's "our thing."

I take my seat and try not to make it obvious I'm watching her. She's focused and quiet, and it might be silly, but this feels like a big step.

A bit later, a grin spreads across Piper's face as she presses the button on the blender, her carefully cut ingredients getting pulverized.

"I like this part. It's violent," she admits as the blender pulses. She's a cute, excited little thing. She turns quickly toward me, and her elbow bumps the blender, but her other hand flies out and catches it as it wobbles. Her eyes dart to me, and she looks like she's waiting for me to finally kick her out of the kitchen.

I give her the slightest shake of my head with an encouraging smile and see her release the breath she was holding.

"Ok," she says with obviously feigned confidence. "What's next?"

"For the soup? We just chill it and then eat it. There's a bit more on the salad if you'd like to keep going, though."

"Yeah, let's do it," she answers, her voice strong, determined.

I wonder if this is what it felt like when my brother got me to stop stomping to my bedroom and slamming the door after school.

As Piper starts picking cilantro leaves, I decide to press my luck. "Tell me about your family. I already know you don't have any siblings, but are you close with your parents?"

"Not so much. They moved to Florida once I started college and are living their best old people lives. My dad is an anesthesiologist, and my mom was a stay-at-home mom, so I was her job. Dad always wanted me to be a doctor, like him, or a lawyer or a financial analyst, or something else impressive. Librarian wasn't really up to snuff, and he's made his disappointment in my career path very apparent. Maybe I embarrass them. It's fine."

I stop trimming the beef I'm working on and look at Piper, my flabbers completely gasted. How anybody could look at all Piper is and not sing her praises confuses the shit out of me. She's kind, driven, beautiful, wild—what more would somebody want?

"No disrespect, but… what?"

Piper finally catches sight of my expression and cracks a laugh. She shrugs again. "Who knows, man." Then she makes that beautiful laugh again, but her eyes are sad. "My dad worked incredibly hard and overcame a lot to become a respected doctor. Being a Black man in the medical field is profound, but it comes with a lot of obstacles. He wanted to provide for us and make sure I didn't have hurdles, financial or otherwise, to achieving greatness."

"That's an incredible amount of pressure to put on you. You have to take the right path for you. You know that, right?"

"No, I do," Piper says with a sigh. "My mom understands I need to do my own thing a little more than he does, and she tries to play peacekeeper. Doesn't make it easier though. It's still pretty tense." She pauses before pivoting the conversation. "Tell me something fun about living in New York."

"It's got to be the accessibility of good food," I say, daydreaming about the perfect meatball sub I would regularly get from a street cart a few blocks away from my apartment.

Our night continues like that, with busy hands and taking

turns asking questions—nothing too deep after the disappointed dad conversation.

The wind is blowing in the right direction to allow us to open the back door before we eat. We watch the thunderstorm over the lake from the safety of the house, samesiding at the table so we can both look outside. The temperature drops and the sound of the rain is rhythmic and soothing.

The night is just the conclusion to a regular day, but I think it is pretty perfect.

CHAPTER 14

Piper

Scott is stubborn, and it is *infuriating*.

We just finished breakfast and are now having it out once again about his insistence I use his car. While I was in the zone yesterday at work, he told Mads I wouldn't need a ride this morning. There's no way I can ask her to come now, this close to when we need to be at the store, and Scott won't drop me off because he wants me to take the car myself instead.

I just can't. It's too much. He'll need it someday, and I'll have it hostage. I don't care that he could take the Trans Am. It's not the same as his big Range Rover. What if he needs to pick something big up? Or help a friend move? No matter what I say, none of my arguments are having any impact.

"What if I wreck it?" I'm basically shouting.

"Have you crashed many cars?" Scott asks, sounding calm, cool, and collected. It makes me want to shake him.

"No. Never, but—"

"But nothing. I've been in two accidents, and I still let myself drive the car. If potential crashes prevent you from being eligible to drive my car, then actual crashes should bench me permanently. You should be the one driving *me* around."

"Two accidents? Really?" I'm surprised. He seems like such a responsible guy.

"I hit a curb when I was learning and popped the tire. That hardly counts. And the other time was a little fender bender during a snowstorm when I hit some ice. That's not the point. Take the car." Scott is determined to keep me on topic.

"I caaaaaan't." This man is stressing me out. "I don't know how else to explain it. It's just too much."

"I'll be personally insulted if you don't." Scott tries a different tactic, letting gravity pull him bonelessly onto the couch like the mere weight of my rejection is too heavy to stand through. "My ancestors will be insulted. My future descendants will be insulted. My dead parents will be insulted. You might be cursing us to be haunted forever."

The entire production is ridiculous, but I don't know what to say. Playing the dead parents card is cold. How the fuck do I fight back against the threat of ghost parents?

I look at the clock on the oven. I need to *go*. Scott follows my line of sight and grins when he sees the time. He knows I'm getting desperate to leave. I don't like being late, though it happens often. I want to start good habits with this new job. This is some younger sibling wait-until-they-give-up bullshit he's pulling, and as an only child, I have no practice dealing with it.

"Fine! Give me the damn keys. But if something happens to this car, it's your fault."

"I take full responsibility. But nothing is going to happen. If it does, it's a good car, and at least you'll be safe. Remember. It's just a thing."

It's just a thing. Like it's no problem to replace a whole-ass car.

I stomp out of the house and let the door swing shut a little harder than is necessary. It feels stupid to be mad about him doing something nice, but I want to throttle him just a little bit for being such a pain in the ass about it.

That is, until I climb in the car, feel the soft leather on my legs, and realize how freeing the independence of having a car will be.

Damn you, Scott. I look back at the house and see his stupid face peeking through the front curtains.

I worry on my drive to work that living with him will be difficult if this is how disagreements go, but once I'm at the bookstore, I'm too busy to give it much more thought.

When I get home in the late afternoon, the house is quiet, and I realize it's my first time there without Scott. After searching upstairs and out back to confirm I'm actually solo, I connect my phone to the Bluetooth speaker in the living room and crank up some Taylor Swift loud enough so I can't hear my off-key singing.

I'm self-aware about my messiness, and I want to make sure I'm pulling my weight, so I start tidying up around the living room. I don't want to be dead weight dragging Scott's house down.

I fold my favorite tv-watching blanket and tuck it in the basket where it's supposed to live, clean the television, and dust everything I can reach. I'm dancing with the vacuum when I turn around and find Scott standing in the kitchen, just inside the back door.

I shriek and drop the upright vacuum on my foot before quickly grabbing my phone and turning down the music volume.

"I'm so sorry. I didn't hear you come home," I breathe out, huffing and puffing from being startled.

Scott shakes his head, smiling brightly at me and placing a hand over his heart. "No, no. I'm the sorry one—for interrupting that *incredible* performance."

I stick my tongue out at him.

He crosses the space toward me and passes by, stopping in front of the speaker. He turns the volume right back up to where it was.

"Carry on!" he shouts over the sound before dancing his way upstairs and into the bathroom.

I scooch to the bottom of the stairs, where I can see the closed bathroom door, and wait for a minute, fully expecting Scott to reemerge and change his mind about the decibel of the music, but he doesn't. The pipe makes the grumbling clang it does when somebody turns on the water, and I realize he's really going to let me have my little noise-fest down here without complaint.

Huh.

It's leftovers for dinner tonight, and I'm guzzling water between bites of the salad we made last night. The dressing is spicy, but so damn delicious.

"Are you good?" Scott asks when I start fanning myself.

"Yep. Doing fantastic." I'm already on my way to refill my glass at the sink. I spot the dish towel crumpled on the counter where I must have left it earlier and quickly hang it neatly on the oven door handle. I down the glass of water and fill another.

Scott slides up next to me with our empty dishes, placing them in the sink. He plucks the dish towel from where I just hung it and reaches around me to drop it back on the counter beside the sink.

"A little untidiness is ok, you know," he says softly as his fingers brush my forearm.

I hear an echo of being scolded for having something just a bit out of line, but it's faint and fading. Is this what healing feels like?

I clear my throat loudly (because of the spicy dressing, nothing else) and abruptly change the subject.

"Where did you head out to this afternoon? Did you need the car while I had it?" I ask.

"Nope." Scott pops the p like he does when he's pleased with himself. "You're still stuck with it. I was just on a walk around the lake. Being outside helps me clear my head, especially since my job involves staring at a screen by myself for hours on end. I feel like the walks help refill the creative well."

I want to say something supportive, but I can't really relate. Maybe we're just wired differently.

Scott isn't deterred by my lack of response. "You should come with me sometime."

"Yeah, maybe," I say noncommittally, trying to keep the instinctual grimace off my face.

The invitation is sweet, but I doubt that's going to happen. My idea of a good time rarely takes place in the great outdoors.

Piper

Since Scott works from home, I try to stay out of the house during working hours as much as possible. On my days off, I like to lovingly bug Alice. I'll often go to her house, but she's also been showing me different places to chill around Wilcox Grove. It's been steadily getting warmer, and Wilcox Grove is charming from every angle.

Sometimes, it's just the two of us. Other times, her friend, Ila, or even Grateful Bob will join us. We have one of those friendships where we don't have to do anything when we're together, so sometimes, we just loaf and doom scroll on our phones together.

If I am home when Scott is working, I try to be as unobtrusive as possible. I think it's helping me build up some self-restraint. Now when I read a particularly misogynistic manuscript for my editing job, I groan *inwardly* instead of swearing *outwardly*. Growth, am I right?

In all honesty, my daytime down time hasn't been that significant. Literary Lake is doing a great job keeping me busy, and I stay after the end of my shift basically every time I work.

The overtime at the bookstore isn't because Hannah and Leslie are demanding. I just like being there, and there's so much to do. My days have developed a rhythm, and that's exactly what I need to keep focused.

After Hannah and Leslie gave me the green light to update the store, I looped Emily in and we scheduled team meetings with the booksellers to loop them in and get their feedback. Everybody is really excited about the changes. We all dive in, updating our collection, making displays, and ordering fun bookish stuff to keep things exciting.

I'm arranging some of the plants on the current features table—Beach Reads to Get You Ready for Summer—when Scott slides up behind me. He's stopped in a couple of times before, usually in the morning or just before I leave on days when we carpool together.

"Hi, roomie," I say without turning. I know it's him. The cadence of his footsteps and the smell of his cologne, fresh, light, and crisp, have become familiar over the past two weeks.

"Hello, princess," he replies, helpfully taking the plant I have wedged between my side and elbow. I'm still not sure where the nickname came from, but I like it and haven't questioned it.

"Ugh, thank you. I've been juggling these things for like fifteen minutes trying to make them all fit. It's impossible." I finally turn to face him.

He's in a sky blue button-down with the sleeves rolled up and khaki-colored pants, a change from what he was wearing when I left this morning. The light blue shirt makes his eyes vibrant, and having his full attention on me is a little jarring. He looks *good*.

Does he have a date or something tonight? Does he date? I haven't even considered the possibility. I turned him down weeks ago, and summer is the time for flings. Is he going to bring somebody back to the house?

"You changed," I say, trying to sound casual when I feel anything but. "Big plans tonight?"

Scott looks down at himself, like he's just noticed he's not in basketball shorts and a t-shirt.

"I was just going to ask you if you were ok with me inviting Jake and Alice over for dinner but otherwise no. I had a video call with a client, so I put on the top half of a suit before. This is just the leftovers from that." He looks me up and down, taking in my lemon-print sundress. "You, on the other hand, look lovely."

I flush, both from the compliment and from getting so needlessly worked up over the prospect of Scott having plans. It'd be none of my business anyway. He walks with me over to a shelf with some space on it so we can rearrange the plants that wouldn't fit on the table.

"Just trying to not embarrass Hannah and Leslie." I brush off his comment on how I look, telling myself it's nothing but politeness. "And of course. You don't need my permission to have your family over."

"It's your home, too," Scott says softly. He's always so gentle with me. "I'd be a dick if I didn't at least check in."

"That's nice of you. I'd always check in with you, too. But you can assume it's a blanket yes for those two."

Jake approaches us from the café, balancing two coffee cups and what looks like iced tea in his hands. I guess he was Scott's ride here since I have the car.

Scott takes one of the coffee cups and the cold drink from Jake, handing the latter to me.

"I know you don't like coffee in the afternoons," he says nonchalantly.

He's right. I don't. I shouldn't be surprised he knows that with all the things he picks up on, but there's still a pleasant feeling spreading through me from him noticing.

I take the cup and thank him.

He then turns to Jake. "Do you and Alice want to come by for dinner tonight? I was thinking of making ribs, if that works."

"Ribs are good," he says bluntly. "I'll check with Alice to make sure, but I'd bet she'll say yes."

He turns away to fire off a text, and Scott's attention falls back to me.

"I was going to go check things out at the nursery with Jake before getting the ribs and going back, but do you need extra hands here?"

"We're all set, but thank you for the tea." It's something floral and fruity, perfect for the warming spring weather.

"You're very welcome. I'll see you back home later."

I nod, and he heads out with Jake.

When I think about it, I realize there's been a lot of help with the bookstore these past couple of weeks. Alice comes by whenever she can, and Scott always finds some way to lend a hand when he stops in, even just with little things like today. So do Jake and Grateful Bob. But they're not the only ones. People I've never seen before seem to hear about the new opportunities I'm trying to create for the bookstore and offer their congratulations and support. It's been special to witness.

When I get home, Jake, Alice, and Scott are crowded around the grill on the back patio. The back door is open and the delicious smell of barbeque is wafting in.

"Piper, get your butt out here!" Alice yells, her face appearing on the other side of the screen door. "I've got a cheese plate!"

That girl's first true love will always be cheese. I'm about to obey her command when my phone buzzes. I check the screen. It's Mommy dearest.

"One second. Mother calls," I say and hear Alice's dramatic groan. She's been with me for a lot of lectures from my parents and knows our chats don't often go well.

I'm on the stairs before I answer the call. Nobody needs to hear what is undoubtedly going to be an unpleasant conversation.

"Hey, Mom," I say.

"Hey? That's how you greet your mother? You have better manners than that," Dad's voice is stern. I guess they're together.

Oh yes. This is going swimmingly.

"Good afternoon, Wendy, Cameron. I hope your day is lovely," I try again, unable to keep the snip out of my voice.

"Don't take a tone, Piper. It's unbecoming." He sounds bored.

"*Cameron,*" I hear my mom scold him softly.

"What can I do for you both?" I ignore the critique. It's not quite standing up for myself, but at least I don't apologize.

"Your father has a work conference in Boston in a couple of weeks, and we'd like to drive up to see you after," my mom says cheerfully.

"Oh. When exactly do you think you'd be here?" I ask, already feeling the increase in anxiety that comes with a parental visit. Everything needs to be perfect, and even if it is, there's still a good chance I'll do something wrong. I love my parents. I do. Our relationship is just difficult.

"Your mother already told you. At the end of the month. I need you to pay attention. This is what happens when you fill your time with nonsense. I can't watch you lose the focus we taught you when you were growing up." Dad is back.

I'm already exhausted.

"Ok," I say, trying to figure out whether I can search for the conference online and figure out the dates of their visit from that.

"It'll probably be that last weekend in June," my mom says, gently as ever. It's always been like this, with my mother trying to inject her calmness into me and my father, ignoring our sharp comments. I know our tension is hard on her.

I hear my father's muffled voice in the background, and before I can reply, Mom says, "I'm so sorry. We've got to run. But I'm excited to see you soon. I miss you. Do you think you could send me information about hotels in the area?"

"Um, yeah. I'll ask around and send you something," I say quickly. "I miss you, too."

There's a pause during which I can hear her breathing, and I wonder if Dad will say anything, but the line goes dead. The conversation is so short I don't even make it all the way into my room. I lean back against the wall in the upstairs hallway and close my eyes for a few deep breaths before plastering on a smile and heading to the back patio.

The second I'm out the door, Alice pops the cap off a beer bottle and shoves it into my hand.

"I've got a feeling you need that," she says softly while the guys are still focused on poking at the grill. "What did she need?"

"It was the both of them. They're coming to visit," I say without emotion before taking a long drink from the cool brown bottle.

"Oh, great," Alice says, taking a drink of her own. Solidarity, sister. "When?"

I shrug. "Dunno exactly."

"What do you mean, you don't know?" Alice is perplexed like any reasonable person would be.

"Dad has some work thing in Boston at the end of the month, and then they're coming here. Mom said probably the last weekend of June, but I'm not sure if that's decided or something she said as an option."

Jake catches my attention when he places a platter of ribs in the middle of the table. Thankfully, a pound of barbeque sauce just might be the thing to improve my mood. They smell divine. We've also got coleslaw (lemon dressing, no mayo), potato wedges, and those little Hawaiian rolls.

Scott walks over and looks between me and Alice.

"Weird vibe, ladies," he notices.

"Are there any hotels in Wilcox Grove?" I ask, finally raising my voice enough to include everybody in the conversation.

"Hotels?" Jake asks with a scoff. Considering the size of Wilcox Grove, the question really wasn't necessary. I could guess the answer. "There's a tiny inn, but no. No hotels. Why?"

"My parents are coming to visit," I say with as much enthusiasm as one would have announcing an upcoming root canal.

"Oh yeah?" Scott says with some excitement like the thought of meeting them is neat. Then he sees my face. "Oh… no?"

Nodding, I confirm, "That's the ticket. But let's talk about something else. Jake, what's cooking at the nursery?"

I transform into Fun Piper (TM), so I don't bring down the whole dinner and take my seat. Just like we did at Alice and Jake's house, Scott and I sit side by side across from Alice and Jake.

"Right now, the tulip fields are a huge hit," Jake answers once we're settled.

As he dives into way more detail than I knew existed about tulips, I realize the trick to getting him to talk seems to be asking about plants. I don't mind him running the show. I don't have the emotional bandwidth to think of things to say right now, anyway.

I let the warmth of the day seep into my skin, the soft sound of the leaves rustling in the breeze hush the noise in my head. This is a level of nature I can tolerate, even enjoy.

After a very domestic family dinner, I'm rinsing dishes while Scott wraps up leftovers and the BBC Pride and Prejudice mini-series plays in the background. It's my comfort show, and mercifully Scott doesn't mind that I keep playing it over and over again. I look at the dark window in front of the sink, unable to see out back with the kitchen lights on. Instead, I see Scott's reflection from behind me. He smiles softly to himself, and I feel just a bit lighter.

I can't stop thinking about how this town and its people have quickly and efficiently weaseled their way into my life, and how much I'm enjoying feeling like I'm a part of this place. Then, I feel a sense of impending doom over my parents entering this safe space. I know I won't be able to show them the life they wanted me to have. Nonetheless, I text Mom the info about Wilcox Grove's only inn.

I'm eager to figure out what social events we can start hosting at Literary Lake, and I make it my focus the next day at work. I think community events are good starters, and maybe we can work our way up to hosting a special guest. Mia Lane, a new but wildly popular mystery author, has a spooky book coming out just in time for fall, and it's now my mission to convince her to visit our little store on her book tour at the end of the summer. First, I need to prove we can handle the marketing and the crowd she would draw in.

"So, where do we start?" Mads asks me.

"Well, damn. I was about to ask *you* that," I admit, nervously laughing. Mads has been with Literary Lake for a while and volunteered to help with some of the new event planning responsibilities.

We're sitting at one of the bookstore's little tables crouched over the store laptop, scrolling through the list of event ideas the bookstore staff came up with.

"Maybe something with little setup?" Mads suggests. She points to some of the themed nights people suggested. "I feel like it could take a lot of time to make props for some of these ideas, and they'd only appeal to some people."

"That's a good point. I also don't want to ask the café to figure out how to make a full *Game of Thrones* menu for our first event."

We alternate removing options until we're left with just one—trivia.

"It's perfect." Mads sighs. "You'd be shocked by how competitive all these sweet small-town people can get. I think this could be something great… and maybe violent. You've got bar fight experience though!"

I smack Mads on the arm. "That was *one* time! How did you even know about that?"

"Oh, Piper. This is a small town. Everybody knows everything about everybody."

We pick a Wednesday in two weeks for our trivia night and immediately get to work. It's less lead time than I'd like to have to advertise an event, but this is a small town, and I don't want to wait. Over the next several days, I write the questions, Hannah works on a menu of snack foods, and Leslie starts drawing up seating plans and calling vendors for the extra equipment we'll need to rent. Even though Mads and I picked trivia because it would have minimal setup, this undertaking feels intimidating, and I worry I won't be able to bring all the parts together.

I am eternally grateful for Mads taking point on the store's new social media pages. She's convinced—or bribed? Threatened? I didn't ask—her friends and some of the other booksellers to help make fun videos and posts for our pages, too.

I'm scrolling through our stories when I come across a new graphic advertising the trivia night. It has an impressively accurate drawing of the café. Little tables are packed, and I can almost hear the excited chattering from the roughly drawn attendees.

Scott made this. I'm sure of it.

I take a screenshot and text it over to him.

ME

Thank you.

The dots at the bottom of my screen start bouncing right away.

SCOTT
Proud of you.

I look at the to-do list in my little notebook, and I feel for the first time since we scheduled trivia night that we can pull this off.

Scott

"Goooooooooooaaaaaaaaal!" I call out as I race around the field, curving in a wide arc until I reach my teammate, Marty, and give her a high five.

Eli, Jake, Marty, and I are playing two-on-two soccer in one of the fields at Wilcox Nursery. I came with Jake again today so he could continue his walkthrough of everything in the business that Eli, Jake, and I *technically* own together. I've spent several days here since returning home, while Jake walks me through every detail of the business, and then makes Eli explain everything he's in charge of behind the scenes.

The nursery is run exclusively by Eli and Jake, which is why we basically always say they're the co-owners without mentioning me, and the only reason I'm on the books as an owner is because we agreed to use our joint inheritance and insurance money from our parents' death to buy the place with Eli. I haven't practically contributed to this place since I finished painting the sign out front the first year we owned it.

I've known Eli for my entire life. The story goes that Eli walked up to Jake on the first day of kindergarten and declared them best friends. Jake said "ok," and the rest is history. Eli's basically been my second older brother, and I trust him as much as I trust Jake. So, I have no desire to look over Jake's and Eli's shoulders when it comes to this business. It's in very capable hands.

Still, Jake insists on these check-ins, no matter how awkward it feels to be walked through books I have nothing to do with and shown plants I know nothing about. Eli and Jake have put their hearts and souls into this place, and I'd have transferred my share of the business to them ages ago if I wasn't worried it would break Jake's heart for me to officially step away.

Because of other financial circumstances, I don't need the income from here, and I donate it back to the business or use it to help community service organizations around Wilcox Grove. I think it makes for complications when Eli does our accounting, but that sounds like an Eli problem.

So, we go through this ordeal from time to time, and I tell the other men how proud I am of them until Jake is as uncomfortable with the attention as I am with my unwilling intrusion in the business, and he inevitably suggests we do something else.

Today, it's soccer. As soon as Jake pulled out the ball, I recruited Marty, who is conveniently working today, to my team. It's been a very quiet day, and the field gives us a good view of the parking lot outside of the office, so there's no harm in all of us playing.

Eli thought he got the good teammate in Jake, since my brother is a giant of a man, strong, burly, and competitive, same as Eli. But Marty's older sister and I were the same year in high school, and I happen to know Marty started playing soccer when she was four and is exceptionally good at it, even though she isn't playing on her high school team. I also know Marty is quiet and private, so I was banking on Eli and Jake not having the same insight I do.

Considering how we have absolutely demolished my brother

and Eli, I'd say I was right. Eli is standing with his hands on his knees, huffing and puffing, and Jake looks a little like he wants to switch to playing tackle football so he can flatten me. I'm feeling damn good, and Marty seems pretty pleased about having shown up her two bosses so spectacularly.

"How… the hell… are you so damn fast?" Eli finally asks Marty between gasps for air.

The girl shrugs. "You need some water, old man?" she taunts, but sits in the grass herself for some rest.

"Ohhhhhh!" I say before howling with laughter, but Eli stares Marty dead in the eye, looking like he might keel over, his blond hair plastered to his head with sweat.

"Yes, please! I'm dying over here." He wheezes, but laughs, too. "God almighty. You are impressive, miss."

It's Jake who ends up jogging back to the office and returning with four water bottles, tossing one to each of us.

Youth recovers quickly, so Marty heaves herself up and heads back inside to tidy up before we close up and all head home. I pull my phone out of my pocket and see a text from Piper. I feel a sharp swoop in my chest just from seeing her name.

PRINCESS

I'm going to be at the store late tonight, so don't wait for me for dinner.

ME

Do you need me to bring you something to eat?

PRINCESS

Thanks, but Alice and Ila are coming by with food, and we're going to make sure all the equipment works for trivia.

ME

Sounds like fun. I'll see you later.

Piper has been working so hard to make sure everything is perfect for Literary Lake's first event. I'm a little worried she's been working *too* hard, but I've been focusing hard on minding my own business and offering a reasonable friend-level amount of help. It's in my nature to lend a hand, but I know this event is *her* thing. I'm banking on her asking if she really does need help.

I look up and see Jake's brow furrow as he checks his own phone. I expect he was just informed about Alice's participation in girls' work night at the bookstore. Eli is simply starfished on the ground.

"Eli, what happened to your football prowess?" I poke just a little more fun at him. He was a talented quarterback all through high school. Enough so, he earned himself a full ride to the school of his choosing. After playing four more years at the collegiate level, he walked away, seemingly uninterested in playing professionally.

"They destroyed every joint in my body. I'm lucky to walk at all," he scoffs with a smile. Eli has always been lighthearted, especially about himself, but I wonder if I hear a bit of bitterness in his tone.

"Would food help?" I ask, hoping my teasing didn't unintentionally tip over into cruelty.

That gets Eli bouncing to his feet like a jackrabbit.

"Always yes. Jake?"

"Yeah, I'm in," my brother agrees. "But both of you are showering before we go if I'm supposed to share a table with you."

"Oh yeah, because I'm sure you smell like fresh cut roses," I throw back. He's right, though. We're ripe. "Showers and then we meet at the Corner Post in like forty-five minutes?"

Grunts all around mean yes.

"Are you here to wreck my bar, Scotty boy?" Penny calls out to me the second I'm through the doors to her bar. I know it's all in good fun. Thankfully, the fight I partook in last year didn't result in any permanent damage to her business, and the other guys are the ones who got banned. Not to sound like a child, but they *did* start it.

"Penny, my love, I would never. I am only here to defend your fine establishment, if you'll forgive me for my prior indiscretions?" I proclaim as I dramatically approach her, reaching out until I can clasp her hand in both of mine across the bar. She and this bar have been here longer than I've been alive. It's her pride and joy.

The space is welcoming, filled with dark wood and lit with warm lights. Behind the bar is a wall of overlapping photographs pinned and taped up, showing Wilcox Grove and its residents over the years. Every time I come here, I find the one of my parents from before Jake was born. They were high school sweethearts, soulmates, clear as day in the way they looked at each other, even in the faded photo. I want to have a love like theirs—perfect and strong.

Penny pulls her fingers from mine to swat my arm. "Oh, sit down, Scott. You know I only have eyes for Grateful Bob." She winks at the man who's seated just to my left, before placing a pint of beer in front of him.

I clap Grateful Bob on the shoulder.

"Good evening, sir," I say. Grateful Bob is another staple in my life. He's always been around, and I know I can rely on him for a wisecrack just as much as I can for sage advice. Like I said —family.

"Right back at ya, boy." He turns in his chair toward me.

"Wanna join me, Jake, and Eli for a bite?" I nod my head over to the guys, where they've claimed a table.

Grateful Bob looks past me and shrugs. "Might as well. Somebody's got to keep an eye on you troublemakers." His laugh is deep and raspy and sounds like home.

He stands with ease, unfolding to a tall height. He's an old man, though I have no clue exactly how old, but he's lean and strong. Solid. He swings his low ponytail of stark white hair over his shoulder and straightens his patch-covered—most of them loons—jacket before walking to the table.

I follow a step behind once I collect the three beers Penny wordlessly brings to me. It's good to be back in a place where I feel known and welcome. Where everybody knows my name or something.

"Eli, Jake," Grateful Bob greets them as we sit down, and I dole out the beers to my fellow soccer players. "All good with you? Alice?"

"All good," Jake replies. "Alice will be disappointed she missed you, though."

"Shows what you know," the old man scoffs back. "She brought me banana nut muffins earlier today. You can't convince me I'm not her favorite."

Jake rolls his eyes, but I know he loves Grateful Bob as much as I do. That doesn't stop Jake from grumbling something about knowing there are muffins waiting at home for him too, in the house he *shares* with Alice.

"And you're still breaking hearts?" Grateful Bob directs this one to Eli.

"Never. Nobody ever leaves disappointed." Eli feigns offense. He means it, though. While he's not a relationship guy, he doesn't break hearts. Being up-front and having clear communication are steadfast rules he has with women. "Isn't that how *you* told Scott you got your nickname?"

Grateful Bob shakes his head. "That's ridiculous. I'm called

Grateful Bob after a cowboy from an old Texas comic strip my uncle was obsessed with. He said my nose was identical to the character's. Me being named Robert was a happy coincidence."

"What if I just called you Robert instead?" I ask.

His expression gets stern. "The only person who calls me Robert is Ila. Don't make me smack you upside the head."

I raise my hands in surrender, though I expect the smack is inevitable. They're never hard, but there are very few conversations I've had with him that haven't included me saying something dumb enough to warrant one. Maybe I could have been an astronaut or something if I hadn't lost so many brain cells from this man being in my life.

"Enough stupid questions, what mayhem have you been getting up to," Grateful Bob asks me next.

"No more than you, sir," I quip back, and he laughs a hearty laugh.

"What about with your new roomie," Eli asks suggestively. I see Jake's eyebrows quirk up though he stays quiet. Even Grateful Bob shows interest.

"She's a good roommate," I offer, putting on my best poker face. Spoiler: I have no poker face.

"You're telling me there's nothing happening there?" Eli presses. "Most of the town saw you fight Troy here for her last year."

"I fought Troy because he's an asshole," I correct. Though I'd absolutely have fought him for Piper, I don't think she needed the protecting. "And no, nothing's happening."

Penny comes by the table and saves me from having to explain that Piper friend-zoned me, hard. After we order dinner, we fall into that kind of easy, honest conversation that comes when the people you're with already know all there is to know about you, and they don't judge you for it.

It feels good to be back in Wilcox Grove.

When we get home later, Jake stops me before we part ways.

"Are you actually doing alright with the Piper situation?" he asks now that we're alone, concern etched in the lines on his brow.

"I am. I like being her friend." It's the truth. Sharing a space with Piper has been great. Whenever she's around, the house is brighter, happier. We cook together, chat about our days, watch TV together. I feel lucky just being able to be around her.

He doesn't look convinced, but Jake grunts a good night, and I walk across the gravel space separating our homes. I see the living room light on through the window.

Once inside, I find Piper wrapped in her favorite blanket on the couch, out cold, and with the projector instruction manual laying open on her chest. She looks like she belongs here, in this house.

I gently shake her shoulder without garnering a response.

"Piper," I say, shaking her harder before sharply tapping her arm a few times and repeating, "Piper!"

She jolts awake, whipping her head back and forth, and I step back.

"I think it's time to go to bed," I offer.

She's looking around the room, clearly confused, but she eventually finds me. She blinks blearily a few times before seeming to figure out what's happening and checking the time on her phone.

"Oh. Yes, bed is good. Many thanks, sir," she says as she unwraps the blanket and stands. Apparently sleepy Piper is amusingly proper. She begins folding the blanket, likely to put it back in the basket by the television.

"You don't need to do that," I say, and she pauses. "Just leave it on the back of the couch. You use it basically every night anyway. You live here, and it's ok if it looks like it."

Her face softens, and I wonder if this is what it would be like to wake up with a sleepy Piper.

Mentally berating myself for being a creep, I run like a coward to the library.

"Well, good night." I stumble in and close the door, falling back against it.

Smooth.

CHAPTER 17

Piper

Contrary to my earlier concerns, living with a man—at least living with *this* man—has been surprisingly easy. Sometimes, he's a little all over the place, but he's never unkind, and his floundering is kind of cute. Besides, who am I to judge? I've never been put together for a moment in my life.

After a long day, I look forward to coming back to our shared house, hearing about his day, making dinner together. I wouldn't say I'm a good cook, yet, but I think there's the potential for me to become a not terrible cook in the distant future. In my twenty-nine years of life, I've written off a number of things as out of my grasp, and I'm finding myself wondering whether any of those could be a possibility with the right teacher, too.

This isn't just a place where I can store my crap and sleep out of the elements, either. It feels safe. Once I step through that doorway, I can just be. Whether I'm moody, anxious, loud, overwhelmed, or elated, Scott hasn't tried to make me more manageable.

Every once in a while, I catch myself waiting for the other shoe to drop. Something tells me at some point, I'm going to be *too* moody, anxious, loud, overwhelmed, elated. But so far, the only things that have dropped are things I've knocked over.

There's the smallest possibility Scott is different than the exes, than my parents, than the girls—except Alice—I never quite fit in with. The less I think about that dropping shoe, the more I think about Scott and whether it was a mistake to turn him down so quickly.

Maybe I can be better for a man like Scott. If I opened up, maybe he *would* want to stay, and maybe I could let him.

"Scott?" I call out when I get home on the evening before Literary Lake's debut trivia night. There's no response. He must still be on his creativity walk.

I'd *like* to say I feel completely prepared for trivia night, and that I can't wait for it to be tomorrow evening so I can show all of Wilcox Grove what I can do, but my nerves are through the *roof*. As I was leaving work, I was going to call Alice since spending time with her would likely help keep my mind off everything that could go wrong, but I found myself wanting to come home instead… to Scott. It's possible I'm in the tiniest bit of trouble when it comes to him.

Partially as a thank you for all the little things Scott has done to make me feel at home here and partially to avoid the additional task of cooking this evening, I brought home a mountain of Chinese food, even though I know Scott would make a full dinner for me while I sat on my duff if I gave the smallest hint that I wasn't up to cooking.

Some people can't eat when they're anxious. I'm the opposite.

I set the numerous bags on the kitchen table before hurrying upstairs for a shower, hoping I can be done and out of the way before Scott gets back and needs the bathroom himself. I'm just finishing dressing when I hear the back door close downstairs.

"Piper?" Scott's voice carries up the stairs.

"I'm up here! I'll be down in a minute," I call back and hang my towel on its hook before heading to the kitchen.

When I get to the bottom of the stairs, I freeze. Apparently, Scott went for a run today instead of a walk. Usually, when he gets back, he looks refreshed and windswept. Today, his shirt is off and tucked into the waistband of his shorts and every inch of him is glistening.

He's facing away from me, toward the table, and I suddenly remember the feel of every ridge and divot of his shoulders under my fingertips from my first night here.

Lord above. I need to get it together.

I compose myself just before he turns to me.

"What's up?" I ask, hoping my voice doesn't sound as croaky as I fear it does.

"Are you doing alright?" he asks, pointing over his shoulder toward the table. "That's enough food to feed a platoon, and you told me you get a lot of food when you're nervous."

I did tell him that—once. And it was weeks ago while we were cooking on some unmemorable day. Still, he stored away that fact. Kept it safe like he seems to have kept everything I've told him.

"I want tomorrow to go well." It's the truth, but honestly not the main factor turning me upside down at this precise moment. Scott remembering what I do when I'm nervous and checking in on me is making me get all in my feelings. That on top of his sweaty half-nakedness right now is doing things to my brain. I will say it's an extremely effective combination for keeping me from worrying about trivia.

"I've seen how hard you've been working, so I have no doubt you're as prepared as possible. I got you something as a congratu-lations on planning your first event, and for your one-month anniversary in Wilcox Grove."

I check the date on my watch while he collects something

from his work bag. It is indeed exactly one month since I broke into this house.

"Is it shampoo to commemorate our reunion?" I laugh, trying to break the tension building around us. Humor is a tried-and-true shield.

"That was the backup option," he says before passing me a brown paper bag wrapped around—well, I'd know a book anywhere. The bag has the store name printed on it, and I can make out *rare books* from between Scott's fingers.

"Scott…" I hesitate, knowing he's about to crash through those shields with a very thoughtful, personal, and likely expensive gift.

"Take it." There's a touch of an order in his tone, something that's rarely slipped out over the last several weeks, and something that sends a sharp heat right down my spine every time. I refuse to think about where that heat settles.

I take the package and carefully open it, pulling out a gorgeous leather-bound special edition of *Pride and Prejudice*. The title and the edges of the pages are gilded, and the rich brown cover has the most intricate foliate design pressed into it.

Oh.

It's stunning.

"With how happy the show makes you, I thought the book might be a favorite, too. I've said it before, but it's worth repeating. I'm proud of you."

There's pressure behind my eyes and a tingle on the bridge of my nose.

I will not cry.

"How do you know I don't just have a thing for soaking wet men wearing pirate shirts?" I hope the joke will make the situation feel less meaningful.

"Do you? Because I will absolutely wear that for you." Scott doesn't even hesitate, and I catch the ways his eyes darken. He really would… and I think I'd like it very much indeed.

Unable to hold his intense gaze, I look back down at the gorgeous book and run my thumb over the detailed cover.

"This book is my absolute favorite. Thank you." My words are soft. I glance from the book up to Scott. Have we always been standing this close? I swear I can feel the heat radiating off him.

"Open it. Part two is inside."

I flip open the cover and choke on my snort before a barked laugh bursts from me, the risk of tears is forgotten. I pick up the bookmark and turn it over. Scott's drawn us and one side has a cartoon mugshot of me, while the other side has a mugshot of him. He even included his black eye and my post-fight hair looking exactly the way I remember it from the end of the night.

"So you don't take yourself too seriously, my little almost criminal," Scott says. "Tomorrow is going to go great."

"This is truly the best gift I've ever gotten," I say, holding both items in one hand. I rest my other against the side of his shoulder. His skin is like fire.

Ignoring the fact that I'm freshly showered, and Scott is post-workout sweaty, I fling my arms around his neck. His strong arm snaps around my waist.

"Thank you, Scott," I say against his hair.

"You're very welcome, Piper."

He's looking directly at me when I pull back, and my cheek brushes his nose. I think I hear his breath catch. Meanwhile, I've stopped breathing entirely. My gaze snaps to his eyes and finds them hooded, molten.

I could just…

What am I thinking? I step back, breaking our contact, and clear my throat.

"Um, why don't you go grab a shower, and I'll unpack the food?" I offer.

Scott keeps staring at me for a second, and it feels like he can see all the way through me to my deepest, darkest secrets.

"Uh-huh." He blinks, and the world seems to focus for him. "Right. Sounds good."

He rubs the back of his neck, just like Alice said Jake does when he's nervous. He turns to go upstairs, and when he trips on the first step, I pretend not to notice.

The next morning is sent by the universe to test me. I'm woken up by a call from Leslie, who's just realized we don't have the final permits we need to use the café as an event space with the capacity we expect tonight. In the background, I can hear Hannah shouting at her to stop trying to get up with two broken legs. There's a scuffling sound, and Leslie drops the phone.

"Can you please get to the store as soon as possible before I push my wife out a window and break more of her bones? *Please*?" Hannah's voice comes back on the line, but she is clearly still doing some kind of battle with Leslie, whose protests I can hear every few seconds.

"I'll be there in fifteen minutes." I'm already out of bed and shoving my legs into some denim shorts, the phone wedged between my face and my shoulder.

"Oh, thank god. Liz, the fire marshal, said she can meet one of us there, and Leslie seems to keep *FORGETTING* her only job right now is to heal. I'm going to see if Emily can come by to help out, too."

"I'll call Emily on the way. You just deal with whatever you've got going on over there." I pull on a t-shirt and gracelessly crash into the dresser.

"Piper, you can never leave Wilcox Grove ever. You are a lifesaver," Hannah breathes out heavily.

I know it's hyperbole, but it's good to feel needed, wanted.

"I've got your back. I'll let you know how it goes."

We hang up, and I throw open my bedroom door to find Scott standing rumpled in his own doorway, his hair flat on one side and sticking straight out on the other. He's still anti-shirt, and his pajama pants hang *low*.

I *really* wish I had more time to enjoy that view, but I need to go.

"Everything ok?" he calls as I trample down the stairs.

"Yup. Bookstore stuff. Sorry!" I cry as I grab a pair of sandals and the car keys before flying out the door.

I wish I could say otherwise, but the morning doesn't improve.

Liz isn't unkind, but she is strict and has Emily and me running around the store and café, measuring the width of walkways and adding signage to clearly mark exits everywhere. Café deliveries for the menu tonight are delayed and then incomplete, so we have to send somebody to the store to get the things we're missing. Then, one of our servers calls out, stuck home sick with the flu.

With all the moving pieces and cafe troubles, Hannah ends up having to come in anyway, but she somehow manages to get Leslie to stay home for now, promising to pick her up before trivia starts.

Finally getting Liz's stamp of approval feels like we've won the Nobel Prize. Hannah and I physically sag against the wall as we wave to the fire marshal's retreating back before sharing a well-deserved high-five. It's already two in the afternoon, and it feels like we've endured a long battle.

"Go home. Go shower and get ready for tonight the way you'd planned to before I dragged you in here this morning. Eat something and then come back," Hannah says as she pushes off the wall. I wonder how haggard I look and feel the tiniest bit self-conscious.

"Are you sure? I don't want to abandon you," I protest, but I really could use a minute to collect myself before hosting tonight. The stores are still bustling around us, and the noise is beginning to rattle my brain.

"Emily and I have things covered for now, and I promise to call you if anything else comes up."

I look at her with fear in my eyes.

"But it won't," she quickly amends. "It won't. Go."

"Ok," I concede. "I'll be back in like two hours."

"Make it three!" Hannah demands.

The second I step outside, and the door closes behind me, I feel a bit better. The quiet of the street is like a glass of ice water at high noon on a scalding day. I hurry to the Range Rover and shove in my earbud so I can call Alice for some emotional support.

"Hey Pipe." She picks up on the first ring. "Today's the big day!"

"Yeah, and I'm kind of freaking the fuck out a little bit," I admit.

"Of course you are," Alice says with a laugh, like this is no big deal. "That's what you do. But you also work unbelievably hard and plan like your life depends on it. Don't you?"

"I don't know," I hesitate.

"No, I want to hear you say it. You're ready for tonight."

"A bunch of things went wrong this morning, and it has me convinced there's more that's going to blow up in my face. Maybe I forgot something," I counter.

"Do you need any help putting out fires?"

"No. As of right now, we're ok," I admit.

"Look, bumps in the road happen. This is Literary Lake's first event. Expecting no hurdles was unrealistic. That doesn't mean you didn't do all you could to make this event a success. I've been running errands today, and people are talking about it everywhere. I think Bets is telling every single person who comes into the post office she's going to kick their ass at trivia tonight."

That makes me smile. "Are people really excited?"

"Extremely. I can't tell you nothing else will go wrong. It might. What I can tell you is that it's ok if it does. You'll learn from it and be better prepared next time. You're smart and capable. Now, I want to hear you tell me tonight is going to be great."

"Tonight is going to be great," I say mechanically without believing it.

"That was the most pathetic mantra I've ever heard," Alice says. "Do I need to come to you and get you to believe it?"

I take a deep breath. Alice does have a point about the impracticality of expecting a perfect night.

"No, I'm ok. Hannah's ordered me to go home and rest before tonight. It's going to be great."

Alice clears her throat, still unimpressed with my outlook.

I try again, shouting a little. "TONIGHT IS GOING TO BE GREAT!"

"That's my girl!" Alice cheers. "This town is small. I can be at your side in twenty minutes or less. Call if you need me, ok?"

"I will. I love you."

"Love you, too." She hangs up as I'm pulling between the trees toward our houses.

I'm careful to be as quiet as possible when I ascend the front steps and open the door at the house in case Scott is working, but I find him on the couch, finishing a sandwich and watching a documentary on Formula 1 racing.

"Hey!" He pauses the show as I kick off my sandals. "I didn't expect to see you until trivia. Everything ok?"

"For the moment, yes," I say, coming over and flopping on the couch next to him. "We had some last-minute snafus, but we're currently ok. Hannah kicked me out and told me to clean up so I don't scare the customers later."

"But you're such a cute bridge troll." Scott laughs, and I slap the side of his thigh.

"Way to kick a bridge troll when she's down." But I'm laughing, too. It could be a result of delirium since the adrenaline has left my system, but it feels good, nonetheless. "I'm going to go take that shower. I need to rally for tonight."

"You got this!" Scott calls after me as I trudge upstairs.

The juxtaposition of my energy flying down these stairs this morning compared to the slug crawl back up isn't lost on me.

All I want is the coziest, boiling hot shower where I stand under the water for thirty to forty minutes and contemplate the meaning of life, followed by a nap that feels a little bit like temporary death, but that's not in the cards for me today, so I turn the temperature to ice cold… and then make it a moderate luke-warm. I don't hate myself. I still stand under the water until it runs cold.

I'll admit I feel rejuvenated after the shower. I even take the time to blow dry my hair straight, something I very rarely do, relishing the calm monotony and warm air, and allow myself a little bit of time to lie on my fluffy bed and just stare at the ceiling. It's therapeutic. By the time I'm heading back downstairs, I feel much more confident, in white calf-length jeans, wedges, and a pink plaid button-up with sleeves cuffed halfway. I'm ready to take on the world.

Scott is in the kitchen when I return.

"Hey, I made you—" He cuts off when he sees me, his mouth remaining slightly ajar as his eyes scan all the way down me and back up.

I cock my head when he gets back to my eyes. "Yes? You made me…?"

He drags a hand down the lower part of his face and stares for another second. The fact that I affect him like this does great things for my confidence.

"I made you a caprese sandwich and filled the biggest cup we have with iced coffee how you like it," he says after a beat.

My eyes fall to the plate and glass near Scott on the table. "Oh my god, I love you," I rush out, suddenly feeling the full impact of not having eaten a single thing all day.

I hug him from the side and throw myself in my chair before I realize what I said. I shove the sandwich in my mouth before I can say something else stupid, though I'm pretty sure nothing can be worse than a rogue "I love you." I didn't mean it like *that*. I glance at Scott, and he looks a little dazed.

I'm such an idiot!

Scott holds up a paper bag, and kindly ignores what I blurted out, though it takes a second for him to compose himself. "I—uh —also made you some more coffee in a thermos to keep it cold and threw an energy drink in here in case we need the big guns. There are some snacks, too, so you don't get jittery."

Maybe I *did* mean it like that. This man is a godsend. But I try to pick a safer response.

"You've earned yourself a gold star, mister," I say, and I can guarantee it sounds as weird as you'd think it would.

"I will now expect a gold star sticker, you know." Scott is a good egg. "I'm going to wrap up some work stuff but let me know when it's time to go."

I stop scarfing down my sandwich. "You're coming?" I'm genuinely surprised. He hasn't said so before.

"Oh, princess, I wouldn't miss it for the world. Alice, Jake, Eli, Grateful Bob, and I made a team, and we're coming to win." He says over his shoulder before disappearing into the library.

I didn't realize how badly I wanted them all to be there until he confirmed it. My people are showing up for me.

I *have* people.

CHAPTER 18

As I drive me and Piper back to the bookstore, I notice she seems much calmer than when she got home just a couple of hours ago. I'm still floating on air replaying her slipped "I love you" from earlier. I know she didn't mean it *that* way, but it garbled my brain in the best way, nonetheless.

"Is there anything you need me to stop and pick up for tonight before we go back?" I ask, focusing on reality, here and now.

Piper thinks about it for a second before responding.

"Nah, I think I'm actually all set." She raises the bag of snacks and caffeine I'd given her earlier today.

"You feel like giving me any hints about what the categories will be tonight?"

"Scott Preston! I know you are not trying to *cheat* right now. Do you really have such little faith in your team?" Piper is outraged by me, and she's all kinds of fired up. I like it.

I find a parking space on the street near the store and pull in.

"I'm sure we'll do fine. I just happen to know you're a crafty woman, and I had to try."

"Well, you'll get no special treatment from me. You'll have to rely on your collective knowledge of random, mostly useless facts," she scolds before narrowing her eyes at me. "I've got my eye on you, so everything better be above board."

"Always, your honor," I promise, hand over my heart.

She merely points two fingers at her eyes and then at me and gets out of the car. Trivia starts at seven, but it's only five, and the bookstore is packed. Clusters of people are milling about everywhere, including outside the door. It seems like the whole town has turned up for this.

Piper is looking at a wild success for tonight, and she deserves nothing less.

The café is wrapping up its regular service for the day, so Hannah is trying her best to corral the trivia teams into a line and out of the café so the tables can be rearranged and extra chairs can be set up. It's not going well. Leslie is safely behind the café counter in her wheelchair, but she looks like she wants to jump up and help her wife.

"Oh, thank goodness, Piper," Hannah breathes out when she sees us. "We're good to start setting up so we can sign in teams and seat people, but nobody will *move* out of the way."

"If you can get me hands to help set up the tables, I can move the people," Piper promises.

Looking around, I spot Jake, Alice, and Grateful Bob through the front window, just arriving.

"I've got the hands covered," I say, waving and catching my brother's eye. His size helps to part the clusters of people, and they get to us quickly. Hannah gives me a copy of the floor plan.

"Thank you," Piper says, touching my arm. "Consider yourselves signed up. Please help Hannah."

I'm about to show the modified café layout to Jake when Piper's voice cuts through the cacophony in the store from beside me.

"Hey!" she shouts quite impressively and then starts moving toward the registers in the bookstore. "If you want to play trivia, follow the sound of my voice and line up in the bookstore *only*. If you're in the café while we set up chairs, I cannot guarantee you will not be hit with a chair, but I can guarantee your team will *not* be playing tonight unless you are all together and sign in directly with me."

Her voice projects through the store, and miraculously. the mob shuts up and begins following her like she's the Pied Piper.

I quickly pass the layout diagram around our group, and we jump to work, shifting tables and chairs in the café and the bookstore's seating area, and unloading additional folding chairs from the rental van out front. When Eli arrives, we task him with placing little tents with the trivia menu on each table, as well as a pen and packet of answer sheets for each team.

Finally, we set up screens and projectors to show each question where every table can see and speakers for the microphone Piper will be using.

In just over half an hour, it feels like we're ready to go, and people are finding their seats and ordering all kinds of bar appetizer snacks, Hannah's chosen menu for the evening. For the first time ever, Barefoot Bake is suddenly churning out wings, baked potato skins, and mozzarella sticks.

"We have a *waiting list!*" Piper squeals, breathless, as she runs up to me and Alice waving a sheet of paper in her hands.

"Aw, congratulations, Pipe," Alice says, hugging her best friend.

"Thank you, I—" Piper starts to answer but is cut off by a loud voice I'd know anywhere.

"What do you mean there's no beer?" Troy Basel's oaf grunt barrels through the happy chatter, and I turn toward the cause of the Corner Post Bar Fight of 2024. He's standing, bearing down on Hannah.

"Troy, we're a breakfast and lunch café. Of course there's no beer. Sit your ass down," Hannah growls back, clearly having no issue handling the brute.

I *hate* that guy. He's been an asshole for his entire life, like it was written into his DNA. He's always the loudest voice in every room, especially when he has nothing productive to say.

"Yeah. I was going to tell you. Troy and his friends are here," Piper mutters, sounding disgusted.

"Couldn't you just tell them \no?" Alice says what I'm thinking before I can.

"They haven't technically done anything wrong here, yet. I didn't want there to be any chance we get accused of mishandling things for our first event." She sneers toward Troy's team. "Based on how things are going, I expect we won't have to wait long for him or one of the others to cause a scene and get kicked out."

"Don't let them ruin this," I say. "It's going to be a great night."

The kitchen gets a little backed up as everybody orders all at once, but the pre-trivia socializing otherwise goes well. At one point, there's the clear sound of shattering glass, but Troy's friend insists he *accidentally* bumped his soda with his elbow. If I didn't know better, I'd say the guy sounds drunk.

At 6:45, Hannah and Leslie take center stage to thank everybody for coming and to introduce Piper as host. Piper is beaming, but I can her anxiousness in the way she's tapping her finger against her thigh from our table right up front. She takes the microphone.

"Gooooooooood evening, Wilcox Grove!" Piper does a great Robin Williams impression, her voice steady and strong, and the café explodes with cheering. "I am so excited to have you all here for Literary Lake's inaugural trivia night. Tonight is general trivia, but if things go well, we'd love to host themed trivia nights in the future, so be sure to give us any suggestions for what you'd like to see. I'm just going to take a few minutes to explain the format and rules, so who's ready?"

It's surround sound clapping and cheering. As it dies down, there's a distinct voice in a not-so-quiet whisper shout.

"I wish she would shut up, already! She's *so* obnoxious." It's Troy's female friend from the bar last year complaining to her friends. If memory serves correctly, Piper got at least one good hit in with that one.

"HEY!" I shout, the same time another voice yells, "How about *YOU* shut up!" It's Ila. I spot her at another table with her husband and what looks like the whole team from the tattoo shop.

I watch Piper visibly retreat into herself and remember her saying people think she's too much.

Come on, Piper. You know this is just Troy being a piece of shit. You are perfect.

"Sorry, um—" Piper is shaken, and I'm furious. "I'll try to be quick."

She rushes through the format and rules, explaining the different rounds, the specialty picture round, and that each team needs to bring up their answer sheet before the next round begins or it will not be counted. There will be a stretch break halfway through and, of course, looking up answers isn't allowed.

I try to focus solely on Piper, but the snickering and muttering from Troy's table is about to make me flip *our* table. It's made worse by the fact that Piper's eyes keep flitting over in that direction. She can hear them, too.

"Ok, well, we're going to play a couple of songs so you can think of your team names, and then we'll get started. Please make sure to write your team name on every answer sheet so you get credit for your responses."

The volume of Troy's obnoxious chortling keeps increasing, as does the sound of their chairs scraping back and forth, and the clank of their glasses and dishes knocking together.

Leslie, who's sitting up front with Piper ready to help her keep score, gets Hannah's attention and points as Troy gets more animated, flailing his arms around. Like it's happening in slow motion, Troy's arm shoots out while he guffaws, and his meaty hand connects with a tray in a passing server's hands, sending several glasses crashing to the ground.

The room goes silent, and every head turns in that direction. Piper rushes over to the server, making sure she's alright while Hannah gets rags and a broom. As Hannah gets to the table, her irritation is clear.

"Come on, dude. Get it together. I need you to settle down if you want to stay," she says firmly.

"Jeez, lighten up, lady! Isn't this supposed to be *fun*? So far, all that's happened is me and my friends getting denied our order, and some hag screaming rules at us."

I'm standing before I register that I've pushed back from the table, and Alice is at my side. Jake and Eli are both poised to back us up. I'm ready to go round two with this piece of shit, but Hannah steps in again, and Leslie is deftly wheeling herself over to the commotion.

"Get out. You and your team need to go, now," Hannah says, seething.

"You've got no right!" Troy yells, shoving into the table and standing. As he does, a flask slides off his lap, spilling brown liquid across the floor as it bounces away from him. Hannah picks up the flask and smells it, just to be sure.

"I've got every right. And because of this"—she gestures to the flask brought into her liquor-license-less business—"I can also say you're all officially unwelcome at any other evening event hosted by Literary Lake. Now, get *out*."

Troy looks around, maybe realizing for the first time he's the center of some very undesirable attention, and his expression contorts into something ugly.

"Fine!" he bellows. "I should have known anything planned by this bitch would be trash anyway." He gestures toward Piper, and I just about snap. I step toward him, but Grateful Bob gets a firm grip on my wrist, his attention focused on Troy.

"Boy, you want to get out of here, I think. You don't have good odds." The old man's voice is the most menacing I've heard in a while, and I finally take a minute to look around.

Alice and I aren't the only ones standing. Jake and Eli have gotten to their feet, and so have Ila and her husband, Marty and Tim (the two nursery workers looking rather cozy), Mads, and even the quiet librarian, Molly, from the school.

Next to Hannah and Leslie, Piper is standing with her arms crossed over her middle, white as a sheet. It doesn't make sense. Last year, when this gargoyle and his friends were coming after me, Piper came out swinging to defend us—literally. But now that they're spewing their vitriol at her, it's like she's become a shadow of herself.

I just want her to look up, to look around. To see these people have her back and value every part of who she is. But she doesn't. I'm not sure she can.

"Whatever," Troy grumbles. "Let's go."

Miraculously, they all leave. The applause for their departure is even louder than the cheering Piper received before.

With the mess cleaned up, and a team called up from the waitlist, Piper and Leslie make their way back to the front. I catch Piper's arm as she passes by our table. She's still folded in on herself, and her eyes are trained on her shoes.

"Pickles?" I whisper so only she can hear.

She shakes her head and lifts her gaze.

"Not yet. I can do this." Her voice is soft, but there's still strength there.

Once Piper is back at the microphone, her eyes find mine, and

I can't help myself. I wink. She rolls her eyes, but a hint of a smile peeks through.

Let's go, baby.

CHAPTER 19

Piper

After a rocky and dramatic start, the rest of trivia night is a blast. It takes me until the second round of questions, but the music and energy in the room finally pull me out of my funk. Everybody is cheering and screaming when I share the mid-way point totals, and the team names have me cracking up.

It gets even louder at the end of the night, when I announce "Three children in a trench coat" have won our first trivia night and a gift card for the café. Several attendees demanded to know when the next trivia night will be, and Grateful Bob, who has an alarming amount of useless trivia packed in his brain, is determined to win, even if that means kicking Eli off the team and replacing him with "somebody who knows more than pop music facts."

As the kids would say, the vibes are immaculate (Do the kids still say that?). I'm still riding the high of the night as we're stacking chairs, wiping tables, and taking out the trash.

I look around at everybody who chose to hang around to help with cleanup, and I feel that pinch behind my eyes again. It's the same group of people who stood up for me without hesitation earlier, and right by my side, beaming at me, is Scott.

Catching me looking at him, Scott reaches out and squeezes my elbow.

"You accomplished an incredible thing tonight, and you deserve all your success. I know Troy is a piece of crap, but don't let him or people like him make you smaller. I see all of you, and I think you're spectacular."

I'm trying to figure out what to say to that when a loud crash has both me and Scott spinning around.

"Sorry!" Alice calls out from beside a stack of folded chairs that just tumbled off the cart they were piled on. "Pipe, can you give me a hand?"

Girl... have better timing, damnit!

"Yup!" I quickly turn back to Scott. "Um, thank you."

It's not enough, and it feels like I'm brushing him off, but I flee to Alice anyway, kicking myself the whole way across the café.

"Did I interrupt something?" Alice whispers when I'm by her side.

"Nope," I reply too quickly.

"Not for nothing," she continues. "I think he could make you really happy."

Jake pops up out of nowhere to bring the chairs out to the rental service's truck, so I don't answer Alice. When I give her a questioning look behind Jake's back, she just shrugs like *it's your call.*

I don't have a chance to talk to Alice or Scott again as we finish cleaning and everybody takes a turn thanking and congratulating me before heading home. It's thrilling but a little overwhelming. It's a relief when we're outside on the sidewalk standing beside Leslie as Hannah locks up.

The street is deserted, and it's blissfully quiet. I take a few long, deep breaths, urging my body to step away from the flight part of fight-or-flight.

Scott drives the two of us back, rolling down the windows the second he turns the key in the ignition and quietly putting on some R&B. I want to tell him what him—and the rest of the town, but mostly him—standing up for me meant, but when I glance his way, he's focusing so intently on the road that I wonder if he regrets the almost moment we had inside.

The car's tires on the asphalt and the soft notes from the radio are the only sounds on the drive home.

I'm still restless once we're inside, and when Scott goes upstairs, I head out back and climb onto the swing bench at the corner of the back porch, folding my legs under me until I'm kind of contorted, but snugly wrapped around myself. I reach out for the standing post and push against it to lazily begin swinging.

I don't know how long I'm out here, but Scott eventually comes looking for me.

"There you are," he says from the doorway before disappearing back inside for a moment. When he re-emerges, he's holding a plate of cinnamon buns in one hand and two mugs in the other.

"Did you just make those?" I ask, gesturing to the plate, shocked and impressed.

"Nah," he laughs. "I mean, yes, but they're from a tube."

I scoot to one side of the swing, and Scott takes a seat beside me. He holds out the mugs first, and I take the one with the teabag inside. I can see a couple of ice cubes melting, just how I like it.

Scott wedges the other mug between his knees before lifting one of the buns, the one basically dripping frosting, and holding it out to me. I look at him quizzically. It's clearly the best one on the plate.

"What? You can't tell me you don't want the one with the

most frosting. Isn't that the main reason you have desserts?" he asks.

I think back to every pastry and dessert I've selected in his presence over the last few weeks. Of course, he's right. Most of my food only serves as a vehicle for sauce, frosting, icing, or syrup.

I hadn't realized he was paying that much attention.

"I love frosting," I confirm, taking the treat from Scott's hand. "Thank you."

I stare at it while Scott begins devouring another one. Thinking more about it, maybe he's always paying attention to me. When I'm talking too much. When I'm dancing like a lunatic. When I'm letting my every thought play across my over-expressive face. I'd bet Scott sees it all.

Scott realizes I haven't taken a bite yet.

"Is something wrong?"

"No—" I start.

"If this is about before, I'm sorry for making you uncomfortable. I just hated seeing how Troy's bullshit affected you. He and his cronies are wrong. You deserve to take up as much space as you want. Your voice deserves to be heard. You…" He trails off and shakes his head like he's holding himself back from saying more.

Alice's words echo in my head, and I think she's right. He could make me really happy.

"Ok," I blurt suddenly. It's a bad idea. I'm not worth the effort, and, more likely than not, this will end with soul-crushing disappointment or betrayal, but I say it again anyway. "Ok."

"Ok?"

I take a deep breath, hold it for a moment, and let it out.

"I wasn't uncomfortable before. I just don't quite know how to react to somebody being as nice to me as you always are. And now, I'm saying yes."

"Yes?"

Clearly my attempt at being subtle is going splendidly.

"You can woo me, if you still want to." I peek over at him.

He's smiling, and there's frosting on his lip. He leans back in his seat and looks out over the lake. I look too, wondering if he can hear my thundering heart. Has he changed his mind? Out of the corner of my eye, I see him lick the frosting.

"There's nothing I want more, princess."

Maybe he's just being nice. I can't bear to look at him and risk confirming my suspicion.

"You know I'm older than you," I remind him.

"Yup."

"And I'm taller than you."

"Ok."

"I'm loud."

"Fantastic."

"I don't know what I'm doing with my life."

"We can figure it out, if you want help."

"Those things would bother some guys." A lot of guys, actually. All the previous guys, at least.

"Not me."

I take a quick peek, and Scott is staring at me, beaming. His joy is so infectious I can't help but smile back.

"Yeah?"

"Yeah."

Here goes everything.

Scott

Piper and I are quiet as we eat more than the recommended amount of cinnamon buns each, and I do an exceptional job of playing the part of "relaxed guy." Meanwhile, I am losing my fucking mind.

Immediately after Piper said she wanted me to woo her, I pinched my leg as hard as I could to make sure I wasn't dreaming. Thankfully, she wasn't looking at me because it hurt like a bitch, and I didn't need her to see my eyes water.

I don't know if the "no pain in a dream" rule applies to comas, though, so there's always a chance I'm unconscious in a hospital bed following significant brain trauma. It would make sense this is the circumstance my brain would create to give me comfort while it heals.

I'm grateful Piper isn't feeling chatty while we sit side-by-side because I'm confident I can process neither speech nor comprehension at this moment. I'm fully occupied with the pit of panic I'm steadily descending into.

After sitting peacefully for a few minutes or sixteen hours—it's impossible to know—Piper gets up.

"Goodnight, Scott," she says, no different than any other night.

But when she brushes her fingertips against my shoulder on her way inside, I feel them sear me right down to my soul. Eventually, I must follow her into the house because I end up in my room, showered, teeth brushed, and ready for bed.

How? Couldn't tell you.

I can't fuck this up with her. I'm confident I'll never have another chance like this because I know there isn't another person like her.

I wake up the next morning, feeling jittery and confused, like I got really drunk last night and forgot something extremely important.

You can woo me, if you still want to.

Piper's invitation slams into me like a freight train, and I wonder again if I dreamed it all up. It felt awfully real, but I'd done my best for weeks to convince myself that a future with Piper as more than my friend was off the table. I needed to, or I'd have done something like swear myself body and soul to her until the end of time. Nothing dramatic or anything.

I head downstairs to get started on breakfast, like usual, and am surprised to find Piper already sitting at the kitchen table with two plates of scrambled eggs, bacon, and toast in front of her. A steaming mug of coffee sits before my seat, and she holds a second mug, the sound of ice clinking against the ceramic filling the space.

"It's one of the few things I could always make," Piper explains, gesturing to our plates. "I just took it out of the pan like a minute ago, so come eat while it's still hot. We should talk."

My stomach drops. She's going to change her mind. My face must give me away, because she rolls her eyes.

"Oh my god, will you sit down? I just want to lay out the ground rules," she banters, and her impatience puts me at ease. This is the Piper I know.

But, what? Rules?

"Do you mean like hard and soft limits?" I ask.

Piper chokes on her coffee.

"What? No!" She flushes from her hairline to the top of her shirt. She pauses, and her eyebrows draw together. "Is that a conversation we should be having right now?"

"You can do whatever you want to do to me, Piper," I say honestly, finally taking the seat across from her and leaning back in the chair.

Piper scrutinizes my every movement, and I smirk, watching her trail her eyes down my torso until she reaches the tabletop.

"I think this is a conversation everybody should have with their partner, but it's something we can discuss… later." She takes a huge gulp of her iced coffee and visibly collects herself. "I mean for this wooing thing. Dating."

Oh. I can't think of a single rule I'd want to impose.

Piper purses her lips and raises her eyebrows, jerking her head toward my plate. The message is clear. She's not saying a word until I eat. So, I pick up my fork and dig in.

"Good. Ok…" Piper takes out her phone and starts reading. "First up—if we're trying this thing, it's staying between us. I will not be town gossip, and I will not have the pressure of everybody's expectations on this."

I make a sour face. I already hate the first rule. No part of me wants to hide dating Piper from anybody. And it's a good thing I didn't already text Jake to tell him. The only reason I haven't is because I want to tell him in person. Jake isn't a talker, and he's an even worse texter. I wasn't going to give him a chance to leave me on read.

I look into the brightest chocolate brown eyes I've ever seen, expectation and anticipation staring back at me. She's scared. She needs the security of privacy. I fix my face.

"Ok. This can be private… for now. But that rule will be revisited later. You are not something to hide away." I reach across the table and brush my fingers over the back of her hand where she clutches her phone. She softens, but she doesn't take back the rule. "What's next?"

"I want to keep separate rooms. And we're not changing any of what we arranged for roommate responsibilities and bills."

That one is an easy yes. "I respect your space and privacy entirely. This will not affect your living situation. Agreed."

"Lastly, we keep things casual," she says after glancing back down at the list on her screen.

I stop moving my thumb over her soft skin.

"What does that mean?"

"No labels or expectations. Not exclusive. Not a relationship."

I hate this one even more than her first rule. When I said I loved the people of this town, I wasn't picturing any of them with their hands on Piper, stealing her smiles, making her laugh. I might actually *hate* the people of this town if *that's* a possibility.

I scrutinize Piper's face. She's chewing her lip, but her expression is determined. When her eyes flick up to mine, I realize she needs this rule, too, for comfort, to feel in control. I shift my hand so I can slide my fingers between Piper's, and her phone slips out of her grasp, hitting the table with a quiet thud.

"Piper, you can make all the rules that you want, and you can call this casual if that makes you feel better, but in the end, it's not going to matter. I'm a patient person. I'm all in, and I'm going to show you that I'm the man for you."

Maybe what I see in her eyes now is hope.

Because of the event last night, Hannah banned Piper from coming into Literary Lake today, giving her a boss-mandated break after all the extra time Piper's been committing to the first event launch. I think the idea is for Piper to relax, but the woman seems determined to do anything but.

Up until now, Piper has spent most of her days out of the house, whether working or not. Today, though, she's hanging around, and I feel hyper aware of her presence. It's nearly impossible to focus, even when I close myself in the library and put in earbuds.

All I want to do is find excuses to be around her. But I expect the reason she clears out so often is to avoid disturbing me, so I mentally chain myself to my desk so I can prove to her that we can exist together and still function. Or, in my case, pretend to function.

After we finish breakfast, Piper begins a frenzied deep clean of the kitchen. When I emerge from my working cave for a coffee refill—an entirely reasonable thing to do—I find her standing on the counters, dusting the tops of the upper cabinets. With her back to me, I shamelessly stop and stare, coffee all but forgotten.

When she turns to hop down, I realize that permission to woo her means I don't have to avoid being near her anymore. I step closer and feel a rush when she immediately reaches towards me. Today, we are in sync, and without needing to discuss it, I help her off the counter.

I slowly lower her to the floor, but she keeps her hands on my shoulders as I release her legs and straighten. She's looking at me quizzically, like I'm a puzzle she's trying to solve. For just a second, her grip tightens, and all my focus shoots to the ten tips of her fingers and the mental image of her squeezing my shoulders like that once before. She rolls her lips together, and I wonder if she's thinking of it too.

Fuuuuck.

Somehow, I drag myself away and close myself back in the library… office… whatever it is. Instead of working, I pace. I sit in one of the reading chairs, and I try to think of what I can do for Piper to show her how I see her. I want to know every inch of her soul and give her mine. All this talk about her being the one for me, and now I've got to back up my words.

I'm looking out the window when a soft knock on the door makes me jump. I turn away from the lake as the door cracks open, and Piper pokes her head in.

"Hey, sorry. It's almost two and you haven't eaten. Maybe you're one of those people who doesn't eat when you're working, but that's a terrible way to live. I made some sandwiches, and you need to have one. If you don't want one, please eat *something*." She's unwavering and a little stern, and I love it. I want to push her buttons, challenge her.

I cross the room in a few strides, but she doesn't back up when I take the door in my hand and open it fully, so we're nearly chest to chest.

"Pack them up. We're going for a walk."

Piper makes a face. "Scott, I know you love your walks, but I'm perfectly fine eating in here."

"I didn't ask. You're coming with me."

She pouts, and her brow furrows, eyes narrowed. For a second, I think she's going to tell me to go fuck myself. I'm taking a risk here, but it's one that feels right.

"Fine. But only because I want to see what you think you're playing at."

She relents, ceding control, and I relish my victory.

I take Piper by her shoulders, gently turn her around, and lightly push her. She takes a small step forward.

"Now, go put your shoes on. I'll wrap up the sandwiches."

She groans and drops her head forward like she's already regretting agreeing to walk with me, so I swiftly swat her ass and urge her forward again.

Her head whips toward me, and the sparkle in her eye tells me she's ready to play.

This is going to be a game, and it's one I intend to win.

It's a good thing I decide to carry the bag with our stuff in it because I'm again comparing Piper to a baby deer as she clambers down the hill behind the house, ignoring the perfectly functional steps right next to her out of sheer stubbornness.

I hold out my empty hand for her, but she waves me off.

"I can manage," she insists.

"I know. I help because I like to, not because you're incapable of doing something yourself." I keep my hand extended, and Piper eyes it like my fingers will morph into talons the second she touches them. She considers for just another moment before grasping it and letting me usher us down the slope.

"Sorry. I have trouble accepting help," Piper reluctantly admits.

"You don't say?"

Piper shoots a glare at me in response to my thick sarcasm.

"People who give help always want something in return. I also want to prove I can do this on my own." Her tone doesn't match the glare. It's wounded.

It hurts to hear she's been treated badly enough to make her so mistrustful.

"Do you think Alice is like that? You seem ok with her help."

"Alice is the exception," Piper relents, fiercely protective of her friend. Their bond is clearly special. "But it's like, I already found one person who is wholly good in my life. It's hard to believe I'd be lucky enough to find more."

Piper winces when she finishes, likely realizing she just said she doesn't think I'm wholly good.

"Sorry," she mutters.

"Oh, no offense taken. I'm definitely not as good as Alice is, but you can still trust me. I told you already. I'm a patient man, and if you need time, that won't scare me off."

I think we can get there. After all, Piper hasn't let go of my hand yet, even though we've been on the flat path around the lake for several minutes now.

"I've got my eye on you, Scott," she jokes, veering us away from deeper conversation.

"Hopefully both eyes. I look fantastic." I hit her with my best Flynn Rider smolder.

She laughs, and it sounds like bells in the wind. She playfully smacks my chest, and the contact feels natural.

Piper looks up and must see we're approaching the next pair of houses around the lake because she drops my hand. I agreed to the rules, so I get it, even if I miss the feel of her skin against mine.

A loon calls out across the lake, and Piper's attention follows the sound. There's a splash against a dock and a flock of birds take flight from a tree on a small island in the water. She turns toward both of those sounds, too. She looks curious, not disgusted or afraid, the way I'd expect somebody who allegedly hates nature to look.

She's still looking toward the island of trees as we get closer to it.

"Look," I say softly as I point to the top of one of the large trees on the spit of land. "If you look closely, you can see an eagle's nest on the far left tree. Sometimes you can even spot one of them flying."

"There are *eagles* up here just flying around in the wild?" She sounds awestruck.

"As opposed to what?" I chuckle. She looks thoughtful for a moment.

"I guess I'm not sure. They just seem like such a majestic creature. I never really thought of one just chilling on a lake."

Her eyes stay glued to the tree, even as we pass the island, like she's willing one to show itself. She turns for a few steps before tearing her gaze away.

"What do the different buoys mean?" Piper asks, nodding toward the different colored markers bobbing on the lake.

"They indicate safe places to drive, rocks, and when you're entering or exiting a slow speed zone."

Piper stops and squints at the lake. "I couldn't identify a path among those if you paid me," she admits.

"I felt the same way when I was learning to drive, but I promise it eventually becomes second nature, the same way you know what lines on a road mean without having to think about it."

We walk a while more, and she asks me other questions about the lake. I point out animals and unique plants, historical homes, or ones with dramatic pasts. The sun is bright, but there's a cooling breeze, and the whole lake is alive. Everything is beautiful and serene, like Barefoot Lake wanted to show off for our little skeptic.

Eventually, we get to a park I loved to play at when I was younger, and I lead Piper to a picnic table. As I unpack our food, Piper crouches down and thoroughly inspects the underside of the table and bench.

As I watch the spectacle, I finally have to ask, "What exactly are you looking for, princess?"

"Massive swarms of spiders. I am *not* interested in having one crawl up my shorts while I'm trying to eat." She shudders, and uses her phone flashlight to check again, just to be sure.

I take my seat. The spiders and I are tight.

"So, are bugs why you claim to dislike nature? Because it seemed like you were interested in the lake and the wildlife on the walk over here." I'm truly perplexed. I thought things were going well, but Piper seems uneasy now.

Finally, she sits, too.

"It's not bugs, per se. It just always feels like something can jump out at me. It's worse at night. *Anything* could happen, and I don't like feeling like I constantly need to look over my shoulder. I like knowing what to expect." Piper unwraps her sandwich as she explains, avoiding eye contact.

"It takes time, but things can become somewhat predictable. I honestly feel like people are more unpredictable than elements of nature."

"Well, I'm not overly fond of most people, either," Piper says with a huff, but her smile peeks through anyway, and her eyes flash to mine.

"I don't believe that for a second. Maybe they frustrate you, but you love people, love helping them. And you're good at it. You're approachable, easy to talk to."

Piper's eyes fall again, suddenly finding the mozzarella on her caprese sandwich fascinating. She shrugs, and her cheeks stain the faintest pink, like delicate rose petals. This strong, fierce woman struggles with compliments.

"I could teach you some of the nature stuff you can come to expect, so it's not all so jarring. If you want," I offer. She doesn't have to like being outdoors if it's really not her thing, but I'd like to help her be more comfortable if she's interested.

"I'll think about it," she says. And when she smiles at me, it feels as warm as the sun's rays.

CHAPTER 21

Piper

Barefoot Lake has its own little song, and for nature, it's not so bad.

As I walk beside Scott back toward the house, I sneak a peek at him. It's just the very start of summer, but his hair is already lightening from the sun, and the breeze lifts the ends that rest against his neck. He looks peaceful, and a soft smile graces his lips. He's wearing a light grey t-shirt and pale blue shorts. The hand between us is casually in his pocket.

If it wasn't, I think I'd want to hold it again.

Today is no different from yesterday, but at the same time, it feels like everything has changed. Maybe in some ways, it has.

It's clear he was keeping me at arm's length before, at my own request, because there's a new warmth now that wasn't there before. I feel a pull toward this genuinely happy man next to me, like he's magnetic. As I look at him, I wonder if this time can be different, if I can have something real with Scott. Or is this just the excitement from the prospect of somebody new?

Even though our friendship is young, it feels different from other ones I've had with men. He's never tried to fit any part of me into a box, and he's made it clear I'm in the driver's seat.

Once I started college, I moved out of my parents' house and haven't moved back since. I've been determined to make it all on my own, probably because my dad made it clear he thought I'd *need* to come ask for help unless I picked a more serious and respectable (according to him) career. That might mean I lived in more than one really shitty apartment, and I have a small mountain of student loan debt, *and* this isn't the first time I've had to have two jobs at once, but I've still done it.

Control and independence are important to me. Scott seems to get that in a way few others have. He offers help, but he's never forced it. And when I do take his offered hand, I don't feel like less of a person for doing so. It's this acceptance of me and my quirks that made me want to try with him and his kind-hearted soul.

"What are you thinking about?" Scott asks suddenly. I must have been wearing what Alice calls my "thinking face."

"You," I say honestly.

"Oh yeah?" Scott says, seemingly elated by my answer. "What about me?"

"Don't break my heart, Scott." I don't know why I say it, but the words tumble from my lips. "I can't be let down again."

He stops and turns to face me fully. He takes his hand out of his pocket and lightly touches his fingertips to my elbow when I stop, too.

"I won't, princess. I couldn't stand it either," he says.

When I look into his shining blue eyes, I believe him.

After we get back to the house, I make myself a little reading nook at the corner of the couch, surrounded by a pile of pillows and my favorite blanket wrapped around me. I'm extra cozy with my skin warmed from the sun. I need to force myself to finish the first read-through of my current manuscript for my editing job. It's due basically now, and I usually provide feedback early, but this one is just painful.

I read all kinds of stories and know everything isn't for everybody, but this author really seems to hate women. It certainly seemed that way when we had our consultation call after his book was assigned to me, and he made his displeasure about not being assigned a *competent male editor* very clear.

The portrayal of all females in this book—even the animals—is abysmal. Every single one is stupid, catty, vapid, and helpless, with the personality of a wet paper towel. And the plot doesn't even make sense.

Did he just say the queen's "ovaries jiggled" because she saw the prince without a shirt on?

I groan and throw my head back. I need to think of a way to provide constructive feedback here, but the struggle is real. I think I'd be justified if I replied with an audio message of me screaming for a solid minute.

Suddenly, I'm looking at an upside-down Scott, standing behind my head by the arm of the couch. He's holding a large mug in one hand and a dangerously familiar light blue glass bottle in the other.

"Tea or tequila?" he offers, looking down at me.

"Tequila got me in trouble last time," I grumble. "Tea, please."

He steps around the couch and hands me the mug, setting the tequila bottle on the coffee table.

"It was some damn good trouble, if you ask me," he says smoothly.

That night leaps to the front of my mind, and I can almost feel the pressure of Scott's palm as he dragged his hand up the outside of my thigh. I quickly take a gulp of the tea to try and hide my face behind the gargantuan mug. It would be a blatant lie to say I hadn't thought of another night like that with Scott several times since I gave him the green light to be *more* with me.

And *yes*, I know it's been less than a day. He looks—and was—that good.

Scott sinks down onto the couch near my feet and slings one of his arms across the back cushions. He looks effortlessly cool, and I find myself staring at the hand extended toward me, thinking, again, about it on me. Scott has *good* hands.

I realize Scott is looking at me expectantly, and I think I missed a question.

"What's that?" I ask, trying to be cool, too, and failing. That's ok. I've never needed to be cool before.

"I just asked what's got you so peeved."

"I'm a freelance editor with this service that pairs writers with low-cost editors. Because it's cheap, assignments are made randomly and there is no vetting process. Anybody who pays will get their story read. The current one is just really degrading, and the author is kind of an asshole," I explain bluntly.

Scott slides his arm down to catch my ankle and pull my leg toward him, propping my heel on his thigh. He begins pressing his thumbs into the arch of my foot, rubbing slow circles. His skin is so soft, but those fingers are strong, and goosebumps erupt up my legs. I pray my feet aren't gross from the walk, but if they are, Scott doesn't seem to mind in the slightest.

"Can you reject the submission yourself or trade for another one?" he asks without explaining the impromptu foot massage.

"What are you doing?" I ask, looking at my foot and wiggling my toes.

"Does it feel good?" he answers my question with a question.

"Immensely," I admit.

"I don't know anything about editing a book, but I figured this wouldn't make things *worse*, so here we are."

"I can't argue with that logic," I concede and prop my other heel on his leg, too, so it can have a turn next. "And no, I'm not allowed to turn down books. It's a very simplistic system and not my favorite thing, but it's a paycheck."

"You can't leave it now that you have Literary Lake?"

"With my amount of student loan debt from undergrad and my masters?" I scoff. "Sadly, no. I need to take whatever I can get."

"Do you want me to take a look at your loans? I could see if there are refinancing options that could help. I have a finance guy."

He has a finance guy? Something tells me Scott and I are *very* different in some ways, and I feel myself instinctively getting defensive. Before responding, I remind myself he's just trying to help.

"No, thank you. I need to handle my financial stuff myself. My dad decided I wouldn't get parental help with school if I wasn't going to pick something more serious than creative writing and librarianship, so I need to show that I can do this and pay off my loans myself. You're already helping by not charging me rent. Now I can put what would have been rent money toward paying down my loans."

Scott looks like he wants to keep talking about this, but his face relaxes, and he says, "Alright. The offer stands. I want to help you, and I think I really could." He switches to rubbing the other foot.

I drag my attention back to the story. Getting a massage while reading improves the experience, even if character development is nowhere to be found among these pages. Eventually Scott sets my feet back on the couch and stands.

The feeling of sadness from his absence is both surprising and ridiculous, since he's probably just going back to work ten feet away in the library. But I liked the contact of our skin, and not just because I was getting a damn good massage. It was comforting and something I didn't realize I wanted so badly.

When he returns a few minutes later holding his tablet, I find myself smiling at him. He gestures back to the couch.

"Do you mind if I work here with you?"

"Not at all," I say, wriggling deeper into the couch. Once seated, he pulls my feet back onto his lap and drapes an arm across my shins.

Maybe he wants to stay touching as much as I do.

The next morning, for the first time since I came to Wilcox Grove, I don't want to go to Literary Lake. It's not that I love it any less than I did two days ago, but I find I really wouldn't mind just hanging out with Scott again. I stayed home all day yesterday, and never once did he make me feel like I was in the way. Instead, he made it abundantly clear my presence was enjoyable and desired.

Sadly, I do have responsibilities, and as much as I want to bask in attention from Scott, after having breakfast together— bagels with cream cheese, lox, red onions, and capers—I've got to go.

As soon as I sit in the driver's seat of the Range Rover, my phone buzzes. I pull it out after I start the car and see Scott's name.

SCOTT

Have a good day today. And if you don't already have plans for the evening, please do me a favor and don't make any.

I smile stupidly at my phone before I feel eyes on me and look up. Scott is standing at the open side door, leaning on the frame. He's still in a t-shirt and his pajama pants, and he's looking at me like I'm something he wants to devour. I *really* want to get out of this car and let him.

ME

Should I be nervous?

I watch him read my text and lick his lips.

SCOTT

Not in the slightest.

He winks before turning and going back inside, leaving me to crank the AC as high as it will go and point all the vents at myself.

· ┼ ✳ ┼ ·

I focus well enough to drive safely, but Scott is still on my mind until I pull up outside Barefoot Bake and Literary Lake and see Hannah standing there with a police officer. Another café manager was opening earlier today, so they must have called her in for whatever is happening. I park quickly and leap from the car the second it's off.

"Hannah!" I call as I jog up to her. "What happened?"

The words leave my lips a second before I see the spiderweb of shattered glass on the bakery's front window. A few pieces even fell out and are lying on the sidewalk beside a hunk of broken brick. Thankfully the chunk of rock didn't go completely through the thick glass window.

I quickly look at neighboring stores and across the street, but there isn't a camera in sight. In a town like Wilcox Grove, I guess they never felt necessary.

The police officer clears his throat to draw my attention back to him. It's then that I notice it's one of the two officers who responded to the bar fight last year—Mike Andersen.

Greaaaaat.

"Officer Andersen," I greet him with the world's most awkward wave. Even though I didn't get in trouble, this is mortifying. "It's so super duper to see you."

He thankfully chuckles. "We've got to meet under better circumstances one of these days," he says, flashing me a dazzling smile. "At least I don't need to put you in the back of my squad car today." His expression turns mischievous and a little playful.

Is he *flirting*? I chuckle awkwardly. That's better than being rude, I guess, but *what*?

Andersen—Mike—slips back into professionalism. "Do you have any ideas on who might have done this, Miss Price?" he asks.

Immediately Troy and his goons enter my mind, but I have no evidence against them other than the fact that they suck. I hesitate to start something nasty in a town this small without more to go on.

Mike notices I'm holding back.

"Anything could be helpful," he encourages.

"Troy Basel got a little unruly at trivia two days ago," I say.

"He was an ass," Hannah supplements. "And he brought a flask, so we had to ask him and his friends to leave."

"Ask?" Andersen is skeptical.

"We kicked them all out," Hannah corrects herself. "He wasn't pleased about it."

"And if memory serves correctly, he and some others with him were involved in the fight at the Corner Post last year." Officer Andersen pretends he doesn't know *exactly* who was involved. He makes notes on his pad as Hannah provides the names of the other people Troy was with on Wednesday.

"We'll talk to them and let you know if there are any developments. I'll email a copy of the police report for insurance as soon as I have it finalized," he promises.

"Thanks, Andersen," Hannah and I say together. It's cute.

He gives us a little salute. "I'll see you around. Hannah..." He pauses. "Piper."

We watch as he walks back to his cruiser and drives away.

"Piper Price, that man was just *flirting* with you!" Hannah squeals as soon as the taillights disappear around a corner.

"Well, I guess that's better than him almost arresting me," I say, turning back to her. I bend and pick up the brick. "I'll get a broom."

As I clean up, Hannah calls Jake to see if he can bring over wood to board up the window in the meantime. I hear her side of the conversation. She's laughing through the whole thing.

"Yeah, I know a nursery and a lumber yard aren't the same thing... well, trees make wood... look, can you help me out or n—thank you, Jake!"

She hangs up and turns to me. "He'll be here in ten."

I hold out a roll of masking tape, and we begin taping over the cracked part of the pane. I don't know if that's proper procedure, but I've seen it on TV.

Fifteen minutes later, a small, old, blue pickup truck with rusted bumpers pulls up in front of the store and double parks. Jake throws himself out of the passenger side while Tim casually slides from the driver's seat. He was at trivia night, but I also remember him from Alice's stories. He's another high school kid who works at the nursery. He's got a good heart, is usually high, and comes with a strong work ethic and great sense of humor.

Jake catches my eye, and I notice he looks a little haggard. "You good?" I ask.

"He's a nice kid, but he drives like a lunatic," he explains, dragging a hand down his face before shaking his head.

"Where's your truck?"

A guilty look flashes on Jake's face for a split second before he slips back into a blank expression. He almost looked... busted?

"I asked Scott to do a favor for me today, so he has it," Jake says after some hesitation. I don't feel like I know him well enough to question the momentary shadiness. It was also so quick I could have imagined it.

"Is this it?" Jake asks, nodding toward the poorly taped window and hastily changing the subject.

"Yeah," I say, and Hannah and I step aside.

"What happened?" he asks as he unclips a tape measure from his belt.

"Vandalism," Hannah answers.

"Troy?"

"Probably."

"Ok."

He really is a man of few words. Hannah seems to get it, giving the facts without any flourish.

Jake gestures to Tim at the back of the pickup, and the teen flips down the hatch and begins unloading what they'll need to fit a piece of plywood over the cracked window.

"We'll leave you to it," Hannah says, holding open the café door. "Holler if we can help."

This time, Jake only grunts, already bent over the wood and marking off the measurements to match the broken window. My bestie's soulmate, ladies and gents.

I pull out my phone and text Scott.

ME

Hey, what are you doing?

A minute later, the response comes through.

SCOTT

Helping Jake haul some stuff. He said somebody broke a window over there? Are you ok?

I look through the window beside the broken glass and see Jake slip his phone into his front pocket. Why does it feel like they're up to something? I quickly update Scott before hurrying into the bookstore and getting to work. I've already lost some time today, and there's a lot to do.

After I check in with the team, I steal away behind the front desk for a moment and pull up the bookstore's email. Weeks ago, when I first made my dream list of bookstore events, I had looked up Mia Lane's contact information. Still riding the high of such a successful trivia night, I decide to be bold and reach out, pitching Literary Lake as the perfect stop on her book tour. Before I can talk myself out of it, I hit send on the email.

The day moves along surprisingly quickly despite how eager I am to find out whatever Scott has planned for this afternoon. I'm also nervous, but in the best way possible.

As I water the many plants around the bookstore, I whisper to them about Scott. I regularly talk to the bookstore plants. I read somewhere it helps with plant growth if you talk to them about positive topics, and this is the happiest topic I have right now. Plus, they're excellent secret-keepers.

CHAPTER 22

Scott

I've never been this worried about a date. Piper and I have been living together for a month, and I've been doing my best to keep my distance the whole time. Now, I've got the green light to move forward with her, and it is *terrifying*.

I'm slightly less useless than I was two days ago, when she told me to woo her, but not by much. I did finally come up with a plan for today and having that to focus on helped ground me. I didn't really have time to panic while I ran around getting things set up.

Now, though, as I wait for Piper to get home, I have nothing but time. I've already fucked with my hair more than is reasonably acceptable and unpacked and repacked our cooler at least four times. I'm giving myself a pep talk in the bathroom mirror when I hear the familiar sound of the Range Rover's tires crunching over gravel outside.

She's here.

As I hear keys jiggling in the side door, I slip out the front, silently closing the door behind me. I press myself against the door, so I can peek in the front window without being seen. Piper sets her bag on the table and looks around.

"Scott?" she calls out, and the hopefulness in her voice makes my chest feel tight. She spots the cooler sitting by the back door, and when she starts walking toward it, I step away from the door and knock.

Piper's whole expression brightens when she sees me through the very same window I was using to spy. Never in a million years did I think a woman like her would look at me like that. She opens the door, and I'm hit with the full force of her beauty, like I am every time I lay eyes on her. Knowing that, tonight, she's mine, makes it that much more powerful.

"Hi," I breathe and am impressed I remember how to.

"Hi," she says sweetly. "What are you doing out there, knocking?"

"I'm here to pick you up for our date, of course. May I come in?"

The smile Piper gives me could power a city. She steps aside.

"Please, come in."

I enter our home and close the door behind me, turning and presenting my gift to her. It's a tiny succulent in a hand painted ceramic pot, not unlike the ones the café and bookstore are decorated with.

"This is for you."

She takes it and examines it carefully. She's looking at it lovingly, wearing the same expression she has when she finds a video online of baby animals.

"It's precious, but isn't it standard to bring flowers for the first date?"

"It might be, but you're not standard. You love the plants at work, so I wanted you to have one here, too. You can talk to it like you talk to them."

"… you've seen me doing that? Is it weird?"

"I see *you*, Piper. And there's nothing I don't like."

She cradles the little plant to her chest and pulls me to her with her other hand on my neck, lightly kissing my cheek.

"I love him."

"Him?" I ask, looking at her, my nose brushing against her cheek.

"Obviously," she scoffs.

She seems reluctant to do so, but she slides her hand off me and steps back before hurrying across the room to place her new plant-child on the kitchen windowsill where it'll get the most direct sunlight. I cross the room until I'm before her and take her hand, sliding my fingers between hers.

"Eight months ago, the day after we met, I told Jake I wanted to take you out on the lake. I wanted to steal you for myself and convince you to stay in Wilcox Grove. He told me I was a moron because it was way too cold in October for a boat ride, and I chickened out on stealing you and convincing you to stay. I think I still owe you that boat ride. What do you say?"

My heart is hammering in my chest, and I hope she can't feel the unsteadiness in my hand.

"I say yes." Her fingers tighten around mine. "I say yes," she repeats, softer.

She looks into my eyes, and I fall even harder. Her pupils are wide and I can feel her breath on my face. I consider throwing out the boat idea and hauling Piper upstairs, but I want more for us.

I lift our linked hands and twirl her, leading her to the stairs before letting go. She looks back at me, pouting. I think she might have been just fine staying in, too.

"Go put on a bathing suit and something you don't mind getting wet," I instruct. Every word I say sounds suggestive, and the look on Piper's face tells me she's thinking the same thing. I close my eyes and count to five. I hear Piper's soft laugh as she pads upstairs.

I compose myself just as she reappears at the top of the staircase in a sheer white tunic over a yellow bikini that makes her skin glow and my heart stop. The v-neck cover-up has billowing sleeves that go to Piper's elbows and tiny tassels along the bottom hem that brush against her perfect thighs with every step. Piper has washed off any makeup she was wearing and braided her hair so it falls over one shoulder.

I might call her princess, but this woman before me is a fucking goddess.

I am *so* out of my league.

I swallow hard, but my mouth feels like I've never had a drop of water.

"You ok, Scotty boy?" Piper purrs as she descends one step at a time.

Is this happening in slow motion? It feels like it's happening in slow motion. I should have worn compression shorts under my swim trunks.

When Piper is finally before me, she twirls around.

"What do you think?"

She knows *exactly* what she's done to me, and she *loves* it. She has all the power right now, and I'm man enough to admit it thrills me.

"I actually don't believe I've ever had a single thought in my entire life," I murmur as I drink her in.

"Oh?" she says sweetly, now slowly walking around me, dragging one finger across my chest, and then my back, from shoulder to shoulder. My feet are cemented to the floor, but I feel a line of fire everywhere she touches, even through my shirt. She flattens her palm on me and slides it down my arm until she grasps my hand.

She turns toward the back door and tugs me behind her.

"Show me your boat," she instructs. The command is enough to get my legs functioning, and I trail after her.

I'd follow her anywhere.

Yet again, I need to compose myself, and I use our walk down the slope to the lake to do so. I carry the cooler in one hand while Piper keeps my other clasped in hers. Alice and Jake are both out and since we're at the end of the lake, it's rare for people to wander all the way down here without a specific purpose. Either she's determined our chances of being spotted are slim, or she doesn't care about our linked fingers being seen.

I hope it's the latter, but I expect it's the former. We just need time.

I direct Piper to the dock at the back of Jake's house and help her board. Even though I also put Alice's boat back in the water today and have permission to take it out, I'm not familiar with it. And I'm not about to figure it out while I'm trying to impress Piper. I've taken mine and Jake's boat out more times than I can count. I know how she handles, and I'm hoping the familiarity will help my confidence.

"Is this why you needed Jake's truck today?" Piper asks from her seat by the steering wheel as I tuck some life jackets under a bench on the boat.

"Yeah, I offered to get both ours and Alice's boats back in the water if he'd let me borrow it."

"He covered for you earlier, you know. He said he gave you the truck because he asked you to do him a favor. He didn't mention the boats at all, like he knew you were surprising me." She looks warily up at me while I'm still standing on the dock. "Did you… tell him about this being a date?"

I stop unwinding the rope from the dock and give her my full attention.

"Piper, I wouldn't do that. You asked me not to tell anybody, and I respect you. I told him you were hesitant to use the Range Rover, and I didn't want you to feel guilty for having the car."

She blinks twice before saying, "Oh."

I hop into the boat. "Piper. You can trust me. We talked about this, and I gave you my word."

"Yeah?"

"Yeah."

"I'm sorry for doubting."

"It's ok," I say, and I mean it. "Just promise me that when you doubt, you'll ask first, ok?"

She nods, and her smile hesitantly returns. I lean forward and kiss her hair.

I finish prepping for our departure and lead Piper to sit at the bow of the boat where she'll have the best view.

"Ready to go?" I ask, taking my spot at the wheel.

She jerks her head so the sunglasses perched in her hair flip down and settle on the bridge of her nose.

"Yes, Captain," she croons, and I'm practically lightheaded with how quickly my blood rushes south.

"Captain, huh?" I manage to ask.

She only shrugs one shoulder, before turning to look out over the front of the boat and letting out a booming laugh.

I take a breath, adjust my shorts, and pull away from the dock. I guide us slowly through the narrow part of the lake, where we can see pairs of houses periodically breaking through the trees on both sides of us. Once we're past the small island with the eagle nest, the lake opens wide.

"Hang on," I warn.

Piper only has a moment to look back at me before I lay on the throttle. She throws her arm out, clutching the railing around the edge of the boat, and we lurch forward, the front lifting out of the water as we speed ahead.

Pieces of Piper's hair pull out of the braid and whip around her face. She's still looking back at me, her nose scrunched with how much she's grinning, and she looks *radiant*.

"Faster," she calls, and I obey. As we bounce on the waves,

she lets loose a whoop. There is nothing on this planet more breathtaking than Piper letting go.

When we finally slow for a narrow part of the lake, I see Piper breathing hard, laughing at nothing, and glistening from the spray of the water. She pulls off her coverup and tucks it away. I actively fight to keep my eyes in my head.

"Scott, this is incredible," she says. And yeah, she is.

"Please, you *have* to teach me how to drive one of these," she begs.

"Come here." I wave her over, and she practically skips to my side.

I explain the controls and the different markers on the water and have her pull out the set of nautical maps we keep on the boat at all times. Those are a little tricky to get used to, but she's focused and determined. As we continue to move along, we rock with the water, and every time any part of her brushes against any part of me, I feel an electric shock through my whole body.

I could spend an eternity on the water with Piper, but driving on the lake is just part of what I have planned for this evening. I guide our boat to a dock on one of the little plots of land in the center of the lake. The banks of the lake are far away enough here that nobody would be able to recognize us if we were spotted.

I cut the engine and tie us to the dock. Piper is looking around, trying to soak everything in. Her eyes are bright, and her expression is curious.

"What's on this island?" she asks, coming to stand at the back of the boat beside me.

I shrug. "Not much—plants—but that's not what we're here for."

She's confused, and I make my move while she's trying to figure me out.

"I hope you can swim," I say before yanking her against me

with an arm banded around her waist and leaping off the back of the boat into the water.

Piper gasps for air as we break the surface together, my arm still clinging to her waist. I wonder if I've made a massive miscalculation when she shoves away from me hard and roughly wipes the water from her face. She takes several more gasping breaths, desperately pulling in air. The water is still pretty cold.

"I can't believe you did that," she shrieks, treading water. She looks at me, aghast, and I very quickly and deeply regret my decision to throw us in the lake.

What have I done?

"Piper, I'm so sorry. I meant for it to be fun. I—" The rest of my apology is only gurgling as Piper launches toward me and shoves hard on my shoulders. Her cackling is the last thing I hear before she pushes my head under water.

My legs knock against hers as I go down, and I take a knee to the solar plexus, but it's all worth it when she drags me back to the surface, and loops an arm over my shoulders, hanging on to me.

"You're insane, Scotty." She's still laughing. Water slides from her hair down her neck and back into the lake, and I'm soaring high. "This could have gone very badly for you, you know."

I breathe a sigh of relief at her amusement.

"I know. I was betting on me knowing you as well as I think I do."

"We love a confident man." She smirks.

I don't know who "we" is, but as long as it includes her, I'm on cloud nine. I want to be everything she wants. She looks around us in the water. It's not very deep by the island and the water is relatively clear.

"Nothing living in here better touch me…" she says.

"I'll protect you," I offer. "Or we can get back on the boat if you're uncomfortable."

"I think I'd like to stay in the water for a bit," she says, and I like that she's testing the waters—pun intended.

We swim for a bit, tackling and splashing each other, and finally just lazily floating, but eventually, we both start shivering, even with the sun shining down on us. Later in the summer, the water will be pleasantly cool, but it's still pretty nippy now. I help Piper climb back into the boat and unload gigantic towels from under one of the seats.

Once we've both toweled off. I begin unpacking the cooler. Out of the corner of my eye, I see Piper stretch out across the warm bow of the boat, like a languid cat, while I take plastic off a plate of cheese, fruit, and crackers. I make the mistake of glancing up at her and nearly drop the whole charcuterie setup when I'm hit with the full impact of her.

"Like what you see, Scotty boy?" Piper asks. My eyes dart to her face, but she hasn't even opened her eyes, like she could just feel my gaze raking over her flawless body. Her lips are tipped up in a cocky smirk.

"I really fucking do, princess."

After we eat, we lie on the boat until the sun shifts low across the sky, and it's time to head back. Piper stands beside me the whole way, and squeals when I offer her the controls. We're on the open water without any other boats around, and she does wonderfully, carefully aware of everything around her, and fully focused on the feel of the waves beneath us.

By the time I pull up beside Jake's dock, Piper's pulled her hair out of the braid, and her loose curls are bouncing around her shoulders. Both of us have warm skin from too much sun and not enough shade, and sore cheeks from smiling so much.

Alice waves from her back patio, where she's lounging with Waffles, so Piper and I don't hold hands as we walk back to our house, instead walking quietly side by side.

Once we're inside, Piper takes our towels straight to the washer, and I follow her upstairs. When we're outside her closed door, she pauses and turns to me.

"Thank you for today, Scott," she says quietly, her chest rising and falling quickly.

"It was incredible," I say, stepping into her space. I brush her hair away from her face and slide my hand to the back of her neck.

"I'm going to kiss you now," I say.

"Ok," she breathes a moment before I pull her toward me and press my lips to hers.

Her hands fly to my sides, tightly gripping handfuls of my swim shorts and pulling me flush against her. Her nails scratch against me, and I relish the feeling. We fit together perfectly, her chest pressed against mine, my leg sliding between her thighs.

When she gasps, I tilt her head and swallow the sound. My other hand wraps around behind her, the pads of my fingers pressing against her hot skin. I can't get enough of her. I want to be *consumed* by her.

She releases one side of my shorts to reach behind her. She fumbles for a moment before finding her handle and turning it. I remove my hand from her back to encircle hers on the doorknob. I pull the door closed.

We break apart, both of our chests heaving, and she looks at me, confused. I place another light kiss right on the corner of her mouth. Then another under her chin. Her head falls back and thuds lightly against the door.

"Not tonight," I whisper against her skin. "Not yet. I haven't earned you yet."

CHAPTER 23

Piper

Scott is the embodiment of "if he wanted to, he would." I just can't figure out why he wants to.

I know Scott likes me. I've known for a while. I mean, he's told me repeatedly. I wouldn't be surprised if most of Wilcox Grove knows. I just didn't expect it to last. Especially after we had sex a month ago. I thought that would take the novelty out of the situation, and he'd move on.

When that didn't seem to do the trick, I was sure living with me would put him off. I'm not a great roommate, and that's not some self-depreciation talking. I'm awkward and loud and not very neat. Despite trying to be better about it, I leave things where they don't belong, sprawl across more than my fair share of the couch, and hog the shower. I've tried to be better about it, but I know I've still messed up.

Still, Scott hasn't seemed to mind. Actually, he's encouraged me to take up space.

At one point, I was sure he was only interested because I had made it clear that I was not. But saying yes to Scott only seems to have made him more enamored.

And *then*, four days ago, he took me on the most perfect first date of my life. I don't know what to do with him. I keep waiting for him to be done, but he just keeps getting in deeper, and he seems awfully comfortable with that.

Maybe there's something wrong with him. Could short-term memory loss be regularly erasing all my annoying habits?

I'm working today, and Scott is sitting in the café, smiling while he talks softly on his phone. He suddenly looks at me and winks when he catches me staring.

I don't want to admit it, but I *like* that he's here. I like that he *wants* to be here, near me, in spite of my rules about keeping our distance in public.

As I drag my gaze away and look back at the shelf in front of me, I wonder if I've made a huge mistake. At some point, he *is* going to tire of me. And I'm afraid it's going to hurt a lot when he does.

"*Piper.*"

I turn and jump when I see Alice looking at me expectantly. When did she get here?

"Jesus, Alice," I hiss, clutching my chest over my pounding heart. "Way to sneak up on someone."

"Girl, I said your name like four times," she says, putting her hands on her hips. "What's got you so distracted?"

Ever so slowly, her eyes slip from my face and inch toward where I was looking a moment ago. Thankfully, Scott is back to focusing on his laptop screen, nodding along to whatever the person on the phone is saying, so he doesn't see Alice, but she certainly sees him.

"Oh…" Her grin becomes wide, and she accusatorily turns back to me. "I see now."

I grab her arm and pull her further into the bookstore. "I was just checking on the café," I pathetically lie.

"Hi Scott!" Alice is overly enthusiastic, looking over my shoulder.

"Oh yeah, sure. Pretend he's behind me." I roll my eyes. What is this, elementary school?

"Hi Alice." Scott's smooth voice is—you guessed it—right behind me.

"Scott!" I squeak, facing him. "Did you need something?"

"I have to head back to the house to deal with something for work and wanted to see if you needed me to pick you up when you're done here," he says. Scott and I drove in together today, so the question is reasonable. I can't figure out how he's being so calm, though, like we're not standing right in front of my best friend, hiding our secret whatever-we're-doing-together.

"I was planning on hanging out here, so I can drive you back if that helps," Alice offers.

"That would be great," I accept, hoping I seem as nonchalant as Scott does. I turn back to him. "I guess I'll see you when I get back then. Good luck with your work thing."

"See you at home. Alice." And Scott is gone. The second the bookstore door closes behind him, Alice pounces.

"And *what* precisely was *that*?"

"Car coordination," I say, quickly fixing some out-of-place books on the shelf beside us.

"That boy wears every emotion on his face, and he was looking at you like you're the brightest star in the sky. He hasn't looked that smitten since you first got into town. Don't tell me it's nothing," Alice presses.

"Not *here*," I urge, looking around to make sure nobody overheard anything.

"Suit yourself, but you're not off the hook." Alice snaps back. When I don't budge, she shrugs. "Fine. Where can I help out?"

"Children's picture books need to be alphabetized." It's a small punishment that my petty ass takes pleasure in bestowing. Children's picture books *always* need to be alphabetized. It takes forever, and they're back out of order within an hour.

"You're evil, Piper Price," Alice says.

"I know." I smile.

"I don't think it's a bad thing, you know. Whatever's happening, I mean," she continues, her voice lower. "You deserve to have somebody make you feel like a star every minute of every damn day."

As I sit in Alice's passenger seat, listening to how Waffles is being a little terror for Jake (according to the texts he just sent Alice), I wonder if she forgot about the Scott interrogation she promised earlier.

So, I slap on a smile and tell her I know she and Jake would let Waffles chew off their arms if he wanted to.

"We would," she admits. "I just wish we could bottle his energy. I swear he's never tired."

"I think we were like that at some point." I laugh, thinking back to our early college years when we'd stay out until three am and then still roll into class by eight. It feels like another lifetime.

"There's no way. Those must have been other people," she says.

"How's your dad doing?" I ask after a bit of quiet. Alice is the product of a one-night stand and only found her father, William, a few years ago, after her mom got sick, and she kept his discovery a secret. William has dementia and usually believes he's still teaching his college classes. He doesn't even know Alice is his daughter, or that he has a daughter, but I know she cherishes the bits of him she does get to know anyway.

"It seems like he's doing as well as can be expected. He's comfortable at the new facility, and I try to visit him as much as I can. Jake usually comes with me."

One of the main reasons Alice thought she'd have to stay in

Boston last year is because her father was in a facility near the city. She's all he has left. Thankfully, Jake was able to find a place much closer to Wilcox Grove that has been able to take care of him and keep him comfortable.

"I'd love to meet him if you think it would be ok," I say, knowing it can be difficult to navigate his illness.

"I'd like that a lot." She reaches across the front seat to squeeze my hand. I keep hers in mine the rest of the way home.

She sighs contentedly as she turns off the road to our houses. "I'm going to take Waffles out back to try to burn off some of his energy. Meet me back there with wine."

Watching a wacko puppy sprint around like a lunatic beside my bestie might be just what the doctor ordered to get me out of my head. If not, at least there's wine.

"That isn't a question, is it?" I check, suddenly a bit suspicious of the invitation.

"Nope! You and I need to talk about Scott," Alice says, and I can see the determination in her eyes.

I weirdly kind of hope she's figured it out. All I want to do is tell her about him and get her advice, but I'm afraid of admitting it could be something just for it to fall apart. So, I only nod. She stops between our houses so I can run inside to drop my stuff off and grab wine before meeting her out back.

I soundlessly open the front door in case Scott is still working, and find him on the couch, phone again pressed to his ear.

He grins when he sees me, and my heart leaps into my throat. He's always beautiful, but he's devastating when he smiles.

I wave at him, intending to slip by, but he holds out his hand to me, continuing his description of some marketing campaign to the person on the other end of the line without pause. My legs carry me to him, like I have no choice in the matter, and he lifts my hand once I'm within arm's reach, flipping it over and pressing a kiss to my palm.

He looks up at me through unfairly long eyelashes, and Alice's words echo in my mind.

You deserve somebody who makes you feel like a star every minute of every damn day.

Do I?

Scott squeezes my hand once before releasing it, and I continue into the kitchen. I pull a bottle of rosé from the fridge and walk back into Scott's line of sight so I can point to the bottle, the back of the house, and then Alice's house.

He nods, immediately understanding my terrible pantomime. I smile, and he winks, reaching out again to brush his knuckle down my forearm as I go, like he can't let me pass by without putting his hands on me. The tenderness of his touch makes me feel like I'm melting. I need to figure out what I'm doing here.

As soon as I'm outside, I unscrew the cap on the wine and take a long pull. Jeeee-zus…

I jog over to Alice's yard, where she's already sitting in the grass, throwing a ball for Waffles. He's not great at returning it yet, but he loves to chase and attack whatever she flings. Occasionally, she can wrestle it back from him. It's another gorgeous day, warm with a vibrant blue sky, and I think Waffles is happy to be outside enjoying it.

I flop down next to her, where she's drinking straight from her own bottle. She does a double take when I do.

"You ok?" she asks. "You look flustered."

Crap.

"Oh yeah. First gulp of wine just went down the wrong pipe," I lie smoothly.

Waffles finally notices my arrival and comes barreling over. He leaps up on me, dropping a wet kiss on my cheek before sprinting across the grass to chase dandelion fuzz or something. Thankfully he's never been interested in taking off, so we can sit back here with him off-leash.

Alice takes another long drink before fixing me with an intense stare.

"Alright. Time to spill what's been going on with Scott."

"I don't know," I say, and it's only half a lie.

"Don't play dumb. Are you in love yet?" She is the opposite of subtle.

"No!" I cough, choking on more wine. "He's a good roommate, a nice guy."

She stares me down. I feel like Cady in *Mean Girls*, knowing the word vomit is coming but being unable to stop it.

"We slept together," I blurt

Alice's wine bottle slips down in her grasp, but she catches it before it falls to the grass.

"I *knew* it! But damn, the standards for good roommate sure have changed," she shrieks before I slap my hand over her mouth.

"Will you *shut up*! I don't want the whole damn town knowing. I don't want anybody to know. Actually, would it be possible for you to not tell Jake? Like, I'm not asking you to *lie* to him, but maybe don't offer it?"

Alice waves her hand in the air like I've got nothing to worry about. "Jake doesn't pry into stuff like that. He won't ask. Your secrets are my secrets, and this is yours and Scott's business. But, if he sees Scott looking like he was at the bookstore today, he's going to know. What happened? When was this?"

I go back to my poorly timed arrival in Wilcox Grove and the tequila-induced decisions that followed and how I shoved him firmly into the friendzone after that.

"After trivia night, I told him we could try," I murmur, hoping if I admit it quietly, it won't be that big of a deal.

"What did he do to change your mind?" Alice sounds curious, not a drop of judgment in her voice. I'm back to loving her again.

"I dunno. He gives me my space, but doesn't ignore me?"

"Piper, have some standards. That's basic decency."

I'm not explaining it right. Scott isn't just decent. Waffles trots back to us and flops on his side, pressed up against our backs. I lazily run my fingers through his fur.

"It's more." I sigh, frustrated that I don't know how to describe exactly how Scott has made me feel. "He makes it impossible to feel uncomfortable here. I've been so afraid of overstaying my welcome, but I don't think *anything* rattles him. It doesn't seem to bother him that I'm such a pain in the ass. He's even joined me in watching the *Pride and Prejudice* miniseries *multiple* times already without complaint because I can't stop rewatching it."

"Piper, you are *not* a pain in the ass. You need to stop being so cruel to yourself," Alice interjects, but I keep going. She's always had more tolerance for me than others.

"He keeps making space for me. He emptied a shelf in the kitchen cabinets, one of the junk baskets in the living room, a ton of space in the bathroom, and in the linen closet. I told him he doesn't have to. I can keep my stuff in my room, but he seems to have selective hearing about it. It's… I dunno. He makes me feel like I belong." I take another drink from my bottle. I feel warm talking about the quiet ways Scott has welcomed me, and I don't think it's from the wine.

"He's become my self-appointed cooking instructor," I continue. "I think it's his way of bonding because it's how he and Jake connected when they were younger. Almost every evening, and on weekend mornings, we cook together. And you've seen me in the kitchen. I can promise I have not improved. It's possible I've gotten even more disastrous. I think I drop or break something every single time we cook. Scott is still patient with me. If I didn't see him fight Troy last year or yell at trivia, I'd swear he was incapable of getting angry."

By the time I finish, I can basically *feel* Alice vibrating with excitement across the space between us. Alice finally shoves her shoulder into me to get me to look at her. When I do, I see she's got a maniacal look in her eye.

"What?" I ask.

"*He's a good roommate.*" she mimics me from before, shaking her head and chortling as she lifts her bottle again.

"What did I say?" I demand.

She only laughs harder and then excitedly hisses, "We're going to really be *sisters* someday."

"You are getting *way* ahead of yourself. It is not that serious. It's not serious at all," I protest, ignoring how her statement makes me feel.

"You keep telling yourself that." She sounds so smug. "You like him."

"He's not… unlikable," I finally admit.

"No, no he is not," Alice agrees. "So, what's the problem? Why is it *not serious at all*?"

"I don't want to ruin things." It's the truth. "You know how I am with guys, how they are with me. It's not exactly healthy."

Alice has seen me do everything in my power to convince myself guys can't hurt me, that they don't matter… usually after they hurt me.

"I think you spend a lot of your time expecting a mistake, so you keep yourself closed off in anticipation of that pain. It kind of becomes a self-fulfilling prophecy. Scott isn't like your usual guy," she says. "I'm fairly certain there's nothing you could do that would scare him, and with him, I don't think you need those walls you keep throwing up." She leans her cheek against the side of my arm.

And I think, just maybe, she could be right.

I don't know how long we're sitting out here just looking at the lake, but Jake eventually comes out on his and Alice's back porch to let her know they need to head out soon if they want to catch some movie they planned to see tonight. Waffles immediately hops up and takes off toward Jake.

Alice invites me to join them, but I decline, kissing Alice on her cheek before she goes to her man. She flashes me a knowing smile, and I'm glad I told her.

I… want to see Scott.

I stand and brush off the back of my pants. Turning toward the house, I see the man on my mind leaning against the back door frame, arms crossed, just watching me. The sun is nearly set, and the pink sky reflects off the lake to bathe him in a warm glow. He really is something to see. Kindness and sex personified.

"Hey you," I greet him as I trudge up the steps to the house, feeling gloriously peaceful. "Whatcha looking at?"

"A beautiful sunset," he says simply. I look back over my shoulder at the lake. He's right. It is very beautiful.

When I turn back to Scott, he's just looking at me.

I look down to hide my sudden bashfulness. Scott steps aside, opening the screen door and guiding me inside ahead of him. I can feel the heat of his body as I brush past. It feels like a magnet pulling me closer to him. I just need a second to think without picturing him naked and above me.

Once inside, I see the light in the library is off.

"Are you done working?" I ask, turning to face him.

"I am," Scott answers.

I need to tell him I told Alice. I did just break my own rule, the very first rule, less than a week after laying down the law. I feel like a little hypocrite.

"There's something else I need to tell you, and you might be upset."

"Ok…" Scott looks confused.

"I told Alice about us, even though it's against the rules. I'm s—"

Scott cuts off my apology and my airflow with the strength of the hug he wraps me in.

He steps back after a moment, keeping his hands on my upper arms, and he's radiant with joy.

"That's fantastic." He beams. "I've already told you I don't think you're some secret. I want to tell the world that I'm with you."

"No, Scott—"

He's so excited, I don't think he hears me. He's talking about taking me out and showing me off. My voice is strangely meek.

Has this kitchen always been so small? Has the humidity been this suffocating *all day*? I didn't mean to open this whole thing. I just—I need—

I lurch back and out of his grasp.

"Pickles!" I shout. My voice is loud and clear this time, and Scott cuts off whatever wild fantasy he's been rambling about. "I just need a minute," I gasp.

I make some vague gestures toward the library door before I finally turn and head toward it, unable to get a full breath until I hear the resounding click of the closed door.

I move toward the back of the room and open the blinds, so the light from the low sun creates a soft glow by the two chairs at the back of the room. I heave open the sticky window and turn on the overhead fan. I need some *air*. The earthy smell of summer floats in.

I pull the copy of *Pride and Prejudice* Scott got me off the shelf and fold myself as small as I can into one of the armchairs by the window, but I just stare at the cover. I shouldn't have let him give me this. It's too much for a friend. For a casual… whatever we are.

After some time, a soft tap on the door startles me. When I open my eyes, I realize it's much darker, and I wonder how long I've been in here.

"Yeah?" I call, but it comes out as a muffled croak. I clear my throat and try again. "Yeah?"

The door slowly cracks open, and a floating plate appears through the gap.

"You can come in, Scott."

The plate is, in fact, attached to a hand, arm, and gorgeous man.

"I'm sorry," he says. "I brought you melted cheese as an apology." He holds the grilled cheese before him like a peace offering.

"No, I'm sorry for running out like that," I say, standing and approaching Scott. "It's not you."

"I know." He shrugs. "But it is what I said. I freaked you out, didn't I?"

"Just a bit," I admit.

"I shouldn't have gone overboard before. I *am* happy you spoke with Alice about us. I'm hoping it means you're realizing I'm sticking around. But we don't need to tell more people until you're comfortable."

"I feel like I'm holding you back," I admit. It hurts. I don't want to make this wonderful man unhappy.

"You could never," he says. I know he means it kindly, but it feels like a lot of pressure.

Looking at him feels too intense, so my eyes fall on the shelves, still mostly empty.

"You should fill them," Scott says, offering me a distraction from *us*.

"I already added all my books." I point to the shelf I commandeered once my boxes arrived in Wilcox Grove. "My apartment in Boston was small, so I couldn't buy many books of my own. I'd usually read ebooks or borrow from the library. Don't you have books?"

"I have some." He gestures to a sad little shelf with a few

books stacked. "I like tech, and most of my materials for that are in the baby." He points to his computer.

"Baby?" I question.

"Hey, don't judge. She and I have been through it."

I hold up my hands in surrender before reaching for the plate Scott is still holding, but he steps back.

"You want to come out of here and eat with me in the kitchen, maybe?"

I really do. I nod.

"Let's go."

I follow him into the kitchen, where he places my grilled cheese on the counter before turning to me, and placing his hands on my waist.

"Jump," he instructs.

When I hop, he places me on the counter beside the plate and steps between my knees.

"I'm here, Piper," he says, holding my face in his hands. "Before, during, and after this and any other freak outs. I'm here."

He's got to have the lines written down somewhere. He always knows exactly what to say. I'm still not sure this is a good idea, but I remember my rule to keep this casual. Maybe it wouldn't be the worst to let myself have a beautiful man while I figure things out.

I nod again and bend to press my forehead against his. I just need to figure it out.

CHAPTER 24

Piper

After my chat with Alice on Tuesday and the subsequent freak-out, I've been trying to figure out a nice gesture to show Scott I care, maybe put a crack in those walls Alice says I have. For the last few days, the bookstore, editing, and helping Alice with her syllabus for the fall have kept me busy, but I feel like I'm running out of time. Scott needs to go to New York for a few days for some of the in-person work stuff he told me about, and he's leaving tomorrow.

When my alarm goes off far too early for a Saturday that's also a day off, I silence it almost immediately. I need to make sure I get up before Scott does. In honor of his patience with teaching me cooking, I've decided to make him a breakfast in bed that isn't scrambled eggs or a cold sandwich. I want to make him something he taught me.

Today is the day I conquer pancakes—making them. I'm already an expert at housing them.

Scott and I have made pancakes together multiple times, and I feel like I might be able to do this. I open the notes app on my phone, where I've memorized all of Scott's cooking tips and skim the section for pancakes before gathering what I need.

I *can* do this.

I definitely flip the pancakes too many times, paranoid I'm going to burn them, but I do eventually end up with a solid mountain of golden brown pancakes cooked all the way through, and only a few in the trash that we don't need to talk about. It's a frickin' miracle, and I am so damn proud of myself.

I'm cleaning up near the sink when there's a sound behind me.

"Good morning, princess." Scott's raspy voice startles me, and the mixing bowl tumbles from my soap-slicked hand, splattering water on me. I'm grateful I didn't sleep in a white shirt, but the grey tee is still sufficiently soaked.

"God *damn*it," I whine. Propping the back of my hands against my hips as I look down.

"I was doing so well…"

I hear Scott approach me and turn. While I look like a drowned rat, there he is, bed-rumpled and with those fucking pajama pants held on his hips with nothing but a prayer.

Suddenly, I'm thinking of a very different, special way to spend the morning. Since our kiss against my bedroom door after the boat ride a *week* ago, we haven't been physical. I can't say I haven't thought about it, but I didn't want to push things after he pumped the brakes, and I think he didn't want to move too quickly after I wigged out a few days ago.

But now…

I see barely-held restraint in his eyes after they flash down to my shirt, and I'm pretty sure I'm not the only one thinking about how this morning could go.

"Did you make breakfast for me? I'm *starving*," he says, licking his lips slowly. I nod.

The way he says *starving* has me thinking all kinds of non-breakfast-related things. Scott reaches behind me to turn off the faucet, effectively trapping me between his body and the countertop.

I tilt my head toward his, so our noses brush. "What are you playing at, Mr. Preston?"

"I'm not playing at anything, Miss Price." He's cocky, and I like it. "I'm just thinking of how lovely today is."

"And what makes today special?" I ask, sliding my hand up his ribcage.

"Today is special," he says slowly and purposefully. "Because of how much *time* I have to spend on you."

Oh.

He leans forward, and I lean back, the counter biting into the back of my hips. His hands grip it on either side of me, caging me in. And then he kisses me. It's claiming, punishing, perfect. I pull his hips flush against mine and feel that he wants me. The shift presses my cold shirt against me, and I gasp. Scott takes the opportunity to deepen the kiss, sliding his tongue against mine.

I want *more*.

I move a hand between us to take him in my hand through his shorts, and he positively growls.

Vaguely, my brain registers another sound, but I ignore it. I can't ignore, however, the firm knock on the front door a minute later.

Scott and I pull apart.

"Who the hell is that?" he says, breathing hard, irritated by the interruption. I look at him, dazed, and wonder if my lips are as puffy as his are.

With sudden realization, my eyes fly to the calendar on the wall. It's the end of June. The sound I ignored was tires on gravel.

"Scott," I say with horror. "I think my parents are here."

"Shit—what?" he questions, stepping away from me, confirming the front shades are closed, and adjusting himself.

"I'm like ninety-nine percent sure that's my dad's knock," I say as the knock sounds again. It's for sure Dad.

"Go get a shirt," I whisper, pushing Scott toward the stairs as I head to the front door. Thankfully, Scott's brain reengages as he hurries upstairs.

I swing open the front door, and there they are, looking the same as they always have. My mom's slight frame is wrapped in a floral dress, her light skin is rosy like it gets every summer, and her straight, blonde hair is as pristine as ever. Other than my mother's thin stature, I physically take after my father. I got my height, brown skin, brown eyes, and dark hair all from him. In a polo and slacks, I think this is the most casual I've ever seen him dress.

"Mom, Dad," I greet, stepping aside. "Welcome to Wilcox Grove! Come on in. I've, uh, got pancakes."

My mom slowly takes in my damp appearance and Scott coming back downstairs—now with a shirt.

"Did we interrupt something?" she asks, the redness on her cheeks darkening as she and my father come inside. "Did you forget we were coming?"

"No," I quickly answer and close the door. I don't know how I could "forget" they were coming when they never confirmed what day they'd arrive, but that's neither here nor there.

Scott reaches us now and holds out his hand. "It's very nice to meet you, Dr. and Mrs. Price," he says. "I'm Scott, Piper's roommate."

"You can call them Cameron and Wendy," I correct as my mom shakes Scott's hand first.

When it's Dad's turn, he says, "Dr. and Mrs. Price will do just fine." I just about die of mortification.

"Of course." Scott takes it in stride.

"You should get dressed," my mother says, turning toward me, unease written across her face. We both know my appearance isn't going to put Dad in a good mood. This is *not* going well.

"Um—" I hesitate to leave Scott alone with them, but I know I'll have to get ready eventually. "I'll be right back."

I hurry upstairs and likely set the world record for getting dressed. I'm still tying my hair into a ponytail when I'm back on the stairs, but I can't have been gone more than five minutes. I find Scott and my parents at the kitchen table, four plates laid out with the pancakes I'd made with coffee and juice beside each.

Scott seems to be telling my dad about his art and his upcoming trip to New York.

Scott notices me first and stops speaking, but everyone is looking at me after a moment. I take my seat at the most uncomfortable table ever.

"Piper made these pancakes, you know," Scott says to restart conversation.

"Yeah," I try to help. "Scott's been teaching me to cook."

"You were always too busy with your studies when you were growing up to cook," my dad says smoothly. "I suppose you have more free time, now." And there's the stab.

We eat our cold pancakes in silence after that.

"What would you like to do today?" I ask as Scott and I clear the table.

"Why don't you show us your life here," Mom suggests with a kind smile.

It's pathetic how this hint of interest in what I'm doing lights me up. "Ok," I perkily agree and start making a mental list of places to show them. I turn to Scott. "Do you need the car today?"

Scott starts to shake his head, but my dad interjects. "We have a rental car. We can use that since you two *share* a vehicle."

I know I was vehemently against using Scott's Range Rover at one time, but hearing my dad say *share* like it's a dirty word makes me want to live in that damn car. I take a breath to calm down. This can still be a pleasant day.

My parents stand from the table, making it clear they're ready to go now.

"Thank you for your hospitality," Mom says as Dad shakes Scott's hand again.

Mom comes to my side and pulls me into a hug, placing a comforting hand on the back of my head. I sink a little into her warmth.

"It was lovely meeting you," Scott lies through his teeth.

I collect my bag and some shoes, and the Price trio sets out.

Even though I'm the one who lives here and knows where we're going, my dad insists on driving. Sitting in the middle of the back seat of their small SUV with my mom in the passenger seat up front, I feel like a child again. It's not a good feeling.

I decide we should circle the lake before heading over to Wilcox Nursery, where Jake and Alice will both be today but wonder if that was a mistake as I watch both of my parents bounce around in their seats. Surprisingly, neither one of them criticizes the uneven dirt road as I explain the layout of the pairs of houses around the water. I point out the park Scott and I had walked to, and they even make humming sounds of… approval? I don't know.

Next, we head over to the nursery. It's too late for the tulips, but there are still giant fields of beautiful flowers I want to show them. I shoot Alice a heads-up text on our way, and she must warn Jake because the two of them are waiting outside the office when we pull up.

"Mom, Dad, you remember Alice from college," I say once we're all together. Alice shakes both of their hands, and neither protests when she uses their first names. "And this is Jake. He's Scott's older brother and Alice's boyfriend," I continue introductions.

Unlike with Scott, *both* of my parents are cordial with both Jake and Alice, though I guess they've always liked Alice. As we walk through the fields together, my mom compliments Jake on the wide variety of flowers the nursery has. Once we reach the blooming apple trees, my dad asks about the different varieties in the orchard. It's the most engaged I've seen him in a long time.

As Alice and I trail behind everyone, Alice shoots me a *what's going on* look, and I silently give her a *I have no clue* shrug back. I do my best to school my face when Dad claps Jake on the shoulder while Mom hugs Alice before we leave.

In spite of our successful visit to the nursery, I'm still worried about my parents' reaction to the bookstore. But that worry turns out to be unwarranted.

When we walk through the front door—thank goodness the window out front has been fixed already—my parents thoughtfully take in the space. My mom looks over toward the café space before walking further into the bookstore and running a hand over one of the nearby plants.

"This is very tasteful," she says, and my father nods in agreement. They also have nice things to say about the book lending program and its contributions to the community. I'm beaming with pride.

If I'm showing off Wilcox Grove, I have to feed them one of Hannah's pastries, so we head into Barefoot Bake after touring the bookstore. I'm pleasantly surprised to find Leslie with Hannah at one of the tables. She waves us over.

"Leslie, Hannah, these are my parents." It's been a day of introductions. "Leslie and Hannah own the café and the bookstore."

"Hi!" Hannah says brightly. "Piper has been an absolute lifesaver since she showed up. With Leslie off her feet, I don't know what we would have done without Piper."

I don't know if Alice tipped them off, or if my luck is just that good, but Leslie starts praising the changes I've made in the bookstore while Hannah retrieves some pie for us all. Though my mom carries the conversation for my dad, they're both kind, *and* I find myself starting to relax.

The rest of the day is shockingly uneventful, in a good way. There are no snide remarks, backhanded compliments, or criticisms at all.

When we walk through the main stretch of town, familiar faces from the bookstore wave and say hello. Families are playing in the field beside the part of Barefoot Lake that stretches this way. The sun is bright and warm. It really feels like Wilcox Grove and its citizens put their best foot forward for my parents.

Both Mom and Dad ask questions about the people who greet us and different shops and landmarks around town. An early dinner at Papa's is excellent as always, but Dad even goes out of his way to say so to our server. It feels like we might be starting to connect. *Maybe* I've been able to finally get through to them.

As the sun continues to set on our walk back to their car, some early summer fireflies start to light up around us.

"We saw most of town today, but we have some options for things to do tomorrow. I should be able to leave work early," I offer. "Maybe we can go out on the boat, and—"

"I think we've seen all we need to see today, so we'll be returning to Boston tonight so we can fly home tomorrow," my dad interrupts.

"What do you mean?" I ask, my heart sinking. I guess the day didn't improve after all. "You're not staying the night?"

"It's for the best. The inn you sent over was hardly suitable. This whole town is hardly suitable. I love you. You are my *whole world*, but you're playing make believe with your future here." Dad's voice is laced with exhaustion.

"But I'm *happy* here," I argue, wanting to fiercely defend Wilcox Grove. It may be small, but it's a *good* place with *good* people.

"Piper, we know. We just want to make sure you're safe, that your future is safe," Mom tries to soften Dad's critique, but I know that isn't what he's saying at all. He thinks I've failed him, failed our family, by choosing the path I have.

"We're always going to have to work twice as hard as everyone else, but I tried to make sure you had as few hurdles to success as possible." My father's deep baritone cuts deeper. "We had the finances for you to go to medical school like I did. I have a network of prominent doctors who would have mentored you. If you didn't want that, I had a network of people in other professions ready to *help* you."

"I *did* work hard, Dad. I still work hard every single day. I did well in school—the best. I graduated at the top of my master's program. I'm *running* the bookstore here and helping it grow. I don't understand why you don't see that." I'm on the brink of tears, but I will not cry.

"And what is your plan? Work at this bookstore for the rest of your life? What about when Leslie is healed? Are you going to continue living off some artist? What are you going to *do* with your life?" My dad is in peak form.

I don't have an answer, and it hurts. I want to defend Scott and tell Dad I have a place in this town, but the words don't come. He takes my pause as a sign of his victory, turning away from me and getting in the car.

"We'll drive you back," my mom says softly, but neither of us moves toward the car. "He does love you, so much. I know he has a poor way of expressing that. I'll talk to him."

I nod, but I get in the car and feel like I've lost.

After a quiet drive back and a curt goodbye as I get out of their car, I drag my feet all the way to the front door. It feels like it weighs a hundred pounds as I push it open and basically fall inside. Scott is working on his tablet on the couch.

"Piper! I have a surprise for you," he says, hopping to his feet and setting the tablet on the coffee table. He quickly scans my face, and his expression falls. "You ok?"

"They already left." I consider lying but take a leap and decide to give him the truth. "My dad basically said this trip confirmed I'm wasting my life, and they didn't need to spend another day here, watching me pretend I was living up to my potential."

"What? How could—" He's outraged on my behalf, but he cuts off when he sees something in my eyes.

He tentatively reaches out and cups my elbows in his hands, running his palms along the back of my arms.

"What do you need?" he asks, and I want to melt into him. The fact that he doesn't just try to fix it means more than it should.

Wordlessly, I slouch and drop my forehead against his shoulder. Yet again understanding me perfectly, he wraps his arms around me and pulls me with him when he sits back on the couch, tucking my legs across his lap and just holding me. His breaths are long and slow, and just listening to them makes me feel better.

"Thank you," Piper mumbles into my hair after we've been sitting silently for almost fifteen minutes. "I'm ok."

"Are you sure?" I ask as she lifts her head, and her eyes find mine. "Do you want to talk about it?"

"I'm too tired tonight, but maybe another time. I'm going to shower and change," Piper says, still sounding so broken.

"Before you go, let me show you your surprise. I think it'll help with the day you've had." I'll do *anything* to make this better for her. It won't help with her parents, but I hope it brings her joy anyway.

I take her hand, help her up, and pull her toward the library, flinging open the door with a flourish.

"Welcome to your new and improved library, princess."

The lamps are already lit, so we can clearly see all the new additions to the shelves—and there are dozens of them. Books.

Piper's mouth falls open as she drifts into the room. She examines the spines, and recognition flashes in her eyes. Her eyes move from shelf to shelf.

"I know these books. I *love* these books," she murmurs, turning to me. "How? How did you know?"

I shrug. "I checked your Instagram and then found your reading tracker. Since you didn't take the car, I went on a little bookstore-hopping adventure out of town, and this is what I came up with."

I couldn't find *every* book she posted about, but I did find a lot of them. Row after row of crisp, new pages.

She shakes her head. "It's too much, Scott. It must have cost a fortune. I can't—I can't accept this."

"It's fine. I *promise* it's fine. I wanted to do this for you." The full explanation is on the tip of my tongue.

"You said you left New York because it's expensive. You shouldn't spend your money on this."

This is my opening. I don't want secrets from Piper.

My hand goes to the back of my neck—the Preston tell. My brother does the same thing when he's feeling awkward.

"I left New York because I was miserable. And yes, it is a very expensive city. But I technically never said that was a problem for me."

Piper stops gaping at the books and focuses back on me. I can't hold her gaze, so I suddenly find my shoes very interesting.

"Wait. Are you saying..." She pauses for a second before blurting, "Are you rich?"

"You make me sound like Scrooge McDuck when you say it like that," I groan. "I just did a project when I was in college that turned out to be... kind of lucrative."

"Oh my god," Piper says, sinking into one of the chairs and lowering her voice. "Are you a drug dealer? We can figure it out if you are. I just need to know," she whispers urgently, looking around like a DEA agent is about to pop out of nowhere.

"Am I a—what? No." I wonder if I should be concerned that

she immediately jumped to drug dealer, but I'm not surprised that Piper was ready to roll with it. "I told you I liked tech stuff. I'm kind of good at it—very good at it, actually. My degree was in cyber security. For my thesis, I did a project examining the security my college had in place for student files, and I found some significant weaknesses. I wrote a program that would patch those holes."

"When the head of the department came to my thesis defense, I thought I was going to get expelled for basically breaking through the school's firewalls," I continue. "Then, when he called me to the president of the university's office, I thought I was getting arrested. Instead, they wanted to buy the program. And then a lot of other colleges did, too. Like, a *lot* of them."

The story pours out of me, like it's eager to finally get loose. I must have started pacing at some point, but Piper just watches me attentively. Back and forth. The way the program ballooned so quickly left me in disbelief, and I've never gotten used to it. It's just always been there, giving me the freedom to do what I love with graphic design and help support the nursery. I have a financial team that invests and donates the profits based on a plan we go over each year.

"From there, things just exploded. I set up a company and got a team to maintain it for me. I never talk about this stuff with anybody. The only person in Wilcox Grove who knows about it is Jake, though I bet Eli has his suspicions I've got *something* going on. Maybe he also thinks I'm a drug dealer."

I can't take it. I stop in front of her. "I'm going to need you to say something, please."

"Huh," she says.

"Huh? That's it?" I know I sound frantic.

"So, buying all these books really won't cause you any kind of distress?"

"No. Unless you hate them. I can return them if you hate them."

She jumps up and puts herself between me and the shelves.

"Don't you dare say that about these babies." She smiles. "I kind of had a hunch for a while now that you were doing alright for yourself, so this does explain a lot of things, like your fancy car. Let's compromise. The books are already here, so they can stay, but no more expensive gifts like this. And these books stay in this library. They're not *mine*, ok?"

I find myself smiling back.

"Ok," I agree. I intend for Piper to stay in this house, too, so if she wants to say the books are mine, that's just a technicality in my mind. "Is this weird for you?" I ask. It's weird for me to share this part of myself with somebody.

"I've never been friends with a billionaire before, but no. It's not weird. You created something successful. You should be proud."

I roll my eyes. "I'm not a billionaire, princess."

She quirks her head to the side, suddenly thoughtful.

"Is that why you call me princess? Because you could buy me a country if the right one was for sale?"

Talking about wealth might make me uncomfortable, but talking about Piper makes me feel confident. It's easy to say exactly how I feel about her and tell her what I see when I look at her.

"No, Piper. I call you princess because you deserve to be treated like one."

"Oh. I'm not…" she protests.

This is familiar territory, seeing her insecurities, and I know how to handle it. I take her hands and guide her back to her chair. She looks around but lets me move her and press her down to sit.

I slowly lower to my knees in front of her.

"You are. And I'm here to serve."

Piper

This is not the first time I've had Scott on his knees in front of me. My mind fills with the image of him in the same position at the base of his bed on my first night at Barefoot Lake. I think my expression must betray what I'm thinking because a wicked grin spreads across Scott's face.

"My princess?" he says like he's asking permission, and my skin erupts in goosebumps. I nod, and Scott shifts forward, placing one hand on each of my knees and slowly pushing them apart.

I think my heart is about to beat right out of my chest. I want this—him—bad.

Scott's thumbs press hard into the inside of my thighs as he moves his hands up to the hem of my shorts. He's moving torturously slow, and I just might die. I press back into the chair and grip the armrests until my knuckles go white.

"Impatient?" Scott chuckles.

"Yes," I breathe.

"Ok…"

In a second, Scott flings one of my legs over each of his elbows and jerks me down until my ass is right at the edge of the seat. I squeal at the sudden movement, clinging to the chair so I don't fly right off it, though I'm pretty sure Scott wouldn't mind one bit if I fell on him pussy first.

Scott places a quick kiss to the inside of my knee before extracting an arm to pop the button and pull on the waistband of my shorts. He lifts my hips right off the chair with his other arm, allowing my legs to fall closed, and yanks the denim down over my ass in one smooth movement. He maneuvers one of my legs free, so the shorts hang uselessly against his arm.

He lays his hand reverently against the front of my pink thong and presses his thumb between my thighs, dragging it up. My head involuntarily smacks back against the chair as an electric shock goes through me.

"Wait, Scott." I abruptly remember what I spent my day doing and try to pull out of his grasp. It's like an iron vice holding me still. "I've been walking around for hours, and I haven't showered. I'm going to be sweaty. We can't. I'm—"

"Shut up, Piper." His voice is commanding but kind, and when I find his eyes, there's a hunger in them I haven't seen before.

"If you want to stop, we stop," he says, separating my legs again and moving forward. "But if you're worried about me not wanting to be here?" He presses his nose against the damp material between my legs before dragging his tongue over the spot. "Don't."

"I—Ah!" My words dissolve into a moan as he repeats the movement. "Are—are you sure?"

The rumble of his laugh against my aching lips is almost painful. He hooks a finger under the material to yank it aside, and immediately clamps his mouth over my clit, letting me feel every moment of his "Mmhmm" in my core.

He slides his fingers to the waistband pressing into my hips from being stretched so far.

"How much do you like these?" he asks, still against my skin, rubbing the lace between his thumb and forefinger.

"Not that much," I gasp out a second before he shoves his thumb through the delicate material and rips. He pulls them away so they hang destroyed near my shorts.

"Hang on," he warns before driving a finger into me and dragging his teeth against my clit. My hand flies to the back of his head, and I'm eternally grateful he grew out his hair as I twist my fingers in it and squeeze.

My hips buck against his face, and I'm mortified by the movement until Scott hums and presses another finger into my cunt, curling them suddenly against my front wall and making me see stars.

I cry out again, beyond words, and squeeze my eyes shut. Scott lifts his head just enough to instruct me.

"Take it, princess," he demands, working his fingers in and out of me, over and over again, hitting my clit with the heel of his palm every time he rocks forward. I roll my hips against him, increasing the pressure each time we connect.

His tongue is on me again, working with his fingers against my skin, inside me, between his fingers. His other hand works up to the outside of my thigh and holds me tight, gripping me like he knows I'm his.

With my hand in his hair, I pull Scott against me and rock my hips again, seeking more—more friction, more of him. Stretching me with a third finger, Scott delivers, playing me like an instrument. He alternates between letting me fuck myself on him and trapping my clit between his teeth, creating the most mind-blowing suction.

"I, I—" I don't know why I think words will work now. They don't, but Scott understands anyway.

He finds a rhythm and holds it while the tension inside me builds higher and higher. At the last second, he presses the heel of his hand to my clit so I can grind against it. His mouth falls to the inside of my thigh, and he bites down hard. The sharp pain has me tumbling over the edge, and my walls clamp down on Scott's fingers.

He keeps moving within me, helping me ride out my orgasm, until I'm a boneless puddle, about to slip off my chair. He releases my thigh and presses a kiss to the sore skin before resting his cheek against my leg. Slowly, he draws his fingers out of me. I groan at the sensitivity and the loss of fullness.

One by one, he licks his fingers clean, still resting his head against my leg, but our eyes are locked. Watching him savor every drop has me ready to go again. This man loves to eat pussy.

"Next time we do this, princess, you'll be sitting on my face properly," he promises.

CHAPTER 27

Scott

The next morning, as I come downstairs and find Piper curled up on the couch reading, I strongly consider firing my clients, so I don't have to go down to New York for the next two days. My taste of Piper yesterday has left me wanting more. I could happily waste away in a bed with the woman before me and live a completely fulfilled life.

I come up behind her and wrap my hand below her chin to gently guide her head back until I can bend over her and claim her lips. This strong-willed, stubborn woman is completely pliable under my fingers, arching off the arm of the couch to press up toward me. She hums greedily into my mouth. With a frustrated noise, I finally release her lips, looking down as her eyes lazily flutter open.

"Good morning," I say, and she hums again in response. "What are you doing up? It's not even six."

"I wanted to see you off," she says sweetly, and it shoots right through me, making me want to climb over her on this couch.

"What if I didn't go?"

Her laugh is like a siren's call. She sits up and rotates toward me.

"You have to go, and it's only two days," she says, telling me what I told her to say last night when I correctly guessed I wouldn't want to leave come morning.

After our very educational experience in the library last night, I was tempted to lift Piper in my arms and continue our night in my bedroom, but I couldn't do that knowing I was leaving first thing this morning. When I have her back in my bed, I don't intend to let her leave it for at least twenty-four hours.

Beside that, though, she had a rough day yesterday.

"Are you ok after everything with your parents? I don't want to abandon you." Piper's brief summary of what happened sounded harsh, but we haven't really talked about it.

"It's fine." She shrugs. "It's not the first time they've said things like that. I think it just hit me harder because they had seemed to like Wilcox Grove all day."

"I still don't like that it happened. You don't deserve that."

"I know," she says, and I hope she does. When I don't move, she repeats. "It's just two days. Go."

"It's going to be a long two days," I grumble and stand, but she's right. I should go, have some face time with my corporate clients, and check in with my team about the privacy program. Hackers get more and more creative every day and trying to stay a step ahead makes me feel like we're always a step behind.

"You sure you're all set without the car?" I ask. To make the trip as quick as possible, I decided to drive. I'm not about to waste time on a bus that Piper isn't on with me.

"Yup! Alice is giving me a ride in a few hours, and Mads will drive me back tonight. Since my parents aren't here, maybe she, Alice, and Ila will want to stay over. Then Mads and I could go in together tomorrow afternoon instead. Jake said he'll scoop me on his way home tomorrow evening. I'm all set here."

"You should definitely have them over. It sounds like it would be a fun night," I say. Then, I huff playfully. "You don't seem to need me at all."

"I don't. I just *want* you here." She stands and walks to the kitchen, where she collects a travel mug and a lunch bag. "But you need to go. I packed snacks and made you some coffee."

I take my treats, feeling some kind of warm from her having made the time to take care of me. She starts ushering me toward the door.

"Alright, alright. I'll go," I relent and let her push me.

I pick up my bag from beside the door as I slide on my shoes.

"Just two days," I say, reminding myself more than her as I turn to go.

Piper's hand reaches out for the far side of my collar, yanking me back toward her. She kisses me quickly but fiercely, leaving me stunned as she pulls back just as abruptly.

"And I'll be here when you get back."

It feels like a promise.

New York in the summer isn't my favorite. It's always a busy city, but it's *extra* packed with tourists during the summer, and it's a Sunday, so it's even worse. Plus, the heat doesn't do any favors for the various unsavory aromas that can pop up without warning around any corner.

Traffic wasn't bad, so I have a few minutes to check into my hotel before heading to a lunch meeting with my team. I'm eternally grateful they made themselves available to meet with me on a Sunday so I can see my clients on Monday and get back to Wilcox Grove with a few days to spare before the Fourth of July madness descends.

I climb the stairs out of the depths of sweaty hell—the subway

—and take in gulps of what passes for fresh air around here. I pull out my phone and start recording myself.

"Alright, princess. Here's New York." I swing around to show her the block. "Since you couldn't come with me, I wanted to show you some important spots. For example"—I zoom in on a park bench—"I regularly cried here when I was studying for finals."

I step back into frame and wink before sending the clip off to Piper. When I got into New York, I texted Jake as requested to let him know of my safe arrival but also texted Piper. The photo she sent in response of her giving me a thumbs up gave me the idea to take her along with me as I venture through the city.

On the next block, I send her a picture of my favorite place to get bagels first thing in the morning. On the one after that, I record another video of the pizza place I picked for lunch.

"Usually, a place this good in midtown at lunch would be impossible to get into, but it's owned by somebody I went to school with. We were randomly assigned as roommates our freshman year. Odin was on track to become a hotshot at his father's hedge fund, but he decided to buy a pizzeria instead. Let me tell you, he makes some of the best fucking pizza I've ever eaten."

This one gets me a response text.

PRINCESS

Show me everything, and I'll show you some
things you're missing here, too.

Following that is a picture taken in the upstairs bathroom at home. Piper is leaning back against the counter, peeking over her shoulder so she's just barely looking at me in the mirror… and she's completely naked.

I almost drop my phone.

I quickly look around to make sure nobody else can see my screen before staring at the perfect line of her spine down to her thin waist, my eyes snagging on the dimples at her lower back, just visible above the edge of the countertop.

ME

Good lord above.

After messing it up more times than I care to admit, I hammer out a reply.

ME

Fuck! Warn a man, princess!

PRINCESS

Consider this your warning, Scotty.

I'm thinking of something clever enough to reply with when there's a hand on my shoulder. I immediately close my text with Piper and turn. Of course, it's my head of HR. Behind him, I see my accountant and lawyer walking up. After hellos and a few more arrivals, I hold open the pizzeria door.

"Ready to head in?" I ask, catching Odin's eye as I look inside. He jerks his head toward the back, where a table will be waiting for us. The large man looks too big to fit in a place this crowded, but he moves through the space with ease.

I let everybody file ahead of me, so I can safely fire off an answer to Piper.

ME

I will deal with you later.

She only answers with the laughing emoji.

I finally reach Odin, getting swallowed in his hug. He's basically a current-day Viking, tall and stern, with his blond hair tightly tied up and arms as thick as sturdy tree branches. Looking at him here, confident in his element, you'd never guess he'd been the insecure kid who got conned out of his clothes by some girls and had to run two city blocks barefoot in his underwear to get back to our shared room.

We catch up for just a few minutes before making plans for a late lunch back here tomorrow so we can have a full conversation.

Today's working lunch goes well—as well as things can go when I have half a dozen people throwing a mountain of information at me for multiple hours. Long story short, the program is working, schools and their students are happy, attacks on the program have been unsuccessful, but not unheard of, feedback on customer service has been relatively positive. All in all, it really is good.

I stretch when I stand from the table and finally get feeling back in my feet. I check my phone and am a little disappointed to only find a slew of work emails waiting for me. I open my conversation with Piper and see her laughing emoji still mocking me.

ME

You get cold feet?

PRINCESS

You haven't shown me anything since I gave my offer, so as far as I can tell, the ball is in your court.

ME

Touché. Let me up my game.

I have some time before evening drinks with a client, so I need to think of something good to show Piper. I certainly don't want to disappoint.

The idea hits me like a ton of bricks—of course! I start walking.

When I get to Bryant Park, I'm pleasantly surprised to find a collection of pop-up shops. I take a video walking by them before coming to a row of hot dog carts and proudly proclaiming them the ideal college lunch spot.

I send the goofy clip before coming around the corner and starting a new video. "I think you'll like this one," I say, slowly panning across the front of the New York Public Library.

For the next, I silently shush the camera and share one of my favorite places in the city, The Rose Main Reading Room inside the library. The space itself is a work of art, and I know without a doubt Piper will love it as much as I do.

PRINCESS

Well, Scott, you came to play. Be patient. I'll send a treat when I'm home.

I'm not done yet, though. Back on the street, I make my way to a bookstore I know used to host a lot of author events. Once inside, I quickly find the table labeled *Signed Books* and send a picture of it to Piper.

ME

Pick one.

Piper's response pops up quickly. Then another.

PRINCESS

Sir, you were complaining about me not warning you? That text was positively pornographic.

Surprise me.

After spending so much quality time with Piper's TBR yesterday, I know just the one I want to get her. Thankfully, I have time to bring it back to the hotel and suit up before I need to head back out.

I always love the fit of a good suit, so, feeling confident, I send her a mirror selfie.

It's the truth. I must have spent too much time getting ready because when I catch sight of the time, I realize I'm going to be late. Shoving my phone in my pocket, I hurry from the hotel and into the night.

I'm standing in a swanky bar with dim lights and dark wood, among a number of cookie-cutter men in tightly-buttoned suits when my phone starts vibrating repeatedly in my pocket. I try to focus on what the man across from me is saying, but all I can think about is the image that could be waiting for me from Piper.

Maybe I can just sneak a peek…

I hold my phone close to me as I type in my password. Several messages are waiting for me.

There's a picture of several wine glasses cheersing in the living room. It looks like the girls did end up coming over.

The next picture is Piper back in our bathroom upstairs. She's wearing denim cutoff shorts… but nothing else. Her hand is draped across her chest, and her head is tilted to the side.

My mouth goes dry and my pants get tighter. This is *not* the time.

"Hey Scott?" Somebody touches my arm, and I just about

jump through the ceiling, my phone sliding from my grasp and crashing onto the exposed concrete floor. Everybody around me is looking at me like they're waiting for me to say something brilliant, but my eyes are on my shattered screen lying between my feet.

Shit.

CHAPTER 28

Piper

As soon as Scott drives away, I miss him. Obviously, we aren't together all the time. I go to work five days a week, we have our own lives, and we see our friends separately, but just knowing he's leaving the state causes a sudden, surprising feeling of sadness. I meant what I said before he left—I don't *need* him. But I also meant it when I said I want him. It's a weird feeling to allow myself to want. The people closest to you have the most opportunity to hurt you, so I rarely let anybody get close. With Scott, I'm trying.

I plan on distracting myself from Scott's departure and my dad's brutal evaluation of my life by finalizing the bookstore's second and third evening events—a paint night and a movie screening—as well as its participation in this town summer bazaar happening on July fifth. I want to make sure everything is perfect. It has to be.

So, after putzing around the house, cleaning, wasting time all morning, and getting ready, I'm eager to get to the bookstore. Just before I head over to Alice's house to pester her until it's time to leave, Scott surprises me with his first video message, and I feel the tiniest spark of hope that he's maybe thinking of me as much as I'm thinking of him. Of course, the text might be a one-off, but then the picture comes through, and then he sends more.

Before I can lose my nerve, I run upstairs, strip down, snap my photo, and send it off. Then I get dressed again and flee to Alice's house. She answers the door with a bagel hanging out of her mouth and ushers me inside. A blender is loudly whirring in the kitchen, and it makes me think of making gazpacho with Scott.

I hope he likes my picture. I check my phone and find back-to-back messages from Scott, which I quickly respond to.

SCOTT

Good lord above.

Fuck! Warn a man, princess!

ME

Consider this your warning, Scotty.

"Smoothie?" Alice offers, turning off the blender, and jolting me out of my flirty texting haze. "It's pineapple-banana-mango."

"Immediately yes," I say. Something cold sounds perfect right now. Is it hot in here?

I take a seat at her kitchen island. This house is laid out the same as the one Scott and I live in, but it has a large, high-top kitchen island where our table sits.

"So—" Alice hesitates as she hands me my smoothie. "Were your parents body-snatched or something yesterday?"

"You'd think, right?" I start, and Alice nods. "But don't worry. They were their usual selves by the end of the day, right before they took off back to Boston. Dad was disappointed and Mom was unsuccessfully trying to smooth things over. So, I won't be entertaining them today. I was actually wondering if you'd like to stay over with me tonight. I was also going to ask Mads and Ila since Scott is away. Maybe Hannah and Leslie, too."

"While I'm really sorry your dad is back to his old game—sad but not surprised—I *love* the slumber party idea! Count me in." Alice comes to my side and squeezes me in a hug. "What did dear ol' Wendy and Cameron say this time?"

"Same old from him." I shrug. "*You're wasting your life. This place is crap. Why didn't you become a doctor?* Mom reminded me that Dad loves me, though."

"How sad for them that they can't see all you are," Alice says with her face pressed against my hair. She's always had unwavering faith in me. But a prickle of doubt still rests somewhere deep in my brain, questioning if there isn't some validity to what my parents said.

At work, I dive in, ready to prove Cameron Price wrong. Checking the store email doesn't help my confidence, though.

Mia Lane's manager, Susan, has gotten back to me, telling me it would be very difficult to squeeze such a small venue into Mia's schedule. Still, she sent a list of insane demands, requesting all kinds of statistics about prior events the bookstore has held, a list of other authors that have signed at the store, transportation and lodging options including confirmation the store would pay for both, sales numbers, our offer for author compensation, and more.

Part of me wants to abandon the whole idea, since I'm certain this isn't industry standard, but today is not the day for me to quit at anything. Instead, I start brainstorming how I can best sell our venue. For some of the questions, I know I won't have good answers, but I believe in Literary Lake, and I think it deserves a chance, even if I can't say that we've sold out theaters welcoming a dozen bestselling authors in the last year.

The afternoon and evening pass by quickly between regular store tasks and my event-planning agenda. Paint night sign-ups went live today, and there was a lot of interest.

Still, I can't keep Scott off my mind. My heart speeds up

when he picks our tour back up. The park. The *library*. The *bookstore?!*

I'm still not sure how much I like my mood being so heavily influenced by the attention of another person. Like… can I turn that off?

Maybe not, but it turns out you can ignore it for a few hours with the right people.

"Ready, Piper?" Mads says, flinging an arm around my shoulders and grinning a megawatt smile at me. Both she and Ila jumped at the sleepover plan. Hannah and Leslie had to take a rain check, which I hope means we will plan another of these nights someday.

I've already checked in with the closers, so I take a quick glance around and scurry out of the store with Mads, like we're two kids released for summer break. We have a couple of pit stops for Mads's overnight bag and an obscene amount of takeout from the Corner Post before heading back to the house.

Alice's car is by her house, and Ila's is parked by my lawn, but there's no sign of the women when we pull up. Once inside, I'm about to text the group chat when I hear a thumping against the siding of the house out back. I curiously open the back door and poke my head out to find Ila and Alice sitting on the swing, splitting a bottle of pink bubbly.

"Took you long enough," Ila scolds before holding out the bottle for me. "We got bored and started without you."

"Will you forgive us if I tell you we brought like two pounds of fries?"

"Sold." The two women clamber up and hurry inside.

Ila and Mads are new friends, but it's unexpectedly easy to be around them. We've hung out outside of work before, but nothing as monumental as a girls' night slumber party. I want to get out of my head, and this is the perfect remedy. As is the absurd amount of wine we consume. We watch movies—mostly talking over them to share town gossip—and eat anything we can dip in ranch, marinara sauce, or cheese.

We're finally all entering food comas when I pick up my phone to check the time and see texts from Scott. I unlock the screen and almost audibly gasp.

The. Suit. Picture.

It's just a mirror selfie, but there he is in a suit I'd bet was literally custom-made for him, a crisp white shirt unbuttoned at the top, his hand casually in his pocket, and one ankle crossed in front of the other. I've never really been one for full suits.

But this man? This suit? I'm a goner.

I've seen him look nice—it's a cute, preppy thing he has going for him. His mini mullet works exceptionally well with it. But this?

The wine-induced giggles cover for me as I flee from the room, back to my own little boudoir studio upstairs—aka the bathroom. I send the wine picture I'd taken earlier, teasing Scott.

But I want to do more.

I want to be rash, daring. So, I am.

Once I'm fully dressed again, I fling my phone in my room, a bit manic about what I'd just done, and barrel down the stairs. When the opening credits for *Grease* start playing, I settle back in with the girls and push Scott and that wicked suit out of my mind.

I wake up with a thrumming pain behind my left eye that can only be the result of drinking copious amounts of cheap wine. I try to roll over, but I appear to have fallen asleep beside a boa constrictor.

No. It's just my best friend who's koalaed herself to my side. Alice is a stage five clinger in her sleep, especially when she's been drinking. I try to extract myself from my human blanket, but she won't budge.

When I stretch my neck so far that it feels like I'm about to pull something, I can just barely see my phone lying where I'd chucked it, face down on the carpet beside my bed. Last night, I simply *couldn't* know Scott's response. Now it feels like I might perish if I don't get my hands on that phone immediately.

"Alice," I hiss.

Nothing.

"Alice," I say more forcefully and casually drive my finger into her side.

Alice squawks and jerks, lurching away from me and curling around her side.

Sorry babe. It's an emergency. I'm freaking the fuck out over here.

"*Ow*, Piper! I had an organ there, you know," she growls at me, but I've already thrown myself to the floor and bear-walked (more like galloped) over to my phone. The fucker is dead!

I do a barrel roll. Yes, a real barrel roll—everybody's nude-photo-induced panic looks different, ok?—over to my charger and practically violate my phone plugging it in.

"Come on come on come on," I urge as it starts up.

"What the hell is happening over there?" Alice's head pops out over the edge of the beg.

I keep tapping impatiently on my screen. I give it a second to load and find… nothing? My email is a mess. I get one for every confirmed registration for one of the bookstore's events and another for each confirmed payment for the paint night materials. I reload the screen, but there's nothing there. Scott… didn't… answer.

When I look up, I see Alice still peering at me, concern written across her face.

"What happened?" she asked.

"Nothing," I try, but Alice gives me her best serious face. There's little point in trying to hide things from her. I show her the screen of my phone. "I sent Scott a spicy picture last night, and he didn't answer."

She snatches the phone out of my hand, zooming in on the photo I sent.

"Hot *damn*, woman! Is it possible you gave him a heart attack and killed the poor boy?"

At least I know Alice will always love me.

Her attempt at humor is sweet, but it doesn't make me feel any better. Why didn't he answer? Did I go too far? Does he think I'm a slut?

I must say at least the last part out loud because in a flash, Alice is off the bed and in a fury.

"He would never. And if he does, I'll murder him. I'm adorable. Nobody would ever suspect me."

"You threatened his brother with a frying pan the first time you met." I lean into the joke (at least, I think it's a joke), but her support means everything to me.

"Nonsense." Alice waves vaguely before her voice gets soft. "I'm sure there's an explanation."

"I hope so," I say mostly to myself. "Do you think he's ok? Maybe something happened?"

Alice shakes her head. "Don't think like that. I'm sure he's fine. I was just joking about the heart attack."

I tell myself she's right, so I don't worry. But if he's fine… My dad's words are right there, waiting to taunt me. *Are you going to continue living off some artist? What are you going to do with your life?*

"I think I might really like him, Alice. Something like this shouldn't bother me—not that I've sent pictures like this around before—but I wouldn't *think* it would bother me."

"You care what he thinks," Alice says.

"Ew, gross," I immediately reply, making a face to go with my very mature response. "I don't want to be interested in a man's opinion."

"I know the feeling. I'm trying to be cool right now, but I'm gonna be honest. I'm *giddy* for you." She still has her arm around me, cradling me to her like I'm not half a foot taller than she is. She squeezes me as she talks. It's nice. "Scott will come through. I know it. Just be patient."

I look at her with skepticism.

"First time catching feelings?" she asks with a playful bump against my side.

"You know it is," I groan. "If this is what maturing is like, I'd like to go back to being immature, please. I was much better at our one-night-stand situation."

"About that, wanna share the deets?"

"I absolutely do not," I say, pushing her so she rolls onto her side.

"You wouldn't take *no* as my answer after Jake and I got naked," she argues, rolling back toward me.

"Thankfully, you respect boundaries more than I do."

"I don't need to respect shit." She grabs my ankle and yanks, poising her little claws over the bottom of my foot and knowing being tickled there is my kryptonite.

"Don't you dare!" I squawk.

Just as she barely touches my skin, there's a shout from downstairs.

"You guys up?" It's Mads. She and Ila must be awake now. They'd taken the couch and air mattress in the living room last night.

Alice's gaze darts between me and the door, and she tightens her grip on my ankle.

"Thankfully, I have better distractions." I steal my leg back and flee down the stairs, Alice hot on my heels.

Back in Mads's and Ila's presence, I know I'm safe. Alice won't pry now, knowing my arrangement is still a secret.

It feels like she opened a locked box, though. I can't stop thinking of that first night with Scott. He seemed pretty into things, like he did in the library two nights ago.

So, why did he ignore my picture?

Eventually, Mads and I need to go to work. Alice whispers that she'll tell me if Jake hears from Scott, and I promise not to mope or worry (at least I'll try).

CHAPTER 29

Scott

It's weird that bumping along an unpaved road is what finally releases the tension from my shoulders. Two days back in The Big Apple were enough for me. Sure, checking in was important and catching up with Odin was nice. There's no denying there's something unique and magical about that small island, but it feels damn good to be home.

I turn toward the house, and once the trees break, I know I'm just feet away from my (sort of) girl. The Range Rover is barely off before I'm out of my seat and hurrying to the side door of the house, not even bothering to get my bag first. It can wait.

Piper's name is already on my lips as I'm stepping inside.

"Piper?" I ask a second time, once I'm fully inside, not having heard a response to my first attempt.

"Yup," Piper mutters from the couch, where she's lying down.

She doesn't owe me anything, but her unenthusiastic greeting *is* a little disappointing, especially after she sent that picture the other night. She almost sounds… mad? Did I say something wrong?

I walk further into the house until I can see Piper. She's

holding her book uncomfortably close to her face, so it completely blocks her view of not only me but the whole room.

Oh yeah, I fucked something up.

"I'm sorry," I blurt. I don't know what I did, but the apology is authentic. I really am sorry for whatever it is.

"Hm."

Piper doesn't move, and I briefly think the sound is all I'm going to get. I stay put, just in case. After the longest minute ever, Piper huffs and lowers her book. Her eyebrows quirk up like she's just noticing I'm here.

"Oh look. You *are* fine. When Alice told me Jake heard from you yesterday, I thought he must be mistaken. What happened then?" If looks could kill…

I rack my brain trying to figure out what she's talking about. I did email Jake yesterday to check in, sure, but is that bad? I know my confusion is painted on my face because Piper gets more irritated. She abruptly sits up, snapping her book closed and slapping it on the couch cushion beside her.

"What the hell happened, Scott?" she repeats. "Did Manhattan lose all cell reception? Did your phone break or something? Did—"

"Yes," I interrupt, surprised.

Piper starts. She should know that already. Unless...

Oh *no*.

"What?" Piper snaps, dumbfounded.

I dig my phone out of my front pocket and hold it up for her to see, completely shattered with a piece of packing tape slapped across the front so glass shards don't fall out.

"Yes. My phone broke. I emailed you Sunday night, as soon as I got back to my hotel to tell you. I sent it to your store email because I don't know your personal one. I stupidly don't have your number memorized, or Alice's, and I didn't want to ask Jake for it and have him start asking questions. I figured the email would cover things until I got back this morning."

Piper is frozen for my whole explanation, but she jumps into action as soon as I finish, scrambling to get her phone. I watch her eyes dart around the screen as she furiously taps.

"Oh," she finally says. Then, she starts reading under her breath. "'*Piper, your last correspondence was so pleasantly surprising. Unfortunately, it was followed by the immediate and complete destruction of my phone. I'm going to try to get a replacement tomorrow, but there might not be time. Either way, I wholeheartedly hope we can continue our conversation in person once I'm back home. I have some thoughts on arrangements you might find interesting. Always, Scott.*' It's so formal."

She looks up at me, equal parts stunned and embarrassed.

"I was trying to be subtle in case anybody else in the store checked your email for you. I was *trying* to tell you I loved the photo so much it stunned me stupid and I dropped my phone. But then, when you didn't answer, I was worried I'd been too forward about my suggestions for once I was back, so I figured we should just talk in person to avoid misunderstandings," I try to explain.

"Too forward? I just… I didn't see it. I got dozens of emails yesterday because of store event registrations. I missed it. I— UGH." Piper plops her head into her hands, but her muffled voice still makes its way to me. "I feel like such a *drama queen*."

"It's ok, Piper. I could have done more, like looking up the store phone number or something." I move her book out of the way and sit beside her, placing my hand on her pajama-clad knee. "I need you to have the tiniest bit of faith in me. I'm not the kind of guy who would just ghost you, and I feel like I've made that clear. Things have been pretty good so far, right?"

"Yeah," she admits.

"Ok then. Have some confidence I don't suck." I reach up to

cup her face, tipping her head toward me so I can kiss her temple. I thought we were making progress, but right now it feels like she's still miles away. Hopefully my surprise for today makes us a little more solid. "You're still off today, right?"

I feel her nod.

"Good. Get dressed. I made plans for us. And then hopefully you don't mind coming with me to get a new phone?"

"Ok." Her voice is small. She's embarrassed, ashamed.

I can practically hear the gears turning from her overthinking about the picture, her assumptions about my silence, getting so angry, the missed email. She shuffles over to the stairs, and I call out when her foot hits the first step.

"Wear pants. We're going horseback riding on some nature trails."

I'm not sure I've ever seen anybody move as fast as she does when she whips around toward me.

"We're what?" Her voice has jumped at least an octave. Maybe two. And her face is fully animated once more, like the life has been shocked back into her.

"I was just trying to get you out of your head," I say, satisfied. "Don't worry. We're not going horseback riding. I found a nice, unique indoor activity for us. I just couldn't have you in this funk all day, worried that you overreacted or something. I'm still here."

Everything about Piper softens. She opens and closes her mouth twice before deciding to scurry back to the couch instead. Her soft fingers slide over my cheeks as she tips my head back and kisses me gently.

"Thank you," she whispers before running away again. "I'll just be two minutes," she calls from upstairs.

"Wear something comfortable that isn't your favorite," I call back. "Things could get messy, and I mean it this time."

As soon as we get in the car, Piper asks if there was time to stop for *a little treat*, and I have no desire to deny her anything, so the entire car is filled with the smell of fast food. Bad for your body, but sometimes good for your soul.

"So, how was your unplugged day yesterday?" Piper asks before popping a French fry into her mouth.

"An absolute menace," I say honestly, chuckling at how much such a small device can impact my life in one day. "I wasn't unplugged because I still had my email on my laptop. Since I was in back-to-back meetings almost all day, notifications were constant. I basically only got the negatives of a broken phone. I had hardly anybody's number—do you realize how hard it is to be without a cell phone these days? All the things we use apps for? It was a huge pain in the ass."

"We'll get you hooked up again soon. Do you want to take care of that before whatever you have planned?"

"Nah." And I really don't. "Right now, I'm *actually* unplugged, for just a few hours, and it's not so bad. You're the person I'd most want to talk to anyway, and you're here."

I glance over at Piper and see her trying to hide her smile. With her hair pulled back, she can't hide the flushed tips of her ears though.

"Besides, I'm not interested in postponing something with you for something that isn't an emergency." I need her to know she isn't an afterthought here. She's my top priority.

I ask what I missed while I was in New York, and she tells me about the bookstore, its events, and the difficult woman she's trying to impress so she can get a superstar author into Literary Lake. If you ask me, this manager sounds unreasonable, but I don't know how these things work. I didn't even know authors *had* managers. I just hope the author isn't a diva since Piper seems to be a big fan.

After almost an hour of driving, I exit the highway, drive for a bit more, enter a neighborhood, and follow a few winding roads before pulling to a stop in front of a beautiful green lawn and cutting the engine.

"Where are we?" Piper asks, leaning forward and looking around.

"What does it look like?" I ask.

She does another sweep of the area, looking for something she missed, before answering.

"It looks like a house." Suddenly, she gasps and smacks my arm. "You did *not* buy me a house Mr. Fancy New York Rich Man," she yelps, horrified.

"What? No. I like you living right where you're at now." Like hell I'm encouraging her to move out. I want to wife her up, not kick her out. "I'll give you an unhelpful hint. Our date is behind the house."

"Oh my god. You're going to murder me in the woods." She seems elated by the idea.

"Yes," I deadpan. "I wanted to make sure it was something you hadn't done before."

"I knew it. You're so thoughtful." She thinks some more before giving up. "I've got nothing."

"Then this is a successful surprise. Let's go." I reach for my door handle before turning back to her. "Wait right there."

I'm surprised, but she obeys. Not wanting to push my luck, I rush out of the car and around the front. I open her door and find her still patiently waiting for me. She keeps eye contact when I reach across her to unbuckle her seatbelt, our faces just inches apart. Then, I hold out my hand and help her out of the car.

"Huh," she finally says. "That was kind of nice."

"Good," I gloat a little bit. "Get used to it, princess."

I loop her arm through mine and lead her along a pebble-laden path to a multi-car garage-sized structure behind the house. A middle-aged woman with grey hair and a kind face comes out the door to greet us as we approach.

"You must be Scott and Piper. I'm Kathy," she says warmly. She's wearing overall shorts, a sleeveless top, and a heavy tan apron, splattered with grey. "I'd shake your hands, but…" She shows us her palms, similarly grey, though still wet in some places.

"It's wonderful to finally meet you in person, Kathy," I respond, and Piper says hello.

"Alright." Kathy claps her hands together. "Let's get messy!"

I feel Piper hesitate beside me and chuckle a bit.

"I haven't exactly told the lady what we're here for," I admit.

"Oh," Kathy says with delight. "Well, come on in. It's much more fun to show than to tell. We're going to have a great time."

Piper lets me lead her into the building after Kathy. The space inside is open, without any internal walls but still divided into clear quadrants by the objects around the room. Pottery wheels, worktables, shelves, and kilns cluster around the space.

"Welcome to my studio," Kathy announces with flourish. "I've been working with clay since I was a teenager, and now I divide my time between restoring historic pottery for various museums, creating custom art, and teaching classes of all levels. You are here today to create with me."

I look over to Piper as Kathy finishes and find her eyes sparkling with wonder.

"This is *so cool*," she exclaims, slipping her arm out of mine to move further into the building, her head on a swivel between the beautiful ceramic pieces on the shelves and the lumps of clay waiting for her eager hands on the tables.

She looks back at me and mouths an awed *thank you*.

I could spend my life making this woman happy.

Kathy has us wash our hands and then suits us up with aprons of our own before leading us to the tables. She talks about the different types of clay, the tools available to us, and the danger of air bubbles in our projects. Then, she has us just play with some clay to get the feel for how it reacts to pressure and water, to understand what it takes to hold pieces together, and how easy it is to crush delicate work.

Piper is attentive and focused, but most importantly, her smile never leaves her face. In no time at all, both of us have flecked clay on our aprons, up our arms, and somehow also on Piper's forehead.

Kathy is an excellent teacher, encouraging and knowledge-able. She insists there's no wrong way to create with this medium, so long as we remain safe, and stresses that we should go where the clay guides us. She notices Piper's eyes darting to the potters' wheels.

"Is your clay guiding you to throw?" Kathy asks.

"No," Piper protests at once. "I'd never throw it."

Kathy smiles. "That's one of my favorite jokes for newbies," she says. "It's terrible, honestly, but I'm a simple woman. Throwing clay is what we call it when you form the clay using the potter's wheel."

"Oh, then yes. I wish to throw clay very badly." Piper looks like she's vibrating with excitement.

"Then grab a hunk of clay each, and let's go."

It is soon abundantly clear I am not good at using the potter's wheel at all. For an artist, I have an abysmally heavy touch and keep crushing anything I'm able to form. I also have a lead foot and seem determined to stomp on the pedal that controls the wheel's speed. I nearly sent my clay flying once from the force with which the wheel abruptly started, but thankfully Kathy had her back to me and didn't notice.

When Kathy shifts to the side, I let my curiosity get the best of me and sneak a peek at Piper's clay and then bark a laugh. Hers is as lopsided and lumpy as mine is.

"What?" Piper hollers at me, her face appearing from behind Kathy. "Let me guess. You're a natural?"

"No." I laugh back. "I'm frickin' *awful*."

Her eyes go down to my hands and see the truth of my words. We both burst out laughing so hard it takes several minutes before we can try making something again. I don't remember the last time I've had this much fun.

Somehow, at the end of our three-hour class, Piper has managed to create a very passable flowerpot (she said we'll have to get her succulent a friend once the pot is fired and glazed), and I created a quite lopsided trinket tray.

We carefully carve our initials into the bottoms of our projects and set them on the shelf with the other projects waiting to be fired. A quick glance at Piper's, and I realize P.P. could stand for Piper Preston just as easily as it could stand for Piper Price.

As we wash up, Kathy promises to email me so we can schedule a time to come back to glaze our creations, and then we head back to the car. Once we're outside, Piper snatches up my hand, pulling it up to her mouth so she can press a kiss to the inside of my wrist.

"That was absolutely *perfect*," she says. "Thank you so much."

"You are very welcome. I saw how much you liked all the different flowerpots at the store, and I thought you might like to try making something yourself. I didn't expect it to be so much fun." And I *did* have fun. Not just squeezing clay between my fingers—which was extremely satisfying—but watching Piper have fun, too.

"I can't wait until we can come back to finish them," she says wistfully.

And just like that, we have a little future together. It's not very far out in the future, but it's something, and Piper wants to do it with me.

On our way back, we stop and get me a new phone. Back at the house, I set up my phone's data transfer while Piper and I start dinner together.

We move easily with one another in the space, and it's impossible to miss how much Piper's confidence has grown in the kitchen. She still asks me to double-check everything, but she is no longer unwilling to dive in. More importantly, mistakes don't paralyze her. She even sings a little while we work.

It's this life in her that first drew me in. It's enigmatic, and I love that about her. I don't *need* to figure her out, so long as she lets me come along for the ride.

After we eat, we queue up a movie, and Piper curls into the spot at my side where she seems to fit just perfectly. Her hand falls to my thigh, and mine brushes over her hair, but I stop when my fingers slip among her curls and find a chunk of—

"How the hell did you get clay in your hair?" I ask, trying to pick the crumbling pieces out.

Piper reaches up, feels what I found, and groans.

"Pause the movie," she grumbles like a child. "I need to go shower."

I'm amused by how annoyed she is at having to vacate the movie-watching spot she worked so hard to find. She even stomps up the stairs. A moment later, I hear the telltale pipe thud from the shower.

A bit later, I'm checking on my phone's progress (it's almost finished) when Piper calls my name from the base of the stairs. I hadn't even heard her come down.

When I glance up, I nearly shatter another phone because Piper is standing before me, glistening and wet, in nothing but a towel that's far too short for her tall frame. Her hair is twisted up, but the short pieces at the nape of her neck stick to the long column of her beautiful throat, and I swear I can see her pulse fluttering.

"I'd like you to come back upstairs with me," Piper says confidently, and my need for her is immediate.

I'm moving toward her before I can even register directing my legs to function. I capture her face in my hand, so I can angle her head just right for me to crash my lips to hers the second I'm close enough. Piper's hand that isn't holding her towel up finds my empty one and slides it between the terry cloth folds until I'm holding her waist, remembering the feel of her side, back, ribs, breast with my palm. Her skin is hot from the shower, and I need more, more.

I haul her against me so she can feel just how badly I want her, and she moans, a rumbling, unconscious sound. I love her sounds. I want to draw them out of her one by one.

Vaguely, I register hearing the chime of my phone getting a new text message. It must have finished transferring my old data. It chimes again, and again, but I ignore it.

My whole world starts and ends with the feel of Piper in my arms. I move from her lips, kissing and nipping down her neck and across her collarbone, until I get to the place normally covered with her shirt, and I bite, lick, kiss, grin at the mark I've made. She writhes against me, relishing the sting.

"More…" she moans, mimicking my thoughts. "Mor-"

My fucking phone is going off again, shrill and continuous. A call. I'm very tempted to shove it in the garbage disposal. The tone cuts off just to pick up again. I growl angrily.

"Upstairs," I insist. We need to get away from the goddamn racket. "Let's go upstairs."

It's ringing again.

"Scott," Piper pants, clearly the more responsible one between the two of us. "You should check it. Somebody seems to *really* want to get a hold of you."

"I couldn't care less," I hiss. I straighten to look into her flawless brown eyes, and she touches her forehead to mine.

"I know, but I think you should make sure it's ok that you don't care. Just make sure it's not an emergency. I won't be able to stop thinking about it if you don't."

My hands squeeze once more before I drag myself away and stomp over to my phone just as it stops ringing. Something had better be fucking imploding. My screen is filled with new text messages. I start with the most recent and work my way back.

Oh shit.

The phone rings again in my hand, but I pick up this time.

"Now?" I say in lieu of greeting.

"Yes, now." It's my top technician.

"Fuck. *Fuck!*" I shout. This is not good.

"I know. How soon can you get here?"

"Three hours if I push it and don't hit traffic."

"Ok. I'll have an update when you get here. And, sir?"

"Yeah?"

"Please answer your fucking phone."

"I know."

I hang up and look at Piper, but she already knows something's wrong and has my car keys in one hand. Her other is holding out my laptop bag.

"There was a cyberattack on one of the Massachusetts schools using my program. We don't know if they got through or not, but I need to go. Now." I take the bag and begin shoving everything in it that I might need.

She holds out the keys to me. "It's ok. Go."

It's torture to leave her, but I have to go. This is one of those rare emergencies, and I can't let these people down. I take the keys. "I'm sorry."

"You have nothing to be sorry for. I mean it. Call me when you know more."

I press my lips to hers in a brief kiss and leave.

CHAPTER 30

Piper

Scott texts me to let me know he gets to the school, but it's radio silence for a while after that. I'm restless waiting for an update, knowing a breach of his system could have major impacts on his business and the students whose information was compromised.

Other than generally not being stupid online, I've never given much thought to the privacy protections I assume are in place around my information. They just kind of exist… hopefully. Now, I'm sitting up in the middle of the night, worried about a bunch of students I have no connection to, spiraling thinking of what could happen to their private information in the wrong hands.

The sky is just starting to glow a faint orange when I get another update from Scott.

SCOTT

Good news. They didn't get any real information, just the dummy files we have in place to distract hackers. Bad news. I don't think I can get back until tomorrow. We still need to figure out what happened and talk to the right authorities. I'm sorry.

> It's great they didn't get anything! And don't worry. Do your thing. I'll be waiting for you.

After double-checking my morning alarms, I flop back onto my pillows to try to get a couple hours of sleep before Alice picks me up for work. I pass out before my phone screen has enough time to go dark.

When my buzzing phone wakes me up, I'm convinced I slept through my alarms. Heart hammering, I blink hard to bring the screen into focus. It's still early, but Hannah is calling.

"Whazwrong?" I jumble together.

"The store got hit again," Hannah answers grimly. I sit up.

"Shit. How bad?"

"Thankfully no permanent damage, but it might make your day really bad. Somebody wrote *Cancelled* over the fliers you had in the window for the paint night tonight and the movie screening next week. They also commented on our socials saying everything is indefinitely postponed. The phone's already been ringing off the hook, and everybody who's come in to the café is confused. There's a lot of misinformation going around."

"How did they cause this much damage this early in the morning? Was it Troy?" I ask, frustrated and confused. We did end up installing security cameras, so hopefully we at least got a clear shot of somebody this time.

"I checked the cameras, and it looks like they came by shortly after we closed yesterday. They're wearing sunglasses and a hood, all black clothing. It's hard to tell, but they don't look as big as Troy. And maybe I'm being judgy, but the handwriting is nicer than I'd expect from him. The account online is anonymous. I can't figure out a connection to anybody. I already called the police, and Mike is on his way."

I'd bet real money his bitchy friend is the one on the tape, and he's behind the account.

I take a deep breath to switch into problem-solving mode. This could be worse. I throw off my covers and start getting dressed.

"Ok," I say, a to-do list already forming in my head. "Ok. We can fix this. I'm coming in now. Once Mike sees it and takes whatever pictures he needs, let's get the fliers down and replaced with a new sign saying *Not Cancelled*—something big and bold. I will call Mads and get her on our socials clarifying that everything is still on, and when I get in, I will call and confirm with each attendee personally. We should also call the painting instructor and make sure there are no issues with our supplies or the rentals or the staff scheduled for the events, just in case."

"On it," Hannah says, and I hear typing in the background, and expect she's making the new sign. "I don't know what I'd do if I didn't have you."

"You don't have to. We're in this together," I say. It's good to have a partner. Another idea hits me. "Oh! Can you also call Bets and Grateful Bob? Bets is the biggest gossip we've got, and Grateful Bob knows everybody. There's no faster way to get the word out that somebody is pulling a malicious prank."

"You're a genius, Piper! Great idea. I'll call them now. See you soon."

I hang up with her, wake Alice up to beg to borrow her car (bless her, she says yes), and speed off into town.

And that's how my day descends directly into chaos.

Many hours later, when I'm looking out at our still fully-booked and very successful paint night, I feel like I was shoved through one of those rolling paper presses.

Somehow, comments from the new, fake Instagram account are enough to create doubt about the accuracy of information given personally from me. I had the same conversation over and over and had to field questions I didn't have answers to about why somebody said the events were cancelled if they weren't. It was *exhausting*.

On top of all of that, Mike was also back to laying on the charm when he came to the bookstore this morning. It felt weird. He's good looking, nice, and respectable, and the uniform looks good on him, sure, *and* I did specify that things with Scott are casual, but I'm not interested. I haven't been interested in anybody other than Scott since coming to Wilcox Grove, actually.

Mike promised to come visit me at the Independence Day Weekend Fair on Saturday, but I'm hoping he forgets.

I'd prefer if Mike spent his time trying to figure out who our vandal is. He said he questioned Troy after the broken window incident, and that he claimed absolute ignorance. I have no doubt Troy is ignorant, but I also have no doubt he's involved in terrorizing the bookstore. Mike said he can't call Troy in for this one since he's clearly not the person in the video, but that he has eyes on the brute to see if he does anything suspicious, and he will talk to the woman, Lauren.

Emily slides into a chair next to me where I'm sitting against a wall, overseeing the event. She's helping out on the café side tonight since Hannah came in early to deal with our latest case of vandalism.

"Eat," she instructs, placing a panini in front of me. I get hit with the smell of warm pesto and melted cheese, and my stomach growls loudly.

"You are heaven-sent," I say, and it's unclear whether I mean Emily or the sandwich she brought me. Drained but starving, I take an enormous bite.

It feels like I've lived a week in this one day when I finally crawl into bed a few hours later. I'm plugging in my phone when a text message pops up.

SCOTT

Can I call you?

Instead of answering, I dial his number.

"Hi princess." His voice is soft, sleepy.

"Hey." I cut myself off with a gigantic yawn. Who am I to say somebody sounds sleepy? "Is something wrong?"

"No, thank goodness. The program did exactly what it's supposed to. I just wanted to hear your voice and tell you I didn't break my phone today."

The smile on my lips is automatic. I didn't know it until he answered, but I wanted to hear his voice, too.

"I'm very proud of you." I chuckle.

"How was paint night?" he asks, and I'm impressed he remembered in the midst of what was likely an insane day for him.

"After some hiccups, it ended up going really well. I'd like to host it again, I think. People seemed to have fun."

"Hiccups?"

"Yeah." I yawn again. "I'll explain when you're back. Tell me about your day instead."

Scott starts walking through what happened, beginning with his late-night arrival at the university last night. His voice is smooth and even, soft, comforting… I'm asleep before he can tell me about his breakfast.

I'm hit with a wave of guilt when I wake up with my phone still stuck to the side of my face. I can't believe I fell asleep. When I check the screen, there's a text from Scott.

SCOTT

Good night, princess. I'll see you tomorrow evening.

Ugh, that just makes me feel worse. It's so damn *cute*. At least I'm rested enough to function better today because I have a plan for Scott's arrival that I'm hoping will more than make up for my untimely snooze. I text Scott an apology and tell him I'm counting down the minutes until he's back. It's sappy and not something I'd usually say, but it feels nice. More importantly, it's true.

But I've got work to do until then. I get ready for my day and head out. Thankfully, I still have Alice's car (she and Waffles went with Jake to the nursery today) because I have some shopping to do before I go to the bookstore, and what I have to get isn't something I'm willing to buy within this town's city limits. There are too many nosy gossips around here.

By the time I park on Wilcox Grove's Main Street for my shift at the store, I'm giddy with excitement. Caffeine probably isn't wise with how wired I am, but I grab an iced coffee anyway before I go to check in with Mads at the register.

I must have crazy eyes because she's looking at me like I might attack.

"Please tell me that's at least decaf," she begs, eyeing the cup in my hands.

"Can't a girl just be in a good mood?" I roll my eyes at her, but I can't force the smile off my face.

"*That* good of a mood is cause for alarm. Did you get Mia to agree to come or something?"

Well, that's one way to throw a wet blanket on a good day. Goodbye, smile.

"Not yet, but I'm going to win over her manager if it's the last thing I do. Maybe I'll start with her today. I can talk up our event successes, but I want as much time as possible to convince her if she's still hesitant. At least I can honestly tell her Mia's other books have been selling like crazy, so there's clearly interest in Mia from the town."

Mads retrieves the store laptop and hands it over to me.

"Well, you have fun with that," she says, looking at me like I'm about to go to the gallows. "I'm happy just being with the books and am very grateful you're here to do the schmoozing stuff."

It's not my favorite either, but I'm determined to get Mia. For me, for Literary Lake, for Wilcox Grove. I just don't want to fail.

Perhaps fueled by my excitement to get home, the day moves quickly. I'd been warned by Hannah that summer would pick up, with people visiting the lake, wanting to escape busy cities and enjoy some small-town simplicity. With the long holiday weekend about to be upon us, that tourist rush seems to have started.

I had Mads prop the doors and move a cart of discount books to the curb, beside the few tables the café has outside in the warmer months. People are coming and going all day, and I'm grateful for the additional traffic. Hopefully it helps convince Susan we're worth her and Mia's time.

Today keeps me a good kind of busy, but I'm still ready to fly out our door when closing time rolls around. Scott had texted me just before he hit the road to come back, and I should have plenty of time to beat him back, but I want everything to be perfect. It's more than I've done for a hookup before, but Scott maybe isn't just a hookup. I know he wants to be.

Scott is the kind of man who makes me want to try to be more.

That's why, when he opens the door, I'm standing in the candle-lit living room in a black silk robe.

When he freezes, one hand still on the open door, I pray he's the good kind of surprised, because there's no turning back now.

When Scott's eyes track down my body, I can feel how intensely he's looking at me.

His bags drop off his shoulder with a thud, and he clumsily kicks the door shut behind him. The air becomes heavy the moment the lock clicks.

I slip my finger into the knot at my waist and pull, tugging so the slippery material shifts off my shoulders and pools at my feet, my new bralette and panty set, bought just for Scott earlier today, on full display.

"Welcome home, Scott."

CHAPTER 31

Scott

I must be the luckiest man alive.

Every frustration about my traffic-laden drive is gone as I take in Piper, seemingly all wrapped up just for me in black lace, delicate straps, and the thinnest ribbon choker around her neck. She even has garters and thigh-high black stockings on.

Fuck.

"Piper, you look…" I pause. "There aren't words for how you look. Shit. I should go away more often if this is the homecoming I get."

Piper grins, and she exudes confidence. It's one of the sexiest things I've ever seen.

"I would suggest you stay."

Her voice is molten, dragging me to her, pulling me in. I'm so far gone I might not be able to find my way back out.

"I'm definitely staying." Somehow, I've made my way to her, and my hands fall to her waist, sliding down until they rest on the flair of her hips. I bend and kiss her, slowly, memorizing every movement of her lips.

"You're sure?" I murmur, finding her eyes.

"Very sure, but this is as much as I'd planned. So, how do you want me, Scotty boy?"

I am grateful I stuck with hockey for as long as I did as I scoop Piper up and fold her over my shoulder, wrapping my arms around the back of her knees to hold her steady.

"I have a promise to keep, princess." I think back to what I said in the library as I carry her up the stairs, her squealing laughter music to my ears.

I take her straight to my room and toss her onto the center of my bed. She bounces when she lands, head thrown back and hair haloed around her. The image undoes me. I yank my shirt over my head while I kick off my shoes.

After pulling off my socks, I press a hand into the mattress on each side of Piper's thighs and bend over her until I can press my lips into the exposed skin below her navel. One of Piper's legs, previously hanging off the bottom of the bed, runs up the inside of mine, pushing the material of my pants up as she goes. I shift so I can catch that ankle and hook it around my hip. Piper immediately flexes, pulling me closer to the apex of her thighs.

"Somebody's greedy," I say, pressing away from her so she can't get the friction she's looking for.

I reach between us and press my thumb against the scrap of material between her legs, finding it absolutely soaked.

"You make me crazy," Piper says, fire behind her eyes. "I don't want to wait."

Well, fuck, I don't either, but I *do* want to savor her—sober and with all my sensibilities. I want to remember every moment of this.

"I'll make it worth your patience," I vow, and try my hardest not to blow in my pants when she bites her lip and squirms below me.

My eyes dart down, and my hand moves to the elastic garter. I snap the material against Piper's leg, making her gasp.

"These are doing something to me, princess," I say, kissing where the band wraps around her waist. I place another kiss lower, against the front of her thong. It looks expensive. "These, though, I could do without."

"If you rip these ones, I swear to god I'll—"

I cut her off by dragging my tongue up the material between her legs.

"Don't worry," I say, playing with the little tied bow by her hip. I pull the end, and am pleased to discover the design is functional, not just decorative. I untie the matching one on her other hip and drag the material away slowly.

I unhook Piper's leg from around me and stand, holding the scrap of lace between two fingers.

"See? Unharmed."

I slip it into the back pocket of my pants before pulling those and my boxers down and out of the way. Piper's eyes immediately fall to my cock, already hard and leaking for her. She looks hungry.

Approaching her again, I move with slow deliberation, bending her legs until her feet are flat on my mattress. She looks confused but curious and positively shudders when I blow cool air against her exposed cunt. I lie forward and hook one arm under each of her knees, wrapping a hand around each thigh.

Before she can tense, I flip over, taking her with me and positioning that glistening pink pussy over my face. Off balance, Piper tips forward, and her hands slap against my headboard. She looks down at me, and the image of her surprised face from my place between her thighs just might be ingrained in my brain forever.

"I suggest you hang on," I recommend before tightening my grip on her legs and pulling her down onto my tongue.

Piper groans loudly, and I hear her nails dragging against the back of the wooden headboard. That's my girl. I suck her clit into my mouth as a reward, and she grinds down against my face, her thighs tightening against my ears.

I love that she knows what she likes and isn't afraid to chase it. Still, I press my fingers into the insides of her thighs and open her to me because I also love that she wants me to fight her.

Piper's thighs shake in my hands from the effort to resist me until I thrust my tongue into her and scrape my teeth against her swollen core. One of her hands releases the headboard to find a fistful of my hair as I continue to work her. She begins rocking again, her clit rolling against my face. I take a deep breath through my nose and devour her until that hand tightens against my scalp and a moan rolls off Piper's tongue. I release my hands, so she can squeeze her thighs against me again, while I lap every drop of her up.

She lifts herself up on unsteady legs and looks down at me, satiated.

"You alright down there?" she breathes.

"Never better."

Piper shimmies down my body until her pussy bumps against the head of my straining cock. She lifts and slides against my shaft, making me slick as I brush between her legs. I'm surprised I don't crack a tooth with how tense my jaw is.

"Condom," I say, reaching for my nightstand.

"Or…" Piper says, rubbing my cock against her pussy again. This is how I'm going to die. Right here, right now.

"Or?" I quirk an eyebrow. Surely she isn't saying…

"I'm clear, and I'm on the pill. I take it *religiously*."

"I haven't been with anybody other than you since I was last tested—also clear."

Piper grins devilishly.

"Perfect," she says as she reaches between us to grasp my length and raise above it. "Yes?" she asks.

"Oh *god* yes," I pray, and she presses down onto me.

No *this* is how I die.

"Fuck," I draw out, my breaths coming in gasps. "I've missed you."

I've never been bare before, but I think the out-of-body experience I'm having is entirely because this is with Piper. I can't take my eyes off her. I need more.

My hands find hers, and I lace our fingers together pulling her forward until she presses the backs of my hands into the mattress beside my head.

Just as Piper sinks all the way onto me, I thrust my hips up, and Piper's mouth pops open. Her eyes lock on mine as she begins sliding up and down and throws her head back.

"Piper. Piper. Piper." Her name has become my salvation.

She begins moving quicker, her pussy working my cock. She looks back down, and her eyes find mine. She shifts, bending and kissing me roughly. She's taken full control now, and it is a sight to see. She moves faster, harder, on me. I feel the rough lace covering her breasts against my chest, the brush of her curls against my face, and I think I might combust.

I squeeze her hands and love that she squeezes right back, her nails biting into my skin. She clenches around me, and I drive up into her.

Piper's mouth pops open in a silent cry before she gasps, "Again."

We somehow find a perfect rhythm, Piper's forehead pressed to mine.

"Piper, I'm..." I warn.

"Me too," she breathes against my face. "I—"

She becomes a vice around me, and her walls flutter. Her breaths are ragged gasps. It undoes me, and I come hard, spilling inside her.

When we finally still, we're both breathing hard, our chests pressed together, our shallow breaths sharing air. My fingers are stiff from gripping hers so hard, but I don't dare let go.

As her eyes open, I can see clearly that she feels the same as I do.

It has *never* been like that.

CHAPTER 32

Scott

When I wake the following morning, the first thing I do is reach out to make sure Piper is still beside me. My heart sinks when I find warm but empty sheets. I'm about to get up and check Piper's bed to make sure she didn't bolt again when I hear the toilet flush, followed by running water.

A minute later, the bathroom door opens and a stunningly naked Piper prowls back into my room, a crumpled ball of cloth in her hands. I grin with male pride when I see she's walking just a little bit gingerly.

"Sore?" I tease, leading to Piper flinging the item in her hands at me with a playful swear. It hits me squarely in the face. I shake it out and discover it's one of my t-shirts. I raise my eyebrow at her in question.

"I thought I'd steal one of your shirts to be all cute with it barely covering me, but the damn thing fucking fit. Tall girl problems... One of these days, I *will* find something oversized that you own so I can feel dainty in it."

"I'll buy a whole collection of shirts multiple sizes larger than

I need if it'll make you happy," I offer. I'd love her wearing anything… or nothing.

She rolls her eyes as she climbs onto the bed, kneeling beside me, and I can't figure out where to look. Every inch of her is perfect and on display for me, but I drag my gaze to her eyes, expecting to find some panic there. What happened last night was intense.

"Are you… ok after that?" I ask tentatively. She seems relaxed, but I'm not going to make assumptions about something this important. I need to know she feels comfortable and safe here.

"I am *excellent*," she says, clasping her hands together and reaching up in a languid stretch.

I won't lie. I look down her body. I'm just a man.

She snickers when she catches me and shifts her knees apart, ever so slightly. My eyes jump back to hers.

"I mean it. This," she says more seriously, gesturing to our nakedness and the bed, "was never one of the things I was worried about. You're very good at *this*."

"I'm glad you enjoyed yourself."

That earns me a pillow to the side of the head.

"Cocky ass…" she mutters, but she's still smiling. "Are you hungry?"

She moves to get out of bed, but I clasp her wrist and flip her to her back.

"Absolutely starved," I say, and I crawl over her body.

It's several hours later when Piper physically shoves me out of bed and sends me in search of sustenance. I throw on my boxers and head downstairs. Ever the thoughtful woman, she had picked up baked ziti from Papa's for us for dinner last night, but we never got around to eating it. I heat some up, grab water (we need to hydrate) and the gift I'd gotten her from New York, and head back upstairs. As I walk past it, I snatch up Piper's black silk robe, too.

I set the food and book on the dresser and the robe on my bed but hear Piper showering in the bathroom. I knock softly on the door, and she calls me in. The room is steamy from her scalding shower, but I can still see her blurry image through the glass shower walls. I start to open the shower door, but Piper puts a wet hand on my chest.

"Oh no, I need a break from you and"—she glances down at my boxers—"and that. You stay out there."

"Ok, ok." I hold up my hands in surrender. "I'll just watch."

I close the bathroom door but open the shower door all the way. Water is spraying onto the floor, but I couldn't care less. I lean against the counter behind me and cross my arms over my chest.

"Have it your way," Piper says, turning away from me.

"Still a great view," I say, humming appreciatively.

Piper shoots a glare at me over her shoulder.

"Fine," she says, and turns to face me again. She keeps her tied-up hair out of the stream of water but tips her head back and slides her hands down the sides of her neck and to her breasts. She presses them together and pinches her nipples for just a moment before continuing her path down her stomach.

I swallow hard. It is possible I've bitten off more than I can chew here.

I feel my cock start to thicken and try to adjust myself to make it less obvious. Of course, Piper's eyes pop right open and fall to my lap. Her gaze works its way back up my torso as she slips her right hand between her closed thighs.

With the soap and water, her fingers slide easily against her curls as she moves her hand forward and back. I look back at her face and find her staring me down. Her tongue slowly moves across her bottom lip, and I am completely entranced.

Before I can blink, she extracts her hand, rinses off, and smacks the handle to turn off the water.

"All done," she chirps as she snatches her towel from where it hangs over the shower wall and wraps it around her body. "I'm starving. Let's eat."

"I—w-what?" She can't possibly expect me to function after that, can she?

She lightly pats my chest before kicking the shower door shut and leaving the bathroom, letting in a wave of cool air. I should just turn the shower to ice and step inside.

"You are a cruel, cruel woman," I say, but there's no bite to the words.

I take a couple of steadying breaths and splash water on my face before I head back into my room. Piper is sitting cross-legged on my bed in the robe and already has one of the bowls of ziti in her hands. She's doing her happy food dance. I pick up the other bowl and a water bottle before sitting across from her.

The last several hours have been incredible, and not just for obvious reasons. It has felt like Piper is really mine, in the least controlling and misogynistic way that can be said. She's felt like my equal, my confidant, my partner.

"I'd like to ask you something," I say. It's only been a little over a week since I royally fucked up telling her I want to be public, so I'm careful to handle this conversation differently, calmer.

Piper stops eating, her fork hovering halfway between the bowl and her mouth.

"Okaaaaay," she says, her unease obvious, and sets her fork back in her bowl.

"The last couple of weeks have been incredible. I don't think you're ready to go public, but would you go with me to watch the

Fourth of July fireworks over the lake tonight? People usually gather at the park for the best view, and friends very often stand near one another when watching something like a fireworks display."

Piper pulls some pasta from her bowl until the string of mozzarella snaps. She uses the bite to consider her answer, and I force myself to wait silently.

"Ok, yeah," she finally says. "I'd like that."

Finally remembering her gift, I retrieve the brown paper wrapped book from the dresser.

"I got this for you when I was in New York," I say,

handing it to her.

She sets her food down and tears into the wrapping, gasping when she sees the cover. She quickly flips it open to the title page and runs her fingers over the signature written there. Based on her review, it's one of my favorites—a small town romance about a struggling Christmas tree farm and two friends who don't realize they're madly in love with each other. I saw her copy in the library, and it's well-worn.

"Scott," she breathes, hugging the book to her chest reverently. "I love it. Thank you."

"You're very welcome." I swear her smile could heal people.

We can do this.

CHAPTER 33

Piper

here's a boy in my bed. Granted, it's Scott, and I invited him to be in my bed and didn't tell him to leave and just last night I was in *his* bed, but… there's a boy in my bed. It's been a while since that's happened.

I need to get up and go to the bookstore to cart things to our booth for the fair, but he's warm, and his arm across my torso is comforting. How he didn't wake up to my alarm going off a few minutes ago is beyond me. It's peaceful in here. In here, even with the boy in my bed situation, things are so much easier than out there.

Last night's fireworks were beautiful and watching them while standing between Scott and Alice should have been a dream come true, but I was incapable of shutting my mind off. Scott wants more. I know that. Of course I know that, but I've been enjoying our banter and the dates and the attentiveness. So, it's been kind of easy to pretend things are just fine.

Even though we didn't touch, standing beside him in front of most of the town last night felt like a lot of pressure. We had an agreement when we became more than friends, but it feels like Scott wants to push those rules, and it scares me. I feel weak.

It's not like I've been dating other people or even been interested in dating other people. Scott has been nothing but wonderful, and I feel like a schmuck for holding us back. He keeps telling me how perfect I am, and it makes me scared to be anything less.

Scott's arm tightens around my middle, sliding me even closer to him, and I smile. It's like even sleeping Scott is attuned to my distress.

Do you see that, brain? This is a *good man!*

Brain doesn't answer. While that's probably a good thing generally, it's unbelievably frustrating right now, and I let out a petulant huff.

Scott hums into my hair.

"What time is it?" His voice is scratchy, and I hate that I find that sexy.

"Almost six," I say after checking my phone.

"We need to get up so we can set up the booth," he mumbles, but the way he nuzzles against me tells me he doesn't want to follow his own advice.

"We?" I ask. I'd been planning to spend today working so hard I could ignore my Scott conundrum. That's harder to do when he's right there.

"Oh, sorry." Scott props up on one arm to look at me now. "Jake asked me to help man the nursery's booth, so I just figured I'd head into town with you and help set up the books first. I assumed you'd need extra hands. I can go with Jake and Alice later if you'd prefer."

He's right. We can use all the help we can get, and any sane person would jump at his offer to pitch in. I need to stop being ridiculous and think about what's best for the store.

"Don't be silly," I say, convincing myself I'm unbothered. "I would really appreciate the help. But, we do need to get going."

And that's when the calm expires, because I launch out of

bed, grab my clothes, and flee to the bathroom to get dressed even though Scott is intimately familiar with every inch of my body.

I tie my hair up in a ponytail as I walk down the steps, a laugh tumbling past my lips when I spot Scott wrapping two bagels in aluminum foil.

Even though today is the fifth, this is a Fourth of July themed fair, so I chose white denim shorts, a red off-the-shoulder over-sized tee, and a blue bandana tied like a headband in front of my ponytail. Scott is in white shorts that go just past his knees, a red polo, and a blue baseball cap.

We match.

At the sound of my laughter, Scott looks over at me and then down at himself.

"Aww, we're cuuute," he teases, turning back to the counter. "A proper couple."

I'm glad he's looking away, because I guarantee my face has subtitles.

What did he just call us?

There's a lot to do today, so I choose not to acknowledge the label, instead scooping up the travel cup of iced coffee from the table and taking a long drink. "Ok, let's go."

"Lead the way," Scott says and follows me out the door and into the car, a definite pep in his step.

We eat our bagels on the way, and it's-all-hands-on-deck the second we park outside the bookstore. Emily and Mads both walk up a few minutes after we arrive and everybody begins moving boxes of books into the Range Rover and Emily's SUV. Mads shoves a few displays into the back of her car, and we're on the move again.

The town set up booths for the fair in the park along Barefoot Lake in the middle of town—the park I brought my parents to last weekend. The usually peaceful expanse of grass is unrecognizable now. It's covered in several rows of red, white, and blue wooden booths, linked together by archways of matching balloons. Every park bench and light post has been draped in patriotic ribbon and flags, and I can already smell charcoal grills starting up. The place is bustling with everybody setting up. It has everything I'd hoped a small-town fair would deliver.

We temporarily grab some street parking so we can unload and get to work. Hannah and Leslie are already at our adjoining booths—one for Barefoot Bake and one for Literary Lake—and I'm thrilled to see Leslie out of her wheelchair.

"Look at you!" I say as I get close enough, pushing a handcart of books in front of me.

Leslie is balanced between her crutches and leaning on the wooden counter of the booth, but she's grinning like a fox. She bows as much as she can.

"Thank you, thank you. I still have the chair behind the booth for when I get tired, but the doc said it's good for me to try to be upright whenever I can."

"I have zero medical authority to say this, but I think you're doing great."

Leslie, Hannah, and Paul are putting out cookies for sale as well as setting up a decorate-your-own sugar cookie station. Since the entire town is expected to come here, the physical stores are closed today, so everybody can focus on the fair.

It is surprisingly quick to get the Literary Lake booth put together. We have a bunch of summer themed sections and a table with Literary Lake and Wilcox Grove souvenirs for tourists. For our interactive craft, we have little books of paper stapled together and all kinds of pens, markers, and stickers for kids to make their own stories.

In no time at all, we're ready to go. And it's a good thing, because people arrive to this shindig early and don't stop coming all day long. Music blares through speakers, and children run by shrieking with glee every fifteen seconds. Even with Scott splitting his time between our booth and the nursery's, I really don't have time to spiral about the status of our non-relationship or his misunderstanding about what's happening here.

That is, until Mike makes good on his promise and shows up with a little girl in tow.

"Hey," he says, playing it cool as he leans against the table where I'm manning our portable register.

"Hello," I say, glancing between him, the little girl, and the general direction of the nursery booth where Scott is. With Scott calling us a couple this morning, I don't know how he'd react to Flirty the Cop trying to be suave in my booth.

"I'm going to draw books someday," the little girl announces proudly. Oh, to have the confidence of a child. She looks like she could be six or seven.

"That's so cool! Would you like to make a book now?" I ask her and point to the table of supplies within the booth, eternally grateful for a buffer with Mike. Is she his?

"Yeah, I do!" she exclaims, releasing Mike's hand and taking off for the table.

Crap. I just sent my buffer away.

When I turn back to Mike, he's looking at me expectantly.

"Um…" What the hell am I supposed to say? I look back at the girl, but she's deeply invested in her little book and won't be bailing me out.

"Oh, she's my niece, not my daughter," Mike offers, misinterpreting my discomfort for judgment about his potential fatherhood. "My older brother, his wife, and their new baby are still picking out cookies, but Kate is obsessed with books. Insisted I bring her over here immediately."

"Oh. She seems sweet," I offer. I literally have nothing to say.

"You've done a great job with Literary Lake these last few weeks." Mike seems comfortable enough carrying on the conversation for me. He really is a nice guy.

"It's been my pleasure. I just wish people would stop trying to wreck it. I half expected to find our booth in pieces when I got here today." Vandalism is a safe topic. "Any update on the investigation?"

"I wish there was, but there's hardly anything to go on. No fingerprints, no clear images from the cameras, no witnesses. I'm sorry I don't have better news."

Mike does look genuinely frustrated on my behalf. Then, his expression morphs and a smirk slides across his face.

Shit. He's going to hit on me.

I feel my flight response kicking in. I've gotta get the heck out of here, but I can't exactly run away from my own booth.

"I'd like to talk to you when there isn't damage to the store," he starts.

Oh shit oh shit oh shit. Don't ask me out right now!

This is the *last* thing I need right now.

"Maybe sometime you and I could—"

"Hey, Piper! Do you need the second box of blind dates with a book from the car yet?" Scott's shout completely drowns out whatever Mike was about to say, and I lean to the side to peer around Mike. There's Scotty, sauntering up like he owns the place.

"Hey Mike," Scott greets, clapping the taller man on his back before shaking his hand. Is it just me, or did Scott hit him kind of hard?

"Hey," Mike says politely, but he keeps looking between me and his hand clasped with Scott's, like he's trying to figure out if he can finish his proposition now that we have an audience.

He releases Scott's hand and opens his mouth but is miraculously interrupted again.

"Look Uncle Mike! I made my book about the police, just like you!" Kate has returned and is waving a little book in the air, a stick figure in blue clothes on the cover.

"Aw, that's great, sweetie," Mike says, but he sounds disappointed.

Not as disappointed as you would have been if you had finished your question, buddy. Trust me.

"Thank you!" She squeals with delight. "Can we get food? I'm hungry."

I will be personally writing to Santa later this year to make sure this girl gets on the good list.

"For sure. Thank Miss Piper, and then we'll go get your parents and little brother."

"Thank you, Miss Piper!"

"You don't know how welcome you are, young lady," I say, and they leave before anybody questions why I said that.

Scott turns back to me after watching the pair leave the Barefoot Bake booth with two other adults and an infant.

"The blind dates are good," I say, answering Scott's earlier question, still trying to figure out what he's playing at. "And I don't think we left anything in the car. I'm pretty sure we brought everything over here with us."

"Oh," he says, not sounding at all surprised. "I must have been mistaken." It sounds like a lie.

"What was up with Mike?" he asks abruptly.

There it is. Scott came over here to mark his territory—me. I bristle at the thought.

"Scott, you have nothing to worry about there," I speak slowly and clearly, wanting to make sure he hears me. "But even if there was something there, you coming over here to stake a claim on me isn't what we agreed on. That isn't what I need right now. If your needs have changed, we need to talk because I will not put up with whatever you intended *that* to be."

"No, Piper," he backtracks. "I didn't mean—"

"You did," I cut him off. "Don't tell me this is all in my head."

"Scott. Your brother is looking for you." Grateful Bob's voice calls from behind Scott. I wonder how much he heard.

"I'm sorry, Piper," Scott says.

"Ok." I nod. We shouldn't talk about this here.

Scott turns and meets up with Grateful Bob.

"Not your best showing there, boy," I hear Grateful Bob say as he puts a reassuring hand on Scott's shoulder.

Fuck. I guess he heard enough.

CHAPTER 34

Scott

I feel like I've put my foot in my mouth again, and I don't know what to do about it. It seemed like there was a clear shift in my relationship with Piper this past week, and I had been excited to move forward, but now we're a giant step back.

Jake gave me a ride back last night after I helped him break down a bunch of the booths, and Piper was already in her room with the light off when I got in. It was late, sure, but I thought maybe she'd want to talk.

I hear Piper get up and start getting ready for work, but I stay in my room like a fucking coward. Talking last night seemed good, but after her isolation, part of me is worried if she sees me, she'll call this whole thing quits, and I can't let her do that before I figure out a way to fix everything and get us back on track.

I hear her footsteps as she heads downstairs and almost immediately hear the door open and close. It's early. Much earlier than when she'd need to leave for an opening shift at the store. And her taking off without a word and without breakfast doesn't bode well for me. The pit in my stomach gets materially worse.

I haul myself out of bed, deciding a too-long shower is my best bet for a clear head. I'm uselessly running through every moment I've spent with Piper when my phone buzzes on the bathroom countertop. Through the steam, I see it's Jake and turn off the water.

"Hey, what's up?" I ask. Jake doesn't often call, and it's even more rare early on a Sunday.

"You busy? I need your help with something." Vague statements with few details, though, *are* common with him.

"I'm free. What happened?"

"I'll tell you on the way. Meet me out front in ten. Thanks." And he's gone.

Maybe a distraction is what I need today. Then Piper and I can talk about this rift tonight with clear heads.

When I walk outside, Jake is already waiting in his truck with Alice. I climb in the back seat and give Alice a quick hug around her seat before tapping Jake's shoulder in greeting. He shifts into gear, and we pull away.

"You both look pissed," I observe. I hope their relationship isn't in trouble, too. "Care to fill me in?"

"It seems like *somebody* targeted the bookstore and café again," Alice says, fuming. "I mean, let's just call them Troy."

"Oh shit," I say. That's the last thing Piper needs to deal with. "What did they do?"

"We're not sure yet," Jake answers. "But none of the doors will open. I've got tools in the back, so we can hopefully figure it out."

Then it hits me. "We're going to the bookstore?" I ask, even though the answer is obvious. So much for avoiding Piper.

"Yup. That's where the bookstore and café doors are," Jake says, suspicion in his tone and in his eyes, which catch mine in the rearview mirror.

Smooth.

I shut up for the rest of the drive.

Piper, Hannah, Allen, *Mike*, and a small crowd of townspeople are standing on the sidewalk when Jake pulls up and double-parks. A barrier between townspeople and their coffee is an emergency worthy of bending parking rules on Main Street. Piper homes in on me the second my feet hit the pavement. Her attention something physical I can feel on my skin. I give her a small smile, relief punching me in the chest when she returns it and starts walking toward me.

"Hi," she says softly.

"Hey," I answer. I want to touch her, hold her hand, something, but there are too many people around. Jake is on his way to talk to Hannah and the police, but Alice is lingering near us by the truck. She catches my eye and quickly looks between me and Piper. I wonder if she can feel something's off, too.

"I'll go with Jake," she says before hightailing it toward the crowd.

"Are you ok?" I ask. I'm not sure what I'm asking about. This? Last night? Life in general? I'll take anything.

"Yeah. The doors are fucking superglued shut." She chooses to focus on the present, practical issue.

I don't know what more we can say without being in private.

"Scott!" Jake's voice shouts over to us. "Can you bring me the toolbox from the back?"

Piper is already on the move to the back of the truck. I guess we'll talk later.

With a chisel, a very heavy hammer, and some aggressive thwacking, Jake eventually gets the café's wooden door pried open. The second Jake gets the door fully off the frame, opening staff and customers pour through the doorway.

Leaning the door toward me, Jake suggests, "Why don't you and Piper take this one behind the store and try to chip the glue off. You can use the sander after you get the chunks off. Hopefully it didn't damage more than the paint and we can get it back up. Alice and I can work on the bookstore door, and then we can try the back door."

"Sounds good," I reply. When Mike steps forward to help me carry the door around back, I avoid looking at Piper and make sure I stay as friendly as humanly possible. "Thanks, man."

Once he heads back up front, it's just me and Piper and this lumpy door. The silence is deafening, only broken by the sound of chisels and hammers.

"I didn't see you last night," I say pathetically.

"I'm sorry. I was beat after being at the fair all day, and I opened today, so I wanted to get to bed early."

Is it just me or is she avoiding eye contact?

"And you weren't steering clear of me this morning?" I sound needy even in my own ears. *Get it together, Scott.*

"I didn't mean to." Piper's eyes flash to mine for a second before she's focused on her chisel again, scraping at a blob of glue. The chisel rubs against the metal hinge, making the *worst* screeching noise. Piper winces but continues. "It was *really* early. I didn't know how late you got in last night, and I didn't want to wake you. I also wanted to get here quickly after Hannah called to tell me the doors wouldn't open."

I guess that makes sense. We keep working until Jake appears, carrying the second door with Alice in tow behind him holding the electric sander. We all look at each other.

"Weird vibe," Alice mutters, but neither Piper nor I answers.

After a while of working in silence, we have three stripped down doors. They'll need to be repainted, but they're sturdy enough to safely go back up. When Jake and Alice disappear to bring the tools back to the truck, I cave.

"Are we ok?" I ask outright.

"Scott." Piper softens. "Yeah. We're ok. I just need to know we're on the same page, and I'm sorry if I was unclear."

"You weren't. You're great," I insist, eager to reassure her. "I'm sorry again."

"Thank you for coming to my rescue." Her smile warms all of me.

"Always," I promise.

Unfortunately, Piper's week doesn't improve. On Monday, she comes home ranting about Mia Lane's manager again. I guess the ogre of a woman answered Piper's latest email in the most condescending way, calling a visit to Literary Lake a waste of the author's time.

"I'm sure there has to be another author who isn't so pompous." The look on Piper's face tells me I've said the wrong thing as soon as it leaves my mouth.

"This isn't Mia's fault," she defends, though I'm not sure she knows that's true. "And I cannot just *give up*. This is important for Literary Lake, and I will not fail them."

I'm not sure I fully understand, but I can tell it's important to Piper.

"Ok. How can I help?" I hate seeing Piper this unhappy.

"You can't. But I'm going to *make* Susan see our worth." She's so determined. If anybody can convince this woman, it's Piper.

Tuesday is Piper's off day this week, but she spends a couple of hours in the morning drafting a response to Susan, including more statistics about the store and the town, as well as pictures showcasing Wilcox Grove's charm.

Once that's done, I hope Piper will relax, but she ends up on a video call with her author from the editing company she works for. She has headphones in for the call, so I can only hear her side, but the number of times she's seemingly cut off is infuriating, and

I'm not even the person being interrupted. I head into the office to give her some privacy, and to avoid interjecting to tell this guy to shut up.

When I come back out, Piper is screaming into a couch pillow.

"Piper, this isn't healthy," I say, looking at the red splotches on her cheeks. Not even Susan got her this angry. *Maybe* Bernard did, and that was a bad situation.

"Do you think I don't know that?" she snaps, frustrated. "Do you think I do this because I want to? I *have* to have this job."

"I just don't think there's any way whatever they're paying you could be worth what they're putting you through." I want better for her. She deserves better.

Piper angrily presses some keys on her computer before flipping the screen to me.

"Do you see this?" she asks. It's a rhetorical question. The screen shows six figures of student loan debt and a criminal interest rate. "I need something that's flexible enough to let me work two jobs at once and still gives me a little bit of time each week to not be working, eating, or sleeping. Don't talk to me like I haven't tried to think of other options. I've *tried* to think of a way out. This is what I get for not doing what my parents told me to do."

I sit down next to her and gently take the laptop from her hands, setting it on the coffee table.

"I'm sorry," I say, and I hate how many times I've had to say those words to Piper recently.

My sympathy doesn't make things better. Still, when I wrap an arm around her shoulders, she does let me pull her against my chest and hold her until she's calmed down.

There has to be some way for me to practically help her.

CHAPTER 35

Piper

I'm having a really shitty week. There's no denying it. I lie in Scott's bed, staring at a text on my phone, somehow still surprised by the things my dad will say with his whole chest.

The problem is Dad isn't a bad person, so I feel guilty being frustrated with him. He's loyal, loving, devoted, and so, so proud. He should be more supportive of me, yes, but him wanting more for me isn't inherently cruel, and it's not at all malicious.

I close out of my messages, get up, and go through my workday in a haze.

Alice always helps pull me out of these funks, but I don't want to tell her I'm also freaking out about Scott. She's been so supportive and excited about the prospect of the two of us. Me falling back into old patterns would crush her. I also don't want to bitch about my parents. She's clocked a lot of hours listening to me complain about them, and there's really nothing new to say.

Friday brings more traveling summer families into Wilcox Grove, and I swear I make it through cleaning up the store just for every display to be a disaster again by the time I circle back around. Partway through the afternoon, I get a weird email from my loan service provider, but I don't even have time to figure out what's gone wrong there. It really feels like everything is crashing down on me during this one freaking week.

By the time I finally get home, I am exhausted and raw. I closed, and it's late.

I'm reading the loan email for the third time as I open the door to the house, and I still can't figure out what it's going on about. It has all kinds of payment plans and interest rates, fixed and floating, and a whole section on investment opportunities. In the past, my loans and I have had an understanding. The payment is automatically taken out of my account each month, and I try to avoid looking at the number so I don't cry. So far, it's worked. Did something go wrong? I cannot afford to take a credit hit from a failed payment on top of everything else.

"Hey," Scott greets from the kitchen once I'm inside. "What's up?"

"Hey, can you take a look at this? I'm trying to figure out if I somehow messed up my loans, and I can't even tell what this says." I hold out my phone to him, feeling proud of myself for asking for help. It's a big step for me.

Scott's face falls before it takes on an expression I immediately know I don't like.

"They weren't supposed to email you directly," he says. He looks over his shoulder back into the kitchen. "I was actually making dinner so I could talk to you about this myself first."

No, I do not like this at all.

"Talk to me about *what*, exactly?" I ask, my hackles raised.

Scott's hand goes to the back of his neck, and he won't make eye contact.

"After Tuesday, I might have looked into some options you have available for managing your student debt. There are some refinancing opportunities that will make things much more manageable, and then maybe you could stop editing those terrible pieces if you wanted."

There's a loud buzzing in my ears. There's no way I heard that right.

"You did what?" The sound of my own voice cuts through the buzzing.

"They're just options, and I was only trying to help. I'd never actually change anything."

I can't believe this. I couldn't have been more clear about how I felt about my financial situation.

"How—how did you even get into my accounts to see them? Isn't that *private*?"

"When you showed me your loan account earlier this week, I saw the bank details and—"

"You *broke* into my accounts?" This is getting worse by the second. This is the shoe dropping I had *almost* stupidly tricked myself into believing didn't exist. "I can't believe you'd do this to me."

"I didn't actually do anything. I was just getting options. I did this *for* you." He's seriously defending himself.

"Why, because you're Mr. Hotshot Millionaire? I'm *not* your wife. I'm not even your girlfriend! You had no right." It's blunt, and it's mean. But I don't care. My eyes burn, and my chest feels tight.

"Trust me. You've made that very clear," Scott snaps back, before clamping his mouth shut, like he didn't mean to say it. "I'm sorry. I just thought I'd have access to options that might not otherwise be available. I've clearly made a huge mistake, and I'm so sorry."

He's looking toward me, now. I can feel it. I drag my eyes to his.

"I trusted you," I whisper. This is excruciating. "I trusted you to let me be independent, to figure it out on my own. I wanted you to see me as a whole person, just the way I am."

"Piper, I'm so sorry. I do see you as a whole person." He looks like I've stabbed him. It feels like he's shot me.

"I really don't think you do. You see me as the dream of a person you've made in your head and not as an actual human being. It's like you have me on some pedestal with an entirely unrealistic vision of who I am. You keep telling me I'm perfect, and I'm it for you, and you *see* me, but it really doesn't feel like you do. It feels like you haven't heard a word I've said about what I need to feel in control of my life." I look around, frantic, without a clue of what I'm trying to find. "I need a minute. I need you to leave, please."

I can't believe I'm trying to kick this man out of his own house. I don't even know why I say it when it's the last thing I want. I think I might be testing him, to see if he'll fight again, if he'll stay. It's cruel and immature, but I can't stop myself.

He looks stunned, broken.

"Get out," I say again, my voice dripping with acid I don't feel, acid he doesn't deserve.

"I'm sorry." He sighs, looking defeated, but I don't feel like a victor.

And then he walks out the front door.

The click of the door closing snaps something within me, and I sink to my knees, gasping for air. Hot tears sear their way down my face, and I clutch my stomach, trying to figure out why this hurts so badly.

I've always known the ones you let closest can hurt you the worst, but I never imagined it would be *this* painful for Scott to violate my privacy like that and then act like I'm wrong for rejecting his intrusion. This is why I didn't want something more serious with him—something *else* he ignored, in spite of our very clear rules. I didn't want to leave myself vulnerable to feeling like this when it inevitably blew up.

This isn't what I wanted. This isn't what I wanted. *This isn't what I wanted.*

The pot Scott left on the stove suddenly begins spitting and hissing, startling the shit out of me. I look over and see whatever was cooking is now violently boiling over. I roughly wipe my cheeks as I stand, hurrying to turn off the stove and remove the lid from the pot.

The starchy foam recedes, and I see potatoes through the bubbling water. Scott was making mashed potatoes for us to eat with dinner. Together. Like a couple. Where he wanted to discuss my finances, without having my consent to hack into my private accounts. The steam is uncomfortably hot on my face, and I take a step back. The air is cooler away from the stove, and it soothes the warmth on my skin.

That's what I need to do with Scott. I need to take a step back. What we had—have?—wasn't public. It wasn't serious. It wasn't exclusive. He can only hurt me if I let him be that close, but he's *not* that close. He *can't* hurt me.

I quickly make sure no other appliance is on in the kitchen, so I don't burn the house down, and I run upstairs to change into something slutty.

A minute later, I'm pulling up different rideshare apps, finding somebody anonymous who can pick me up in this fucking middle-of-nowhere town and take me somewhere that serves cheap liquor and isn't afraid to keep pouring when I've had enough.

It's sickeningly easy to fall into old habits. I thought I'd grown over the past few weeks, but I'm about to make some really bad decisions again.

CHAPTER 36

Scott

I don't have a destination in mind when I get in the car and drive away from the house. I roll to a halt at the stop sign before the paved road leading into town. Now that I've stopped moving, I realize my heart is racing, and my hands have a shake to them.

I *really* messed up with Piper. I had good intentions, but I can't figure out, in this moment, why I ever thought going behind her back was the right choice. Frustration bubbles up in me, and I roughly hit the heel of my hand against the steering wheel until it burns.

"*FUCK*," I bellow where there's nobody to hear it except the birds in the trees around me.

I have to fix this. I start driving again and find myself in the Corner Post parking lot a few minutes later. It's the only place I could think of to sit at that would be open this late. I just need to think, and then I can see if Piper is willing to let me grovel.

It's only when I push through the doors do I remember it's Friday. The place is packed. Coming here was a mistake. There are too many eyes on me. I don't even see an empty table I can hide at.

"Scotty boy!" a familiar voice calls out, and I spot Grateful Bob flagging me down. He's got a small table in the corner, the seat across from him empty. I could make an excuse and try to dip out, but I don't know where else I'd go beside just sitting in my car…

I maneuver through the busy bar and plop into the empty chair. Grateful Bob's eyes narrow on me.

"What have you done?"

I shake my head. "I fucked up, sir."

"Care to elaborate?"

I really don't. "No disrespect whatsoever, but I think I need to try to figure this one out myself. Can I just sit here for a bit?"

"Of course you can," he says, standing. He puts a hand on my shoulder, and the squeeze is comforting. "You stay here, and I'll get you something."

I press my fists against my forehead and squeeze my eyes shut. I keep seeing myself looking into Piper's loans and want to scream at myself to *stop*.

Grateful Bob pulls me out of my self-loathing when he returns to the table and slaps a giant chocolate milkshake before me.

"A milkshake?" I ask, perplexed.

"You're way too depressed for alcohol," he says wisely. "Chocolate will help more. Trust me."

I do trust Grateful Bob, so I take a long drink. It could be all in my head, but I might feel the tiniest bit better. "Thank you."

"Did you know loons have different calls depending on who they're trying to communicate with and what they're trying to say? A hoot is pretty common." He makes this short, musical but almost bark-like sound.

I can't help it. A laugh bursts out of me. "What on earth are you doing?"

"What does it sound like I'm doing? I'm educating you, boy." Grateful Bob repeats the noise. "That one is a…?"

"A hoot," I answer dutifully. Grateful Bob is distracting me. He's a good man.

After midnight, I offer Grateful Bob a ride back home, which he accepts. The drive is quiet, and my thoughts go right back to Piper, especially on the short leg of the trip from Grateful Bob's house back to ours. If she's still awake, I hope she'll want to talk.

I know going through Piper's loans and other financial information was an enormous breach of trust. I really did think I could help her. The plans I put together would significantly lessen the financial burden she has, but I know that's not the point. I handled it really fucking badly. There's nothing I can do to undo that mistake or justify it, so I'm just going to go to her, hat in hand, and ask for another chance to prove to her that my indiscretion was a one-time thing. I've set us massively back, but I hope she'll let me fix it.

The many different ways this conversation could go are still playing in my head when I break through the trees that lead to the house. I slow as soon as I do, wondering if I somehow went to the wrong place, because there's some shitty little grey sedan parked with two of its tires on my lawn. I'm sure I've never seen it before.

I double check the numbers on the house. It's mine.

I don't understand.

I pull beside the house and cut the engine before heading over to the car to see where it might have come from. I'm nearly at its back bumper when my front door opens, and a man steps out, shrugging on his jacket.

The stranger pauses when he sees me before raising a hand.

"Hey," he says, pulling keys out of his pocket.

I think I've grown roots because I can't move. The man watches me warily as he circles the hood of his car and opens the driver's door.

Who are you? What are you doing here? Where's Piper?

I don't ask any of these questions, though, because my vocal cords are as frozen as my legs.

Just before he gets in the car, the man turns to me.

"I'm sorry," he says, and then he leaves.

… Piper? *Piper!*

Suddenly I'm sprinting to the house and throwing open the door. What if she's not ok?

"Look, thanks for the ride, but I changed my mind, and I need you to leave. Did you forget something?"

Piper doesn't turn around when she speaks. She's in a sparkling red cocktail dress, standing at the kitchen sink with her back to me.

She didn't…

I close the front door.

"Are you listening to me?" Her tone is sharper, and she finally turns around. Her hands are covered in soap, and she's holding the pot I was using earlier tonight.

The faucet is still on, and it sounds like a waterfall is in the room. I trail up from Piper's bare feet all the way to her shocked face.

"Oh my god," she mouths, but I don't hear words. The world's volume rights itself. A glob of soap suds splatters on the floor by Piper's toes. "Scott. I didn't—"

"Who was that?" I cut her off.

"I don't know." Another splatter of soapy water.

"You don't know? Why was he in *our house*?"

"Scott, I was upset. I went out to a bar and—"

She stops speaking when I squeeze my eyes shut. I hear her set the pot down and the space falls into silence when she turns the tap off.

"He just drove me home and used the bathroom before leaving. I didn't sleep with him."

My eyes fly open at those words.

"Oh, well, that's good at least. You didn't *fuck* some other man in our house. *Thank you.*" It doesn't feel like I'm speaking. Why would I? This couldn't happen to me, to us. It must be somebody else's life.

"Hey!" Piper shouts. "You do *not* speak to me that way. Ever."

"I'm sorry. That was out of line." She's right.

"We agreed things were casual, non-exclusive. I didn't do anything wrong here." It doesn't even sound like she believes what she's saying.

"Don't you give me that!" I'm raising my voice again, and I hate it. "That's bullshit, and you know it. There's nothing about what we've been doing that was *that* casual, and you *damn well know it*. Even if it was, you know that didn't include bringing strangers from some bar back here where we both live. How would you feel if I brought some woman back here from a club?"

She opens her mouth like she's going to yell at me, but she closes it again. There's a storm in her eyes.

"I don't know what you want from me." Her voice is soft, and it sounds particularly delicate after my yelling. It pulls all the steam right out of me.

"Not this," I reply just as softly. I turn back to the door.

"Scott!" Piper's voice carries over to me. She's getting closer. "Scott. Where are you going?"

"I told you this thing between us wouldn't impact your living situation, so I am not asking you to leave. But I can't be here right now."

"Scott," she pleads. "Don't leave like this. We both fucked up."

I stop just outside the door. "Don't you pretend that me making a mistake, granted a *big* mistake, when I was honest-to-god trying to help you is anything like you bringing some other guy here to purposefully hurt me. That is some vindictive shit, and I've got to go." I start walking down the steps out front.

"Go?" she asks, still following me. "What does that even mean?"

"You needed time before. I need time now." I get in the car and slam the door behind me.

I can't face Jake and Alice right now, so I head for my other family, Eli. The drive isn't long, but I don't remember any of it anyway. As I climb the stairs to the second-floor condo, I pray he's alone.

It takes a minute of knocking before Eli answers.

"What the—Scott?" Thankfully it doesn't seem like he was asleep, but his expression is painted with confusion.

"Hey, I'm sorry to show up like this. Can I crash here tonight?"

He moves aside automatically. "Always. You don't even need to ask. Do you want me to call Jake?"

"No."

"Are you ok?"

"I'm not sure." It's as honest as I can be.

"Do I need to be worried?"

"No."

"Ok. But we're talking in the morning." The few hours of reprieve he's giving me are a kindness. "And you wake me up if you need anything. Ok?"

"I will," I say, and I remind myself of Jake with my short answers. I don't want Eli worrying, but I don't have any more words right now. He pulls me into a fierce hug before heading to his room. I notice he leaves the door cracked, so he can keep an eye on me.

CHAPTER 37

Piper

What have I done?

I sink into a chair at the table and stare at the door Scott disappeared through. I keep playing Scott's words over and over in my head. Did I really go out last night to hurt him? I want to say I didn't, but I didn't go out with good intentions. I was purposefully reckless and destructive, determined to show myself I didn't care about Scott. Even before he asked how I'd feel if he brought somebody back here (there would be blood), I knew what I was doing was beyond the understanding of *casual*.

Shit!

I'm still the same fucked up person I always thought I was. I never should have trusted I'd be good enough to have something real with Scott. He badly overstepped, sure, but I dropped a fucking nuke on everything we'd built.

Closing my eyes doesn't help. I just see the stricken look on his face when he asked who that guy was. And I honestly don't even know. He was decent-looking and interested. It was late. I was buzzed and angry. So, I'd led him out of the bar and let him drive me here.

I lurch out of my chair and just barely make it to the downstairs toilet before I empty the contents of my stomach into it. I heave again and again, my body determined to purge itself of as much as it can. Eventually, I crumble to the floor, skin clammy and throat sore, and press my cheek to the cold tile. No matter how much I want to, I can't undo the last few hours.

Sure, I didn't go through with it—I couldn't. But that doesn't make me feel any better. I never should have gone out in the first place.

My bones feel like they're made of lead, but I drag myself up. I think it's a mixture of the weight of my guilt and the disgusting turpentine masquerading as liquor that I poured down my throat. I pick up the tiny bag I'd taken with me and trudge my way upstairs, throwing myself in the shower the second I've stripped, deserving the blast of cold water on my skin.

Once I no longer smell like the floor of a trashy bar, I stumble out of the shower and into my room. After dropping my bag and dress on the floor in a lump, I fall soaking wet onto my bed somewhere in the very early hours of morning. I hug a pillow to my chest and clutch it, like the pressure might piece my heart back together. I squeeze my eyes shut, but hot tears slide down my face anyway.

The angry rattle of my phone vibrating against the contents of my clutch eventually drags me out of sleep I don't remember slipping into. When I retrieve my phone from the floor, I see Mads's name on the illuminated screen, and I realize I'm late for opening the bookstore. Goddamn it!

Briefly, I consider calling out sick, but I really don't think I could survive disappointing more people today, so I answer, mutter my way around a vague excuse, and promise to be there as soon as I can. My hair is a disaster, and I don't even look at what I pick to wear, but I'm dressed and outside before I realize the Range Rover is gone.

Of course it is. It's Scott's car. And Scott is gone, too.

I look over at Alice and Jake's place, but both of their cars are also gone. Mads is already at the bookstore, holding down the fort solo since I'm not there with her, and it'll take too long for Ila or Hannah to get over here.

Ughhhhh!

I swallow my pride and call Grateful Bob. He answers on the first ring.

"What can I do for you, Piper?"

His cheerful voice makes me feel worse, and I didn't think that was even possible. He certainly wouldn't be so kind to me if he knew what I did to Scott. He *warned* me. I'm tempted to just hang up, but I really need to get to the bookstore. The movie screening is tonight, and I volunteered to show Emily how to set up the projector, extra speakers, and screen.

"I, um, I was hoping you could give me a ride to the bookstore. I'm already super late. I'm so sorry."

I hear keys jingling in the background.

"I'll be right over. Are you alright?" His concern is another stab.

"Yeah, I'm good. Thank you. I'll be outside when you get here." I hang up before he can be nice again.

A minute later, Grateful Bob's truck barely rolls to a stop before I jump inside, and he pulls back onto the road. He keeps glancing at me, and I know I'm not getting away with this. We're over halfway to the store when he dives in.

"Is it Scott?" he asks to be polite, but I can tell he already knows. Grateful Bob is incredibly intuitive.

"Yeah." My shame is limitless.

"Piper…" he starts, and his tone carries so much emotion with those two syllables.

"I know, Grateful Bob. I did a bad thing," I admit as a tear rolls down my cheek. I could be imagining it, but he looks surprised by my admission.

Don't be surprised, Grateful Bob. I'm a bad person. You were right when you warned me against hurting Scott. You saw what I am back then.

I expect him to yell at me or even pull over and tell me to get out of the car. Instead, he reaches into the pocket of his door and passes me a travel pack of tissues. I pull one out and cover my whole face with it.

I feel like a cat, hiding by shoving its head behind the drapes. If I can't see you, you can't see me.

"You know, we all do bad things from time to time." Grateful Bob's deep voice is gentle. "What matters is what we do after that."

"But I don't know *what* to do," I sob.

"You'll figure it out," he says with such surety. I want to believe him. Then he asks, "You care about him?"

"Yeah," I admit, still blubbering.

"Then you'll figure it out. Now, I'm going to go around the block again, and unless you want the whole town knowing your business and making up their own stories, you need to pull it together, ok?"

The world does not deserve Grateful Bob. I know I certainly don't.

"Ok," I agree anyway.

By the time we come around to the front of the store again, I've stopped crying, but I know my whole face is still puffy. I'll take what I can get. I just need to make it until Emily can take over later.

"What time are you done today?"

"You don't have to come get me," I protest, and slide out of the truck.

"What time?" Grateful Bob kindly repeats before I can close the door.

"Four o'clock. Thank you."

By the end of my shift, I wonder if calling out would have been the kinder thing to do for the bookstore. I felt like a walking disaster all day. I was distracted, kept running back and forth, posted a half-ready caption on our Instagram, and messed up two online orders. I also knocked over two coffees and a plate of cookies from café tables and accidentally unplugged our register when I was trying to find somewhere to charge my phone.

It's a miracle the store is still standing when Emily shoos me away, insisting I take my bad luck far away from her movie night. When I asked Hannah if I could possibly take a few days off, she said yes before I could finish the question.

I'm shocked when I find Alice waiting outside for me, leaning against the side of her CRV.

"Grateful Bob called me," she explains. "He wouldn't say why, but he told me you needed me. Are you ok?"

I take long strides to meet her, tears already falling before we touch. Her arms are strong around me, like they're holding the pieces of me together. We stand wrapped around one another for a few minutes, the only sounds are my gasping breaths between sobs.

"Let me get you home," she murmurs against my hair as she shifts me so she can open the passenger door and usher me inside.

Once Alice is behind the wheel, she immediately reaches across the seat to take my hand.

"Pipe," Alice says, hesitantly. "What happened?"

"Scott did something he shouldn't have, and I royally fucked up in response."

"What does that mean?" Alice asks softly. "What did Scott do?"

I shake my head.

It doesn't matter what he did. It doesn't justify what I did, and I can't bear to say the details of that out loud. That I went out to find some guy to hook up with so I could pretend Scott didn't matter and then brought him back to *our* house. It doesn't matter that I ultimately kicked him out instead. I don't deserve anybody's understanding.

"Let's go home," Alice says, not pushing me to talk.

"I can't go to his house." He said he wasn't making me leave, but I can't face him.

"You can stay with me. I'll get some of your stuff."

Everybody needs a friend like Alice. Even if I'm questioning whether I deserve her at all.

CHAPTER 38

Scott

As I start waking up, I can *feel* I'm not alone in the room. Even before I'm fully conscious, I can tell that the other person here isn't Piper. Thinking about her brings the rush of memories from last night back, so I feel like shit from the second I crack open my eyes.

When I find two concerned faces staring at me, I feel worse. I pull a pillow over my face.

Eli called Jake.

"I'm sorry," Eli says. "I had to."

"What the fuck happened?" Jake is much less gentle.

I groan into the pillow, but Jake snatches it away.

"What. Happened."

I sit up and take a deep breath.

"Piper and I have been seeing each other since trivia night at the bookstore." I might as well just lay it out there.

"We know. What did you do?" It's Eli who says this, and I'm in shock.

"You what?"

"Well, he figured it out." Eli nods to Jake. "And then he told me."

I look over to Jake, completely dumbfounded.

"Have you seen your face? It was obvious."

They're both leaning toward me, eager for the story and still looking alarmingly concerned, so I take only a second to absorb the fact that I wasn't sneaky at all before I dive in. I tell them about Piper's rules, my trip to New York, our dates, getting closer (though I keep our private life private), the way I got a bit green-eyed when Mike was hitting on her, the bad week, my intrusion into her loans, and her visitor from the bar.

While neither interrupts as I talk, I can see Jake's face tightening more and more as I go, so I'm not surprised when he pops first.

"So, she got what she wanted, and you had to settle for whatever she'd give you? That's fucking manipulative," he barks, standing in anger.

"Now hold on just a second." Eli surprises me again by speaking up before I can defend Piper myself. "It sounds to me like Piper laid out exactly what she was looking for and offered Scott an out if it didn't work for him. It's not her fault he accepted knowing full well he wanted more."

"It felt like we were working toward that more together," I interject.

"But did she agree to that? Did you ever talk about changing the arrangement?" Eli looks at me like he knows we didn't.

"I'm just saying it sounds like Scott was always going to lose in this arrangement," Jake argues back.

"Do you think it's manipulative when I offer women a hook-up, telling them from the beginning that it'll never be something more?"

"That's different," Jake scoffs, putting his hands on his hips and turning away.

"Why? Because Piper's a woman?" Eli's words hit hard.

"No!" Jake and I say together, but Eli raises his eyebrows.

We've known and supported that Eli enjoys casual hook-ups for years. He respects the *hell* out of women, but he's not looking for a relationship. That's never once been a problem for either me or Jake.

"Is it possible you may have had different standards without realizing it?" Eli presses, and I don't like it. Neither Jake nor I answer, so Eli continues.

"The way I see it, you wanted Piper to be your perfect woman, your life partner, so you kept seeing her that way. But Piper isn't a fantasy. She's a person, and you pigeonholing her into being your future wife wasn't healthy or fair. Is it fucked up that she picked up some guy to hook up with? Yeah. But she's a grown woman, and you're *not* together, so she can do whatever she wants. *And* I'd like to point out that what she chose to do was send that guy packing. Seems to me she went back to what's always worked for her—hookups—and maybe realized it's not what's working for her now."

Jake turns back toward me and Eli, and his furrowed brows tell me he's absorbing what Eli said just like I am. I feel like such an asshole. I think women are incredible, and I'd never want to hold any woman to a different standard than a man, but I think Eli's has a point about how I was treating Piper. I was so convinced we'd eventually be in the type of relationship that I foresaw that I acted like we already were, ignoring what she asked for.

I drop my head into my hands. "I'm still just so angry with her. I think I just thought it'd be easier. When I found my soul-mate, I thought it'd be easy to love them, like it was for Mom and Dad. I want with Piper what they had."

"What are you talking about?" Jake finally speaks.

"They were perfect together," I say. Jake and I don't purposefully shy away from talking about our parents, but we don't talk about them as much as we did when I was a kid. All these years later, the stab of missing them still hurts something fierce.

"Now that you're a whole-ass adult, I sometimes forget how young you were when we lost them. Mom and Dad were *not* perfect, Scott." My head jerks up at Jake's words. I don't remember our parents ever even fighting.

"Dad was unbelievably careless. He'd always forget the keys in the car or leave the garage door open all night or forget to turn off the oven after cooking. It drove Mom insane. And Dad always thought Mom was a perfectionist. Her need to have a schedule planned out for everything infuriated him. They were always butting heads over the most random things. Getting along all the time isn't why they were solid. They were solid because they *chose* to love one another every single day in *spite* of those arguments."

His words hit me hard, so contrary to how I remember our parents. Hearing they weren't perfect hurts a little, but knowing they had the love I saw anyway gives me hope. I wish they were here for me to talk to. Instead, I look to the family I *do* have.

"You've got to stop holding her to impossible standards," Eli says, but he doesn't need to. I know I've fucked up. I also don't know if I can get past what she did, even knowing that.

"It doesn't matter. I can't change what I already did or what she did. I don't know if we can get past this. I don't know if she wants to. I don't know if *I* want to, and with how I left, it's pretty over." The pain of seeing that guy walk out of our house is fresh and fierce.

"You don't have to decide right now," Eli says. "You could take some time. You *should* take some time. I think you should try to figure out what you're unwilling to live without, and then do your best to earn that. You're welcome to stay here while you do."

Eli's offer is kind, but couch surfing doesn't seem like the right answer. "Maybe I'll go camping. Going back to the basics always helps clear my mind." I turn to Jake. "Would you be able to get my gear from the house? I don't want to run into Piper."

"Of course," he says.

By mid-afternoon, I'm situated at a campsite not too far out of town, and for the first time since moving back to Wilcox Grove, being alone feels lonely. I don't exactly want to be around people, though. According to Lorelai Gilmore, people need to wallow. At this exact moment, I think I agree with her because I'm getting some sick comfort from my own misery and anger.

I absentmindedly pick at some cheese puffs and listen to a random sports broadcast coming out of my portable radio. I'm somehow both restless and lethargic at the same time. Usually, I can enjoy the peace of nature, even when I camp alone, but it doesn't feel very enjoyable today. I don't want to draw or read or go for a walk or cook or do yoga or really do much of anything, but I also hate doing nothing.

Barefoot Lake is massive, and there's a lagoon nearby that's generally good for fishing. Restlessness wins out, I secure my campsite, and I take the fifteen-minute walk over to the shore. I bring my rod and bait as well as my sketchbook, just in case I can gather the motivation to do something.

When the dirt beneath my feet gives way to sand, I know I'm almost there. The sun is bright, warm when I break the tree line. The lake sparkles as the sun's rays bounce off the slow waves moving across its surface. When I hear soft loon calls, I think of Grateful Bob. They're calling for one another, communicating. I have nothing to say.

I take off my shoes and socks, carrying them to the empty dock jutting out into the lake.

I walk to the end and take a seat, setting up my rod and

looking down at my sketchbook. Even with the beauty all around me, I can only picture Piper's face, bright and smiling and then crushed when I walked out the door last night. There's a persistent ache in my chest. I hurt from what we both did, but I also hurt because I miss her. I close the notebook.

My toes just brush the water as I sit there, and I enjoy the gentle waves lapping against my feet. Sitting in silence over here feels less morose than doing so back at the campsite, so I let myself bask in the peace. It's a stark contrast to how I feel. After a couple of hours, I feel stiff from sitting so motionless and decide to head back to camp. The sun is only just starting to set, but I'm exhausted.

I eat a few bites of beef jerky before securing my food in the locker at the campsite. I don't have much of an appetite. It's warm and quiet, so I set my air mattress just outside of the tent and lay back fully clothed. I watch the sky grow darker and count the stars as they begin to appear.

Eventually, I fall asleep.

CHAPTER 39

Piper

"Piper," Alice's usually kind voice is stern. "You *need* to eat something. I did not invite you over here so you can die in my guestroom."

I tighten the plush comforter around my head, hoping she'll take the hint and leave. In fact, the opposite occurs. Since she's smaller than I am, I always forget how strong Alice is. Then she does something like grabbing the blanket and yanking it clean off me in one swoop.

"Hey! Give that back," I jolt up angrily. I want to be left *alone*.

"No!" she shouts back. "I love you too much to let you wither away in here. What is *wrong* with you?"

"I'm a stupid whore," I yell back and watch Alice shrink.

After she took me in yesterday, she convinced me to tell her what happened between me and Scott. She's been incredibly supportive, staying with me last night and holding me until I ran out of tears. I guess this afternoon is the start of the tough love portion of her care.

"Babe, you are not." She lets the comforter fall to the ground, and she crawls on the mattress to sit beside me. "You know you're not."

"I don't know what I'm doing," I try again. While I do feel slimy for going to that bar, I don't *really* think I'm a whore. I *do* think I'm a trainwreck though.

"What do you mean? With Scott?"

"With everything. What am I even doing here, Alice? I ran away to Wilcox Grove because *you* ran away to Wilcox Grove. I came with no plan, and I haven't even tried to make a plan since coming here, and it's been over two months. I've just been winging it."

"So?" Alice says. When I give her a "what do you mean, *so*" look, she continues, "Let's say you've been flying by the seat of your pants for two months. Setting aside this weekend, how has that been a problem? What has gone wrong for you?"

"I have no career, the bookstore is being vandalized, I can't get *one* author to come here, and—since we cannot just set aside this weekend—the thing I had going with a nice man has imploded." I count off each disaster on a separate finger.

"No." Alice shakes her head, like that makes what I said untrue. "I don't see that at all. Both Leslie and Hannah have told anybody who will stand still long enough how invaluable you are. I'm guessing you've got a future with Literary Lake if you want it. If not, you're qualified, talented, driven, and personable. There are other places for you to go. I'm not even justifying the vandalism argument with a rebuttal. There is a criminal targeting the store.

"As for Mia, that's her loss. What are you doing focusing on this one author whose manager sucks? You won't get everything you wanted, and it's nuts to think you will. If this falls through, there will be other authors. And you're completely overlooking the events you *have* put on. Every single one sold out and had a waiting list. People can't stop talking about how excited they are to see what you come up with next. Don't discredit that."

"And what about Scott?" I argue. "Are you going to tell me that isn't a mess, too?"

"No, what's happening with Scott is a mess. But it's not your fault alone. You both made mistakes here. Refusing to shower and staying in this bed won't change that." Then, she asks the hard question. "Do you want to fix things with him?"

"I don't know," I say. In spite of Alice's reassurances, I still feel like I'm floundering. I was fooling myself when I was playing girlfriend to Scott. Even if I decided I wanted to be serious, I'm wrong for him. I think my behavior the past few days proves I'm still too much for anybody to have to handle.

"I see those gears turning. Tell me what's happening in your head," Alice urges.

"I'm wasting my time in this town, and I was wasting my time playing house with Scott," I say bitterly.

"Ok, Cameron," Piper quips, and the dig cuts deep.

"What?"

"You sound like your father. Do you want to try again with your own opinions this time?"

"No," I snap. Saying I sound like my father was a low blow. I lay down and turn away from Alice.

I hear her huff but leave. I snatch the comforter off the floor and wrap it around myself again, pitifully lying in silence for who knows how long.

"Hey." When I look up this time, Jake is standing in the doorway. I've been expecting a visit from him, but I thought it would consist of him yelling at me for hurting his brother.

"Hi," I reply, uncovering my head and sitting up. I have no clue where this is going.

"It's time to come downstairs and eat, now. Alice is worried sick about you, and I can't have that." His deep voice is smooth, even.

"I'd think you'd want me to suffer for what I did to Scott." The words fall out of me. "You've been giving me side-eye for weeks. I figured it was because you knew he had feelings and didn't approve."

"It was. But, no, I don't want you to suffer." Jake shakes his head. "I think it's possible I might have misjudged you. I might have also underestimated Scott. It's hard not to protect him after all he's been through, but he's got to make his own choices, and this is one I don't think needs my input. I've seen the friend you are for Alice, so I know you're a good person."

That might be the most I've heard Jake say at one time that isn't about plants.

"Oh."

"So, are you coming?" Jake jerks his head toward the stairs.

"Yeah. Let me shower quickly, and then I'll be down."

Dinner was quiet, but a shower, a good meal, and a decent night's sleep did wonders for resetting my brain, and in the morning, I voluntarily leave the guest room and go downstairs. Jake is mowing the grass out back, but Alice is sitting at the island in the kitchen.

"I feel like I took a big stand against my parents when I decided to get my master's in library science. I went out on my own, walked away from their money, and told them I'd be making my own choices. Since then, it feels like I've failed. I'm not a librarian, I didn't make it in the city, and I'm starting over in this teeny tiny town, crawling to my best friend because I can't be on my own," I ramble. "I've always had a plan, but when my last plan ran out of steps, I just kind of kept falling forward until I got here."

"Are you happy?" Alice asks.

"At this moment? No."

"*Were* you happy?"

I think back over my time in Wilcox Grove. I've felt more grounded here than I have anywhere else. "Yes. But—"

"But nothing. What do you want?"

I've been asking myself the same question since yesterday evening and again this morning. I think I know, but the answer is scary.

Jake comes inside, but I answer anyway.

"I want to stay in Wilcox Grove, and I want to make things right with Scott."

"Then, do that," Alice says.

I smile. "Maybe the plan can be not having a plan. Maybe it can be just having a next step. I think my next step is going next door and talking to Scott."

"Actually," Jake interjects. "Scott isn't next door."

Both Alice and I snap our heads to him.

"Scott left to go camping and clear his head."

CHAPTER 40

Scott

I'm lying down in the grass, staring at the pristine, blue sky, and ignoring the stick jabbing into my back when I hear the distinct sound of something approaching through the forest and jolt upright. I haven't seen a soul since coming out here, and there hasn't even been anybody camping close enough for me to hear. I suppose that's unlikely to be the case for long in the middle of a gorgeous July. It's *probably* just some other campers.

Another sound comes from between the trees, making me just a little bit uneasy. Campers should be coming down the path, not through the trees. Better safe than sorry, I slowly get to my feet and retrieve the knife I'd intended to use to make lunch before I abandoned the endeavor for some dried fruit. My phone is in my other hand with the rangers' station number already punched in. The sound becomes a racket as whatever's approaching picks up its speed.

All at once, a panicked mass of person and jumbled gear comes crashing over a bush. I blink repeatedly, unable to believe what I'm seeing.

"Piper?" I eventually call out at the lump of bags and limbs on the ground before me.

Her head whips around to me.

"Oh, thank god," she breathes. "I've been wandering for hours."

"What the hell are you doing here?" I'm still not entirely convinced she *is* here.

"Jake helped me figure out what to bring and talked to somebody about paperwork and I don't even know what and then brought me here this morning. We had a big ol' fight because he wanted to take me all the way here, but I had to do this myself. So he begrudgingly showed me a map and told me how to get to you, but then there was a sound, and I ran and tripped and fell down a hill or a ravine,—what even is the difference—and I thought I could figure out where I was going, and then I was convinced I was going to die, and there were more sounds and animals and bugs, and I scared several other campers, I'm sure, and then I ran again, and now I'm here." I don't think Piper breathes once while she tells the whole story.

"I didn't ask *how* you got here," I snap. Seeing her makes the hurt flare up. "I asked *what* you're doing here."

"I'm…" Piper looks like she's going to apologize again, and I really don't think I can bear it. She must see it on my face because she closes her mouth before trying again. "I'm camping."

That response might be even more ridiculous than another apology.

"You're *what*?"

"I'm camping," she repeats. Her eyes fall to the knife in my hand. "I see you've upgraded your weapon of choice against an intruder. Much more effective than a shampoo bottle."

I quickly shove both my knife and phone away.

"I don't think this is the time for jokes or walks down memory lane, Piper." My voice is cold, colder than I expected. I don't even recognize the sound. Piper winces, and guilt burns bright in my chest. "What are you really doing here?"

I watch as Piper drags an enormous backpack that I recognize as Jake's camping bag and the sack for his tent through the dirt to the empty space behind me, just on the other side of an enormous tree trunk laid down to help delineate campsites. Mine and hers are meant for multiple families camping together, so they're kind of like adjoining rooms in a hotel rather than separate spaces.

"I told you. I'm camping," she says, looking at a small square of wood nailed to a tree at the edge of the clearing to check the site number. "And this is my campsite."

I'm going to kill Jake. I can't believe he helped her come here. This is insane.

"This isn't funny. You know nothing about camping, and this can be dangerous. Do you even have the right provisions and gear?"

Stop caring. This isn't your problem.

"I will figure it out," she says stubbornly, dragging the tent poles and tarp out of their bag. "Jake gave me the CliffsNotes version and sent me with some books on how not to die, and he basically packed for me, so I've probably got something useful in that bag."

As if it were a paid actor, the enormous bag slowly tips over, the small pot tied to the outside clanging loudly when it knocks against a rock.

"Fine." I huff. "Have at it."

I drag myself off the ground and shut myself in my own tent.

As soon as I'm inside, I want to leave again. It's stuffy and hot, even with the vents open. It's a comfortable tent usually, but it feels small and confining right now. But I can't go back out there. My pride won't let me. I unzip the side that faces away from where Piper is and lie back on my air mattress, which I had pulled inside this morning after sleeping outside again last night. I consider just packing up and going home, but I'm not quite cruel enough to leave Piper out here alone, though I'm also not nice enough to offer her a ride back yet.

My last couple nights of crappy sleep catch up to me, and when I wake, the sky has a beautiful golden hour glow. I must have been out for hours. I emerge from my tent and resist the urge to immediately check on Piper. I hear noises from that way, so she's either still there or I've now got woodland creature neighbors.

I walk over to the fire area, dropping in fresh wood and kindling. I snatch up my saucepan and fill it at the nearby spigot that provides fresh water. On my way back, I stupidly look away from my own feet for just a second and catch Piper watching me. She got her tent pitched. Good for her.

"Drinking water faucet is five minutes that way." I jerk my thumb over my shoulder, pointing down the little path. There. I helped her not die tonight. "Oh, and make sure you put *any* food, including leftovers, in the—"

"Bear box," Piper finishes for me, holding up a guidebook for this park and pointing to the nearby food locker.

I just grunt and sit near my pile of sticks with my back to Piper. I wonder if this is what it feels like to be Jake. Not talking leaves a lot of time for me to sit with my own thoughts. Not sure I'm a fan of that.

After I get a fire going, I wait for my water to boil so I can cook up some pasta. I pull out one of those Sudoku books you get at an airport to pass the time. I'll now do anything to distract myself from the woman behind me.

Once my pasta is cooked and sauced, and I'm spooning some of it into a bowl, I allow myself a glance over to Piper's site.

"Are you eating?" I shout over. Angry caring? I definitely feel like Jake now.

Piper holds up the apple she just bit into. "I'm good."

"There's pasta in the pot. Either you eat it, or I throw it out." I turn my back on her again and move away to sit near the tent opening, where I can still keep an eye on the flames to make sure nothing gets out of control while pretending to ignore that whole direction.

The fifteen minutes of tense silence I spend eating are awkward as fuck, but eventually Piper comes over with her own bowl and fork.

"Thank you," she reluctantly mutters.

I ignore her.

"We should talk," she says after she's emptied the small pot.

"Piper, don't…" I warn.

I can't. Not yet.

"We both fucked up," she pushes.

"We did," I agree, turning more toward her. "But I never thought you'd do what you did. I honestly don't think you thought you would either, but you did, and here we are."

She just stares back at me. I know I'm right.

"Look, I offered to share my food, not my time." And I turn back around. Eventually, her footsteps fade away as she goes back to her side of the log. I finish eating, extinguish the fire, wash out the pot and my bowl, and retreat to my tent. It's barely dark but today needs to be over.

CHAPTER 41

Piper

Between the bugs, the random noises, and my guilt, I don't think I sleep for more than a few minutes at a time all night. Every crack, creak, and whisper has me convinced some rabid animal is going to descend on my tent and tear both me and it to shreds. And the guilt, the anger? Well, they're self-explanatory.

Maybe coming here was a huge mistake. Hearing how angry Scott is with me has rekindled the betrayal I felt from him. I think I hoped he'd want to make up as much as I did.

I sit up on top of my sleeping bag and drop my head into my hands. I'm exhausted, cranky, and itchy. I'm also feeling just a little bit hopeless. I groan and flop back onto my little pillow. The thin air mattress beneath me squeaks pathetically and provides little cushion.

Ow.

The sudden movement seems to have startled something outside the tent because there's suddenly furious scratching against the nylon behind me. I basically teleport out of the other side of the tent. It would appear squawking is what I do when I get scared by… a squirrel.

I watch as it sprints to a tree and disappears up into the branches.

"You good?" Scott asks, smirking. Apparently, all I need to do to improve his mood is humiliate myself.

"Yup!" I call back. "That was just my attempt at a loon call."

"It needs work." The smile falls, and he turns his back to me yet again.

I guess I'm up for the day, so I retrieve a cup and go brush my teeth by the spigot before filling up my water bottle. Then I clean up with a camping wipe inside my tent. It's hot and humid, and this is the closest I'm going to get to a shower for however long I stay out here. I take a breath, dress, slather on sunscreen and bug spray, and find a lovely private bush for… other reasons.

Camping is *greaaaaat.*

My heart is racing from my brief venture into the woods, so I'm huffing and frustrated when I get back to my tent. I don't notice Scott standing beside it until I've nearly reached him. I stop dead in my tracks.

"Come on, Piper. Let me take you home. You're clearly miserable out here." He sounds exhausted. I think it might be worse than when he was yelling.

"You're ready to go?" I ask.

"I'll come back after I drop you off. If you don't get lost, it's not very far and won't take too long." His eyes are looking in my direction, but I can tell he's not seeing me. He doesn't want to.

I'm not going anywhere. Not like this.

"No thank you." I crouch down so I can get some hand sanitizer from my bag and then pull out my solar-powered battery pack. I'm looking around for the best direct sunlight when Scott finally answers.

"What do you mean *no thank you*?"

"It's pretty self-explanatory. Thank you for the offered ride, but I'm not leaving." I plop down onto a tree stump and brush my hands on my thighs. I pull a paperback out of my bag. "This is lovely reading weather."

"Well, that's just great," Scott huffs before retreating. He pulls out a tackle box and a fishing rod from who knows where. "I'm going fishing. Don't die while I'm gone."

He stomps away before I can answer. He's angry again and out of patience for my stubbornness, but he still cares. A tiny kernel of hope sputters to life in my chest.

I feel anxious while Scott is away. Being in the woods is easier when he's nearby, even if he's on his side of our little clearing, just seeing him helps. Right now, with him wherever he is for however long he plans to be there, I'm jumpy. Knowing he enjoys nature and does this all the time doesn't really help since it's logical and my brain is comfortably vacationing in illogical right now.

I'm about to climb a tree (I cannot climb a tree) when Scott finally returns, rod over his shoulder and presumably a fish wrapped in paper in his hand. I do my best not to react even when I feel a crushing pressure lift from my shoulders. I continue *not* looking when Scott cleans and guts the fish, *right there*. But it does kind of smell good once he has it sizzling in that little pot over the new fire he's built up.

I'm perfectly content with my dried mangos, pretzels, and carrot sticks, but just like last night, Scott leaves some of his food behind.

"Yours." He just says one word this time and again moves away from the fire, like he needs to maintain some minimum distance between us.

I don't know if it's an olive branch or just reluctant aid so he doesn't end up with my corpse to deal with, but I accept the fish nonetheless.

"Thank you," I say as I take the piece and scurry back to my side. Maybe because Scott just caught this, I'm surprised it looks so normal. With the crispy edges and the spices Scott added—of course he brought spices—it's delicious.

The afternoon and evening pass much the same way the morning did. Scott and I ignore each other, keeping to our sides, and Scott feeds me. The next day we rinse and repeat. He goes somewhere in the morning, shares his canned soup with me for lunch, stays quiet in the afternoon, and feeds me again in the evening.

This time, I leave the baggy of dried mangoes when I thank him before retreating to my corner again. He thanks me back.

By my third full day of camping, I'm feeling pretty damn gross, but I don't jump at as many sounds. I've learned many of them are just the music of nature, and none have been followed by a bear charging from between the trees, so that's good. The sun is intense midday, but it's not so bad in the shade. The air smells fresh and the patches of grass are cool and soft. When it's light and Scott is at his campsite, I almost breathe normally.

After collecting some more pasta from Scott's fire in the evening, I stop at the divider log and sit on it. I catch Scott watching me from the corner of my eye, and I wonder if he'll tell me to move further away.

He doesn't.

I stay there after it gets dark, not even retrieving or turning on my emotional support lantern. The only light around us comes from the dying embers of Scott's fire. I look up and see the sky like I've never seen it in real life before. It looks like a painting with how many stars blanket the deep navy above me.

I gasp when a light flashes across the sky. Scott is immediately on his feet, looking at me.

"Sorry," I say and point up. "I think I saw a shooting star."

He follows my finger and looks to the sky.

Somewhere out of sight, somebody starts playing an acoustic

guitar. The notes are faint, but beautiful. It's cooler at night, and a gentle breeze tickles my skin.

"I think I get it now, why you like nature so much." I speak quietly, not wanting to disturb our peaceful little bubble, but I know Scott hears me.

I don't know why, but I start to cry.

He doesn't say anything, but he walks over and sits on the log beside me.

CHAPTER 42

Scott

Piper whispers good night before heading into her tent and zipping it shut. Sharing a quiet moment like we had tonight felt like a turning point. Like Eli suggested, I've been thinking a lot about what I can't live without. It hasn't been easy to sort out how to move forward with Piper in light of her reservations, me projecting on her for weeks, and both of our fuckups, but I think her being here means she'd like to try.

Her determination to stay out here has hit me hard. Not only do I know how much unease the great outdoors gives her, but I've been downright cold to her, mean, and she's persevered. Since that first day, she also hasn't tried to explain herself, ask for an apology (which she certainly deserves), or even talk to me. She's been incredibly patient and committed. The significance of that isn't lost on me.

I drag my hand down my face.

It's clear how much she regrets what happened a few days ago, and I haven't forgotten I fucked up first. With each day she stays out here with me, I feel my anger slip further away. I think I get why Piper's defense mechanism was to distance herself from me, from us, and I have myself to blame for pressuring her so hard. That doesn't justify things, but it does help me understand them. The fact she pulled herself out of those habits before following through isn't nothing.

This woman turns me upside down. I want to believe her, to trust her. I want to beg for her forgiveness, convince her to trust me. I just want—

A coyote howling pierces through the silence. It's not nearby, but the volume of the cry is jarring. I hear a muffled yelp from the darkness on Piper's side of the campsite. I think our canine friend woke her up, if she'd even fallen asleep at all.

Another coyote howls in response to the first, and another.

In the bright moonlight, I can just barely see Piper's tent jostling around. The swishing sound of the nylon is unmistakable.

I stand and check the fire. I've already cleaned up after dinner, and the fire went out, but I pour water on the dirt and turn the ashes with my small shovel anyway.

Piper's tent has stilled. Maybe she'll fall back asleep. I step over the log and listen, just in case. All is silent until I hear a quiet sob.

I'm moving before I can think better of it.

"Piper?" I say when I'm outside her tent. "Are you alright?"

"Uh-huh," she lies.

I turn to go back to my own tent but stop.

I need to mind my own business. She's fine. We're safe here.

I pause. I know she's got to be scared in there.

It's now or never. I turn back to the tent.

"Piper, I'm coming in there."

She doesn't object, so I unzip it and shine my phone's flashlight inside.

Piper's sleeping bag is open and laying flat on top of her little mattress—it's too warm to sleep inside it. She's curled in a ball on one side, squeezing her knees to her chest, and the tears on her face shine in the night.

I turn off the flashlight and get down on my knees so I can crawl inside and zip the door closed behind me. I lie down beside Piper, but don't touch her.

"Coyotes are normal around here. Those ones aren't nearby, and they're not coming this way. That's just how they communicate," I explain.

Piper sniffles loudly.

"I'm sorry I'm so fucked in the head," she whispers, the words breaking around her choked sobs.

My heart cracks at the sound. I turn my head toward her even though it's too dark to see each other.

"You are *not* fucked in the head. It's ok to be afraid. The fact that you came out here has been incredibly brave."

"Not just about that," she murmurs, still fighting to get the words out. "About everything. What I did. I'm fucked in the head. And I'm *so,* so sorry."

"You aren't fucked in the head," I say again. I pause and take a deep breath, making a conscious decision for who I want to be. "I forgive you. And I'm sorry, too. I should never have breached your privacy or broken your trust. I've been pressuring you for a while, not realizing that trying to hold you close was pushing you away."

"You shouldn't forgive me." It sounds like she's crying harder.

My eyes have adjusted a little to the darkness, and I can see the outline of her body. I find her hand clamped against her shin and pull her fingers back, so I can slip her palm into mine.

"Well, I do."

"I forgive you, too," she whispers back.

+ ⁺ ✦ ⁺ +

Like I usually do when camping, I wake up with the sun. Opening my eyes, I see the inside of an unfamiliar tent, and I remember where I fell asleep. I look over at Piper and find her still curled up on her side, facing me now and still clutching my hand. I slowly extract my fingers, careful not to wake her, and silently exit the tent, making sure to close it behind me.

I clean up, change, and have some breakfast while I wait for Piper to wake. I'm collapsing the poles for my tent when Piper emerges from hers, stretching and looking toward me.

"Hi," she says tentatively.

"Good morning," I say back. I meant it when I said I forgave her, but it's not like either of us can just forget the last few days.

"What are you doing?" she asks. "No fishing today?"

"No, not today." I begin carefully folding the material for my tent so it'll fit back into its bag. "I think it's time we both go back home, don't you?"

"Yeah?" she asks, doe-like.

"Yeah. I know *you're* fine out here, but I'm ready for a proper shower."

"Ok. I'll pack up." I think she sounds better, too.

I begin working the tent into its bag. It's always a battle, no matter what I do.

After some time and work, we're both packed up, and I've shown Piper how to make sure we leave nature as close to how we found it as possible. We don't talk as we walk back to the car, partially because our bags are heavy, but partially because I expect neither of us quite knows how to act right now.

We've both given our forgiveness, but what does that mean? We can't just dive back into where we left off. That feels disingenuous.

The drive back is similarly quiet and awkward, but at least it isn't hostile. As we bump along on the gravel leading up to the front of the house, I see Jake come out of his house. With his brow furrowed and his arms crossed, he looks shockingly like how I remember Dad.

"You should take first shower," I say to Piper after I park in front of our garage. "I'm going to go let Jake know we're back."

"Ok." She nods.

I wait until she's safely inside before I walk around the front of the house and meet Jake on the lawn. Ignoring the way I smell, he pulls me into his arms for one of the safest hugs I've come to know.

"You were gone longer than I expected," Jake says as he releases me. "I thought you'd be bringing Piper back within a day."

"I tried," I reply. "She wouldn't have it."

"What happened out there?" he asks like he's asking about a trip to an alternate universe. For Piper, that might be what the last few days felt like.

I tell him everything, and when I get to Piper's unexpected arrival, I feel proud talking about her determination to tough it out.

"So, everything is back to normal with her?" He nods toward the house.

"Definitely not, but I think we can get there."

He looks at me intensely now. "Are you sure you want that? After everything?"

I shrug. The answer is simple really.

"I love her."

When I go back to work, Hannah asks if I'm ok but doesn't otherwise pry about my time off. I'm thankful. It didn't escape the eagle eyes of this town that Scott and I both disappeared for nearly a week, but nobody seems to know why.

I've heard several rumors, including that we went to see my parents, that we were undercover and investigating who has been vandalizing the bookstore, and that we were invited to an exclusive sex club. Taking a page out of Grateful Bob's book of storytelling, I've confirmed every single one of them.

Susan seems to have noticed my absence, too. I have three unread emails from her when I open the store laptop. She's very disappointed in my lack of professionalism by not answering all three emails immediately, even though I had an out of office response up, especially considering the lackluster statistics I've been able to offer regarding Literary Lake. She also thinks Wilcox Grove seems "dumpy," but Mia is nonetheless considering a stop here, in spite of her recommendations. She'll let me know what the author decides.

I don't care how much author ass I'm supposed to kiss in this industry. I hate Susan. She's a grade-A bitch. If Mia is anything like her, I'm not sure I want her at our store anyway. I wish I could just *talk* to her directly and see if we can work something out. Inspired by my chat with Alice, I send a passive aggressive response back to Susan and put her out of my mind.

It takes a couple of days, but Scott and I do find a new normal. It's friendly, hesitant, shy. We are each working to earn back the trust of the other. It'll take time.

I decide I want to show him I'm ready for more, even though I'm not entirely sure what that means. I'm new at this. So, on my first day off since our camping trip, I hide in my room like a coward and try to edit a judgmental and factually inaccurate romance-bashing article that has been assigned to me. It's torture.

A soft tap on my open door catches my attention.

"Hey," Scott says. "I'm sorry to bother you, but I was wondering if you wanted to come cook with me."

He stays at the doorway, not crossing the threshold, and I think it's his way of respecting my space.

"I want nothing more." I slam my laptop closed and hop off the bed to follow him downstairs.

It feels like a good sign my acceptance still makes him smile.

In the kitchen, I learn Scott takes his lasagna very seriously. That's why we're starting in the morning by making our own meat sauce from scratch. I briefly wonder if we're going to churn our own cheese, too, but I see tubs of ricotta in the fridge when I grab the fresh basil.

As I stand at the counter, quickly chopping tomatoes in half, my gazpacho kerfuffle feels like a lifetime ago. Keeping my eyes on my knife, I take a deep breath and start sharing.

"My freshman year of high school, my neighbor and I stole her older brother's motorcycle for a little joyride, and I crashed it in a ditch. I broke my arm and ended up having to work for their mom in her dentist office for months to pay them back for the repairs."

Scott had stopped working when I started my little story, likely wondering what the hell I was talking about. I hear the sound of him resuming moving around the kitchen, and silly as it sounds, I swear I can feel him smile.

"Oh yeah?" he says. "Did that ignite a need for speed?"

"Absolutely not." I laugh. "It was horrifying. I haven't gone near a motorcycle since. I'm not saying it's off the table, but I'm fine with cars for now."

When the room gets quiet again, it's a little bit less tense than before. Scott is leaning against the counter when I straighten from sliding the sheet of tomatoes into the oven to roast.

"Tell me another story," he requests. His smile is shy, and his eyes are hopeful.

So, I do. And then another and another. I tell him about my randomly-assigned freshman year roommate in college and her strict list of roommate rules. I recount my one experience with acting, a school play when I was ten, which ended when I tripped and fell off the stage halfway through opening night. I tell him about the ducks, a bonded male and female, that would visit our backyard pool every summer while I was growing up.

I want him to know everything.

Later, when I'm layering the sauce, cheese, and noodles, Scott comes to check on my technique. He cringes.

"May I?" he asks like I'm the one in charge here. I pass the spoon to him.

"If we're going to have a chance at this friendship working, we're going to have to work on your lasagna layering because this"—he gestures with the spoon—"is not it." The critique is playful, and his smile is infectious.

I think this could be the first time he's outright told me I'm doing something wrong in weeks. The honesty is delightfully refreshing.

"Ok, hotshot. Show me how it's done."

So, he does.

And for the record, when we finally eat it later, the lasagna tastes fucking delicious.

Scott and I continue like that for a few weeks. We cook, we talk, we both share parts of ourselves that were private before. I even show him some short stories I've written and never told anybody about. I've never been this open with anybody before, not even Alice. And Scott has been more aware of himself and what he says. He follows my lead, asks my opinion, and listens when I complain, without trying to rescue me.

It feels like I'm giving Scott little treasures, pieces of myself. I watch him cherish them and protect them. I take little risks, and time and time again, he shows me that it's safe to do so.

Still, we've stayed distinctly on the "friends" side of the line. It's like that big old log from our campsite followed us home and has remained as a barrier between us. I can see this is Scott letting me have the driver's seat, but I'm ready to try for an us again. I just don't know how.

Alice is listening to me fret while I place orders with our different publishers at a café table.

"You could plan something for his birthday," she suggests, and I stop typing.

"His what?"

"His birthday? You know, the anniversary of the day he was born?" She's looking at me like I'm nuts.

How do I not know when his birthday is?

"When is it?"

Alice hesitates, and I know I won't like the answer.

"Tuesday?"

"*Shit*. That's four days away!" I could have missed it if Alice hadn't said something.

I feel badly holing up in my room all weekend after that, but I have some urgent planning to get done, and I can't have Scott finding out about it. I am calling in every favor I've accrued and some I haven't. Scott is a social person, and I want to make him feel like a king.

Scott knocks once to ask if I'm alright. I assure him everything's great. He doesn't press.

On Tuesday morning, Alice picks me up to give me a ride to the bookstore. I pretend not to know what day it is and feel like pond scum for not even wishing Scott a happy birthday before I leave. My ignorance is key to the plan.

Around lunch, Alice gets a text from Jake saying he's picked up Scott to distract him with "birthday hangout stuff" far away from the bookstore. With the all-clear, we draw the curtains over the front windows and prepare the store for Scott's surprise party that evening.

The café works on dozens of cupcakes, and we divide and conquer blowing up balloons, setting up a photo booth, hooking up the projector, and testing the slideshow of Scott-through-the-years photos. After forcing Scott to keep secrets from the people he loves, I want this party to be as boisterous and energetic as the man himself. No more hiding.

I'm standing at the register, working on my personal surprise when Mads comes up to me with the cordless phone.

"Piper, I've got Mia's manager on the phone, and she does not sound happy," she says urgently, but quietly, a hand pressed over the microphone.

"I don't think she knows how to be happy." I sigh. "She's going to deny us. I just know it."

After taking her off hold, I can't even greet Susan before she dives into her rude and insulting denial of our request to participate in Mia's tour next month. I'm in the middle of thanking her for her time when she hangs up on me.

Mads is looking at me expectantly, but I shake my head.

"Mia isn't coming," I say. "We'll have to find another book tour and try again."

"I'm sorry." A sweet voice draws both of our attention. A young woman stands on the other side of the counter, holding the hand of the most darling little girl. "I hate to eavesdrop, but are you talking about Mia Lane? Is she coming here?"

"Unfortunately not. Her manager couldn't work us into the schedule." I feel like I failed.

"Ugh, that woman is the devil."

Huh?

"I went to college with Mia, and we're still good friends," the woman continues as the girl begins twirling back and forth. "I'd bet good money Susan didn't even ask Mia about coming here. If she said she did, she lied. You should try emailing Mia directly at her personal address. I can give it to you. Then you can at least know for sure what's been going on."

Mads and I look at one another, dumbstruck.

"I don't want to invade her space," I say. "Are you sure that would be ok?"

"I'm positive. I can also let her know to look out for your message if it would be helpful."

We profusely thank the woman, Iris, for offering her help, and invite both her and her daughter, Samantha, to come back for Scott's party later.

It feels like things are turning around—everything is going well for Scott's party, and we have a new hope for Mia—until Jake walks into the store.

"Scott gave me the slip," he says. "He said he needed to do something for a client and went back home. I don't know how to get him here later without it being obvious we're up to something."

"It's ok. Inconvenient, but not the end of the world. Leave it to me." I never make a plan without having a backup.

A couple hours later, the store is closed, and it's dark outside. For the umpteenth time, I tell everybody to kindly shut *up*, and I dial Scott's number.

"Hey, is something wrong?" he greets.

"No, not really. Well, kind of. Alice forgot she was supposed to pick me up from the bookstore, and she's on a date with Jake. Everybody else already left, and I don't know what to do."

I hear Scott grabbing his keys and closing the side door. It's working.

"I'm already on my way," he says, starting the car.

"Thank you, Scott," I gush. "I'm going to wait inside, just in case, ok?"

"Sounds good. I'll be there in like ten."

I hang up. "Places, everyone! He's on his way!"

I flick the lights off, so the store looks closed and abandoned.

Maybe five minutes later, there's a crash from behind the store. Alice, Jake, Hannah, and I all turn toward the noise.

"What was that?" Alice hisses.

"I don't know," I whisper back. "There's no way Scott's here already."

There's another crash, and a few other people start whispering about the noises.

"We'll go check it out," Jake offers, elbowing Eli to get his attention.

"No," I protest. "What if you miss Scott?"

"He'll forgive us. What if it's Troy?"

I catch Hannah's gaze, and she shrugs.

"Ok, but hurry up and be careful," I relent.

I think we collectively hold our breath as the two men move as quickly and quietly to the back door.

Suddenly, the world erupts in noise. Everybody jumps to their feet, coming out of hiding places as crashes, bangs, and swearing echo from behind the store. Alice runs to the back door, calling Jake's name, but the guys are already coming back inside when the lights flick on, Troy and a friend held among them.

"What is going *on* in here?" Scott calls from the front of the store, his hand on the light switch.

All heads turn back toward him and silence fills the room.

"Surprise!" we shout in unison.

Scott

The explosion of sound in the room nearly knocks me off my feet. I think the whole town is packed into this bookstore. Front and center is Piper. I expect to see my brother beside her, but I think he's part of whatever's happening at the back of the store.

What I don't expect is for Piper to run forward and throw her arms around my neck, right in front of everybody, but the smell of her shampoo, floral and sweet, is all around me, and I'd know the feel of her in my arms anywhere. I've *missed* her.

"Happy birthday, Scott," she whispers in my ear before pulling back. "I'm so sorry to hug and dash, but I think Eli has Troy in a headlock."

She turns to go, but I clasp her hand. "I'll come with you."

A wall of people stands between us and the top of Jake's head with everybody trying to see what's going on. After attempting to find a path and failing, Piper cups her hands around her face.

"Coming through!" she shouts. "Mingle for a few. We'll start the party as soon as we can."

Mads hurries over to a laptop and starts some music. Bless her.

Like the Red Sea, the crowd parts for us and Piper takes my hand so we can squeeze through. Sure enough, Eli has Troy in a headlock, and Jake is standing over that woman he's always with, Lauren, just inside the back door. Hannah and Leslie are with them, neither looking too pleased, and it sounds like Hannah is on the phone with the police.

"Yeah. We have them by the back door," she says into his cell.

"We weren't doing anything!" Troy bellows.

"Oh, shut up," Eli snaps. "You were literally jimmying the lock."

"Allen and Mike are on their way over," Hannah says as she hangs up.

After that, we all just kind of look at one another, not sure what to do while we wait. Every few seconds, Troy pushes against Eli's arm, trying to catch him off guard, but Eli's not budging.

"Well, happy birthday, Scott," Alice says, patting me on the back. That triggers a wave of birthday wishes from Jake, Eli, Hannah, and Leslie, too. It's hilariously chipper for the weird standoff we're in back here. Another minute later, we hear sirens out front.

Once Allen and Mike make their way over to us, Eli releases Troy, who makes a big show of claiming Eli attacked him and Lauren without reason.

Since there's basically a whole town worth of witnesses to vouch for the fact the two of them were breaking in, it's not looking good for them. Plus, Mike finds Troy's backpack full of fireworks, and we highly doubt he was coming to celebrate my birthday.

Jake slings his arm over my shoulders when he comes to stand beside me. Piper, on my other side, squeezes the hand she's still holding in support. While Troy's most recent targets might be this store and the café, he's been bullying me since grade school, and even Piper has seen some of that.

Mike starts taking photographs as Allen leads Troy and Lauren out to the police car. Troy catches my eye as he passes by and sneers.

"You know, watching Troy get taken out of here in cuffs might make this the best birthday ever," I say smugly.

"Justice is sweet, little brother." Jake sighs.

Once Mike finishes up, he comes over to the cluster of us that have been waiting. "You guys should go back to the party. We'll get things sorted, and whoever wants to make a statement can come by the station tomorrow. We'll at least need ones from Jake and Eli and whoever else directly saw Troy break in. Hannah and Leslie, you can also pursue any civil claims you'd like regarding damages sustained by the store."

The radio on Mike's shoulder crackles, and I think I hear Allen's voice say, "attempted arson."

It's not a good day to be Troy Basel.

Mike shakes our hands, the picture of professionalism, and I feel guilty for being a dick to him at the fair. "Happy birthday, Scott," he says when he gets to me.

"Thanks, Mike," I reply earnestly.

CHAPTER 45

Once the excitement of stopping crime passes, the place becomes a full party. I start making my way around the room with Piper by my side, thanking people for coming and snagging a cupcake.

"Hey Scotland. Happy Birthday," Ila says before giving me a hug.

"Scotland?" Piper asks on a laugh as we continue through the store.

"Ila full-names everybody. Years ago, she decided Scott was short for Scotland, and that was that," I explain before another shouted "Happy Birthday!" draws my attention.

As I look around, I spot Eli trying to talk up some woman I don't recognize. She's clearly giving him shit for something. Eli doesn't get shot down often, so the visual is amusing.

Grateful Bob brushes past, squeezing my arm and giving me a wink when he sees Piper standing beside me. Even Penny showed up.

Some of my favorite songs play in the background, and gigantic pictures from throughout my life are scrolling on the projector screen. In the midst of some very happy attendees, I'm hit with the realization of everything that must have gone into planning tonight.

"Piper, I can't believe you did all this," I say, bent close to her ear so she can hear me over the cacophony around us. "I didn't even know you knew it was my birthday."

"Yeah, what was the big idea with you not telling me?" She smacks me in the arm as she scolds me, and it's playful. The feeling jolts through me. I've felt like a live wire since she hugged me. I think I've been starved for her touch, and I'm thankful she doesn't seem to mind sticking with me today.

"I guess it just never came up?" I shrug. In actuality, as it got closer, I couldn't figure out a good way to say something without making a big deal out of it. There have been more important things on my mind, like proving to Piper that I care about *her* and not the idea of her. I gently guide her to the quietest place I can find in this building, a roped off area by the laptop Mads used to start the music earlier.

I pull her close, so I can lower my voice, and her big, brown eyes bore into mine.

"Piper, you mean the world to me. Not just because of this party or because I got swept up by you last year. I think you're strong, smart, loyal. I see you fight for what you want and stand up for your friends. You're easy to talk to and the most fun to be around. I am so sorry I took our friendship for granted and over-stepped before. I promise I never will again. I will be whatever you need me to be."

"Thank you so much for saying all those things," Piper says, her eyes shining. "But before I answer, there's one more part to tonight that I need to do."

Piper shifts nervously on her feet and glances around.

"Ok. Ok, now is good," she says cryptically. She pivots toward the laptop, tapping something on it to cut the music. She then picks up a microphone from beside it and clicks a couple more things before going to stand beside the screen that has been showing pictures of my life.

"Good evening everyone, and thank you for coming here to help celebrate Scott's birthday." She claps and everybody cheers with her. Her voice is wavering, though, and I wonder what's up. Piper isn't generally a nervous public speaker.

The picture on the screen changes, and I do a double take. It's one from the two of us in Kathy's studio, covered in clay. Is that supposed to be showing? I look around the room, and everybody's eyes are on Piper and that screen.

Piper takes a slow breath and continues.

"When I came to Wilcox Grove, I was desperately looking for a safe place to land after blowing up a large part of the life I knew. My best friend, Alice, did the same thing last year, and since it worked out so well for her, I thought I'd try it out. Upon my unplanned arrival, I found a welcoming kindness, understanding, and acceptance I have known very little of so far in my life. And I found that all in Scott. Of course, that was after he'd hit me with a flying shampoo bottle, but don't hold that against him. I *had* just broken into his house."

Several chuckles bounce around the room, and Alice, who has materialized with Jake near me, elbows me in the side for attacking her bestie. I hardly feel it, though. I can't believe what Piper is doing right now. The images behind her regularly change from one moment to the next, all of the two of us. Cooking, reading, sitting on the couch, on the boat…

"I am, and have always been, unapologetically loud, standoffish, inconsistent, anxious, and generally a loose cannon. Maybe Jake dropped Scott on his head when he was a baby, because in the face of all those qualities, Scott has never judged me. He took me into his house and let me make it my home. This unlikely landlord-slash-roommate quickly became one of my closest friends, sneaking his way into my heart by taking the time to accept me in a way most have shied away from. He welcomed my quirks and showed me incredible patience, never once considering anything owed in return."

Piper is standing up there, laying herself bare, putting herself at the mercy of this entire town, but her eyes stay locked on mine.

"Several weeks ago, Scott and I began seeing each other, and he kept that private solely because I asked him to, going to great lengths to jump through every silly hoop I insisted I needed. It's taken me much longer than it should have, but I now know I don't need any hoops or rules. I just need you, Scott Preston. I love you so much. If you'll have me, I'm yours. Happy Birthday."

The room bursts into cheers and shouts of "happy birthday" all around me. I feel frozen until I catch Piper discretely wipe her eye. In a few large steps, I'm before her, swinging her into my arms and crushing her against me. Her arms latch around me, and she buries her face in my neck.

I set her down and take her face in my hands.

"You're stuck with me Piper Price. I love you, too." And I kiss her for all the world to see.

CHAPTER 46

Piper

ONE MONTH LATER

"But are the gluten free cookies clearly marked? I cannot be poisoning somebody tonight." I know I've already confirmed all the snacks, including that the allergy-and dietary-restriction-friendly ones are clearly marked, but I need somebody to confirm it again, just one more time.

"Princess, are you doing ok?" Scott sounds cautious, speaking very calmly. It's possible I am acting just a little bit feral.

"Yeah, I'm good. I'm good. I just want everything to be perfect."

I look down at my checklist again. Everything has been checked off twice and then crossed out—triple checked. But like, what if something moved itself?

Last month, Iris came through for us and Mia Lane is signing her brand-new thriller at Literary Lake today. Tonight. Now.

I emailed her, and like Iris had predicted, Mia had no clue about my conversations with Susan and was outraged once she learned about Susan's behavior. I guess Susan lied every time she said Mia was considering something. In actuality, Susan was just jerking me around.

Mia and I spoke on the phone two days after Scott's birthday, and she was the nicest person ever. She was so apologetic about the situation with Susan and was thrilled to figure out a way for her to come up to Wilcox Grove in between her Boston and Chicago tour stops. It's been full steam ahead ever since.

"Piper, I think you should take a seat. Maybe have a glass of water before Mia gets here." Scott is already slowly guiding me to the rows of chairs I have set up facing where Mia's Q&A will happen. I sink into one of them and let Scott begin to rub the tension from my neck and shoulders.

"Mia's here!" Mads gasps from where she's been staring out the front window. I'm back on my feet and by her side in a flash.

I hear Scott's resigned sigh from where I abandoned him, but he knew what he was getting with me.

Mads and I not-so-subtly watch Mia climb out of her car. She's short in size, but I can feel the magnitude of her presence from all the way over here. Her shoulder-length, dark hair has a little wave to it, and her inquisitive eyes give her a look of innocence that matches her five-foot-nothing height. The rest of her, though, is in stark contrast.

She's a curvy bombshell, dressed in a fit-and-flare black dress that stops above her knees with a metal belt that looks like it's made of a chainsaw chain, and has tiny, bloodied chef knives dangling from her ears. Her pearl choker similarly has red crystal beads that look shockingly like blood droplets from a distance. She's rocking fishnet stockings, black ankle booties, and a black glittering clutch.

Said simply, I think she'd give Grateful Bob a run for his money in the "coolest person ever" category.

A young man who looks like a professor in his dress pants, button-up, and black-framed glasses gets out of the car at the same time Iris climbs out of the back seat. The second Iris helps her daughter out of her car seat, Samantha darts to Mia and grabs her hand. Mia's face splits into a grin as she bends to scoop the girl up. I hurry to the door before Mia catches us creeping.

"You must be Piper," Mia says, hurrying to me and pulling me into a one-armed hug, holding Samantha to her other side. I think I'm a full foot taller than she is, even with her in heels, but the power with which Mia carries herself is enigmatic.

"It is so wonderful to meet you in person," I say, fangirling just a little bit. "The entire team is here to see you, and I expect most of the town will be showing up soon." I quickly introduce Hannah and Leslie and all our booksellers.

"I'm just glad this could happen. I don't know if power went to Susan's head or if she was always nuts, but she's no longer working with me," Mia explains as I usher her further inside.

"I want to say I feel badly about getting her fired… but I don't. She was horrible," I admit. Is it the most professional thing to say? No. Is it true? Yes.

Mia barks a laugh. "I don't blame you." She turns to her male companion. "This is my friend, Forrest. I bribed him to help me out on the tour since I kicked Susan out."

Judging by the way Forrest is looking at Mia, I doubt she needed to bribe him at all.

"It's nice to meet you, Forrest. Welcome to Wilcox Grove," I say, shaking his hand.

"Is there a place I can set up Mia's things?" he asks politely. He's quiet and reserved but charming.

"Yes, of course. Mads can help you bring anything in," I offer, and Mads eagerly steps forward.

Mia dreamily watches Forrest head back out to the car before shaking her head sharply and focusing back on me.

Oh?

The rest of the night rushes by in a blur. Mia is the kindest, most gracious woman. She browses and praises our little store and even stays on the floor as guests start flooding in, mingling with as many people as she can. Forrest is never far from her, discretely making himself available for whatever she needs. He seems to read Mia like a book, knowing what she needs before she can even ask for it—a pen, a glass of water, somebody to snap a picture of her with a fan. Eventually Mia and Iris take their seats for the Q&A portion of the night, Samantha sitting beside Forrest in the front row of chairs.

Scott, Hannah, Leslie, and I stand at the back, basking in the success of the evening. As I watch Leslie beside Hannah with only a cane as a mobility aid, I realize my time with Literary Lake might be coming to a close. As if she reads my mind, Leslie reaches out to tap on my arm before jerking her head toward the back office in the café. I follow her over there.

"You have to stay," Leslie blurts the second I close the office door behind us.

"What? Is something wrong with your recovery?"

"No, no. I'm doing great. I just can't come back here and run this bookstore. I will gladly take back any financial stuff, and I can help with ordering or something else sometimes if you want, but I think I'll lose my mind if I'm here full time." Leslie has panic in her eyes and is leaning toward me. "Please tell me you're staying here."

"Leslie, calm down." I feel guilty chuckling at her distress, but it's a little funny. "I knew pretty quickly after coming to Wilcox Grove that I'd be sticking around. And if you and Hannah agree, I'd be thrilled to stay on at Literary Lake."

"We've already discussed it, and Hannah is completely on board." Leslie looks like she might hug me, but she isn't much for touchy-feely stuff. She still reaches out and tightly grips my hand. "We actually want to talk to you about becoming our business partner."

"You what?" I'm in shock.

"Take some time to think about it. Then we can sit down and talk about some different ownership options if you're interested."

My mouth hangs open. I don't know what to say.

"Thank you for everything," Leslie plows on. "Now, let's get back out there so you can see the fruits of your labor."

"Thank… you…" I say reverently.

Scott does a double take when he sees my face on my return. Once I'm back by his side, he leans into me and whispers, "What was that all about?"

"Me staying here indefinitely."

"Oh yeah?" he asks, playing it very cool. "You think you will?"

"I mean, at least until a better offer comes around." I shrug. But I can't even imagine a single thing I'd want more, and I think he knows that.

He reaches around to cup the other side of my face so he can lean in and press a kiss to my cheek. "You're a wicked woman."

I pull my phone from my pocket and take a picture of Mia, Iris, and the large crowd before them. I type out a message to my parents, telling them who she is and about the offer to become an owner of Literary Lake. I'm about to send it when I pause. I save the picture for myself but delete the message, realizing I don't need to chase their approval. I'm happy here.

After the talk, questions from the audience, book signing, more mingling, and snacks, Literary Lake is now void of guests, and I am beat. Mia and Forrest had to unfortunately take off to keep to their tour schedule, but they promised to come back as soon as they can.

Coming down from the high of the night, I look at all the chairs and the mess we need to clean up with dread.

Hannah comes over and pats Scott on the arm. "You two get out of here now," she says.

"Wait, what? No. We'll help clean up," I protest, even as Scott takes my hand and pulls me toward the door.

"I've already cleared this with Hannah. I covered the cost for a cleaning team to come by in the morning and break all this down," Scott says while I look over my shoulder and pitifully wave bye to Hannah. She's cracking up laughing, clearly pleased to have helped surprise me.

"You did? Why?"

"Because you and I are going camping, and I didn't want us to leave even later than we are," Scott says, ushering me into the passenger side of his SUV.

I turn around in my seat, and my heart drops when I see those oversized backpacks sitting on the floor in the back seat. I survived camping with Scott in July, sure, but I'm not eager to get back out there. Seeing the glee all over Scott's face as he circles the front of the car, I plaster a smile on mine. I will do this for him.

I fall asleep once we're on the road and don't wake up again until Scott shakes me to tell me we've arrived. Knowing that front seat chair nap was probably the most comfortable sleep I'll have for a few days, I'm reluctant to open my eyes.

When I finally do, I rub them, because I must be seeing things. We are parked outside of a beautiful, A-frame house. I look around, and we're in the middle of the woods, but there's a light glowing through the glass on the front door. This place has *electricity*.

"Scott," I breathe. "What is this?"

"I call it compromise camping."

He gets out and comes around to open my door, too. I hear an owl softly hooting and the sound of nearby running water. Maybe a river?

"We're in the middle of nature, away from people and light pollution. I can fish in the river, there are a ton of beautiful trails if you want a touch of the outdoors, and there's a place to build a fire out back. But there are also walls, a roof, a bed, and indoor plumbing. What do you think?"

I take his hand and slide off my seat. "I think it's perfect."

We carry our bags inside—the use of the backpacks was solely to trick me—and I want to look around, but Scott leads me right upstairs to the loft space and a beautiful king-sized bed.

"I have one more little surprise," he says, digging through a third suitcase he had hidden in the far back of the car. He pulls out a balled-up piece of black and silver material and tosses it to me.

I shake it out and discover it's a hockey jersey with a silver star logo across the front and Preston sewn across the shoulders on the back.

"It's my old jersey from when I played hockey. You said you wanted something oversized that you could steal, and since that had to fit over all my padding..." he trails off because I've already begun stripping and pull it over my head.

The sleeves cover most of my hands and the hem brushes the tops of my thighs.

"What do you think?" I ask, even though I've got a pretty good idea of what he thinks of me in his jersey from the look in his eyes. Nonetheless, I turn around to give him the full three-hundred-sixty-degree view.

"Oh," he breathes when I face away from him.

I look over my shoulder and see him prowling toward me, his coat already in a pile on the floor. His eyes are trained on his name across my back. He reaches over his shoulder and yanks off his shirt.

"I'm going to need you to get on that bed on all fours for me, princess," he says, and I can feel the lick of his words all the way up my body.

I fold forward to slip off my panties and do as I'm told. The bed is plush and soft beneath my knees.

I feel the mattress shift with the weight of Scott coming up behind me. He flips the hem of his jersey up, gripping a fistful of the material at my lower back.

"I'm going to love seeing my name on your back when I've got my cock buried deep inside you," he growls.

His hand smooths over my exposed ass before he runs two fingers between my lips and presses them inside me.

I'm a *huge* fan of compromise camping.

EPILOGUE

CHRISTMAS EVE

My family and Eli's have been spending Thanksgiving and Christmas Eve together for my whole life. Holidays at the Chambers' house have always been warm and safe, especially after Jake and I lost our parents. Helen and Richard, Eli's parents, never made me or Jake feel like we were intruding. We are part of the family. No questions asked.

Recently, the party seems to keep growing in size. A couple of years ago, Grateful Bob started coming with me and Jake. Then, last year, Alice joined us, and now we have Piper and Waffles, too. To nobody's surprise, Eli's parents are thrilled with the additions. They exude "the more the merrier" energy.

Of course, since Jake and I both have dates now, there is a significant amount of teasing, asking Eli when he's going to settle down.

"Hopefully never," he answers with a smile every time he's asked.

Helen shakes her head at her son but kisses his hair nonetheless as she passes him a mug of hot chocolate. She's a happy woman, with well-worn smile creases on her face and a Santa hat over her bob of silver hair. Richard, a spitting image of Eli twenty-something years in the future, stands beside his wife, a tray with more cocoa in his hands.

As per our tradition, family presents are opened tonight, on Christmas Eve, while Santa presents are saved for Christmas Day. The fireplace is roaring to keep the room extra warm in spite of the frigid wind outside. Instrumental versions of holiday songs play softly around us, and we each take a turn saying what we are thankful for from this past year.

Richard starts us off with a classic. "Health, happiness, and good people to share them with."

Then Helen, "I'm thankful for the people in this room, who I get to spend the holidays with, and I'm thankful that the group keeps growing."

"I'm thankful for the family of loons who chose to nest in my yard last spring. Watching them grow was a blessing." That one is Grateful Bob.

"I'm thankful for friends who are family," Eli says, looking at all of us. He's always been a bit of a sentimental guy.

Piper's eyes are glistening as she says, "I'm thankful for new opportunities in Wilcox Grove, with all of you."

Mine is easy. "I'm thankful for Piper."

Alice scratches behind Waffles's ears. "I'm thankful for this little fella and the home we get to share with Jake."

When it's Jake's turn, he nods to me, and I click my tongue to call Waffles over to me and Piper. Piper wraps an arm around his neck to hold him in place, and Alice watches us with a furrowed brow, peeved that we stole away her baby. We both feign innocence.

That is, until Helen gasps, and Alice follows her line of sight to where Jake is on one knee between Alice and the enormous real fir tree we decorated together after Thanksgiving dinner here.

"Alice, you have shown me a love that I never thought was in the cards for me. You came into my life and turned everything upside down, but there's nothing in this universe that would convince me to turn it back. You said you're thankful for our home, so what do you say to sharing it forever? Will you—"

Before he can even finish the question, Alice launches herself into his arms, throwing both of them to the ground, and screaming "yes" over and over again, with a kiss to his face after each one.

"Ace, you didn't even let me finish asking." Jake laughs, entirely unsurprised by the antics of his now fiancée.

"Ok, ok. Try again," Alice says, relenting on the kisses, but keeping her arms around him and her body sprawled across his.

"Will you marry me, Alice McDermott?" Jake asks from the floor.

"A million times yes," Alice answers him.

Piper, fully crying now, releases Waffles so he can congratulate his parents with sloppy licks all over both of their faces.

Acknowledgments

Wow. Wow wow wow wow wow. Kindergarten-age Kim who loudly proclaimed she was going to grow up and be an author would be so proud of 34-year-old Kim publishing her second book. Like Scotty did after Piper finally said yes to dating, I had to pinch myself to make sure this was real. Sure enough, it is.

I owe the biggest thanks to you, reader, for allowing me to bop along on this bumpy trail of authoring. Your choice to read this book has made it possible for me to continue writing, and for that I will be forever grateful. There are no words for the feeling of seeing somebody choosing to visit Wilcox Grove and get to know these precious characters. You are everything.

Ben, you are my rock, my voice of reason, my strongest cheerleader, and the love of my life. I am grateful for you always and know that without your support, I could never do this. Thank you for making me an unbelievably happy woman. You are my everything, and I love you with all that I am.

Ila, my sister author, my best friend, my Jiminy, my life partner always—you are the missing pieces of my soul, and you heal me every day by existing. Our nonsense fuels me, and I am grateful every damn day that I get to know you. I'm not sure we'll ever figure out a way to describe what we have to others, because I just don't think what we found together is anything shy of extraordinary. I could not and will not do this without you. I love you dearly.

Mads and Jessi, my ride-or-die WAGs. Your support and love

have made my life whole, and our group chat with Ila has likely kept me out of prison. I'm always dreaming of the commune.

Mom and Dad, you are the first and longest-lasting supporters of my writing. Thank you for proudly telling everybody you meet, "My daughter is an author."

Georgianna, thank you for giving out my book like you're Oprah and demanding I give you the next story the second you finish anything I write. Fear of your threats is an effective motivation tool.

Lexy, Robin, Emily, and my ARC readers—thank you for gnawing at the bars of your enclosure, screeching inhumanly, blushing when reading in public, *literally* laughing at loud, falling in love with Wilcox Grove, and allowing me to ruin men for you forever (I blame Scotty entirely for that one). The fact that you *want* to read what I write will never not blow my mind. Your support is my life blood.

Lastly, thank you to another absolutely incredible group of women who helped bring this book to life: Annie, Hannah, Lo, Sam, Grace Elena, Nicole, and Kenzie. You have given me, this book, this world, and these characters your patience and wisdom, lending your invaluable skill to crafting it into what it is now. You've also all dealt with my anxiety, imposter syndrome, and endless questions. You are true treasures.

Content Warnings and Spice Guide

In the Stars Rewritten includes references to the following topics:

Off-page parent death (one from cancer and others from an accident)
Off-page mention of parent with dementia
Self-depreciation
Struggles with self-worth and self-image
Anxiety
Self-sabotage
Parental disappointment

Explicit sexual scenes can be found in the following chapters:

Chapter 2
Chapter 26
Chapter 31
Chapter 32
Chapter 46

After nearly half a decade of practicing law, Kim Swizz is now a recovering attorney, living her best life writing small-town romance. Kim has always had a passion for creative writing and has come a long way from the book she wrote and had bound in first grade, a titillating story entitled "The Cat is Eating."

A forever Jersey girl turned former Arizona resident, Kim now calls Boston home with her husband, though they love to travel together.

When she is not writing spicy scenes or making her readers cry, you can find her crocheting tiny things, knitting, embroidering, cross-stitching, bullet journaling—you get the point.

Kim is never without her emotional support Kindle and is an

avid F1 fan, keeping up with news on all the drivers, but mostly Carlos Sainz.

Kim is an unapologetic Disney adult who loves the smell of fall, small animals, and dancing her heart out (and Carlos Sainz).

Website: kimswizz.com
Facebook: Kim Swizz
Facebook Reader's Group: Kim's Swizzles
Socials: @authorkimswizz

www.ingramcontent.com/pod-product-compliance
Lightning Source LLC
Chambersburg PA
CBHW020233010826
48973CB00006B/1498